# The Blue Snow Meltdown

## By Gregory T Glading

# Contents

# Prologue

October 1, 1950

Ebbets Field. Brooklyn, New York.

The sun ruled the ion-free Brooklyn sky. Yet electricity steeped the air as 35,073 people paraded over the Italian marble floor of Ebbets Field's entrance rotunda. Dodger faithful anticipation and Phillies fan trepidation vibrated the ornate chandelier hanging from the ceiling. Dennis Waldron braced his arm around his seven-month-pregnant wife and led her up the first base side spiral staircase to their upper deck seats.

"I've never seen so many people in one place." Patricia held Dennis's arm as she lowered herself into her seat. "Even from up here, we're so close to the players. I feel like I'm in a theater rather than a ballpark."

"It's a good thing I got our tickets in advance. As you can see, it's standing room only." Dennis rubbed his wife's abdomen. "It was risky enough bringing you here. Standing would be an absolute no-no." Dennis squeezed her hand. "You saw how many were turned away. I wonder how many of them traveled all the way from Philadelphia. Well, honey, this is it. Eleven days ago, our Whiz Kids had a seven-and-a-half-game lead. Now it's the last game of the year, and the lead is down to one."

"If they lose, is it all over?"

"Pretty much." Dennis pursed his lips. "A Dodger win forces a three-game playoff. That doesn't bode well for our Phightins. They're out of pitchers. Bubba Church and Bob Miller are injured. Curt Simmons is in the military. Robin Roberts has already pitched three of the last seven games. He's pitching again today. He's got to be his best. The Dodgers are countering with Don Newcombe." Dennis smiled at his wife. "So, the three of us better cheer for the team below," he pointed to the first base bag, "and pray to Heaven above." He pointed upwards. "A victory means our first pennant in thirty-five years."

"New York gets a World Series every year." Patricia pinched her chin. "It doesn't seem fair."

"All we can ask is for a fair game, honey. They're about to play the National Anthem. Can you stand?"

"Yes." Patricia nodded. "But you'll have to help me."

***

Bottom of the ninth. Tie score. 1-1.

Dennis moved to the edge of his seat and put his chin on his hand. Patricia put her hand on his back. He glanced at her. "It doesn't look good, Pat." He grit his teeth. "The Dodgers have a runner in scoring position, no one out."

"Ouch," Patricia put her hand over her abdomen.

"You okay, honey. This is a critical moment in Phillies history, but it's still just a game. You and our new arrival are more important. Maybe we should leave. If we wait until the end, it will take too much time to get through the crowd."

"It's all right, Dennis." Patricia heaved two breaths of air. "It's all right."

"Unfortunately, the game may end any second. Oh no!" Duke Snider drove an apparent game-winning single to center field. Dennis hit his forehead with the heel of his palm and slumped. Six seconds later, Dennis leaped to his feet and pointed. "Abrams is out at the plate! Yes! Way to go, Richie! Great throw!" Dennis turned to his wife. "How about that! Are you feeling any better?"

"Yes." Patricia beamed. "I think our future arrival is happy too."

"Richie Ashburn doesn't have Baseball's strongest arm, but, as you just saw," he beamed and flapped his hands, "It sure is accurate. We're not out of the woods yet." Dennis pointed to home plate and adjusted his black plastic glasses. "They just intentionally walked Jackie Robinson. That loads the bases, and Carl Furillo is up. Anything hit to the outfield, and we lose."

Dennis shook his crossed fingers. "Yes." He closed his eyes and looked upward as Furillo hit an easy pop-up to Eddie Waitkus at first base. Dennis put his arm around his wife and put his hand and eyes on her abdomen. "Are you happy in there?" He looked back at his wife. "Just one more out. It won't be easy. Gil Hodges is up. He's already driven in 113 runs." Dennis and Patricia gasped as he drove the ball to left field. "He caught it!" Dennis pointed to Phillies left fielder Dick Sisler. "We survived. We're going extras, honey."

"I hope to never go through that again." Patricia wiped her brow.

"Robin Roberts came through; now the hitters must do their part." Dennis pursed his lips. "It won't be easy. Don Newcombe has only allowed one run."

Patricia patted her abdomen. "I feel our new arrival is telling me we're going to win." She smiled.

***

"Two men on, we got a chance. Come on, Dick Sisler." Dennis shook his fist. "Come on." The next sound resembled a cracking whip. Dennis leaped. "It's deep to left! Go baseball. Go! Go! Yeah! Yeah! It's gone. He did it! He did it! Homerun! Three-run homer."

"Dennis! He's kicking! He's kicking!" Patricia smiled from ear to ear. "I think we got ourselves a Phillies fan!"

# **Chapter 1**

"The Year of the Blue Snow, that's when the Phillies
will win."

- Gus Triandos, after being asked about his 1964
trade from the Detroit Tigers to the Philadelphia
Phillies.

Charles Dickens opened his seminal novel, *A Tale of Two Cities,* with, "It was the best of times, it was the worst of times." 1992 was not the best of times or the worst of times. High School English teacher Bill Waldron considered it his worst time. He scanned his 230-square-foot room in the Kesmon Hotel and saw a new paint chip on the wall and another cigarette burn on the carpet. He scratched his head, *'What the hell happened?'*

Deep into his second decade of teaching English for the Philadelphia School District, another pesky thought buzzed in his skull, *'It's late April. I wanted to make a difference...make an impact on my students. I introduced them to A Tale of Two Cities and tried to teach them how it can enrich their lives.'* Bill pursed his lips. *'They only paid enough attention to pass the exam. It looks like making a difference isn't going to happen this year.'* He looked at a *Philadelphia Daily News* sports page lying on the floor, *'and it's not looking good for Phillies either.'* "What the hell happened?" He closed his eyes and looked upward. He pictured his estranged wife, Laura. *'Eighteen years. Eighteen years we were married.'* He hung his head, opened his eyes, and noticed a new scuff on his shoes. *'In just a few days, you'll be my ex-wife.* "Damn Lawyers!" He smacked his head with his palm heel. "What the hell happened?"

An image of his sixteen-year-old son Rory flashed into his head. *'Smart Kid. Lousy Grades. Smokes pot. What can I do? He hates baseball and listens to death metal. I tried, and I'll keep trying. But what the hell happened?'*

Bill picked up a pennant emblazoned with, 'Philadelphia Phillies. 1980 World Champions.' He stared at Pete Rose's signature. "What the hell happened, Pete? What the hell happened to the Phillies?"

He slung his jacket over his shoulders and left his room, singing a paraphrase of a Disney song. "I owe. I owe. It's off to work I go."

# Chapter 2

Constructed of industrial clay brick, Filbert High School had nearly seventy-five years of ground in dirt. Barred windows give it a hybrid factory and penitentiary look.

A shrill bell rang, bringing yet another school day to a close. *'Perfect timing.'* Bill gathered some papers. *'Just enough time to drive home, get out of my work clothes, and catch happy hour at Doc Watson's Pub.'*

Never mistaken for a model or athlete, Bill stood a shade under six feet on a good day. He kept trim by playing recreational softball and pickup basketball.

He once played with vigor. Lately, his two favorite events were the two-ounce shot put and the twelve-ounce curl. Over the past two years, twenty pounds had crept up on him like back taxes. Hard times ravaged his hairline too. Gray streaks infested his thinning dark brown hair. Today, he wore a pair of navy slacks, a white shirt, and a brown tie. He left work with only a few nods to passing students and faculty. He climbed into his rusty and dented Chevy Nova. *'At last!'* He yanked off his tie and flung it onto the passenger-side floor mat. He turned the key. A metallic grind. "Dammit!" He slapped the steering wheel. Another key twist, another grind. His car turned over on the third attempt. "Whoo," he brushed his scalp. He ignored the black smoke billowing from the tailpipe, shifted into gear, and drove to Center City Philadelphia. He turned his radio dial past the all-sports talk station and stopped at an oldies music station. The voice of his long-time favorite disc jockey, Jerry Blavet, made him smile. Bill's memories of Jerry Blavat go back to boyhood. Jerry had a knack for playing Bill's favorite songs when he needed them most. His favorite was a Philly soul group, The Intruders. He even once heard that the Intruders were Dick Allen's favorite group. Bill's friend, Mark "Frog" Carfagno, a groundskeeper at Veteran's Stadium, however, told him The Temptations were Dick Allen's favorite group. Yet for Bill, The Intruders embodied more than just the sound of Philadelphia; they were the sound of Twenty-First and Lehigh.

Bill drove along the trolley tracks of South-West Philadelphia. He beamed. Jerry Blavat treated him to the voices of Little Sonny, Big Sonny, Phil, and Bird. The Intruders. Bill drummed on his steering wheel to their song, "Together." He opened his mind to imbibe what he considered the soul of Philadelphia.

Two minutes into the record came ten seconds of brass heaven, taking Bill to another place, another time...

"...Now batting for the Phillies, Number fifteen, Richie Allen." That announcement stirred a tempest at Connie Mack Stadium (Neé Shibe Park). The crowd worshiped him and vilified him—sometimes both at once.

On this day, the Phillies battled the St. Louis Cardinals. Tie score, last of the ninth, even the most hardened of Philadelphia's "Boo-Birds" and bigots were rooting for Dick Allen.

Bill inched to the edge of his hard, red-painted wooden Shibe Park upper deck seat.

Hall-of-Fame pitcher Bob Gibson was on the mound. Dick Allen described him as "So mean that he would knock you down, then meet you at home plate to see if you wanted to make something of it."

Dick Allen and Bob Gibson glared with laser focus. Allen brandished his forty-two-ounce bat. He locked and loaded it with a jiggle. Gibson drew first. His fastball flashed toward his catcher. Allen had a microsecond to counter. The collision of ash and horsehide snapped like rifle report, but with the decibel of a cannon, high and deep, the baseball soared, out of the playing field, over the left field bleachers ...

*Honk! Screech!*

"Yo! Asshole! How about keepin' ya eye on da road!"

Bill Waldron stuck his left arm out the window and flipped his middle finger.

Six southeast blocks from Philadelphia City Hall, the Kesmon Hotel's brick facade blended into the neighborhood. Its interior exposed its years of neglect. Its gloomy lobby had worn and chipped furniture. Old plaster walls looked as if they hadn't received care since the FDR administration.

The hotel did offer a convenient location, cheap rent, and safety. A passable place to stay only because its manager, Mack Pittman, didn't rent to hookers and junkies. Mack and the Kesmon both have seen better days, albeit many of them. Pittman was a small, graying man in his late sixties. His clothing was worn as his skin. Yet he was well-spoken and polite.

Bill leaned on the counter.

"Afternoon Bill, want ta go up to your room?"

"Yes, please, if you would."

"By the way, you got a message," Mack handed Bill a piece of paper. He opened it and glanced at his scrawl', *Laura wants you at her office right now.'* Bill grimaced and shoved it into his hip pocket.

Mack rode Bill in the seven-story Hotel's manually operated elevator to the third floor. He escorted Bill down the dusky corridor. Each floor of the Kesmon had only a few rooms, each on the same side of the west-facing building. The manager unlocked the door to Bill's room, looked downward, and nodded goodbye.

Bill Waldron ignored the sagging ceiling and a large cockroach scaling the wall. He breathed a sigh of relief. His baseball memorabilia collection was safe. All of it from autographed bats and balls, pictures, uniform shirts, and ticket stubs. He stopped to stare at his most prized piece, a 16" X 24" framed photo of himself as a six-year-old child, his father, and Stan Lopata, the Phillies catcher of the fifties, also known as Stash. Bill cracked his second smile of the day by looking at the image of his father, Dennis Waldron, as a young man with a thin body, wavy black hair atop a lean, angular face, and his Clark Kent-style black glasses. Dennis toasted a beer with Stash. His grin radiated athletic prime. Sitting on his father's lap, Bill radiantly smiled, a bud of purity possible only in life's early spring. Bill's mind drifted back, way back.

## Stash

Shibe Park was known as Connie Mack Stadium in Stash's Day. Philadelphia's devoted boosters considered it a sports shrine. Its wooden seats often symbolized pews girding Elysian Fields with grass greener than the mythical Shangri-La. Here, they hoisted the gonfalon of league titles. The Philadelphia A's won seven pennants here. In 1950, a youthful Phillies team nicknamed the Whiz Kids raised the National League flag. Shibe Park even saw the Philadelphia Eagles win the National Football League championship. Shibe Park has witnessed generations of Philadelphia sports fans' hopes and dreams. Unfortunately, scores of Shibe Park's cash-strapped teams had the proverbial snowball's chance in hell of winning a championship. Many of those teams failed to escape the cellar. Cheers turned sour as defeat followed bitter defeat. A ray of hope was soon lost in the dark cloud of disappointment.

At Shibe Park, the ghosts of baseball past magnified six-year-old Bill Waldron's dreams of the future. Here, his dad's favorite player, Stan Lopata, was immortal.

Don Newcombe, the Brooklyn Dodgers' hulking 6'4", 220-pound right-handed pitcher, checked Richie Ashburn, the Phillies baserunner on first. The pitcher accepted his catcher, Roy Campanella's sign. Stash brazenly dug his rear foot into the batter's box. Newk's first pitch zeroed in on his head. Down he went!

"Boo! Kick his butt Stash! The Bum only did it 'cause he don't have da guts ta throw ya a real pitch!" Dennis put down his empty popcorn container, doubling as a makeshift megaphone, and lifted Bill onto his lap. "He's got to come to him now, Billy Boy. And keep your other eye on Ashburn at first base. He's leading the league in stolen bases."

Stash reasserted his stance. This time, Newk pitched to him. Stash was ready. He drilled Newk's delivery. Dennis leapt, lifting Bill with him. The ball sped with trolley wire trajectory, smashing against the Ballentine beer scoreboard in deep right-center field. Brooklyn right fielder Carl Furillo fielded the rebound. Stash had beaten Newk. Now the clash pitted Carl Furillo, nicknamed the Reading rifle for his hometown and throwing prowess, against Richie Ashburn.

Ashburn's right foot touched inside the third-base bag as he dashed for home; Furillo threw a perfect one-hop strike to Campy. Ashburn slid into home. The crowd quieted, waiting for the umpire's call. "Safe!" The stadium erupted in cheers.

"The Phillies won, Bill! The Phillies just won!" Dennis boosted his little boy skyward

...The multi-decibel shriek of a passing police siren jolted Bill. Hustling to catch Doc Watson's happy hour, he hastily donned an old pair of cotton trousers, a well-worn Temple University sweatshirt, and a blue Sixers satin jacket. Bill glanced at the three-quarter length mirror on the closet door and noticed a bit more droop and line to his Anglo-Italian face. *'Did my nose grow?'* He plugged "The Best of Smokey" cassette into his Walkman, strolled back down the dusky corridor, dimmer now with the gloaming, eschewed the elevator, and loped down the three flights of narrow, creaky stairway that never failed to remind him of a Wildwood Boardwalk funhouse.

# Chapter 3

Doc Watson's Pub was Bill's favorite Center City Philadelphia bar. He liked its genial atmosphere, decent food, and inexpensive drinks. The pub's patrons included laborers, executives, and a few eccentrics. Bill was regarded as the latter.

Doc's had eight TV sets positioned for optimum viewing from the bar and tables. Bill sat at the bar and glanced at the TVs, half showed sports highlights, and the others had an N.Y. Mets vs. the Pittsburgh Pirates baseball game.

"Good afternoon, Bill. The usual?" Fred the bartender's height matched a racehorse jockey. His paunchy waist would preclude him from making weight. He wore a loose-fitting light blue sports shirt. Ruffled, short black hair topped a vacant face.

Bill grinned and pointed his thumb up before putting a twenty-dollar bill on the bar.

Fred served Bill a cold mug of Budweiser and a hot shot of Jack Daniels before taking Bill's twenty and replacing it with his change.

Bill belted down the bourbon.

"Must be another of those days, Bill?" Fred put his thumbs in his pocket.

"Aren't they all?" Bill slid his glass forward for a refill, sipped his new Jack Daniels, and gulped more beer. "Hey, what the hell is with those flippin' Phillies? It's all over before it's over." He finished his second shot and quaffed more beer.

"Guess we have to look forward to the Iggles, and, hey, the O's ain't doin' too bad." Fred pointed to the TV showing highlights of a Baltimore Orioles victory.

"Yeah, but the Eagles are football, and that's Baltimore. I want some decent baseball in Philly."

"Of course, who doesn't?" Fred refilled the shot glass and slid it next to Bill's beer.

"I got to admit. That's not a bad song you're playing." Bill sipped his shot and chased it with beer. "It's kind of hard rock but nothing like the hellish stuff my son listens to."

"It's Guns and Roses, *Sweet Child 'O Mine.*" Fred chuckled. "You need to escape from your oldies bubble. It was a huge hit, and it's already four years old. Now that you're about to be single again, how about you consider getting caught up with the times? Check out Nirvana, The Red Hot Chili Peppers, and Pearl Jam?"

"No thanks." Bill finished his shot and slid his glass to the bar's edge. "I prefer real music."

"My younger customers would have something to say about that." Fred laughed. "You've told me what you think of New York. But Baltimore ain't so bad; I still say ya ought ta drive down I-95 and check out Camden Yards. It's sort of like the old-time ballparks you're always harping about. Baltimore also has great seafood."

"Sure, Fred, but Bookbinder's Seafood Restaurant is just around the corner, and where the hell in Baltimore am I going to find a real South Philly Cheese Steak? Which reminds me." Bill signaled to his favorite waitress, Cynthia.

Cynthia was in her late thirties. Although too short to be a model, she had an attractive face topped by short blonde hair. Bill appreciated her soft blue eyes and gentle nature.

"Hi there, Bill! Guess you want a South Philly cheese steak?"

"Geez Cindy, who taught you to mind read?"

"I can't read everyone's mind. Just yours." She grinned.

"Hope that's a compliment."

"Of course." Cindy nodded.

"How is your daughter doing?" He smiled and looked into her blue eyes.

"She's fine, thank you, studying hard for her exams. Of course, who'd know better than you that it's that time of year again? Tell me, Bill. Any change with Rory?"

"Cindy, I just don't know what to do. Whenever I go over to see him, he's out somewhere. Hey, Lord knows," Bill threw his hands up, "Laura's never there. Do you know what I'd like to do?" He wagged his finger. "I'd like to go to his room and tear his disgusting posters off the wall! Then smash his God-forsaken death metal records!" He brandished a clenched fist. "Sometimes I think I should just grab him and shake some sense into him. Though I can just count the ways his big-shot lawyer mother would use that against me in our divorce case."

"Bill, your frustration couldn't be more apparent than if steam rose from your brow. If there's any way that I can help...just ask." Cynthia gently squeezed his hand.

Cynthia's concern lifted Bill's spirits, as did Mr. Jack Daniel's. Feeling euphoric, Bill finished his third shot of bourbon and guzzled the rest of his beer. He promptly called Fred over for a refill.

Bill watched baseball highlights on a corner TV. As usual, they mentioned the Phillies last. The broadcaster spared his national audience the lowlights, just showing a quick graphic: Chicago eight runs, ten hits, one error; Philadelphia two runs, six hits, three errors. He added that the Cubs held onto fifth place in the National League East. *That's an accomplishment only to the Phillies.'* Bill downed his beer. "Oh, to be in Philadelphia and the cellar," Bill muttered to himself.

Ten minutes later, Cynthia returned with his cheese steak. "You're the best Cindy." The alcohol had Bill feeling like he was in a different body. He leaned across and pecked her cheek.

"Bill! You'll get me fired!" She affectionately cuffed his shoulder. "By the way, did you see this week's trivia question? A free drink if you answer correctly."

He looked over at a green chalkboard in the bar's far corner. Inscribed in chalk, "The last time any major league player had an on-base-pct over 500, two players did it in the same year, same league. Name both players and the year." After thinking for a few seconds, Bill said, "Mickey Mantle and Ted Williams! 1957!"

"We got a winner!" Cynthia put her hand on his shoulder. She pointed to Fred. "Get this man a free drink."

"How did you know?" Fred shrugged.

Bill raised his hands and smirked.

"Tell ya what, Bill. Some places call a bourbon and a beer a boilermaker as if it were one drink. So, I'll give ya both."

Bill quickly leaped off his stool, pointing to the TV. "All right! Yes! Yes!"

Most of the fifteen or so patrons at Doc Watson's glanced at a TV. They saw a Pittsburgh Pirates baserunner getting congratulated for scoring the winning run against the Mets.

A regular at Doc's, JoJo, a husky man in his late forties with a large reddish nose and wearing a blue working outfit, looked over to Bill, Cynthia, and Fred. "I'll second that, Bill. I agree with what you're always sayin'. New Yorkers think the sun shines out of their assholes."

"Yeah! I think this world would be a better place if some intergalactic invaders came over with a giant shovel, scooped up New York, and shoved it right up the back side of a black hole." Bill took another sip of booze, thought of his father, and hated New York even more.

The jolt of a telephone ring broke his recovery

"For you, Bill." Fred handed Bill the receiver.

Bill arced the receiver to his ear. "Yeah."

"Is that you, Bill?"

"Tiz I. Is that you, Laura?"

"Of course, it's me. Didn't you receive my message?"

"Um ...No."

"Nice try, Bill. I phoned Mr. Pittman fifteen minutes ago. Make it easy on yourself, and come to my office right now."

"Okay. Laura." Bill departed Doc's feeling abashed and deflated. He left what remained of his twenty as a tip.

Laura Chilton. Bill recalled the early spring day over two decades past. She was a student at Ivy League Penn and hailed from the Philadelphia area's affluent Main Line suburbs. Laura was a noticeably attractive young lady. Bill? Who noticed? A Temple University student, he came from a modest South Philly row home. She listened to Joan Baez, John Lennon, Bob Dylan, and Buffalo Springfield and claimed membership in the Students for a Democratic Society. He listened to Motown, Philadelphia International Records, and headed the Dick Allen fan club.

Nevertheless, Laura was fed up with fake interest in her causes and doing or saying whatever it took to please her. Laura appreciated Bill's sincerity. She also found his intelligence and independent thinking attractive.

Laura recognized and appreciated Bill's stable and sure influence. Always studious, he delved into the great literature of America and Europe to better converse with her. Bill soon majored in English. He became a teacher and, for a long time, effective. Laura became a successful attorney.

Bill could still remember that first balmy day in early spring. The warm sun's return felt like reuniting with a long-separated loved one. Over two decades ago. He first saw her at the entrance of the University of Pennsylvania Library. Laura, fair as a spring rose. He approached her like a grizzled prospector shuffling through scorpion-infested sands. He considered rejection like a scorpion's sting to the heart.

Laura returned his shy greeting and even spoke with him. Bill found his chest of gold. Alas, both its blessings and curses. Two questions would forever haunt him. "Laura, what do you see in him?" And "Can't you do better, Laura?"

The coldest day in the depth of winter compensates with invigorating air and cleansing white snow. Unfortunately, this early spring day, over two decades after Bill met Laura, was veiled not in white snow but exposed to a nasty scrub-water gray sky. Bill held out his palm. "What next?" He clenched the moisture, "What frickin' next?" A minute later, the rain fell hard enough to sting. He lowered his head and watched the rain sluice into a storm drain.

The offices of the Crane, Alexander, Endicott, and Hurst law firm reflected contemporary Philadelphia style. It blended Colonial American Heritage with modern. The firm was on the twenty-fifth floor. Its interior featured woven wool carpeting and hardwood colonial furniture. The walls featured prints depicting scenes of the American Revolution, the signing of the Declaration of Independence, the founding fathers of American government, and historical Icons such as the Liberty Bell.

Bill stood at the firm's doorway, wringing wet, cold, and disheveled. He resembled a stray mongrel dog that followed a rich kid home.

"Well, Bill, I'll give you credit for method to your madness." Laura no longer looked like a spring rose; the exquisite flower had blossomed to summer splendor. She stood in front of her mahogany desk. Taller than average, she boasted a svelte figure achieved by over a decade of proper diet and physical fitness. Tightly tied back auburn hair gracefully enhanced her sculpted triangular face. Attired in a custom-tailored navy blue skirt and jacket, she looked noble and elegant. Bill, even after over two decades, stood bewitched by her emerald eyes. "If you had come when I asked, my colleagues and clients might have seen you."

Unfortunately for Bill, one of Laura's colleagues was with her. Bill suspected Burt Jenkins and Laura's tie exceeded professional boundaries. Jenkins was forty-something, tall and robust, but still possessed a boyish face that, to Bill, had *hate me* tattooed on his forehead. "Afternoon, Bill." Burt smiled with fake charm. "Looks like you got the worst of this weather. I've got just the thing to warm you up." Burt walked to a liquor cabinet across the office. Seconds later, like an illusionist pulling a rabbit out of a hat, he presented an elegantly curved carafe.

"You can't see that he's had enough?" Laura stepped toward Burt.

"Relax, Laura." He touched her shoulder. "Give the man a break. He looks cold and wet. Moreover, this whole thing's surely been as hard on him as anyone else." Burt grinned at Bill. "Twelve years aged, imported from Northern Scotland." Burt poured the magic potion into a crystal glass and handed it to Bill...

...Bill sniffed before rolling a dram of the Scotch on his tongue. *'Delectable and piquant'*. He took a full sip. "Hmm...Not bad. Pretty fancy stuff ya got here, Burt. Where did you say you got it from? Scotland huh? Well, what I have for you is homegrown American." Bill belted Burt square in the gut with a straight underhand right! Burt groaned in agony while keeling forward. Bill countered with a sizzling left hook to the Jaw!

Burt staggered backward, collapsing unconscious into a plush chair. Bill grabbed Laura, pulled her in, and kissed her. She resisted at first, but his virility soon overwhelmed her. She returned his kisses with a yearning for Paradise lost.

Cradling her in his arms, never yielding their lip lock, he lowered her onto a black leather couch. She assisted in unbuttoning her blouse; he tore off her bra, *'delightfully firm, perfect shape.'* Bill had known her through eighteen years of marriage. His life without her was an arid desert. He buried his face in her breasts. Like a parched desert castaway in an oasis of frosty water, he engrossed their fragrance and imbibed their ambrosia…

"Bill! Burt's offering you a drink. Are you going to take it? Or continue standing there like a zombie?" Laura shook her head. "Oh, never mind."

Bill took the glass from Burt and scornfully slammed down the Scotch. "Hmm, not bad, not bad at all ... But I think I'll stick to drinking American."

"Yes, well, um, nice Sixers jacket, Bill. Pity about the way they blew their series against the Bulls. What do you think? Will Michael Jordan be the all-time great?"

"Yeah, well, you never saw Wilt Chamberlain. I hope the Sixers take Temple's All-American point guard with their first pick..."

"Sorry to interrupt your little chat, guys, but Bill, if you would please sign these papers..." Laura took a folder with legal papers and a fountain pen from her desk and handed them to Bill. "Burt and I are pressed for time."

"Oh, are you? So, what have you and Burty planned that's so urgent?" Bill dumped the clipboard back on Laura's desk and stepped back. He hunched his shoulders and furrowed his brow.

"We have an important cocktail function with senior executives from the V.I.G. Corporation. As if it were any of your business."

"I'll tell you what is my business. Both of our business. Who will be home for Rory?"

"I think Rory's big enough that he doesn't need his mother twenty-four hours a day." Laura scrutinized Bill. She scrunched her nose and lowered her eyebrows. "As if you, in your present state, set an adult example."

*'Don't piss her off but don't be a wimp. And show Burt who's the real man. Rory. Can't let this take him down lower.'* Bill gritted his teeth. *'Gotta be strong. Gotta be strong.'* Bill took one step toward Laura. "That sounds like something you'd say. Always an excuse to put you, or your career, ahead of our son."

"Well, Mister Bigshot," Laura did not flinch. "I don't think we need an accountant to settle whose career paid the bills and whose career is going to pay for his education."

"You think so, Laura? You think my teacher's salary only bought beans on Sundays? Yet another excuse for you to run around with Big Burty," He pointed at Burt, "While those biker freaks corrupt our son."

Burt put his hands on his hips and rolled his eyes.

"I refuse to listen to any more of your drivel. Now, please sign this and leave." Laura waved Bill away. "I only listen to answers, not accusations. Oh, before you close the door behind you, why not suggest some friends for him? I was thinking the kids on Walton Mountain."

Bill squared his feet and hunched his shoulders. "Am I supposed to find that amusing? Our son is running with a pack of sociopaths. Can't you see that? How far do you think that will take him? Skid row? Jail?"

"Bill." Laura lowered her eyes. "Answers please. I'm only hearing paranoid ranting and raving. If you have an intelligent suggestion, put it in the box outside." Laura pointed to the door. "Don't bother telling it to Rory. Anything you say only makes him do the opposite."

"Well, he lives in your house! You can do something! Why don't you start by taking those posters off *your* walls?" Bill swatted his arm past his face. "Then don't allow that ... Devil rock in *your* house."

"Is that the best you can come up with? Hey, why not a little book burning while we're at it? Where did you get your teacher's diploma? Nazi Germany or Soviet Russia?"

"Try right here in the good ol' USA. Let me teach you something about an America you'll never see while sitting in your fancy office and sipping cocktails with rich old men in gray suits. Visit the trenches of Filbert High and witness those kids. Some glassy-eyed! Others rage-filled! Even suicidal! And do you know what? They're all into the same things as Rory!"

"So, while I'm sitting in my professional ivory tower, you just know everything, don't you?" Laura shook her head. "What you're saying is, if someone isn't just like you, there's something wrong with them. What did you ever involve Rory with besides collecting baseball junk? Maybe that's why he suffers the problems you claim. Look, you had your chance with Rory, and you had your chance with life. The one lacking the drive to better himself is you." She prodded. "Who knows? Maybe you could have seen a University Professor ... Instead of a washout bitching about juvenile delinquents."

"Hey? Who the hell's bitching? Those kids need me! Teaching is a vocation! Do you know what that means? Miss Down with the establishment? Miss, I wanna join the Peace Corps. Miss, 'All We Are Saying is Give Peace a Chance'? A vocation! Not a sell-out career!"

"Sell out? Let me tell you Something!" Laura walked toward Bill, wagging her finger. "It's not just rich old men in gray suits that walk into this office ..." She jabbed her finger in Bill's chest. "Sometimes we get dirty, drunk bums! I asked you politely to leave a couple of minutes ago. Now get out!"

"Timeout!" Burt stepped in, shaping a "T" with his hands. "We're not getting anywhere!"

Just as Bill was about to tell him to go to hell, Burt pulled a pair of tickets from his pocket and handed them to Bill, "Why don't you take these? They're for tonight's Phillies game."

His first impulse was to tell him to stick them up the seventh planet from the sun, but a glance revealed they were for deluxe box 1-A. He looked back at Burt, Laura's narrowed eyes, and left.

"Laura, I can't believe what I just saw. We've worked together on some explosive cases, yet never have I seen you that close to losing your aplomb."

"Yes, Burt." Laura looked down. "I do feel embarrassed. Though I'm sure you realize…a divorce is a trying time, especially when it involves children."

"No question about that. When Debra and I split, your spat with Bill was an exchange of sonnets compared to our fights. Meanwhile, I'm going to contact NASA."

"NASA?"

"Yes, NASA. I want to ask them if the Voyager probe solved a mystery more complex than why you spent eighteen years living with that loser."

# Chapter 4

The wind-driven rain felt like steel pellets. The alcohol numbed the physical and emotional pain. *'This damn weather says it all.'* He covered his head with his arms as he made a final dash for the subway portal.

Graffiti scarred the City Hall subway station's walls of gritty cream-colored tiles and bare concrete. A urine stench filled the air. While noxious to the eyes and nose, it provided a spellbinding relief to the ears. An excellent vocal harmony group sang an a capella version of a classic song from a Harlem, NY, doo-wop quintet. The Harptones' lead singer, Willie Winfield, commanded a silky-smooth tenor voice. The "subway" group's lead had a course, earthier voice. Yet he still captured the song's essence.

"I still remember the day that we met. Your smile is something I'll never forget. And since that day, my love grows and grows; that's the way it goes. The way it goes. I spent a lifetime just waiting for you.

But from now on, dear, our waiting is through, for you can make my dreams come true, and that's the way it goes.

From out of nowhere, you came into view; now I'm completely in love with you.

You walked right in; my heart walked out; You took its place without doubt. Oh, won't you please open your heart to me?

For since I've known you, you're all that I see. You are the one girl my heart has chosen. That's the way it goes."

The twenty-five or so commuters who gathered around zealously clapped. Most added loose change or dollar bills to their small aluminum wastepaper basket. Bill envisioned Laura throughout the song. He wiped a solitary tear from his left eye and threw in a dollar.

The singing group thanked their audience by performing their version of "Looking for an Echo." A Brooklyn, NY, vocal quintet, the Persuasions, recorded Bill's favorite version of the song. The Persuasions sang it as a nostalgic anthem about life and du-wop in 1950s Brooklyn. The "Subway" group changed the lyrics somewhat, applying them to themselves growing up in Philadelphia.

"Up on Broad Street in North Philly, we used to harmonize.

Me, Tyrone, Willie, Manny, and some of the guys. We were singing oldies, but they were newies then. And today, when I play my old forty-fives, I remember when,

We practiced in the subway, in lobbies, and in halls, Even in the doorway, singing du-wops to the walls.

And if we went to a party and they wouldn't let us in,

We locked ourselves in a bathroom so nobody could get in.

'Cause we were looking for an echo, an answer to our sound,

A place to be in harmony, a place we almost found.

The girls would gather 'round us, and how our heads would swell; we sang songs by the Moonglows, The Harptones, and The Dells" …

…A rumble and shrill whistle signaled the arriving subway train, ending their harmony. Bill snapped out of his funk, rifled through his wallet, added another buck, and darted into the train just before the automatic doors shut. He collapsed onto a hard, plastic molded seat. He enjoyed riding the subway. The southbound express train made an initial stop at Walnut and Locust Streets, then rambled under Broad Street non-stop to Veterans Stadium. His alcohol-induced state and the dark, underground journey's click-clack drone affected him ...

... Bill and Laura sit together on the lower deck, first-base side. The date is October 1, 1970, Shibe Park's (Connie Mack Stadium) final game. Connie *Mack Jr.* eulogized the Ball Park to the final 31,822 fans: "I feel sadness about this old ballpark that has been so important a part of my life ... I will always have my memories." An Irish wake began.

"It's hard to believe." Bill whimsically looked upward and around the ballpark. "Sixty-one years of history ... After tonight, it's all over. They're gonna tear this grand old place down."

"I can believe it," Laura sipped her soda.

"What?" Bill furrowed his brow.

"Oh, come on, Bill. Admit it. This place is filthy, decrepit even. Let's face it—It's a dump."

"A dump? How can you say that?" Bill pointed toward the infield. "That pitcher's mound was the domain of Lefty Grove, Eddie Plank, Chief Bender, Robin Roberts, and Curt Simmons! Look at that outfield." Bill pointed to center field. "Richie Ashburn made more putouts there than anyone in baseball history! Over there," Bill pointed to right field, "was the great Al Simmons's territory. You've heard of Lou Gehrig, haven't you?"

"Yes, from the Gary Cooper movie."

"Well, I'll have you know that Lou Gehrig once hit four straight homers, right over that very wall," Bill pointed to right field, "and Babe Ruth once hit a ball so far over that wall that it cleared 20th Street, two rows of houses, and landed on Opal Street. Ted Williams secured Baseball's last .400 season by going six for eight in a final day doubleheader." Bill pointed to left field. "They say that Jimmie Foxx cleared those left-field bleachers with some of baseball's longest home runs. You see those Cadillac and Coke signs way up top there? Well, I've seen Dick Allen smash homers clear over them ..."

"That's fine, Bill," Laura interrupted, "Though I'm afraid those names don't mean anything to me."

"No, Laura. It's not just about names and numbers. It's about history. Not just baseball history. A wonderful part of my life, my father's life, even his father's life," Bill raised his hands, "It still lives here. This place has a pulse and heartbeat of its own! Can't you feel it?" Bill shook his hands.

"You're crazy, Bill, but that's what I like about ya." Laura kissed Bill's cheek. "Just for you, I'll try to catch the vibes. One thing still bothers me, though."

"What's that, Laura?

"It's the neighborhood surrounding this place. I refuse to believe that a just society can allow its people to live in such blight and squalor."

"Unfortunately, Laura, it's been that way as long as I can remember. My father always complained about it, though I can't remember him saying it was ever any better. That's the main reason the Phillies are moving out."

"Don't you care?"

"Yeah, sure, but what can we do?" Bill shrugged his shoulders.

"You disappoint me." She pulled her face. "For one thing, we can stop wasting funds on an unjust war over ten thousand miles away and start putting it…"

"Hey! It could drop!" Bill leaped to his feet as the Phillies' Oscar Gamble hit a blooper to shallow center. "Yes! Base hit. How about that! They're getting started, Laura.""Sometimes I lose hope in you."

The Phillies weren't the only ones getting started.

Some used the wooden seat slats handed out before the game. Others used wrenches, hammers, or saws. Before long, the fans ' early dismantlement of Shibe Park sank into an orgasmic bash of destruction. The bedlam sounded like a combination lumberjack convention and urban construction site.

"Please, let's leave. I no longer feel safe here."

"Don't worry, Laura, you're with me. I've been here several hundred times. Nothing to worry about ... Yay! All right!" Bill stood and cheered with 31,820 others, Laura Chilton the lone exception, as Phillies catcher Tim McCarver tripled home Tony Taylor with the game's first run.

Demolition delirium took over. A husky, loose-jowled, unshaven man in an oil-stained jacket sitting in Bill and Laura's row barked, "Okay, everybody! Rock forward! Roll backward!"

"Come on, Laura, this is gonna be fun." Bill grinned at her.

Laura stood, put her hands on her hips, and pulled her face at the adults rocking back and forth in their seats like children in a playground.

"Rock back, roll front," Jowl face egged on, "Rock back, roll front."

With a creak and a crag like an antique rocking chair, the seat's steel bolts lost their grip on the concrete floor. A few minutes later, Bill, jowl face, and the others raised the entire row of wood and steel seats overhead like a prize fighter with his championship belt. Entire sections of fans, even from the upper deck, voiced their approval.

The rollicking crowd was aware of the game on the field. With the Phillies clinging to a one-zero lead, the Expos loaded the bases with only one out in the eighth when a fan ran onto the field and consulted Phillies pitcher Barry Lerch. That stunt was like another break in a pressurized fuselage—now the players on the field were fair game. Nevertheless, Barry Lerch pitched out of the inning despite fan invaders.

In the Expos' ninth, John Bateman hit a one-out routine flyball to left field.

"Laura! Look! What in the hell is that idiot doing to Palm Tree?" Bill said.

An idiot fan tried to steal the Phillies' left-fielder Ron "Palm Tree" Stone's glove. That interference caused the ball to fall safely, putting the tying run on base.

"Now that your game is a farce." Laura pinched his arm. "You can take me home."

"Oh, come on, Laura. This is an important game. The Phillies must win or they finish in last place. You don't want the Phillies to finish their final season here in the cellar, do you?"

"Get real, Bill!" A second later, a thrown seat slat whizzed inches past her ear. "That does it! You better take me home right now." Laura stood and prodded. "Or I'm leaving by myself!" She turned and walked away.

Bill grasped her arm. "You want me to get real?"

"You take your hand off me." She shook her body, breaking his grip. "Now!"

"Yeah, right. You want to walk around in this neighborhood? Alone? After dark? It's seven full blocks from the subway. That's if you know how to find it. " Bill spread his arms. "And that you'd want to ride it alone at this hour."

"I'll take a taxi."

"Yeah, right. You think taxi drivers are dumb enough to cruise these streets after dark? I'm afraid you're here with me for the duration. Relax. It won't be long now. Why not enjoy the game? Hey, they're planning some neat post-game festivities."

"You ..." Laura scowled at Bill while returning to her seat.

"I'm glad you're staying, because what irony we're seeing! Here we are at the ballpark's last game, fighting to avoid the cellar, and the manager of the last Phillies team to fight for the pennant is with the opposition. Look, Laura, Gene Mauch's using his favorite pinch runner from that '64 team." Adolpho Phillips pinch-ran for Bateman. "And look who's batting. Bobby Wine. The '64

Phillies, shortstop. I'll never get over that team for as long as I live."

"Are you still moaning about that team? Here we live in a world beset by war, poverty, and social injustice." Laura sneered and shook her head. "As if some guy stealing home with Willie Mays batting ..."

"Frank Robinson." Bill smiled tightly, more with his left lip.

"Oh really? I see baseball is your only concern. I once considered you a conscientious person. At last, you bare your true . . .

"Oh, no!" Bill yelled as Bobby Wine doubled home the tying run.

Bottom of the Tenth. The Phillies Tim McCarver reached second base; Oscar Gamble batted. The crowd urged the Phillies by pounding wooden seat slats against wood, concrete, or steel with jungle drum rhythm. Bill sat on the edge of his seat, shaking crossed fingers. Laura slumped on the back of her seat, chin on palm.

Ground Ball up the middle! Basehit! Tim McCarver took a wide turn at third. Centerfielder Boots Day bobbled the ball. The Expo relief pitchers fled from their rightfield corner bullpen for the dugout's safety like Impalas from roaring lions. The other Expo players also bolted from their positions. Tim McCarver crossed home plate with the winning run. A fan ran onto the field and attempted to steal home plate. Failing to dislodge it, he stole a bat instead. No one will ever again play Major League baseball on these hallowed grounds.

The Phillies canceled the post-game festivities because of the uprising. Thousands of people charged the field. They tore up sod, ripped signs off the outfield fences, stole turnstiles, pieces of the bullpens—anything they could get their hands on. The riotous contagion infected Bill. He pulled Laura with him to the field. A large, burly fan barreled into her without apology while storming to the melee (It happened too abruptly to identify the culprit, but judging by force of impact, Eagles football legend Chuck Bednarik was a suspect). The hit sprawled Laura across the ground. She ejected her purse like a fumbled football. A teenager scooped it like a linebacker and vanished into the crowd! Laura spurned Bill's help and stood up. Her dress was a soiled, grass-stained mess. Mud smudged her pretty face. She was soaked from sweat, grass dew, and tears. She snapped at Bill with a dry-ice sting in her eyes. "Why didn't you stop him?"

Bill replied feebly. "How could I? He's long gone."

Laura turned to a nearby cop. "Some kid took my purse."

"Lady, you're lucky that's all he took." The uniformed patrolman passively observed the pell-mell.

***

Bill and Laura stood in front of Charlie Quinn's Deep Right Field Cafe, 20th and Lehigh, across the street from the thirty-four-foot high rightfield wall. Laura had warmed from dry-ice cold to blast furnace hot. She angrily put her hands on her hips. "Well, Bill, I'd like to thank you for a wonderful evening. First, someone almost split my head open with a seat slat. Next, I get slammed into the dirt. And I got robbed! All so you could carry on like a hooligan." Laura hunched her shoulders and jutted her jaw. "My evening was *so* wonderful ... I'll make it our last to better remember you by."

"I'm sorry, Laura!"

"Oh, you are sorry, all right. Look, why don't you just go to ... TAXI!" Laura ran to hail a passing cab. She mumbled mild curses as someone got it first.

Bill realized both his blame and the gravity of Laura's position. He ran and pleaded with her. "I said I'm sorry, Laura! I'm sorry! Please understand." He raised his palms. "These things happen—you know!"

"Oh, do they now?" Laura's finger jabbed Bill's chest. "Would they have if you took me home when I asked?" She paused for effect. "Huh?"

"Please understand." Bill steepled his hands. "I had to say goodbye to Shibe Park." He shook his hands. "I just couldn't leave early."

"Say goodbye to Shibe Park! Now you can say goodbye to us!" Laura looked up and down Twentieth Street for a taxicab. "Hey, since when is participating in mob rule saying goodbye?"

"It wasn't a mob! We all loved the place! They're taking Shibe Park away from us." He opened his hands, "So, we all wanted to take it back home with us."

"Love? You call vandalism and looting everything but the kitchen sink—love?

Four seconds later, three fans left the stadium in a procession like the Three Kings in a Christmas pageant. One carried a toilet, the other a urinal, and the third a kitchen sink.

Laura laughed. Next, she eyed Bill. His moist eyes drooped like a puppy dog guilty of pooping on the carpet. "You're all right. You're all right, after all."

They embraced and petted to a gentle harmony singing from Charlie Quinn's Deep Rightfield Cafe's jukebox. The Intruder's "Love is Just Like a Baseball Game."

October 1, 1970. Bill Waldron lost a friend that night but found love...

"Hey buddy, wake up; we're at the last stop."

Bill awakened and looked at his disturber with glazed, glossy eyes.

With his left hand, the stranger gently shook Bill by the shoulder. The stranger spoke with a lucid, baritone timbre. "Come on, my friend, we're not going any farther."

Bill's eyes cleared while staggering to his feet. The impressive gentleman bewildered him. Perhaps in the early sixties, handsome, not just for his age, but because of his age. He was nattily attired in a tweed, charcoal, double-breasted jacket. His shirt had stiff, high, starched collars with pointed ends and a narrow black tie. Narrow suspenders held up his form-fitted trousers, slightly breaking over his Brogue shoes. A matching fedora hat and long trench coat completed his outfit.

Bill rubbed his eyes. *'So formal and couture. Something's not right. Out of time, maybe.'* He jerked his head to circulate blood to his brain. He surmised the stranger matched his height, but his posture made him look taller. *'At least twenty years older but in better shape than me.'* "Uh, thanks, sir." Bill again rubbed his eyes.

"You don't have to call me, sir. My name's Kelly, Michael Joseph Kelly." The gentleman extended his right hand. "Call me Mike."

"Sure thing, Mike." Bill returned Mr. Kelly's firm handshake. "I'm Bill Waldron. Call me Bill."

During their ride up the escalator to the subway exit, Bill asked, "By the way, Mike, are you going to the game?"

"Why yes, thank you, I am."

Bill scratched his head, *'What's a gentleman like him taking the subway to attend a game in a rainstorm to see a team doomed to finish last?*

"Do you have a ticket?"

"Yes, I do, Bill." Mike showed him a yellow ticket.

"You must be kidding me! That's for the seven-hundred level! You don't see baseball from up there; you see a flea circus! Hell, if you sit up there, you'll need supplemental oxygen! Not just because the air is thin." Bill smirked. "It's so you don't smell piss and pot smoke. Tell you what, Mr. Kelly, I mean Mike, why don't you watch the game with me?" Bill then proudly presented Mike with a ticket for deluxe box A- 1.

"Why, thank you, thank you very much, Bill." Mike accepted the ticket and grinned while perusing it. "I guess I can't get any closer than this without playing myself."

Bill and Mike alighted at the Pattison Avenue subway portal, across the street from Veterans Stadium. They stood in the station. Cold, dank rain continued to fall. "We better wait here until this stuff finishes. I'm wearing a hat and a trench coat. You're wearing nothing to keep you dry."

"I always said that no true fan misses batting practice."

"Well said, Bill. I feel likewise. A baseball fan not attending batting practice before a game is tantamount to a horse racing gambler not viewing his thoroughbred in the parade ring before a big race. During pregame batting practice, I could cherish the chimes of leather, horsehide, and ash buffeting in orchestral rhapsody. The chirping of players to and at one another was winsome as the first robins of early spring."

"Yo!" Bill beamed. "You have a way with words! I'm a high school English teacher. I only wish I could have my students describe things like that."

"I know what you do, Bill." Mike chuckled. "I bet they use 'Yo' nonetheless."

"Touche." Bill held out his palm. "It's still raining. The weather gives us a pass on missing batting practice. Besides, I'm sure they canceled it anyway. Well, we're standing in the subway station. The ballpark, if we dare call it that, looks like a scaled-up version of the subway with those bare concrete columns and its donut shape. After over two decades, I still miss the artistic frills of Shibe Park's French Renaissance façade."

"Well, Bill, it's to everything a season. In my day, artistry ruled. Demographic shift, neighborhood flux, and populations wane and wax. When Shibe Park was built, few people owned automobiles. Now, the automobile rules. A greater share of revenue is spent on automobile-based infrastructure. Functionality and multipurpose are the current stadium zeitgeist. Bigger, not intimacy and charm, are considered better. You must admit that the Vet's size is imposing. The Vet will have its day. Another stadium will avoid its mistakes, but new demands, such as corporate boxes that push the everyday fan's seat higher, will prove unavoidable. Moreover, modern fans demand convenience, parking, and comfort."

"You're right, Mike." Bill pursed his lips. "But is commercialization and sterilization of the fan experience necessary? Will the next generation of stadiums still try to replicate theme parks? What happened to just enjoying a ball game? I still love the game. I just wish I could recapture the magic baseball once held for me."

"You're forgetting something. As a child, you saw the players as more than heroes; you looked up to them as demigods. That's a wonder of childhood, but unhealthy in an adult. The players have personal flaws, just like you. Besides, as a youth, you watched games before real-world cynicism raised its ugly head. Are today's exuberant salaries better than yesterday's stingy owners forcing players to fight for an extra nickel or dime? A youngster's world is limited in time and experience and grants a blissful unawareness of real-world issues."

"Now I understand what that song I just heard, *Sweet Child O' Mine*, means. *'She got a smile that, it seems to me, reminds me of childhood memories, where everything was as fresh as a bright blue sky.'*" Bill closed his eyes and pictured Laura on their wedding day. He shifted his thought to Jim Bunning throwing the final pitch of his 1964 Father's Day Perfect Game.

The sound of the Phillies public address announcer Dan Baker broke his reverie.

"Sounds like the game started." George cuffed his shoulder. "You ready to brave the rain and go inside?"

***

Bill and Mike handed their tickets to the taker and clicked through the turnstile. The Chicago Cubs already had runners on first and third with two out. The batter doubled home both runners before Bill and Mike reached their seats.

Bill half-smiled and looked slightly upward as he presented the usher with their tickets.

The weather-worn usher smeared rainwater from only one steel-framed, vinyl-padded seat. Afterward, he looked at Bill with wide eyes and open palm.

"I'll give you something if you wipe off the other seat." The usher complied. Bill gave him a two-dollar tip. They sat directly atop the Phillies dugout.

"I don't get it, Mike. Why didn't the usher wipe off your seat?"

"Maybe because this is your night."

As Bill and Mike sat, the Cubs' next hitter drove in the runner on second by blooping a soft single just between the shortstop and left fielder. The sparse crowd groaned.

"Damn!" Bill slapped his knee, "We've barely sat, and the game's all but decided." Bill threw up his hands. "What should you expect? The Phillies whole damn season is all but decided."

Mike sat. "Bill, is a ballgame only about winning or losing?"

Bill glowered at the scoreboard and shrugged.

"Let me put it to you another way." Mike turned to Bill. "Can you recall that famous football coach? The one with the Italian name?"

"Vince Lombardi?"

"Yes. Vince Lombardi." Mike smiled and nodded. "What was that well-known saying of his?"

31

"Do you mean, 'winning isn't everything: it's the only thing'?"

"Yes, that's the one. Bill, please allow me to reflect on my younger days."

"Please do."

"Bill, I had my days as a player, many of them ..."

"Really? Who did you play for?"

"Who I played for doesn't matter. It's how I played. You talk about a Machiavellian, win-at-all-costs attitude," Mike grinned and shook his head. "Well, can I put it to you another way?"

"Of course." Bill nodded.

"Put a month's pay in your wallet. If a knave picked your pocket, how would he feel?"

"Well, if it's my month's pay, he'll probably want more." Bill chuckled. "I know what you're saying, though."

"Okay, Bill, but do you think he'd feel remorse?"

"Hell no. I bet he'd take pride in getting over on me."

"Exactly! Back then, Bill, I considered chicanery, cunning, and guile as an extension of strength, speed, and skill. Soon after my thirty-sixth birthday, I discovered baseball's more profound purpose ..."

"Oh, nuts, man." Bill reacted to the Phillies' shortstop, allowing a ground ball to trickle through his legs for an error. The Cubs scored another run on the misplay. "Can you believe this? They pay that bum a million bucks a year, and he missed a ball that a little leaguer would've caught."

"Bill, if you paid that shortstop a billion dollars, would it make him a better fielder than Bid McPhee?""Who?"

"Um, The Wizard Oz in his prime."

Bill looked down and shook his head as the Phillies finally retired the Cubs. The score: Cubs five, Phillies zero. "I don't get your point."

"My point is that despite the amount of money invested in a player, he is still human, with intrinsic human limitations."

"Now I hear what you're saying," Bill grinned. "It's like dumping money on chicken shit and expecting it to turn into chicken salad."

Mike chuckled. "That is one way of putting it. Well, we both know that front-office management treats baseball as a business, and the players' main concern is also money. Nevertheless, does that change the quintessence of the action on the field?"

"I don't understand, Mike."

"Well, Bill, what are the players doing on the field?"

"They're playing a game of baseball—a horseshit brand of it—but a *game* just the same."

"Exactly," Mike said.

Bill watched the first Phillies batter pop out; the second batter fanned. "I agree with you philosophically, Mike, but, damn, they stink. I blame it on the skinflints in the front office."

"Bill, I could draft volumes on the stinginess of baseball's erstwhile owners. Their greed led to current player salaries. Do you prefer the dark days when Gerry Nugent and Connie Mack peddled their best players to make ends meet? Those plundered teams were far worse than this one."

"Okay. I agree that those teams were worse. Still, Connie Mack and Gerry Nugent had an excuse. Neither had personal fortunes. Besides, TV money was nonexistent, and they shared a depressed market. This lot has both TV money and the largest sole market in North America." The third Phillies batter also struck out. Bill had to stop talking for five minutes until the multi-decibel organ music finished. He continued, "What's their excuse?"

"Touché Bill. What if a Walter O'Malley type owned the Phillies? Isn't bad baseball, or as you put it, horseshit baseball, better than no baseball?"

"Good point. Although sometimes I wonder." Bill's voice blustered with the fans' moaning at a Cubs home run. "Yes, Mike, you're right. If the Phillies became, let's say, The Vancouver Assholes or something, it would destroy this city. My father used to always talk about how the A's moving out hurt him. No baseball at all in Philly? No way, Jose."

A beer vendor bellowing, "Cold beer, cold beer, cold beer," entered Bill and Mike's box.

"On me, Bill."

"No thanks. I can't let you pay champagne prices for warm, flat horse piss."

"Don't fret, Bill. After all, you gave me my ticket." Mike handed Bill a twenty-dollar bill. He relayed it to the vendor without getting any change back, took two beers, and handed one to Mike. "Bill, in my younger days, I could out revel an entire team of merry men. Unfortunately, we were blissfully unaware of alcoholism's dangers. I can tell that this isn't your first of the day." Mike grinned. "But an extra drink is often the best way to get to know a man."

"Gotcha." Bill gulped some beer. "By the way, where are you from, Mike?"

"I was born in Troy, New York. I've worked in Cincinnati, Chicago, Boston, and New York City. I last lived in Boston. How about yourself?"

"I grew up here in South Philly, about a fifteen-minute walk away. Although my mother sold our house and moved to Florida. Now I live in Center City." Bill swallowed more beer and watched the game. The rain fell harder. "You've watched a lot of baseball; tell me, who's the best player you've ever seen?"

"Buck Ewing."

"Who?"

"DiMaggio. Joe DiMaggio. Bill, the 'Clipper,' sailed across the field like Pegasus galloping through the clouds. His successor, the Commerce Comet, was Hercules in spikes. That other kid. The one who played in the horseshoe across the river. Say Hey, did he play in body and spirit? The Duke of Flatbush was an Olympian in blue. The best? Joe DiMaggio. He swung a bat like Lohengrin sweeping his enchanted sword. Did you know that Joltin' Joe out-hit the Splendid Splinter in neutral parks?

"No. I didn't." "Yes, he did." Mike pointed upward. .333 to .328

"Mike, I got a vision of DiMaggio galloping through the clouds. Can you imagine what this plastic on concrete surface would have done to his feet, heel, and knees?" Bill grimaced as another Phillies error plated two more Cubs runs, upping the score to eight-zero. "Playing baseball on astroturf is like playing ice hockey on a roller rink. Dick Allen summed it up perfectly, 'If a horse can't eat it, don't play baseball on it.'"

"Bill, please allow me to indulge the past."

"Oh, please do, Mr. Kelly. Anything is better than this present." Bill pointed to the field. The Phillies pitcher had just walked the next Cub to load the bases.

"Baseball in Alexander Cartwright, Al Spalding, and Ban Johnson's time was a rural, pastoral game. The early professional owners, however, took their teams to the people. They fitted their ballparks into the most populous parts of cities. Their stadiums seized the pattern of the city blocks where they were built."

Bill responded, but the inning ended. Blaring music accompanying an electronic raffle race reduced his speech to fluttering lips. Bill inhaled deeply. "Has it all finally bottomed out? Bill threw up his hands. Do the fans have nothing better to do than cheer an electronic blip? Every year, I travel up to Boston to watch baseball played in a real Ballpark where the cheering and jeering are over a real game played on a real field.

Fenway Park's wacky contours and that high and dandy green monster in left make every flyball an adventure." Bill sipped some beer. "That always makes for a fun game."

"Bill, I hanker for the old parks because their quirks challenged a player's unique skills."

"Hey, good point, Mike. I can remember Yaz anticipating those fickle rebounds off Fenway's Green Monster. Heck, the old ballparks even tested managerial strategy. I can recall Shibe Park in the early sixties. Gene Mauch moved his bullpen from the leftfield corner to the rightfield corner so that one of his pitchers could signal whether a long fly was caught or hit the rightfield wall by waving a towel."

"Interesting observation, Bill. How about the great Alex winning thirty games a year as a right-handed pitcher at the old Baker Bowl? That rightfield wall was only two hundred and eighty feet away! Yet a pitcher at Brave's field had the Old Professor's fourth outfielder, Old Joe Wind', gusting in off the Charles River, salvaging pitching mistakes into outs. Bill, each park also affected the psychology of the game. Imagine a right-handed slugger's thoughts when faced with 'Death Valley' at Yankee Stadium in Joe DiMaggio's day. Pulling a ball through that monumental distance and heavy air was like pulling a loaded brick cart through a quagmire! Meanwhile, just across the Harlem River, the Polo Ground's sub-two-sixty boundaries down the lines tantalized even the weakest hitter. What about Chicago's Wrigley Field, Bill? Today, the hawk howls in, and it's a pitcher's paradise; tomorrow, the Hawk turns and condemns pitchers to the inferno."

"I first thought that the idea of lights at Wrigley stank," Bill said. "Now, I'll tolerate anything to keep it alive. Another thing, Mike, I've noticed how Fenway and Wrigley have adopted the character of their surrounding community. Mike, now I understand why my father loved talking about his father taking him down to Washington to see the A's play the Senators at Griffith's Field. I guess the Senators and Browns were the only two teams they could beat back then. I digress. My father always talked about sitting in the stands and smelling the aroma from a neighboring commercial bakery."

A recording blaring, "Da-da-da-dot-da-da," butted in on Bill's conversation. The giant animated scoreboard flashed, "Ch-a-a-a-r-ge!" He thought about his father. Burt Jenkins replaced that image. Bill forced back bile and gastric acid.

"Can you stomach that? The stadium is at least nine-tenths empty. We're mired in last place and losing eight-nothing to the next worse team. We're freezing in the rain, and they want me to yell, 'Charge'? Man." Bill shook his head. "Next, they'll want us to do the wave."

"I'll leap from the upper deck with a noose around my neck before I do the wave," Mike said. "Bill, I'm glad you mentioned the neighborhoods. Urban neighborhoods were so much different in the early twentieth century. A fraction of the drugs and ensuing violent crime. People weren't so damn suspicious and paranoid. They were friendlier. We shared a community spirit." The Phillies scored their first run, cutting the gap to seven.

Bill raised his palms, "At least we're not getting shut out. Look, Mike, I wasn't around back then, though I do share your sentiments. But I've heard it all before."

"Bill, the past is a switch-hitter. Pollution control, sanitation engineering, and waste management were either primitive or non-existent ideas back then. And racism and bigotry were real. Still, we had our ballparks! Yes, our ballparks! Luxuriant, fragrant, and perfectly manicured green grass! Basepaths of bucolic brown earth! Freedom *from* the bondage of urban drudgery!"

"Yeah, Mike! Well, take North Philly in the sixties. Take it, please. Hell, it was as blighted then as it is now. Yet we had Shibe Park! They could say anything they wanted about the condition of the building, but no one, not anyone, could fault that gorgeous green diamond."

The Phillies added another run before making the third out. The fans surrounding Bill and Mike mugged for the Panavision (a giant TV screen located in the centerfield upper deck) cameraman. He further annoyed Bill by focusing directly on himself and Mike. Bill glanced up at the screen. Mike was missing from the image. *'What the…?'* Bill quaffed down the rest of his beer. He signaled to the vendor. "Two more, please." After handing one to Mike, Bill downed his in one gulp, drowning the enigma from his mind. "Well, Mike, I'll give this place one thing: it does assume the personality, passions, and emotions of its surrounding community. The ocean-sized parking lot, I-95, and Route 76." Bill held his palm up to the pouring rain. "Damn Mike, you must really love baseball to come out here on a night like this. I feel like I'm sitting in a concrete cavern with plastic stalagmites and groundwater pouring from the ceiling."

"I didn't come to watch the game, Bill."

"What?" Bill jerked his head. "Well, why did you come?"

"To meet you, Bill."

"Me?" Bill pointed to his chest. "Why would you want to meet me?

"Because, Bill, baseball is played not just on a field. Baseball is played in the heart and mind. Despite owners who reduce our great game to a carnival spectacle, despite sportswriters who wreak vengeance for their athletic failures by assailing the players with poisoned pens, despite certain players whose gratitude for gifted ability is ramming coke up their noses or complaining about making more money in a month, than the great DiMaggio in a career; you still love and revere the game. Thus, the game will live on in your heart and mind. I know that you're going through a bad time. Things will get better. We have chosen you for a spiritual journey that only baseball can provide.

Bill watched the game. He turned to Mike. Gone. Vanished. Disappeared. Bill turned to two older, heavy-set women seated in the box behind him. "Did you see where the man sitting next to me went?"

Both women shrugged and shook their heads.

Bill next approached his usher. "Did you see the man I arrived with, you know, the one wearing the fancy but out-of-style suit, leave?"

"What man?"

"Come on now, you wouldn't pull my leg? Would you?"

"Why would I want to do a thing like that? You came here alone. I'm sure of it." The usher nodded and tilted his head.

Bill, while returning to his seat, grabbed two brews from a beer vendor. He gulped the first beer; the Cubs' batter drilled a three-run homer deep into the right-field seats. Enough! He drank the second beer during the fifteen-minute, multi-pitch walk. The rain intensified. The umpires called the game. Final score: Chicago fourteen, Philadelphia two (seven innings rain).

# Chapter 5

Bill placed a twenty on the counter and said to the bartender, "Jack Daniels and a beer."

A great American urban neighborhood, South Philly's vibrant personality and character harmonize with its individuals and families. Here, the residents respect both their neighbors and the community. Italian Americans comprise the principal citizenry, although significant pockets of German, Irish, Polish, Asian, and black people also live in South Philly. Fantastic food is eaten here. Pizza, cheesesteaks, and hoagies are among the many delicacies available at independently owned cafes and luncheonettes on every block. South Philly's corner taverns are akin to the community like the pubs in Olde England.

Bill walked from Veterans Stadium at Broad and Pattison Ave to McCusker's Tavern on Seventeenth and Shunk Streets. McCusker's ranks among America's best neighborhood taverns. Inconspicuously located, the north-facing building is on the southeast corner of a block of two-story residential row houses. Outside is a green-lettered sign simply stating, "McCusker's Tavern." Inside is a bracket (]) shaped bar on its north side, individual tables in its southern area, a jukebox and video games in its southeast corner, and TV sets in its east and west ends. Beach veneer paneling covers its plaster walls.

The patrons make McCusker's special.

"Coming right up." Ted Bodanski, tonight's bartender, is a physical bear of a man, standing 6'5" and weighing close to three hundred pounds. His hair is ultra-short on the back and sides; high, thick bristles of hair standing upright make the top of his head look like an industrial scrub brush. A horse jaw supports a large, square face. Wide, sloping shoulders and overdeveloped trapezoids gave Ted that no-neck look. His chest looks like a beer barrel; his belly looks like he drinks much of that beer. Ted has disproportionately thin legs owing to a serious football knee injury.

Ted starred as a linebacker at Penn State and twice participated in Philadelphia Eagle training camps. He still dreams of playing in the National Football League. Unfortunately, bad knees and time have stacked the odds against him. The bartender is proudly wearing a blue and white Penn State jersey. "You are soaked." He served Bill his shot of Jack Daniel's and a mug of beer. Ted took Bill's twenty and placed the change back on the counter.

"I sat through tonight's Phillies game." Bill slammed down his shot and chased it with a sip of beer.

"Gruesome. Huh? Ya should have watched it here. Heck, ya would've stayed warm and dry, and, hey, we had the Braves-Dodgers game on the other set. They played a real game."

"Yeah, but you wouldn't have believed my seats. We've had some bad teams before, but this one ..." Bill slid his shot glass forward for a refill.

Ted refilled Bill's glass, leaving the bottle of Jack Daniels on the bar counter. "I'll give you a break tonight." Ted examined Bill's Temple University sweatshirt. "I won't mention bad college football teams either."

"Okay, we'll talk about college basketball instead.

"Win a national championship before we compare programs."

"Oh, come on, Ted. Three trips to the elite eight in just six years ... What more do you want?""A national championship."

"Get real, Ted. You know that a school like Temple has no prayer of getting blue-chip recruits."

"Yeah, I gotta give you guys some credit. John Chaney is one hell of a good coach ..."

"Hey, everybody!" Spanky McMullen bellowed into the tavern. Mid-fifties, average height, and sporting a paunchy mid-section, his bald, round head made Spanky's thick, bushy mustache stand out like a palm tree in the Arctic. Spanky is wearing a green bowling shirt and puffing a thick stogie. His loud, high-pitched, rasping voice soothes as fingernails against a chalkboard. "Hey, got a Carson riddle for ya all! What's the connection between a junkie in rehab, a dirty bum, and the Philadelphia Phillies?"

"What?" Ted skewed his face and tilted his head.

"The dopeless, soapless, and hopeless. HA! HA! HA! Bill! Bill Waldron! Hey! Got one for ya in reverse! The shoeless? The clueless? The screwless?"

"I guess I have to hear it."

"Joe Jackson! The Phillies management! And Bill Waldron ... since Laura dumped him!" Spanky slapped Bill on the shoulder and blew a billow of cigar smoke in his face.

Bill clenched his fists and glowered at Spanky.

Ted interjected. "Here we go, everybody! McCusker's Jeopardy! Bald, obnoxious asshole ... Who is Spanky McMullen?"

"Oh Yeah! Well, answer this! Marie Antoinette? A bald tire? The National Football League? The headless! The tread less! And the Tedless! Ha! Ha! Ha!" Spanky walked away.

"There goes the most obnoxious human being since Howard Cosell," Bill put his elbows on the bar."Human?" Ted folded his arms.

George Mueller, a stout, white-haired man in his late sixties, sat a few stools away from Bill. George is wearing an ancient Phillies 'Whiz Kids' jacket. "I see you went to the Phillies game tonight."

"Unfortunately," Bill tapped his forehead.

"Never mind those bums. Yo, got a trivia question for ya. What brother combination hit the most home runs for one team in one year?"

"Hank and Tommie Aaron?"

"Good guess. Wrong answer. I'll give ya a clue. Both played for the BoSox."

"Oh, then it's Billy and Tony 'C.'"

"Yeah, that's it."

"Okay, George, here's one for you. Who had a higher lifetime batting average in neutral parks—Joe DiMaggio or Ted Williams?"

"Ted Williams was the best hitter I've ever seen, so I'm stayin' with the Splendid 'Splinter.'"

"Sorry, George, it was DiMaggio.""Yo, really?"

"Yes, really. The Clipper hit .333 to Teddy Ballgame's .328."

"Okay, Bill, why don't ya answer this one for me? Hank Aaron, Babe Ruth, Willie Mays, and Jimmie Foxx share something unique among Hall-of-Famers. What is it?"

" I think I got it." Bill beamed and pointed upward. "All four finished their careers in the city they started in, but with different franchises. Aaron, Milwaukee Braves, Milwaukee Brewers; Ruth, Boston Red Sox, Boston Braves; Mays, New York Giants, New York Mets; and Foxx, Philadelphia A's, Philadelphia Phillies."

"You're missing one." Ted walked over to them. "Didn't Duke Snider go from the Brooklyn Dodgers to the LA Dodgers, to the New York Mets?"

"Yes, but the Duke finished with the San Francisco Giants in 1964. I know." Bill grimaced. "I'll never forget that season."

"All right." George addressed Bill and Ted, "Answer this one. Nine players have won two consecutive MVP awards. Each played a different position on the diamond. Who were they?"

"An easy one is Mike Schmidt at third base," Bill gulped some beer. "Another player with Phillies connections…Joe Morgan at second base, and Mickey Mantle in the outfield.""Right, so far." George clapped his hands.

"How-a-bout Dick Allen at first base?"

"Nope. But he did play for Philadelphia."

"Ahh…You made it too easy," Bill sipped his shot of Tennessee whisky. "Jimmy Double XX Foxx."

"Yup, Jimmie 'Double X' Foxx …"

Ted polished a glass, "How 'bout Ernie Banks at shortstop and Dale Murphy in the outfield."

"How 'bout Dale Murphy and Ernie Banks. You still need a pitcher, catcher, and outfie ...

Spanky butted in. "Answer this one! Who took the most balls on the chin?"

"Rock Hudson." Ted pulled his face and placed his hands on his hips.

"Yeah, right." Spanky turned away and intruded on another group to tell his repertoire of stale Rock Hudson jokes.

Ted sighed. "Hate to correct you, Bill, but Spanky McMullen is *more* obnoxious than Howard Cosell. All right, George, what about Roy Campanella at catcher?"

"Nope." George shook his head.

"How about Yogi Berra," Bill raised his forefinger.

"Yup." George nodded. "I need an outfielder and a pitcher."

Anthony Malone and Vinnie Romano sat within earshot. An odd couple. Anthony is middle-aged, balding, at least twenty pounds overweight, sloppily dressed, and unshaven. Vinnie, however, is a youthful twenty-one, over six feet tall, lean, boasting a full head of dark brown hair and a clear olive complexion.

Anthony jumped in. "Gotta be the 'Say Hey Kid' in the outfield.""No, it doesn't." George sipped his beer. "Do I have to give you guys a hint?"

"Yeah, give us a hint." Bill gulped some beer.

He played in the same city as Mickey and Willie.”

“The Duke!” Vinnie jumped up from his barstool.“Not even close.” George looked down and shook his head.

“I know!” Bill said. “Roger Maris, the other ‘M’ and ‘M’ boy, 1960 and ’61.”

“Got it.” George folded his arms. “Okay, all I need is a pitcher.”

“Cy Young, Bob Gibson, Walter Johnson, Sandy Koufax,” Ted fired back.

“No, no, no, and no,” George raised his hands. “It is a tough one. He did it in World War II.”

“Hal Newhouser.” Bill slapped his thigh.

“Yup, Hal Newhouser in 1944 and ’45. I remember watching Hal Newhouser pitch against the A's at Shibe Park. Hell of a pitcher. Though Ferris Fain and Sam Chapman used to hit him quite well ...”

“Hell, George, you've been around long enough to see Old Hoss Radbourn pitch to King Kelly.” Anthony hit George with the nineteenth-century ballplayer quip to stop him from blathering for ages about the Philadelphia A's at Shibe Park. Bill, however, enjoyed listening to George's recollections. Sometimes, for over an hour.

Ted poured Bill a refill of both bourbon and beer. “I'm about this close,” Ted held his thumb and forefinger a half inch apart, “to going over there and sticking a sock down McMullen's throat.” He pointed at Spanky, lividly cracking joke after joke at some patrons standing in the southeast corner of the pub.

“Come on, Ted, don't let that loudmouth get to you.” Bill tapped the bar counter. “Yo, when do you start Eagles training camp?”

“Unfortunately, Bill, I'm afraid that it's not a matter of when, but if.” Ted leaned with his elbows on the bar counter. “My knee turned arthritic. The Eagles are giving me a physical next month. It's no pass, no play."

"Are you doing any special training?"

"Yeah, the usual physio'. You know, ultrasound, electro-stimulation, deep heat, anti-inflammation ... that sort of thing. I'm doing some running. Lots of leg extensions—I can't go heavy, and I have to go light on the squats ..."

"It's too bad the mysterious woman my father once mentioned couldn't come in and faith heal your knee like he claims she did Ed Braceland's shoulder."

"Yo! Waldron! Ain't that you!" Vinnie pointed to a TV showing low lights of the night's Phillies game. Included was a long pan of Bill sitting alone on top of the Phillies dugout.

The solo image confounded Bill. He stared jaw agape, at the television. Slamming down his shot, he chased it with an entire mug of beer.

"Hey, we have ourselves a TV star! A round on the house for our new celebrity!" Ted poured Bill another shot of bourbon and drew him another mug of draft beer. "Yo Bill, you weren't kidding about having great seats. Whoever gave you such a ticket?"

Bill gritted his teeth as he envisioned Laura, beautiful Laura, her sexy naked body- sharing it with Burt Jenkins. Bill clenched his teeth before downing his shot. He grabbed his beer, popped out of his bar stool, and wandered toward the jukebox. Hoping to quell the unwanted image, he played his favorite song. The Four Tops' "Ask the Lonely."

Bill sniffled his nose, wiped tears from his eyes with his shirt sleeve, and, as far as pouring water into the radiator can revive an overheated Edsel, poured beer into his belly to collect his emotions. Composure, he needed. He found himself facing Joseph Loviglio. Joseph stood shorter than average but compensated with a trim physique earned by miles of jogging and racquetball. His custom gray suit was a perfect fit. Bill usually enjoyed Joseph's articulate and interesting talk, but he's an attorney and speaks well of Burt Jenkins. "Bill Waldron. How are you?" Joseph extended his right hand.

Bill paused before giving Joseph's hand a cursory shake. "I'm doing great, and I see even better times coming." Bill turned and went back to his barstool. Ted had refilled Bill's bourbon during his absence. He slammed down his Tennessee whisky but stared into his beer.

"Another one?" Ted held a bottle of Jack Daniels. Bill continued contemplating his beer. "Bill! Are you Okay?"

Shaking his head, Bill looked at Ted foggily.

"Bill. What's wrong?"

"Um, Ted ... Ted, it's this divorce busin ... business, and all, um, I will be okay. I'm, um, sure, I'll be okay."

"All right, Bill. I know you're not driving." Ted shook his head. "But I'm afraid I must cut you off. Well, if it makes you feel any better, you're not the only one. Antny is divorced. George also." Ted pointed to George. "And he was married for over twenty-five years! Hey, believe me, I've seen worse cases than you comin' in here. All you guys, cryin' in your beers, 'cause some broad dumped ya. Well, I've already got my girl. She's the only one any man should ever need. My dear mother."

Anthony Malone butted in. "Oh, there you go again, Ted. Hey, if ya ever goes into the motel business, remind me never to shower there."

"What are you worried about, Antny?" George folded his arms. "You never shower anyway."

Bill downed both of his drinks, mustering the courage to sing the chorus from an Intruder's song, "I'll Always Love My Mamma. She's my favorite girl. I'll always love my mama. She brought me into this world…"

"All right, all right, enough! Ted banged on the bar with his right fist. "Hey, since when is there a sign out front saying, 'free drinks for the worst singer'?"

Spanky McMullen jumped in. "Yo, Waldron, did your singing teacher make you give your lessons back? HA! HA! HA! Yo, that's okay, go ahead, sing away—away from me!" Spanky brushed off Bill and returned to the southeast corner of the tavern.

"Yo Bill," Ted held up a bottle of Jack Daniels.

"I changed my mind. I'll serve you a drink on the house if you keep singing ... Anything to keep that bald-headed cretin away from me. Come on, Bill, what are ya waitin' for?" Ted sang, "One thousand bottles of beer on the wall, one thousand bottles of beer ..."

Bill sang, "One thousand bottles of beer ..."

Ted poured.

The fixations returned. Laura and Burt kissed. His hand wrapped around her back and undid...*'No. No.'* He squeezed his temples. *'Yes, Rory, four years old, Laura, young Laura, The Wildwood Boardwalk. The roller coaster over the ocean.* Down, down, down they plummet...Suddenly, into an opening in the Earth. They plunged toward the pit. The tracks trisect. Laura is ripped from Bill's side and into Burt Jenkins's black Porsche; they disappear down the left-bound track. Rory now rode on the back of a demon-driven chopper motorcycle; away they went on the right-bound track. *'I'm alone, down, down...'* His forehead struck the bar counter. The shock returned him to the real world.

Anthony spoke to Vinnie loudly enough for the entire tavern to hear. "Look, kid, if ya wanna score with Gloria, ya gotta change your tactics. Why don't ya borrow my van, take her to da lakes, get her a little drunk, play 'er some Tony Bennett ..."

"Tony Bennett?" Ted interjected. "Yo! Antny! What decade are you living in? Young chicks don't listen to Tony Bennett. Yo Waldron ... Waldron! ... Earth to Waldron ..."

"Um, yeah."

"You're a high school teacher. Do young chicks listen to Tony Bennett?"

"Um, Tony Bennett? They listen to, um, Michael Jackson, um, Madonna, ah, heavy metal, Guns and Roses, Nivana is huge, they like rap, but, um, unfortunately, and, uh, I do mean, un ... unfortunately, not Tony Bennett."

"Yo, right, Waldron," Anthony said. "Rap? I'm tryin' to tell the kid how ta woo the girl—not rape her!" He thrust his hips back and forth, "Do me, do me, bitch, bitch, ho, ho, mudda fukka, mudda fukka, ugh, ugh, ugh."

Vinnie blushed. "Oh, come on, you guys. Lay off, why don't ya? Have some respect for the girl. I'll wait 'till the time is right for both of us."

"Wait 'till the time is right for both of ya?" Anthony asked. "Yo, you're soundin' like a girl, Vinnie. What's a matter? Are ya a homo or somethin'? Yo, if I were young again, I wouldn't pass up a shot at a hot young babe like Gloria."

"Hey, I'm on Social Security," George grinned. "That never stopped me any."

"Yo, you're all a buncha dirty old farts," Vinnie said. "Do you guys have nothin' but sex on the brain or what? Can't a guy respect a girl? Gloria and I are good friends.

"Friends?" Anthony asked. "Look, kid, a man can have whiskey as a friend, and a man can have a dog as a friend—but if he has a woman as a friend ... He ends up drunk and kissing his dog!

"Yo Antny! Judging by how often I've filled your glass tonight, you're a prime example of the first."

Spanky McMullen jumped in. "Ya Ted, now if you'd bring him your mother ... He can do the second! HA! HA! HA!"

Ted vaulted over the bar. He charged Spanky like a semi, going down a seven percent grade.

Resembling a rubber cone roadblock, Joseph Loviglio slid between them. "Hey, come on, Ted! Don't do anything stupid!"

"Don't do anything stupid?" Spanky saw that Joseph stood between him and Ted. "That dumb pollock's been doing nothing but stupid since the day he was born!"

"Nobody! Especially not that bald-headed asshole! Gets away with insultin' my mama!"

"Calm down," Joseph said. "Your mama wouldn't consider your beating the crap out of someone twenty-five years older and over a hundred pounds lighter, defending her honor. Would she now?"

"Whatever it takes!" Ted shouted, raising his fist over Joseph's shoulder.

Spanky, with a safe distance and a clear path to the door, shouted, "The problem with you big, stupid, lug-heads is you can dish it out, but ya can't fuckin' take it!"

Ted recoiled. Joseph's restraint bought a crucial second. "Come on, Ted. Calm down. You know that's not what your mother would want. You can't support her from prison, can you?"

"All right! All right. But I want that bald-headed son-of-a-bitch out of here! That is o-u-t out!""Very good, Ted," George stood. "Last night it was k-a-t cat."

Joseph led Spanky to the northeast door. Spanky grumbled like *Muttley* the cartoon dog. Joseph opened the door. "Yes, all right, he's nothing but a dumb pollock. Let me deal with Ted. Call it a night. Come back tomorrow when things have cooled down."

Ted Bodanski, gritting his teeth and breathing in short gasps, returned to his post. He inhaled deeply, "I know I shouldn't." He poured Bill more Tennessee whiskey before buffing a beer mug with a towel.

"Hey, Pollock!" Spanky, like 'Jason,' 'Michael Myers,' and 'Freddie Krueger' from the slasher films, reappeared through the northwest door. "What do you think of my new mustache?" Spanky pinched his mustache between thumb and forefinger.

Ted hunched his back, jutted his jaw, and clenched his fists. He glared blowtorch eyes and thundered. "Your mustache is as ugly as all damn hell!"

"I guess you'll call it pretty ... When it's as thick and bushy as your mother's!" Spanky bolted out the door.

Ted grabbed a police nightstick from under the bar and, like Thor throwing a thunderbolt, hurled it at where Spanky seconds ago stood. It impaled the wall.

Bill draped his Sixers jacket over the nightstick. The other patrons also. The entire tavern guffawed. Bill, although considering Ted, his friend and disinclined toward Spanky, joined the laughter. *'I hate to think it. Ted's mother is one ugly battleship of a woman.'*

***

Over six hours of alcohol abuse pulsated through Bill's cranium like an over-extended electric generator, impairing perception and thought. The banter of McCusker's deteriorated into a cacophony. Colors faded into depressing shades of gray. He stumbled out of McCusker's. He left his money on the bar counter and his jacket with a Walkman in his pocket on Ted's nightstick. Bill staggered onto Shunk Street. The rain had stopped, although puddles and water slicks soaked the roads. The sidewalk seemed to rock like a wharf boat. He tottered up Shunk Street toward Broad Street. He keeled over and wretched on the sidewalk. His world sank into a blur. His thoughts felt like tires spinning in the mud. Crossing Seventeenth Street, Bill was nearly struck by a speeding, horn-blaring car. He stumbled into a parked car before staggering back to the sidewalk. He heaved again. Three male teens and one female teen watched from a porch. The male with the girlfriend yelled, "I see you got guts." The group laughed at

Bill. "But they're supposed to be on the inside." The teens guffawed.

Oblivious to the mockery, he reeled on and sang loudly and off-key a Gamble and Huff song recorded by an R&B group called *The Formations,* "At the top of the stairs, there's darkness. My life is not based on happiness. My life has been sadly tainted, Now I fear the sight of darkness. Now I fear the shadow of loneliness." A violent heave broke his voice. With his next step, he slipped in his vomit, bashing his face and bloodying his nose on the sidewalk. Clutching his bleeding nose, he rolled off the curb and into the gutter. Bill looked up. Concussive sparks replaced the stars. He puked again. He rolled over and spat it out.

A shrill siren blasted for a split second. Red and Blue flashing lights stung his salty tears. He made out two police officers, a blurry silhouette of a white cop and a black cop. The white cop put his hands on his hips. "It looks like you've had too much to drink. Let's see some ID."

Bill stood, pulled out his wallet and handed the policeman all his cards.

"I don't need all of these." The white cop shuffled through the cards, found his driver's license, and held it up to his eyes. "This is a Society Hill Address. Washington Square. What are you doing in this neighborhood, drunk off your ass? Did Leah the Ghost chase you here?" He sniggered. The two policemen looked at each other and nodded.

The black cop stepped forward. "We have every rhyme and reason to run you in for public drunkenness and charge you with disorderly conduct. Only it would take us half the night to process you. We have crimes to prevent. Where is your car parked?"

"Center city. Spruce Street. Around 12th or 11th Street.

"Good answer. We'd lock you up for even thinking about driving."

"I doubt you're capable of putting a coin in a payphone." The white cop looked Bill over. "And you surely don't look like you have the means to own a cellphone. I saw that you had cash in your wallet. Here's what we're going to do. I'm going to radio for a cab. Stay where you are. Take the cab home."

The Black cop prodded. "If you're still here when we return, we're running your sorry ass in."

After the policemen drove away, Bill keeled over and dry heaved. He looked up. The vision was blurry yet distinct. He rubbed his eyes. He saw a man in his athletic prime. He wore a wool flannel baseball uniform with a high, string-laced collar. Bill rubbed his eyes. He saw he had thick, dark hair protruding from the edges of his high-crowned baseball cap. Bill closed his eyes and put his fingers over his eyelids. He opened his eyes and squinted. The old-time ball player remained. Bill craned his head and looked closer. *The eyes, the shape of the face. It's Mike Kelly.'*

"Back in my playing days, I was quite the reveler. Yet I never did to myself what you've done. You can still make a difference in your students' lives, but not this way. I know your problems. I know all about you. You're close to rock bottom. When things get their worst, your calling will begin."

Bill gasped. "My calling?" He clutched his stomach, fighting a dry spasm. "I don't understand." His brain felt like it was dissolving. "What, what, what do you want with me?"

"You've been chosen. The spirit of Baseball came into your heart when you were in the womb. Your time has arrived. We're about to take you on a journey."

"What do you mean by the 'Spirit of Baseball?" Bill lurched toward Mike. "I never played at a high level. I wasn't even that good in Little League."

"A player and the game on the field exist in a different dimension. You have always respected that. You connected in spirit. Because of your spiritual connection to the game, we trust the game in you."

Mike vanished.

Bill ran to his former spot. He waved his arms, hoping to grasp him, not hearing the blaring horn or the skidding brakes. A van slammed into him. His head dribbled on the street like a basketball.

# End of Part I

# Part II

# Chapter 1

"You okay, Bill?" Bill saw the blurry image of his father. Concern etched Dennis Waldron's angular face. Worried eyes seared the lenses of his plastic, black-framed glasses. "Can you sit up?" Dennis, clenching a yellow plastic whiffle ball bat, helped his son sit. "How do you feel?"

"My head hurts." Bill placed his hand behind his head. "What happened?"

"Try to remember?" Dennis knelt in front of him. "We were playing Whiffle ball. You chased Jeff's hit, slipped on some loose gravel, and fell back on your head."

A motorist turned down S. Colorado Street, halting before the gathering.

"Try to stand. We can't sit here in the street all afternoon." Dennis pulled his son to his feet and helped him stagger to a door stoop. "Sit here."

Bill rubbed his eyes. His father and his two best friends, Jeff and Frank, had gathered around him.

21 September 1964. The best of times. On this first crisp day of Fall, the sycamore, oak, and maple trees flanking South Philadelphia's S. Colorado Street foliage boasted their Autumn tints. A wonderful chapter of thirteen-year-old Bill Waldron's life, invigorating whiffle ball games with his dad and two best buddies, and his heroes, the Philadelphia Phillies, were six and a half games up in first place with only twelve games to play. Pennant bound! The year of the blue snow. "I feel okay, Dad."

"You look better already." Dennis smiled. "Your color is even returning."

"I'm okay now, Dad." Bill smiled. "Really, I am."

"I think you'll live. You had me worrying." Dennis slapped Bill's arm, "But you're a tough kid, aren't you, son?"

"Yes! I am!"

"Well, I've got a surprise for you! Jeff and Frank, you're in on it too. Don't worry. I've cleared it with your parents. Wait right here, boys."

Dennis soon emerged in his gray, top-down Buick Electra convertible. He honked the horn and shouted, "Climb in, boys!"

Bill, Frank, and Jeff glanced at each other. In a flash, they yelled, "All right!" and scrambled into the open convertible. The three sat shotgun atop the back seat as Dennis headed eastbound on Oregon Avenue. The sounds of a Junior Pirolo and the Four J's song, "Precious Moments," blared from the eight-track tape deck. A left on Broad Street and a right up Passyunk Avenue meant only one thing. Pat's Steaks! A second after Dennis parked, the three boys leaped from the car and ran to the counter.

"Cheesesteak, lots of onions, and a chocolate shake," Bill shouted.

"I want extra hot peppers," Frank yelled.

"Give me some cheese fries with mine," Jeff bumped ahead of them.

Bill, Frank, and Jeff devoured their sandwiches. "Hurry up, boys!" Dennis stood by the car door. "We don't wanna be late."

The boys piled back into the car. Dennis drove north on Ninth Street, west on Washington Avenue, and on Broad Street, he steered north instead of south.

Each passing northbound block spurred Bill's anticipation. A left on Lehigh Ave. confirmed first prize. Frank, the sharpest of the three boyhood buddies, spotted the light towers first. Dennis raised the volume of the radio. Future Rock and Roll Hall of Fame disc jockey Jerry Blavat introduced The Four Tops' "Baby I Need Your Loving" in his articulate, signature rapid-fire delivery. The song spiked Bill's anticipation. *'We're* going to a *Phillies game!'*

Dennis orbited the surrounding blocks in search of a parking space. Mission accomplished. His reception committee consisted of two black youths about his son's age. One wore a dirty cotton sweatshirt with "Phillies," and Dick Allen's number *15* felt markered on the back. The other looked tougher. He wore black slacks and a black leather jacket over a white T-shirt. "Watch ya car for a buck?" The kid in the sweatshirt held open his palm.

Dennis looked toward Bill, Frank, and Jeff. "This one's on you, boys. Come on, dig in."

Bill found two quarters and a nickel, Frank thirty-seven cents in pennies, dimes, and nickels, and Jeff a fifty-cent piece.

"Okay. Here's a buck forty-two. Now I expect you guys to watch my car real good." Walking away, Dennis fleetingly glanced back at the black leather-clad youth and realized that the he invested the extra forty-two cents wisely.

Dennis and the boys soon joined about fifty others who assembled to listen to five young men from North Philly singing a capella on the corner of 21st and Lehigh. Philadelphia has been called "Soul-adelphia" because of its music cutting through racial barriers. These young singers were no exception with their interpretation of the song "These will be the good old days," recorded by a local vocal group called "The Dreamlovers."

Their music gave the dingy North Philadelphia neighborhood a festive aura. This took magic, as racial unrest recently hit the area. Although the Phillies had started deferring maintenance on Connie Mack Stadium since the previous decade, in 1964, the ballpark and baseball seemed like the calm before the decade's storm of racial and cultural strife.

The exterior of Shibe Park featured a French Renaissance facade, vaunted spirals, arches, and lavish windows. The cathedral-like dome of Connie Mack's old office acted as the northeast corner of 2lst and Lehigh's centerpiece. Gabled roofs crowned the ballpark.

Inside, 20,067 jubilant spectators from all backgrounds united to boost their pennant-bound heroes. Many sported either souvenir Phillies caps or waved Phillies pennants. Banners hailing their imminent champions hung from the rafters.

The Phillies pitted their number three starter, Art Mahaffey, and his winning 12-8 record against the Cincinnati Reds journeyman spot starter, John Tsitouris, and his losing 7- 11 record.

Dennis, Bill, Frank, and Jeff took their general admission seats thirteen rows up in the upper deck, directly online with the third base bag. "Hey, those guys back on Lehigh Avenue sure sang great."

"Yeah, Dad, they sure did. And I'm glad that the Phillies are back home. That last West Coast trip was a hard one.

"I just hope it wasn't too tough." Frank pointed toward the Phillies bullpen. "Toward the end, those pitchers looked tired."

"Oh, come on," Jeff raised his hands, "Exactly who looked tired?

"How about Ed Roebuck? When's the last time he pitched effectively? Or Jack Baldschun for that matter? And whatever happened to Ray Culp? Even today's pitcher, Art Mahaffey, has been walking people like mad the last couple of weeks."

"So what, Frank, the Phillies are gonna score a ton of runs off John," Bill giggled, "Tit-saurus.

"Hey, watch your mouth, son!"

"Yeah, well, they're gonna kill the bum. Look at him," Bill pointed at the Reds pitcher. "He throws like a girl." He leaped and pointed, "Yeah! Base hit! Way to go, Tony Gonzalez. We're just getting started."

"What do you think, son?" Dennis sipped his beer. Richie Allen is up."

"I think he's going to homer!" Bill pointed over the roof of the left-field bleachers. "Over the Coke sign. I can just feel it! Come on, Richie! A  Bunt?" Bill threw up his hands. "I don't believe it. How can you sacrifice with Richie Allen?"

"Why are you so surprised?" Frank turned to Bill. "Gene Mauch always plays for one run."

"I still say no way ya have Richie Allen bunt. What do ya say, Dad?"

"Hey, the General's got us six and a half games up with the World Series just two weeks away. You can't argue with that, can you?"

Gene Mauch's strategy failed to produce a first inning run. Johnny Callison and Wes Covington stranded Tony Gonzalez at second. Ditto the next inning. The Phillies put Clay Dalrymple on second base and Tony Taylor on first with just one out. Yet shortstop Ruben Amaro skied into the second out. Art Mahaffey then hammered a hard grounder up the middle that Cincinnati shortstop Leo Cardenas caught and flipped across to second baseman Pete Rose for out number three.

The Phillies sizzled in their third. The loudspeaker announced: "Now batting for the Phillies. Number fifteen. Richie Allen."

Nudging Jeff, Bill edged forward. "He ain't bunting this time. Here comes a homer."

On cue came a thunderous crack of the bat.  Allen scorched a rising line drive into the North Philly night. Bill leaped and yelled along with 20,066 other fans. A home run in any other National League Park. Except Shibe Park's fifty-foot-high right-centerfield scoreboard knocked down Allen's homerun bid like a backboard knocking down a basketball. A safe hit, nonetheless, and a good one at that. Allen rounded second base before Frank Robinson's throw reached Pete Rose. "A triple! He's going for a triple!" Bill nudged his father. The second baseman relayed to third baseman Chico Ruiz. Late. Umpire Augie Donatelli disagreed. His right thumb pointed up, signaling the bad news.

"No! No! He was safe, you cripple-eyed dunce!" Dennis shook his fist.

Gene Mauch sprang from the dugout. Like an angry Drill Sergeant dressing down an erring recruit, he spat tirades, eye to eye, nose to nose, cheek to cheek, upon the umpire. Only Dick Allen, Augie Donatelli, and Gene Mauch himself knew the exact words. The angry fans at Connie Mack Stadium shouted their contribution.

"We wuz robbed!" A glassy-eyed Jeff's jaw dropped.

"He looked safe to me." Frank calmly turned to Jeff.

"The blind bum cheats us out of a triple, and that's all you can say?" Bill seethed with anger. "Someone up there's turned against us. I can feel it. Richie was safe. Should have been a triple."

"Cheer up Bill." Dennis patted Bill's back. "It's only the third inning, and it's still a tie ball game. Hey, here comes the hot dog man." Dennis purchased six hot dogs with a five-dollar bill. The hot dog vendor returned ample change. Dennis handed one to Bill. "Just don't choke on it like that blind umpire."

The Phillies' attempts at hitting John Tsitouris's junk curves and screwballs looked as awkward as his pitching. Sportswriter Sandy Grady described Tsitouris as "Having the pitching motion of your Aunt Maude swatting a mosquito."

The Phillies tired and sore-armed Art Mahaffey also proved an unlikely pitching hero by shutting out the Reds until one out in the sixth. Chico Ruiz, a rookie bench warmer enjoying a rare start at third base, blooped a soft single to right. Cincinnati's centerfielder Vada Pinson next smashed a ball up the middle. It deflected off Mahaffey, clear to right field. Ruiz headed for third; Pinson darted for second. Right fielder Johnny Callison gunned out Pinson.

Nevertheless, Ruiz now stood just ninety feet away from scoring the game's first run.

The Reds' best hitter, Frank Robinson, batted. Gene Mauch feared Frank Robinson as the top clutch hitter in the game in addition to creating runs at a Hall-of-Fame clip.

Young Bill Waldron leaned forward in his seat, fingers crossed, fixing his gaze on the dangerous Robinson.

Mahaffey threw the first pitch past the slugger for a strike.

"Yes." Bill closed his eyes, freezing his expression. "Come on, baby, two more; you can do it, Art."

Chico Ruiz audaciously increased his lead off third base.

"Watch him, Art!" Dennis cupped his hands over his mouth and yelled from the upper deck.

Ruiz jigged farther from the base…two steps more…he broke for home.

"No! No! No!" The Reds' third base coach held up his hands.

The act stunned Art Mahaffey. He hastened his pitching motion and heaved the ball past the catcher. It rolled to the backstop. Chico Ruiz scored the game's first run standing.

Frank Robinson and on-deck hitter Deron Johnson, nonplused, didn't congratulate him.

Reds' interim manager, and ironically a former Phillies whiz kid's hero, Dick Sisler, instead of celebrating the go-ahead run, glowered at third base coach Reggie Otero. He shook his head at the manager, denying any foreknowledge.

"I don't believe it!" Dennis smacked his thigh. "I don't stinkin' believe it!" He turned to his bewildered son. "Maybe your premonition wasn't just superstition. Maybe something out there has turned against us."

***

Bottom of the ninth. The score remained one-zero. Tsitouris still baffled the Phillies batters. A voice bellowed from higher in the upper deck, "Come on. It's time to hit this stiff-armed son-of-a-bitch."

"Yeah!" Bill stood. "Kill Tit-saurus!"

"Bill! Watch your mouth! You say another bad word, and I'm taking you home and not bringing you back!"

A fan three rows in front o f Bill and Dennis yelled, "Yeah, listen to the kid. Kill that Tit-saurus."

A meteor boomed off Wes Covington's bat. The Phillies left fielder nailed a Tsitouris delivery against the scoreboard for a leadoff double. Gene Mauch pinch-ran for him with the speedy Adolpho Phillips. "Bunt. He has to bunt." Frank leaned over to Bill.

The next batter, Johnny Hernnstein, didn't bunt. He almost moved the runner anyway, but his grounder to the right side went just foul.

"I don't understand this." Frank shook his head. "Mauch bunts with Richie Allen in the first inning. Now he's losing by one in the ninth, and he lets this oversized bum, who couldn't hit his way out of a wet paper bag, hit away."

"No way, Frank," Bill held up crossed fingers. "Johnny's going to get a hit." Bill dropped his head and groaned as Hernnstein popped out. Clay Dalrymple then advanced Phillips, one out too late, by grounding out to Rose.

Fan favorite Tony Taylor hit next. The crowd chanted, stomped their feet, and hit their seats in a one-beat rhythm, "We want a hit! We want a hit! We want a hit!" Phillips, like Chico Ruiz, danced off third. Tsitouris, unlike Art Mahaffey, paid attention to Phillips. Too vigilantly. Maybe the Phillies didn't need a hit.

"Balk!" Frank stood and pointed at the pitcher. "He just balked!"

Gene Mauch agreed. He charged the field and jawed it out with the umpire.

"You see, he stood behind the rubber and toed it twice." Frank punched his palm. "That's a balk. The ump should wave Phillips home."

"Geez, Frank, I surely hope you know your schoolwork like you do baseball." Dennis shook his head. "And I also wish this umpiring crew knew baseball as well as you."

Gene Mauch again couldn't make the umpires see the light. The Phillies still needed a hit. Tsitouris, distracted, eventually walked Taylor on a 3-2 pitch. Ruben Amaro, the Phillies weak-hitting shortstop and eight-hole hitter, batted next.

"I hope Mauch doesn't let this one hit." Frank gripped the edge of his seat. "He's got two .290 hitters in Alex Johnson and Cookie Rojas on the bench."

"Hey, don't you know, Ruben's been the Phillies hottest batter over the past two weeks," Bill pointed upward.

"Yeah, right." Frank raised his hands. "The day Amaro's a hot hitter is the day it's cold in H-E-Double hockey stick."

"Come on, stop arguing, kids. Hey, come on, we want a hit; we want a hit," Dennis chanted.

The Fans augmented the chant with a rhythmic one-beat clap, but to no avail. Amaro fanned meekly on three pitches.

Some fans booed. Most lowered their heads and trudged to their cars. Dennis muttered to the boys. "It's just one loss? One game at a time. Gotta take it one game at a time."

***

McCuskers Tavern was quiet on this brisk Monday night.

"Scotch on the rocks, Dennis?" Ed Braceland had returned to bartending at McCusker's after a brief stint in the

NFL. He made the Philadelphia Eagles practice squad two years prior and played two sets of downs. After failing to make the squad next season, the Washington Redskins signed him. He got into one game. "How's the wife?" Ed placed Dennis's drink on the counter.

"Fine, just fine." Dennis sipped his scotch.

"Getting along okay?"

"Yeah. The same. The household can't run without the little lady, you know."

"How are the kids?"

"Marie's fine. She's still a bit shy, though I guess that's just her. She always helps Patricia around the house and is getting good grades. I took Bill and a couple of his buddies to the game tonight . . ."

"Hey, Everybody! What did the Spanish fireman name his first son?" Spanky McMullen barged into the tavern, puffing a thick stogie. A New York Yankees baseball cap vainly concealed his prematurely bald scalp.

Dennis slid his glass forward. "Make it a double."

"I'm afraid to ask." Ed lowered his eyes.

"Jose. Now, what did he name his second son? ... Hose B. Get it? Hose A and Hose B. Ha! Ha! Ha!"

"Very funny," Dennis said. "Why don't you cut the jokes and snuff the stogie? Who do you think you are? Groucho Marx?"

"Yeah? Well, who do you think you are? Dennis the Menace's father? Get some human glasses, why don't ya? Hey, I got another. Who invented the toilet seat? ... Believe it or not—the Polish ... Three years later, they put the hole in the center! Ha! Ha! Ha!"

Johnny McCusker, the bar owner, sat in the northeast corner of the bar, face immersed in a page of a *Philadelphia Bulletin* newspaper. He stacked copies of the *Philadelphia Inquirer, the Philadelphia Daily News,* the *New York Times, The Sporting News,* and four racing forms in front of him. He adjusted his glasses and placed his Evening Bulletin on the pile. "Strange game tonight. I listened to it on the radio. When By Saam said that Ruiz had stolen home with Frank Robinson batting, I thought it was an April Fool's joke or Halloween prank. Only it's September, so I guess it happened. And getting shut out by this Tourist, Zorrist, or whatever."

"Tit-saurus," Dennis grinned.

Six patrons seated at the bar laughed.

"Tit-saurus! Ha! Ha! Ha! Good one! Yo, Waldron, I didn't think you had it in ya. Hey, that one was almost as funny as ya look."

"Ya? You want funny, McMullen?" Dennis sighed and turned to Spanky with lowered eyes. "Why don't you take off your hat? I would tell ya to put it over your ass, only you better leave it on your head—it's shinier!" The entire tavern, except Spanky, guffawed.

"Well, as I was saying," Johnny glanced at a racing form, "It's not just that they lost. Even the best team in baseball's gonna lose sixty games. It's the way they lost." Johnny placed his racing form on top of his Philadelphia Inquirer newspaper. "It feels like an omen."

"Oh, come on, Johnny. Omen?" Dennis rolled his eyes and downed his drink. "If I wanted to talk to some profit of doom, I'd go to one of those fake gypsies on South Street."

"Hear me out, Dennis. I said back in spring training that they were, at best, maybe the fourth-best team in the league. Okay, the Phillies have Gonzalez, Callison, and Covington in the outfield. Fair enough, they're good ball players, but they all bat left. Rookie Allen hits great, but defensively, he's out of position. After that, it's a wing and a prayer. Especially first base. Pitching. After Bunning and Short, who on that staff do you want to tell me is throwing well? Off the top of my head, I can rattle off the names of eight Cincinnati

Reds pitchers who are throwing well: O'Toole, Maloney, Purkey, Jay, Nuxhal, Ellis, McCool, and of course, uh, Tit-saurus." Johnny paused to circle a horse in his racing form. "Their line-up has Frank Robinson, Vada Pinson, Johnny Edwards, and Pete Rose. Take first baseman Deron Johnson; he'll drive in more runs in his sleep than an entire bowl of those wet noodles Gene Mauch's runnin' out there to fill Frank Thomas's shoes. Look at the Giants. Hey, as much as I admire Allen and Callison, they'll never be Willie Mays."

"Or Mickey Mantle." Spanky puffed a cloud of cigar smoke.

"Hey, we're talking about the National League." Dennis sneered at Spanky. "You know something, there's something about your kind that turns my stomach. You've lived in Philadelphia all your pathetic life, yet you come here claiming the Yankees as your team. Just where in the hell do you get off anyway?"

"Yeah, well, I've got lots of relatives living in New York."

"McMullen, you don't have any 'living' relatives. Just body parts. Unless you consider the defective brain Igor gave Frankenstein a relative."

"Another one." Johnny slid his glass forward and signaled for a round for Spanky and Dennis. "As I was saying, the Giants have Mays, who's in a class by himself. Plus, McCovey, who's every bit as dangerous a hitter, plus Cepeda, plus Jim Ray Hart, plus Tom Haller, and two pretty fair pitchers named Marichal and Perry. Even Milwaukee. Look at Bobby Bragan's line-up: Aaron, Mathews, Joe Torre, Arthur Lee Maye, and Rico Carty. Their entire outfield's gonna bat damn near .330 collectively." Johnny jotted the name of a jockey on his racing form's margin. "Even their shortstop, Dennis Menke, is on track to hit twenty homers. Hell, if Warren Spahn didn't get old overnight, they'd be making some noise.

"Yeah, well, the Phillies have Milwaukee buried." Dennis gulped the rest of his scotch.

"Fortunately, they are. Unfortunately, St. Louis isn't. Everybody's worrying about Cincinnati right now, but look out for the Cards. For my money, they're the best team in the NL."

George Mueller, a powerfully built, dark-haired man in his mid-thirties, listened in. "Oh, come on, Johnny. They're still five and a half up. Hey, look at it this way, Puddin Head Jones gave me this jacket after their last World Series. I was barely out of my teens back then. I don't intend on being an old man before wearin' it to the next series. So, seeing the only time you ever won a bet was when that computer guy from California gave you results, put your money where your mouth is. Your bet on the Cardinals guarantees us a pennant."

"Yeah, well, the Yankees kicked Puddin' Head Jones and the rest of the so-called 'Whiz Kids' asses." Spanky blanketed Dennis's head with cigar smoke. "And, if, for some strange reason, this team don't choke away the pennant, they're gonna kick your butts again."

"You know something, McMullen." Dennis, like a wild West gunfighter, slowly turned to Spanky. "I can't see any reason, strange or otherwise, to not kick your butt."

"I can think of one, and it's a damn good one! I'd kick yours first! Ya, skinny four-eyed Geek!"

Dennis removed his glasses and slowly placed them on the bar counter. "We'll just see about that!" He stripped the Yankee cap from Spanky's head and flung it against the wall. "Ya bald son-of-a-bitch hairless wonder."

"Yeah! Well, you've also got a bald head. On the Inside!" Spanky shoved Dennis's chest with both hands. "Now pick up my hat and apologize, or you're gonna be yet another skeleton in your family closet."

"Go to Hell. Dennis pushed Spanky clear across the tavern, "Candy ass." Dennis raised clenched fists a n d  t o o k  a fighting posture. "Make a move. Your bald head would make a great tombstone."

"Hey! Hey! Hey!" Ed banged a police nightstick on the bar counter like a judge's gavel. "Enough!"

George wedged between Dennis and Spanky, who now grappled each other's shirts. "Look, McMullen, I've known you for a long time, and I know you're from around here, so I'm just gonna break this up. But I'm also sick of your Yankee garbage. Keep it up, and I'll kick your ass myself."

"Geez ... Testy, testy. Hell, what are ya? Still pissed because the Yanks ran the A's out of town? It's been ten years already."

Two inches taller and forty pounds heavier, George narrowed his eyes, furrowed his brow, and pointed at Spanky.

Spanky slumped his shoulders and sat down on a barstool.

Ed put his hands on his hips. "Look, I don't care who roots for whom. I care nothin' about the Phillies, Reds, Cardinals, or the damn Yankees. I miss playin' football. If anyone fights here, you will make my day. Throwing you out onto Shunk Street will bring back Franklin Field memories."

"Yeah, all six plays of them." Spanky put his Yankees hat back on. "Ha! Ha! Ha!"

Dennis glowered at Spanky before nodding to Ed. "All right, Johnny, we all know you did your homework." He downed his entire drink. "I agree that the Cardinal infield of White, Groat, Javier, and Boyer may be the League's best. Yes, Lou Brock is the best lead-off hitter in the game, and yes, Curt Flood's defense is in a class with Mays. Okay, I do like that McCarver kid a lot at catcher. Sure, no one can fault a starting rotation of Gibson, Simmons, and Sedeki. But if they're all so much better than Allen, Callison, Bunning, Short, and all, why are they six behind?"

Johnny glanced at Spanky and Dennis. "The reason is sitting in the dugout. If you gave Gene Mauch a frontal lobotomy, he'd still be sharper than Johnny Keane. Mauch handled his team brilliantly. Just brilliant. That's another reason tonight's game gives me the willies. Getting shut out by." Johnny scratched his head. "Tit-saurus, and then that crazy steal of home had nothing to do with the manager, but tonight was possibly the first time this year Mauch made a move that backfired. After all, he did bunt with Richie Allen in the first inning, yet he didn't bunt with Herrnstein in the ninth. Then he let Amaro bat in the ninth with Rojas and Johnson available."

"Oh, come on, Johnny," Dennis raised his hands. "It's just one loss. They still have a five-and-a-half game lead with just eleven to go. How can they blow it?"

"I hope you're right, Dennis. I really do. I just don't know. I still got the heebie-jeebies. Every team has at least one losing streak during the season, yet the Phillies haven't. I somehow think their time is due."

"Well, I'll give you credit. I'm impressed that you did your homework and can recite every player in the National League. Nevertheless, you do the same with the horses, and you haven't backed a winner since Mad King Ludwig II backed Wagner."

"Mad King Ludwig the Second?" Johnny folded his racing form. "Yeah, I read about him. Queer as a three-dollar bill."

"Three-dollar bills are less unusual than you winning a bet," Dennis smirked, "any bet." He folded his hands behind his head. "So, I'm backing the Phillies all the way." Dennis shook his head. "They sure better win. Anything else would break my son Bill's heart. Well, talking about my son ..." Dennis glanced at his watch. "I don't think his mother would appreciate my staying out much later. See you 'round, guys."

As Dennis left the tavern, the jukebox played The Rolling Stones' recording, "Time Is on My Side."

# Chapter 2

Tuesday, September 22, 1964

Bill, with a thirteen-year-old's energy, ran all the way home from school. He trudged through the front door of his semi-detached English Tudor-style home in South Philly's Girard Estates neighborhood. "I'm home, Ma. What's for dinner?"

Patricia Waldron sat with her nine-year-old daughter, Marie, helping her with a Jigsaw puzzle. Marie was still dressed in her Catholic school uniform. Patricia fitted a piece of a jigsaw puzzle and glanced up at Bill. Like many opposite-gender siblings, Bill and Marie were like only children. Bill and Marie seldom fought or played together. On this afternoon, he scarcely registered Marie's presence.

"Meatloaf." Patricia smiled at Marie for fitting a piece into the puzzle.

"Meatloaf?" Bill whined.

"Yes, meatloaf." Patricia mimicked Bill's whine. "Look, Bill. You ran into the house without saying 'hi' to me or your sister, and you're already complaining. Your father works hard for grocery money, and I work hard turning it into meals. You know that we love you, and you are our responsibility, but I think it's time that you stop taking us for granted. We aren't your servants, you know."

"I'm sorry, ma." Bill pecked his mother's cheek. "Hey, I wanna watch Superman."

"Marie got here first. You can watch your programs when "Sally Star" is over."

"Oh, come on, Ma." Bill lowered his shoulders and tilted his head. "Sally Star's a crappy show."

"Bill, say another bad word, and you won't watch TV at all."

An hour later, Dennis Waldron entered, cradling a brown grocery bag of cheesesteaks. That struck Bill as Santa Clause shouldering a sack of toys on Christmas morning.

"Yippie! Cheesesteaks!" Bill ran to his father.

"That's right! And from Pat's!" Dennis handed Bill a cheese steak. "All right." Bill beamed and looked at his dinner with wide eyes. "Thanks, Dad."

"Well, all right! You're welcome, son! Now what's a bigger all right?" After pausing for two seconds, Dennis, like a card player presenting his winning hand, flashed two Phillies tickets.

"All right! All right! All right!" Bill jumped up and down.

"I'm not finished ... Now Bill, what's the biggest 'all right you could ever imagine?"

Bill shook his head.

"World Series Tickets!" Dennis played his ace. Out of his back pocket came four tickets, two each for games one and two of the 1964 World Series at Connie Mack Stadium, pitting the National League champion Philadelphia Phillies against the American League Champions.

Bill grabbed the tickets as if they were the keys to the magic kingdom and studied them like a punter would a winning lottery ticket. "Mom! Look at what Dad got me!" Bill ran toward Patricia. "World Series tickets! World Series tickets!"

Patricia took a deep breath before half-smiling. "That's nice, Bill."

Bill sat in a lounge chair with his tickets, admiring them like an art aficionado at a masterpiece.

Patricia walked toward the kitchen. "Dennis, I want to talk to you."

"What is it, honey?"

"In here," Patricia said under her breath. Born Patricia Marie Marconi, she stood over a foot shorter than her husband. Dennis was lanky; Patricia was chunky. Her oval face was pleasantly full. She wore her black hair in a bun and dressed modestly. More than appearance differentiated the two. She hailed from Italian descent. Dennis, Anglo. Patricia was born and raised in South Philly. Her husband was from across the Delaware River in Cumberland County, New Jersey. His family was Baptist; Patricia was from a Roman Catholic household. She met her husband while working as a receptionist at the electronics firm that still employs him as an accounts rep. Upon first meeting, they felt a mysterious chemistry. Despite their differences, they communicated well and discovered they shared similar goals and values. "How long did it take you to stop and pick up those cheesesteaks? As long as it took to find parking? Did you have to wait in line? Well, I've been working in this kitchen all afternoon. Now, my efforts are just a bunch of leftovers to pack in the kids' lunch boxes. Which you know they'll wind up trading to their friends for Tastykakes."

"I'm sorry, but you know how much I've been traveling, and you know what a treat it is for the kids."

"That's not the point. Next time, warn me, please. This is the second school night in a row that you're taking Bill out late. It's wonderful that you're spending time with your son. Yet must I again remind you that you have a daughter?" The children bridged Dennis and Patricia's differences. They named Bill after Dennis's favorite uncle and Marie after Patricia's mother. They agreed to baptize Bill in the Baptist church and send him to public school but raise Marie a Catholic and send her to parochial school. "And do you remember that you have a wife? What with work, your Phillies games, and that taproom, I might as well be a widow."

"Aw, come on, honey. There's lots of time for school. He's only young once. After all, how often do the Phillies win the pennant? The last time you were pregnant with Bill. Now he's a teenager."

"I guess I can't pull the rug out from under him tonight; however, this is the last time on a school night. Furthermore, I don't care if Gene Mack ..."

"Mauch."

"...Whoever," Patricia raised her hands, "invites you to sit next to him in the dugout, you're still taking us on that picnic to the lakes this Saturday."

***

Dennis bought Bill and himself upper reserved seats for Tuesday's game against the Cincinnati Reds. The attendance was similar to Monday night, although most were on edge.

"O'Toole has no tool, ya ball-less wonder!" a leather-lunged fan heckled as the Reds' ace left-handed pitcher, Jim O'Toole, missed outside with his first pitch to Johnny Callison.

"You a Red, or are you yellow?" Another fan yelled through an empty cone-shaped popcorn container, "Throw 'em a Strike? Ya bum!" The fans booed after O'Toole induced the Phillies' Most Valuable Player candidate to hit into an easy out.

The Phillies left-handed ace pitcher Chris Short matched the O'Toole with two shutout innings. The crowd started to murmur as Short opened the third inning by walking his weak-hitting pitching opponent. After a Pete Rose single, Chico Ruiz strode to the plate. The murmurs became a din. "Come on, Short, bust his kneecap!" a fan angry at Ruiz's outlandish theft of home with Frank Robinson batting yelled.

Short walked Ruiz.

Bill put his head on his chin and slumped forward as the Reds threatened to make the game a rout.

"How would you play it if Pinson hits an infield grounder?" Dennis asked. "Would you try and turn two, give up the run, but stay out of the big inning? Or do you cut off the go-ahead run at the plate?"

Bill raised his head. "Turn Two."

Vada Pinson answered with an infield grounder. The Phillies went for two. Out at second. Safe at first. The run scored. Reds one, Phillies zero. Next, Frank Robinson batted with runners on first and third, one out.

"This I don't believe," Dennis said as Vada Pinson attempted yet another stolen base with their most dangerous hitter up. Phillies catcher Clay Dalrymple lofted his throw into center field. Rose scored. Pinson advanced to third.

"Boo! Boo!" The fans voiced their disapproval.

Dennis slapped his leg. "Bill, it looks like the Phillies are standing around letting things happen to them." Dennis stood and yelled, "Come on, Phillies, get a grip!"

Chris Short rejected two signs from his catcher before wasting a pitch by throwing it in the dirt. Frank Robinson, in his best Jack Nicklaus impersonation, golfed the baseball. The champion golfer would have been proud of Robinson's ash-wood shot. It rose steadily, parallel to the left field foul line.

"Go foul. Please go foul." Bill's psychic powers and body language failed. Fair ball. Homerun.

"Dammit!" Denned smacked the side of his seat with a rolled-up program.

A threefold combination of bad Phillies pitching, weak Phillies hitting, and angry Phillies fans marked the remainder of the game. Final score: Reds nine, Phillies two. Lead cut to four and a half games.

Sportswriter Sandy Grady suggested a ton of Red Cross tranquilizers for the Phillies and their fans.

# Chapter 3

Wednesday, September 23, 1964

Frank Ciparoni met Bill in front of his house on S. Colorado Street. Small for his age, Frank took after his father, a history professor at the University of Pennsylvania, in appearance and manner. Like his father, he never used his intellect to show off or antagonize. "Here comes Paul and Tony. Hank and Jimmy said they're gonna play, and Jeff said he's also bringing a friend. Hey, we're going to have ourselves a game!"

"There's Hank and Jimmy!" Bill pointed down the street. "They can be the Reds. You, me, Jeff, and his friend the Phillies!"

Henry Tubbs was the same age as Bill. He weighed nearly eighty pounds more than Bill and nearly a hundred pounds more than Frank. Some of his eighth-grade peers called him names like Fatso and Jelly Belly. On whiffle ball turf, they called him Hank. "You gonna draw the strike zone?"

"It's right here!" Bill pointed to chalk markings on his front steps.

Jimmy Langston, a smallish kid with unkempt black hair and a dirty blue T-shirt, used three bricks for bases, spacing them evenly on the street.

Tony Rocca Jr., the others dared not call him Junior, was as tough as he looked. Tough, but not mean. Tall and lean-muscled, he generously greased back his black hair. "Hey, that Belair is blockin' left field." He opened the door and climbed in. After releasing the parking brake, he shouted to the others, "Come on and push this sucker outta da way."

The five others pushed the car rearward until their left field was clear. Behold! A South Philadelphia whiffle ball diamond. An ideal game was four-on-four. Doorsteps with a chalked rectangle served as catcher, backstop, and balls and strikes umpire. They employed the nearby sidewalk as the batter's box. The street and the far sidewalk fashioned the rest of the playing field. A three-foot garden fence fronting the houses across the road acted as a homerun boundary. It deviated from most baseball diamonds because centerfield was the shortest fence, while the distance increased toward the foul lines.

Paul Castanzo was like Bill in age, height, and build. A prominent pug nose set Paul apart. He pointed down the street. "Is that Jeff?"

Jeff stunned Bill and the gang by walking hand in hand with a girl. "Hi, guys! You all know Dawn." Jeff Giordano lived around the block from Bill. They had always been pals and shared a passion for baseball. Jeff's new passion stunned Bill.

*'Will he still be my pal?'* He scratched his head. *'She's cute. I wish I could meet a girlfriend.'*

Dawn's sanguine complexion framed her bright brown eyes and friendly smile. Nevertheless, she came to the game wearing canvas sneakers, blue jeans, and a yellow sweatshirt.

"She's our eighth player. She'll surprise you guys," Jeff said.

"Hey," Bill put his hands on his hips. "We've never let girls play before."

"Yeah, well, that was before," Frank shouldered his wiffleball bat. "I've seen Dawn play before. She's on her school's field hockey and basketball teams. Let's give her a chance. Besides, we need another player."

"I'm telling you." Jeff turned to Dawn and smiled. "She's going to surprise you."

"All right, Jeff. If you say so." Bill pointed at Jeff. "But she plays on the Reds side."

"Yeah, okay, we'll take her, but you get Hank," Tony pointed at Bill.

The game was set. Their rules were the same as regular baseball, but they played with a yellow plastic bat and a hollow white plastic ball resembling a spherical piece of Swiss cheese. Dawn, Tony, Paul, and Jimmy represented the Cincinnati Reds. Whenever one of the four batted, they wore a souvenir Reds batting helmet. They also announced the name of the coinciding Reds player with the same turn in the line-up. Furthermore, they batted on his concurring side of the plate. Bill, Jeff, Frank, and Hank did the same with the Phillies.

"Okay, guys, we've got to win this one," Bill said. "Because if we win, the Phillies will win tonight. If they win, the Reds beat 'em again."

"If you say so," Frank rolled his eyes.

"First up." Tony donned a Reds helmet and batted left, just like the Reds switch-hitting lead-off hitter would against a right-handed pitcher. "I'm Pete Rose."

Frank curved the first pitch p a s t  h i m . "I'm Jim Bunning, and I'm gonna put two more right by ya."

"Bet ya a pack a baseball cards ya don't." Tony smacked the next pitch between Bill and Jeff, winding up with a double. He grinned widely. "Ya owe me."

Paul then popped up to Jeff. Frank (now Chris Short) struck out Jimmy. Then Dawn stepped in. "I'm Frank Robinson."

*'What a joke,'* Bill squeezed the whiffle ball, *'A girl claiming she's Frank Robinson?'*

Dawn justified her make-believe namesake by smacking a solid line drive in Hank's direction. Like a bowl of gelatine riding atop a pair of ham sides, he waddled after the ball. Dawn ran the bases like a mare, stopping at third before Hank retrieved her hit.

"Why didn't ya catch it ya tub of goo?" Bill glowered at Hank "Anyone could'a made that catch."

"Anyone named Mays, Ashburn, or Flood," Frank replied.

"Hey, quit callin' me names. That was a good hit," Hank pleaded.

"Let me pitch." Bill grabbed the ball from Frank.

"You think you can do better?" Frank dropped the ball in place. "Go ahead and try."

"I'm Jim Bunning." Bill threw Tony a fastball.

He slashed the yellow plastic bat against the whiffle ball like Paul Bunyan against a sequoia. The connection sounded like smashing a pumpkin with a stick. The whiffle ball whistled overhead on a rising line ... over the fence, over ten feet of front yard, crashing just beneath the double-story house's roof. Bill stared at the impact spot. He'd seen grown-ups hit longer home runs. Jeff's cousin, the Teamster pipe fitter, once hit one clear over the roof. Nevertheless, grown-ups don't count. Bill didn't hit his first over-the-fence homerun until age eleven. The next year, he hit twenty-eight homers. He counted. This year he has hit more than he can count. Yet, never had he or his peers driven a whiffle ball this distance.

"Yo, Good one, Bill," Frank walked toward Bill. "Now, why don't you let me pitch."

"Wait a minute." Bill raised his hands. "That don't count! It don't count! You have to announce who you are. You're supposed to say you're Deron Johnson. You never said who you were."

Tony, celebrating his signatory blast with his teammates, sneered at Bill and brushed him off with a right-hand wave.

Bill appealed to his teammates. "He didn't follow the rules. He has to say who he is. It doesn't count!" Bill ceased arguing after getting no support from his teammates.

After a few uncounted innings, Bill's team trailed. He batted with the tying runs on base and confidently announced, "I'm Alex Johnson." He smacked one high and far, farther than he ever hit a whiffle ball. It landed on a porch roof for a three-run homer.

The Kids tirelessly played on. Tony hit home runs almost at will. Dawn more than managed. Bill's team doggedly clawed back, although Hank shifted from slow gear to slower, letting in even more runs for the other side. Then Bill's sister, Marie, arrived on the scene. "Yo Bill, Mommy says you got to come in for dinner."

"Oh, shut up and go inside ya little twerp. I'm playing ball."

"You're gonna get it." Marie wagged her finger. Bill shrugged her off.

About an hour later, the players agreed to make this their last inning. They long ago stopped keeping score and decided that the next run wins.

Tony stood in the batter's box like Goliath girded for battle, the whiffle ball bat his sixteen-pound iron spear. Frank, the diminutive David, slung the plastic sphere at Tony. He bashed it away on a high arc, its apogee roof high. Bill, already playing Tony deep, only backed up a couple of steps before his butt pressed against the garden fence. He leaned back and looked up. Caught. One away.

Frank, shell-shocked from the close call, walked Paul. Jeff appropriated the pitching duties and fanned Jimmy. Dawn stepped up to the plate and announced herself as Vada Pinson.

Bill relaxed and played shallow.

Dawn drove the first pitch high over Bill's head. He ran back like a football wide receiver under a long bomb. Reaching over his shoulder, he grasped the ball in the palm of his hand. It bounced out and fell over the fence. Homerun.

The Reds side leaped up and down and cheered. Jeff hugged Dawn.

Bill ran in. "You grooved it to her."

"I did not!"

"You did too!"

"Forget it, Bill." Frank started walking away. "It's only a game. We had fun. We'll change sides tomorrow anyway."

"Forget it? What do you mean? We still get our last ups.

"That's all right." Frank kept walking. " I better get home. I've got lots of homework."

"Yeah, and I'm gettin' hungry," Hank agreed. "I'm going home for my supper."

"See you later," Jeff waved with his right hand while holding Dawn's hand with his left.

"Yeah, good game, Bill." Dawn flashed a smile. "See you later, alligator."

***

Patricia's face hardened as her son ambled through the front door. "There's your dinner." Patricia pointed to a cold and unappetizing plate of spaghetti and meatballs. "Take it with you to your room, and don't come out until tomorrow morning ... Don't you even think about watching TV."

*'What a sucker,'* Bill thought without realizing that his mother let him play rather than embarrass him before his friends. *Who cares about TV? The Phillies are on the radio.'* Bill tuned his Emerson clock radio to Phillies broadcasters: By Saam, Richie Ashburn, and Bill Campbell to listen to the game.

"It's a lovely night for baseball," Byron Saam said through Bill's radio. "If you're in the area, come on out."

"A lovely night for baseball," Bill muttered. "He would say that in a hurricane."

"Important game, Richie," By Saam continued.

"Yes, it is, By. It's a must-win for the Reds. If they win, they're right back in the hunt. But the Phillies have a chance to knock the Reds out and put this thing away."

"Two young left-handers tonight, Ritchie. For the Phillies, twenty-four-year-old Dennis Bennett and the Reds are countering with a twenty-year-old rookie, Billy McCool."

"Yes, By. Dennis Bennett's been bothered with a sore shoulder, though two weeks ago he shut out the Giants one to nothing and struck out Willie Mays three times."

"What do you know about Billy McCool, Ritchie?"

"He's got a lively arm. Strikes out about a batter an inning. It should be an interesting game."

By Saam said, "Here are the lineups for tonight's game. For the Reds, leading off their second baseman, Pete Rose. Batting second and playing third base, Chico Ruiz. Batting third, the center fielder, Vada Pinson. Frank Robinson is batting cleanup and playing right field. Deron Johnson, the first baseman, bats fifth. Next is Tommy Harper in left field. Johnny Edwards is catching and batting seventh. Leo Cardenas, the shortstop, is eighth. And batting ninth is the young left-hander, Billy McCool. For the Phillies ... Tonight the right-handed batting Cookie Rojas gets the nod in center field, and Ruben Amaro will follow, batting second and playing shortstop. It's Johnny Callison batting third and playing right field. The second baseman, Tony Taylor, is batting fourth tonight, and the sensational rookie, Richie Allen, bats fifth and is starting at third base. Another rookie, Alex Johnson, is starting in left field and batting sixth. Your catcher, Clay Dalrymple, bats seventh; Vic Power is playing first base and batting eighth. And, of course, it's Dennis Bennett pitching and batting ninth."

Clay Dalrymple drove in the Phillies first run with a triple. The Reds, however, quickly tied it on Chico Ruiz's solo home run. Vada Pinson put the Reds up two to one by touching Dennis Bennett for another solo home run in the top of the sixth.

Johnny Callison led off the bottom of the inning by lining a single to right. McCool then retired Taylor and Allen, bringing Alex Johnson to the plate. "Come on, Alex!" Bill leaned toward the radio. Just as he remembered smacking the whiffle ball homer in

Johnson's name, he heard over the radio, "Long drive, high and deep to left, Harper's going a way back…He can't get it ... On the roof! Homerun!"

"Yeah!" Bill yelled. Alex Johnson's homer landing on the left-field bleacher roof and Bill's whiffle ball homer landing on the porch roof confirmed that he had predetermined the Phillies' homerun. Bill trotted around his room's imaginary basepaths to the rabid applause of Shibe Park's 23,000-plus fans. He stopped and collapsed into a chair. He realized the whiffleball game foretelling the Phillies game meant they would lose. A look at the plate of cold spaghetti almost made him vomit. He took it to the bathroom and flushed it down the toilet. Upon his return, the Reds had two men on and Vada Pinson batting. Ed Roebuck pitched for the Phillies. "No way. No stinking way that girl's lucky whiffleball homer means a thing," Bill shook his crossed fingers.

Good radio sports play-by-play broadcasters can replicate the action through vocal inflection as well as words. The way Bill Campbell said, "Pinson hits a long one to right," immediately conveyed that Callison won't catch it, nor would the 34' high spite fence knock it down. Someone on Twentieth Street obtained a bitter souvenir.

"No! No! No!" Bill slammed his fists onto his desktop. "Jeff just had to bring that damn girl." He felt as frustrated as a muzzled pit bull terrier. The Phillies taunted the muzzled beast with a raw steak by loading the bases with only one out in the bottom of the frame. Bill worked on a model airplane while listening to the Reds' twenty-two-year-old right-handed relief ace, Sammy Ellis, fan the Phillie's best left-handed hitter, Johnny Callison, and clean-up hitter Tony Taylor. "Dammit!" Bill threw his airplane against the wall.

Dick Allen hit an eighth-inning double, a scorching line drive off the left field fence that missed a homerun by inches. He later scored on an infield hit.

The Phillies still trailed by two, two out, bottom of the ninth. Bill was repairing the wreckage of his model plane as he had reconciled himself to the tough loss before like a bolt of lightning, Johnny Callison jolted a long, high double off the rightfield wall. Bill stopped working on his model airplane and put his ear to the radio speaker. The Phillies clean-up hitter, Tony Taylor, dug into the batter's box as the tying run.

"Please, God," Bill steepled his hands. "Let him hit a home run,"

"Long drive to right!" Bill Campbell announced.

"Yes! Come on baseball!" Bill picked up his radio and shook it. "Go! Go! Go!"

"Pinson a way back..."

"Please, God. Let it be."

"Pinson's back is against the fence ... He leaps ... Caught! ... Out ... Game over ... Phillies lose six to four."

Bill picked up a baseball bat, tossed his model airplane like a fungo, and smashed it. He then sized up his radio like Dick Allen would a hanging curve. A last-second impulse told Bill the radio was out of the strike zone. Instead, he repeatedly hammered his mattress, yelling "No! No! No! No!"

# Chapter 4

Friday, September 25, 1964

Frank and Jeff sat with Tony on the doorstep of his Porter Street house. Frank shook his fists, "I can't believe the way they blew last night's game to Milwaukee. I'm starting to believe Bill and his jinx stuff."

"Yeah. Especially those cheap triples. Only a jinxed team gets two, not just one, but two bounces goin' against 'em like that," Jeff shrugged. "I just don't know."

Frank opened his hands, "The triple Torre hit should have been an out. Johnny Callison would catch it if he hadn't bruised his foot Wednesday night."

Jeff shook his head and muttered: "What I don't get is twice having baserunners safe, only to have 'em both slide off the base afterward and get tagged out. Again, not just once, but twice."

"At least it's only happening to them in twos, most jinxes are in threes." Frank raised three fingers. "I knew they had limitations, but this losing streak seems like something else altogether."

"Oh, come on Frank, whad da ya mean by this limitations crap?" Tony stood. "They stink. Yo Jeff, whad da ya say? I'm offerin' ya five good cards for just one of yours. Felipe Alou, Arthur Lee Maye, Ron Santo, Frank Howard, and even a good Philly. Tony Taylor."

"Sure, Tony. Except that the one card you want is Roger Maris. I can go to the store and buy five cards for a nickel- and get a slab of bubble gum. But I figure Roger Maris is worth somethin' more." Jeff mused for ten seconds. "Tell ya what. Throw in the other two Alou's, Matty and Jesus, and ya got yourself a Roger Maris."

"No way Jose. Felipe Alou, Ron Santo, Frank Howard, Arthur Lee Maye, and Tony Taylor."

"No Matty and Jesus no Roger Maris."

"What do ya say we flip for it? Come on. Let's see if ya got any guts."

"All right. You're on. But I call."

Tony flipped his Matty Alou card skyward. It descended slowly, spinning end over end.

"Heads," Jeff called. If the card landed player's photo upward, Jeff won the card. If it lands on the flip side, it's tails. Tony's card.

"Tails! It's mine." Tony snatched the card. "Here's to you, Jay Alou." Tony flipped the other Alou card into the air.

"Heads," Jeff called. This time he won. "I want to have all three Alou brothers. Tell ya what, Tony, Roberto Clemente for my Matty Alou back."

"Roberto Clemente? Hell yes! You're on!" Tony pointed down Porter Street. "Yo, here comes Bill. I call first up in half-ball."

"I don't know." Frank stood and held up his hands. "This losing streak is bugging me. I want to get my mind off baseball. Let's play football instead."

"To hell with that," Tony brushed him off. "My dad says Joe Kruharic's a bigger bum than Mauch."

Bill arrived holding a yellow plastic wiffleball bat. "Tony and me stand."

Half-ball is a Philadelphia baseball alternative. Each neighborhood has its own rules, although the game is similar. A hollow rubber ball is first cut in half at the seam. Thus, two half-balls. Each half is resilient while harmless to windows. A half-ball bat is either a broomstick or a wiffleball bat.

In Bill's neighborhood, an ideal game pitted two on two, a pitcher and a fielder on each side. They liked playing on Porter Street because of its triple-storied houses with pitched roofs. Any ball hit off a house's first story was a single, second story a double, third story a triple, and off the roof pitch or on the roof a homerun. A ball landing on the roof was no great loss. It's cheap even before cutting it and getting two for the price of one. When a homeowner employed a roofer, he tossed the half-balls back. Even if they sat on the roof for months, the half-balls remained playable.

An out is either one swinging strike or any batted ball stopping short of the houses, whether by itself or caught by a player. Each team gets three outs an inning.

Urban half-ball has advantages over its rural counterparts. In a nine-on-a-side baseball game, some defensive positions may not even get to touch the ball. A two-on-a-side half-ball player takes part in every play. A player usually bats three to five times in a conventional baseball game. Two-on-a-side half-ball players bat quantum times more.

Jeff, Frank, Tony, and Bill played with enough vigor to lose track of time. Over two hours after they started, Bill stepped up to bat and declared, "I'm Richie Allen."

Frank pitched Bill chest high and across the heart of the plate. Bill snapped his best swing. He saw his bat compress the ball. It sprang off it on a rising line, still rising as it disappeared over the three-story roof.

"Damn." Tony put his hands on his hips.

Frank stood motionless, jaw agape.

Jeff turned to Bill. "Wow! That's quite a hit."

"Yeah, and a game-winner at that." Frank walked over to Bill. "Because it's our last ball. Game over."

"That's it! The Phillies are finally gonna win tonight! See, tonight, they're having Richie Allen night! That's the only time I mentioned a Phillie, and look at what happened! Do you remember the other day when I said I was Alex Johnson? He hit a homer just like me! Then that girl jinxed 'em with that homer after sayin' she was Frank Robinson. Yo, tonight my dad's comin' back from Baltimore, and I'm sure we're gonna go to tonight's game. Hey, let's all go!"

"Not me," Tony said. "Tonight, my old man's takin' me with him to bowling. It means somethin' extra to him. He's goin' up against Spanky McMullen's team. My father says beating him in bowling will hurt him more than punching his loudmouth. If I tell him I don't wanna go, he beats the crap outta me and makes me go anyway."

"Yo? What about you, Frank?"

"Thanks anyway, Bill. But I have a history paper due. I better work on it."

"A history paper? On a Friday night?"

"I think you're forgetting that my dad is an Ivy League professor. Expectations are high, and college applications are only a couple of years away. Last time I checked, Ivy League schools aren't awarding half-ball scholarships." Frank chuckled. "So, it looks like doing homework on a Friday. Besides, I can't stand any more of their choking."

"I just told you; tonight's the night we win." Bill smiled. "The choking is over!"

Frank smirked and shook his head. "I'll leave it to you and the Phillies. Just because they blow the pennant, don't mean I gotta blow my future."

"Oh, come on, Frank." Bill spread his hands. "You can work on your paper another time."

"No, really, Bill. My father will be home tonight to help me. I can't go."

"It looks like it's you and me, Jeff."

"I've already promised Dawn that we're goin' the movies. We're gonna see Andromeda Androids and Martian Colony One. Yo, anyway, Frank's right. This choking's too much for me too."

"Choke? No way they're gonna choke! I just told you guys, Richie Allen's gonna win it for 'em tonight. He must."

"Why?" Jeff put his right hand on his hip.

"Didn't you guys listen? I told ya they're gonna win because of my homerun. And they never would've gotten in this mess to begin with, if ya didn't bring that jinx girl." Bill prodded at Jeff.

"Wooooo!" Tony held up his hand like a police halt signal. "He just called your gal a jinx. Are you gonna take that from him?"

"Nah," Jeff brushed his hand at Tony. "He's just jealous, that's all."

"I am not!" Bill pointed at Jeff. "And why would anyone be jealous of a Jinx?"

"My gal's name is Dawn, and it's time you get over this jinx stuff." Jeff looked away. "Besides, I don't think you even like girls."

"Yes, I do!" Bill prodded.

"Oh really?" Jeff turned back to Bill. "What girl have you ever liked?"

"How 'bout Mary Beth McGovern. I liked her. You remember."

"MaryBeth McGovern? The head cheerleader? Get real. Every guy in school wanted her. She don't even know you're alive. What real girl have you ever liked?"

"How about Sophie Tripodi?"

"You may have talked to her, but you sure as heck never touched her."

"Wait a sec," Tony stepped between Bill and Jeff. "It sounds to me like you're sayin' he's a queer."

"Yeah, maybe you're right." Jeff walked around Tony. "He's a queer."

"Yo Bill, he says you're a queer. Whad are ya gonna do about it? Just stand there and take it?" Tony laughed. "Like a queer?"

Sizing up Jeff, Bill's stomach felt filled with swarming gnats. His fist felt detached from his being as he punched Jeff's jaw.

"Good one!" Tony punched his palm.

Jeff staggered backward. He massaged his jaw, stared Bill down, and charged like a blitzing linebacker. He tackled Bill and pummeled his face.

"All Right, Jeff!" Tony shook his fists. "Let him have it!"

Bill rolled Jeff over. He seized Jeff's shirt with his left hand and bashed his nose with his right fist.

"Good one, Bill!" Tony clapped his hands. "That's the way you do it."

Jeff slipped out from under Bill and scrambled to his knees. "You're nothin' but a punk!" He hooked Bill with a roundhouse right to his mouth.

Bill, also on his knees, spat blood onto the street. He spotted blood dripping from Jeff's nose. Bill struck Jeff's nose, drawing more blood.

Jeff responded by splitting Bill's lip. He tried to counter with a right cross. Frank tread forward and hooked his arm.

Tony grabbed Frank and yanked him back. "Let 'em fight it out like men."

An old lady screamed out of a second-story window. "You kids stop that! Git outta here or I'll call the cops!"

"Shit. That's old lady Doggatelli." Tony lurched in and grabbed Jeff. Frank then did the same with Bill. "That old bag will call the cops. We'd better split." Tony, Jeff, Bill, and Frank left separately.

***

90

Bill staggered through his front door. His head felt foggy.

Patricia covered her face and gasped. Blood drenched her son's tattered shirt. Fresh blood dripped from his mouth; a grotesque purple swell masked his left eye. "My God! What happened?"

"Um ... Some big colored kids beat me up and took my lunch money."

"Oh, my goodness!" Patricia hugged Bill. "Do you know who they are? Do they go to your school? Did you tell the principal?"

"Um ... No. I never saw them before. And, Ugh ... It just happened to me ... On the way home."

"Where did it happen?"

"Ugh…Broad and Oregon."

"Broad and Oregon?" Patricia threw up her hands. Surely somebody saw it. Why didn't anyone stop them? No one called the cops?"

"Ugh ...No Mom. It happened too fast." Bill covered his mouth. "Then they ran away."

"Eww ...Gross ..." Marie ran into the living room. "Who beat you up?"

"Go outside and play," Patricia pointed to the front door.

Marie twirled around and sang. "Bill got beat up. Bill got beat up. Bill got beat up."

"Wait here, Bill." Patricia reappeared two minutes later with a damp towel with diluted rubbing alcohol, a small bottle of iodine, and a box of Q-tip swabs. "This might sting a little."

"Ouch," Bill said as his mother wiped the blood from his face. "Ouch!" he said louder as she applied iodine directly to the cuts.

"Wait here." Patricia left for the kitchen and returned about a minute later with a makeshift ice pack. "Put this over your eye."

She walked over to the TV and clicked on The Flintstones. "Sit still." She watched the cartoon with him.

Fred and Barney fought over who owned a backyard swimming pool. They settled it by dividing it in half. Barney duped Fred into taking the half without a ladder. Fred performed histrionics when he couldn't get out. Patricia laughed. "I think you'll live, Bill."

Twenty minutes later, Dennis arrived home. "Bill! Who'd you get in a fight with? I hope you got in the first punch."

"He didn't get in a fight," Patricia said. "Some big colored kids mugged him by Broad and Oregon."

"Colored kids? In broad daylight? On Broad and Oregon? What's happening to our neighborhood? I'm calling the police. This sort of thing may happen up in North Philly, but it's not going to start happening here, not if I can help it."

"No, Dad, please don't call the cops."

Patricia placed her hand on her son's shoulder. "Rather don't honey. He's been through enough already."

"Okay. Not now anyway, but I am reporting it later as a matter of record. In my day, we never called the cops. The mafia took care of it and did a better job."

"I'm fine, Dad." Bill took the icepack from his eye. "Really," Bill shrugged. "I am."

"Thank goodness!" Patricia steepled her hands. "Your eye looks better already."

"Of course, it's better. I didn't raise a sissy for a son." Dennis slapped Bill on the back.

"Where's Marie?" Dennis adjusted his glasses

"She's outside playing."

"Well, I bought her a little surprise."

"Hey. What about me?" Bill held up his open hands.

"Well, I've got two tickets for Richie Allen night at Connie Mack Stadium." Dennis then joked, "But since you're hurt..."

"No way!" Bill leaped up. "I'm not hurt."

Dennis smiled. "What's for dinner, honey?"

"Last night's chicken cacciatore. And, yes, it's okay to take Bill out for a cheesesteak instead."

"Yeah!" Bill shook his right fist.

***

By the time Dennis drove Bill up Passyunk Ave., his adrenaline and anger had subsided. Disk jockey Jerry Blavat's banter and the music he played over the radio evoked memories of happier times between Jeff and himself. His head slumped forward. "Was it only four days ago?' He recalled riding shotgun through the city in the convertible with Jeff and Frank.

"Why don't we try Geno's Steaks this time?" Dennis glanced at Bill.

"Um ... All right," Bill said. "But can I wait here in the car for you?"

"Wait in the car? Are you sure you're okay?"

"Yeah, Dad. I'm fine."

Dennis raised his eyebrows and tightened his lips. "Okay, if you say so." Dennis disembarked his car and joined the Geno's Steaks queue.

Speakers outside Geno's also played Jerry Blavat's radio show. "This is the Geeter with the heater, I got you a new record from the Marvels, 'Go On and Have Yourself a Ball.'"

The song's cheerfulness had the opposite effect on Bill. He recollected Frank, Jeff, and himself as a team battling Tony, Hank, and Pug Nose Paul in a snowball fight. 'What fun. Okay, so what

93

if Tony threw an ice ball and I got mad and threw an ice ball back, but smacked Hank in the eye by mistake? I never hurt a friend on purpose. Next, Blavat introduced a song by Len Barry, a former high school basketball teammate of National Basketball Association great Wally Jones, and the Dovells, 'The Bristol Stomp.' The song evoked whiffleball memories of Jeff and himself before either could hit one over the fence. 'The dead-ball era,' Bill frowned. After the Bristol Stomp, Blavat introduced the 'Eighty-one', a line dance tune by a group called Candy and the Kisses. 'I wish I had a girlfriend as cute as Dawn.' He remembered the junior high dance and having as much fun as the American Bandstand kids, and the ones on Jerry Blavat and Hy Lit's local spinoffs. But the girls he danced with seemed distant. "How did Jeff get Dawn to like him?"

Jerry Blavat played a song by Tina Britz, 'The Real Thing,' as Dennis returned. "How about this?" He presented a tray with French fries drowning in mozzarella cheese, a large Coke, and a cheesesteak.

Bill finally smiled.

***

Dennis drove them to the ballpark. "I don't want to get your hopes up, but maybe this will cheer you up. I've got tickets to games three, four, and five of the World Series at Yankee Stadium. I may have to use them with business clients, so I don't want to promise you anything, but if I don't—it's you and me."

"World Series tickets in New York! Oh boy! Yankee Stadium! Mickey Mantle! All right! All Right!" Bill beamed. His joy faded when his father stopped at a red light. Bill spotted a group of black youths playing basketball. An empty milk bottle case nailed to a telephone pole served as the hoop and basket. Bill was reminded of his lie. He dropped his head, slumped his shoulders, and covered his face. He felt even worse than when he shoplifted a pack of baseball cards from Testo's market.

Jerry Blavat played Darlene Love's 'Wait Until My Bobby Gets Home' while Bill spotted Shibe Park's light towers shining above the row house roofs. Bill smiled. "Tonight is Richie Allen night, Dad. Like the mighty Thor, he's going to hammer the Milwaukee Braves. I know it. No way Richie Allen's going to let the Phillies choke."

"Sometimes I wish baseball were like your comic books." Dennis found parking but couldn't lose the ubiquitous welcoming committee.

A Black kid, wearing a Philadelphia Warriors basketball shirt with Wilt Chamberlain's number thirteen, ran up to Dennis. "Watch ya car for a buck, mister."

"How is a little guy like you going to keep the big bad guys off my car?" Dennis smirked at him.

"Oh, I give the money to my big brotha. He can whoop anyone on the block."

Dennis looked at Bill's black eye, considered the "reason" for it, and gave the kid two dollars. "Now you make sure your big brother gives a big whoopin' to anyone who even thinks about stealing my car."

***

Bill and Dennis joined the 30,445 fans packing the historic ballpark. Most came to give their support, a few their ire. All suffered a jolt. During the past hundred hours, they witnessed the Phillies' granite six-and-a-half-game lead crumble into a three-game pile of sand. Tonight, the Phillies broke custom by honoring a rookie. Richie Allen. Nevertheless, when is a rookie collecting over two hundred hits, thirty-eight doubles, a league-leading thirteen triples, twenty-nine homers, one hundred and twenty-five runs, and a .318 batting average customary?

Bill cheered a bit louder than the others as each local merchant said an accolade for Dick Allen and presented him with a gift. They gave him a television, snow tires, luggage, and a stereo. Most generous was a thousand-dollar scholarship for his daughter Teri's future education. This was a tremendous blessing for the ballplayer. Richie Allen's salary was only $7,000.00.

Dennis and Bill had a clear view of the Phillies manager from their lower box seats. Gene Mauch straddled the dugout steps, tight-lipped and hands on hips. He squinted up at the Ballentine beer scoreboard, posting a Reds' three-to-zero lead over the New York Mets in game one of their doubleheader. Dennis prodded Bill and pointed to the dugout. "The skipper looks nervous. I can feel his tension from here."

Bill, confident his majestic, half-ball homerun was foretelling, chose to look at Dick Allen. His father continued staring into the Phillies dugout with his chin in his right hand.

"Don't worry, Dad." Bill tapped his father's shoulder. "Richie Allen's gonna win it tonight. I know it."

"It's not Richie Allen who worries me. Chris Short's the one I'm worried about. This is the third damn ...darn time in a row Mauch's pitching him on only two days rest. He's done the same thing with Bunning, and thus far his condensed pitching rotation has been a disaster. Especially last night."

Tonight was Frank Thomas's first game since breaking his thumb on 8 September 1964. To play, he tore off his cast as if removing a leech. Thirty thousand fans cheered for him in the fourth inning when he plated Wes Covington with the game's first run by driving a ball through left fielder Rico Carty's glove. The scoreboard flashed an "E" for error, then an "F" for final next to Cincinnati 3, New York 0, cutting the Phillies' lead to two and a half games.

Chris Short, battling a stiff shoulder, started the seventh with a one-zero shutout. The Braves' inning began with Dennis Menke reaching first base via a fluke catcher's interference call. Mike De La Hoz followed with a solid double to left field. With the go-ahead runs in scoring position, Braves Manager Bobby Bragan challenged the percentages. Left-handed batting Arthur Lee Maye pinch-hit against southpaw Chris Short. Maye hit a shallow pop fly to right-fielder Johnny Callison. If Bragan challenged the percentages, then the Braves' third-base coach defied logic. Johnny Callison had thrown out more baserunners than any other major league outfielder. The Braves' third base coach had Menke attempt to score after the catch. Callison's throw was strong and straight. Unfortunately, straight over the catcher's head. Tie score. Felipe Alou followed with a single. The Braves led.

In the top of the eighth, with Bobby Locke pitching for the Phillies, Hank Aaron attempted a one-out steal of third. Dick Allen covered the base for the tag play. Unfortunately for the Phillies, the Braves batter, Joe Torre, hit a routine grounder where Dick Allen was. He recovered enough to get his glove on the ball. A fraction of an inch more and he catches it. He could only deflect it.

The Braves now led three to one. Bill echoed the sentiments of 30,447 people. "No fair."

The Phillies had won only two pennants and finished in the cellar an astounding nineteen times in their 78 years of existence. Three years prior, Gene Mauch's team won only forty-seven games and lost a dreadful 107 games for an abysmal .305 won/lost percentage. It gets worse. They lost an unfathomable twenty-three straight games—an all-time futility record. How did Philadelphia react? After the '61 Phillies finally won their first game in nearly a month, over 5,000 fans waited hours in the rain at Philadelphia International Airport to greet them. Upon arrival, they hoisted Gene Mauch upon their shoulders and jubilantly ran him through the airport as a conquering hero. Phillies fans had served their time in Hell, and Gene Mauch was their cellmate.

Tonight's crowd refused to let the '64 Phillies slide back to oblivion. 30,447 people crammed into the intimate confines of Shibe Park, creating a human pressure cooker. Their energy was palpable. The Phillies trailed by two, two out, and a runner on first in their eighth. Braves southpaw Billy Hoeft tried to slip a change-up past Johnny Callison. Bat and ball collided like an ignition charge to a blasting cap. Shibe Park exploded in joy as they watched the baseball disappear deep into the North Philadelphia night. They cheered and applauded as if sheer volume and duration alone could liberate the Phillies from destiny's outhouse.

After Waldrons settled back down, Dennis smiled at Bill. "Here, take a sip." He handed his beer to him.

The Phillies' Bobby Locke and the Braves' Bob Sadowski kept the game tied until the Braves' tenth. Ty Cline opened with an infield single. Gary Kolb sacrificed him to second. Joe Torre, the Braves' hottest hitter, stepped up to the plate.

"I bet they walk him, Dad. Joe Torre's been killing us. A walk sets up a double-play, and I think they'll get it. Their next hitter, Gene Oliver, stinks. Not only can't he hit; he runs like a tortoise."

"Well, I can tell you he never bats against righties." Dennis sipped his beer. "Seeing Gene Mauch plays the percentages, I say you're right." Dennis took another sip of beer. "Nope. Looks like we're wrong. They're going to pitch to Torre. This makes no sense." Dennis gulped down the rest of his beer.

Bobby Locke hung Torre a curve. He banged it into the left field upper deck. "Gene Mauch's an Idiot!" Bill shook his fists. "I told him to walk Torre. I told him!"

"You sure know better than that dope. Dammit!" Dennis banged a rolled-up program against the side of his seat. Spotting the beer vendor, he signaled for another.

Bottom of the tenth. Bob Sadowski is still in control. The Phillies have a baserunner in Cookie Rojas, but Sadowski has fanned two batters in the inning. Dick Allen embodied their final hope.

Dennis stood up with a fresh cup of beer. "Come on, Bill. Let's get out of here. I want to beat the traffic; besides, I have to go to the bathroom."

"No, Dad! We can't go!" Bill grabbed Dennis's shirt. "Richie Allen's up. He's going to hit a home run."

"Really? Hey, come on. You're not the one driving home. Let's go."

"Please," Bill pulled on his father's arm. "You see this afternoon in half-ball ..."

Dick Allen suddenly slashed a drive to deep right center. Deep. Deep. Only the fifty-foot-high Ballentine beer scoreboard stood in its path. It ended his home run bid. Allen had a base hit, nonetheless. The ball caromed toward the leftfield stands; Center fielder Ty Cline chased it down; Rojas scored easily; Dick Allen churned for third as if propelled through a molecular vacuum. The crowd sensed something special. Cline's relay eluded the Braves' second baseman. "They're gonna send him! They're gonna send him!" Bill hopped up and down.

Allen bolted for the plate; shortstop Dennis Menke recovered the ball and gunned it homeward ... Offline!

Allen scored standing. Inside the park homerun! Tie Game. The number fifteen on Dick Allen's Atlas wide back spelled hero for Bill better than any combination of letters. Gene Mauch sprang from the dugout and embraced his triumphant rookie. Pandemonium ruled Shibe Park.

"I told you! I told you! I told you he'd do it! I told you!" Bill smiled as wide as Broad Street.

"Yes, you did! Here, son. You earned this one." Dennis filled Bill's empty soda cup with beer.

They toasted Allen's heroics and Bill's premonition.

September 25, 1964. Johnny Callison and Dick Allen took Gene Mauch's Phillies across a continent and an ocean. At midnight, Fate's Mack truck pulverized them crossing the street.

Frank Thomas. The Phillies were 21- 12 with the right-handed slugger in their lineup. They were only 7-9 since injuring his thumb on September 8th. National League managers exploited their mostly left-handed lineup with southpaw pitchers. Even before the injury, Frank Thomas was not nicknamed "The Donkey" for his graceful defense. Now he played rusty and hurt.

Gary Kolb opened the Braves' twelfth with a grounder between second and first. Tony Taylor made a great diving stop and threw in time to first. Only the broken-thumbed Thomas dropped it for an error. Pitcher John Boozer recovered to fan the dangerous Joe Torre but walked the weak-hitting Gene Oliver. Eddie Mathers followed with a slow roller to Thomas for what looked like the second out. Except Frank Thomas clanked it into shallow right, inches beyond the diving second baseman. Kolb scored the go-ahead run, and Oliver took third. With Dennis Menke batting, Dalrymple nailed Mathews attempting to steal second. Oliver tried to score on the tag play. Umpire Ed Vargo bellowed, "Out!" as Taylor gunned down Oliver at the plate.

"That will teach the son-of-a ..." Dennis suddenly gasped. "…What the?" The ball trickled loose from catcher Dalrymple's glove. Vargo changed his out-call to safe, the third steal of home against the Phillies in seven games.

The Phillies did not die. Dick Allen laced a screaming line drive single to left in the bottom of the frame. "That's his fourth hit of the game." Bill shook crossed fingers. Johnny Callison then walked. "I'll take it." Bill turned to his father. "We got the tying runs on base and the winning run at the plate." Bill closed his eyes and looked upward. "We can do it!" Bill shook his fists. "We can do it."

Clamoring for yet another miracle, the fans feverishly chanted, "We want a hit, we want a hit." Unfortunately, Gene Mauch could only draw the .238-hitting Johnny Herrnstein from his quiver. A whimpering ground ball to first later, and the Phillies' lead was cut to one and a half. Dennis stood and pursed his lips. "So much for your half-ball destiny." The lights went out at Shibe Park for the final time in 1964.

# Chapter 5

Saturday, September 26, 1964

FDR Park, aka The Lakes, is located South of residential South Philly. Start at McCusker's Tavern, follow Shunk westbound, then turn south on 20th Street and follow it into the park. Much of its ground lies low and damp. Slight rains turn the park into a quagmire—steady rains, a swamp. It gets its namesake from the small ponds dotting the park. The Lakes are a favorite spot for families by day. By night, young lovers park by a pond to watch the submarine races.

Patricia packed Italian hoagies, another South Philly specialty. A hoagie is stuffed with Italian cold cuts, cheeses, lettuce, tomato slices, onions, and sweet and hot peppers. Elsewhere, hoagies are called a sub, a hero, or a submarine sandwich. Multi-national corporate chains call their Italian sandwiches hoagies. Proof that Philadelphia sets the standard.

The Waldrons ate Patricia's hoagies faster than a master illusionist could make them vanish.

Patricia helped Marie set up a miniature picnic for her Barbie and Ken dolls. If you could reduce a good South Philly Italian hoagie to doll scale, Barbie and Ken might vivify themselves and eat them.

"Pitch it in here." Dennis tapped his glove from a squatting catcher's position.

"All right, here it comes, Jim Bunning with a fastball." Bill hurled his best fastball, exaggerating his follow-through in imitation of the Phillies ace right-hander.

"Steee-rike!" Dennis caught his pitch and threw it back."

"Chris Short with a curveball." Bill threw Dennis his best attempt at a curveball.

"Jim Bunning with a change-up." Bill lobbed Dennis a slow toss. Dennis caught it underhand and threw it back. "Chris Short with a fastball." Bill threw as hard as he could.

***

Later that afternoon, Hugo Tubbs entered McCusker's Tavern while leading his Bulldog on a leash. Hugo Tubbs carried most of his 350 pounds around his waist. Spanky McMullen once cracked, "If he put a hula hoop around his waist, people would mistake him for Saturn," and "He has so many chins that he needs a bookmark to find his mouth." Hugo's dirty white T-shirt hung over soiled beige pants supported by red suspenders.

"Hey, look!" Spanky McMullen puffed his cigar. "Here come the Tubbs twins."

Hugo bent down and pinched his bulldog Ferdi's cheeks. Ferdi was as overweight by canine standards as Hugo by human standards. "Yeah, well, Ferdi here makes a far better companion than your identical twin—your bowling ball."

Everyone in the tavern guffawed.

"Hey, what is it with these Bimbos?" Hugo pointed to the Phillies game on TV. "Here I buy me World Series tickets; I go fishin' in da Poconos for five days; now I come back and they're choking away the whole gaw-damn thing. They's barely still in first. I don't stinkin' believe it. What goes?"

"It looks to me like they're falling apart." Johnny McCusker's eyes remained on his reading material. He had four racing forms, a copy of Life magazine, Sports Illustrated, and three different newspapers stacked on the bar. "This reminds me of the Whiz Kids. Tired pitching staff. Lots of key injuries. Remember when Eddie Sawyer went with Robin Roberts three times in five days? I liken it to Mauch's Bunning and Short rotation. Both staffs were shot to hell. It worked for Sawyer. Barely. Then again, he only had to worry about Brooklyn. Mauch's got three teams on his ass.

102

Everybody's talking about Cincinnati, but for my money, the Cardinals are the team to beat. We'll have to wait and see."

"Wait and see? My ass! For your money? Screw you! Every slimy bookie in town has your money." Hugo heaved his weight onto a barstool. "I got me World Series tickets. Those bimbos best not blow it."

Dennis Waldron walked into the tavern. Spanky stood from his bar stool, squared his feet, and angled his shoulders. "Oh no you don't." Ed Braceland pointed at Spanky. "You two had your fun on Monday night. Any nonsense out of you two, and I have my fun- tossing both of you to the curb."

"You won't get any problems from me." Spanky extended his right hand to Dennis.

Dennis bit his lip and turned away before accepting Spanky's gesture.

"Buzzz."

"Owww!" Dennis jerked his hand away.

"Ha! Ha! Ha!" Spanky revealed a joy buzzer to the tavern.

Dennis flushed as the tavern guffawed.

"Next time, I just squeeze your hand until it breaks. Then I end both your bowling life and your sex life."

"Don't do that, Waldron." Joey Maresco was a hawk-nosed man in his mid-twenties. He wore a black bowling shirt with a burgundy placket. His dark hair was crew cut. "McCusker's bowling team needs him. Crack him in the jaw instead."

"Hey, great idea. Then I can shut him up and stop the other side of his sex life as well."

"Listen here, you ugly bean pole. Why don't I just cut you down to size?" Spanky clenched his fists. "I'll start with twelve, ugly, useless inches off the top."

"Enough!" Ed narrowed his eyes, hunched his shoulders, and prodded.

Just then, a Beatles song, 'She Loves You,' played on the jukebox.

"Yo." Hugo turned on his barstool. "Who's playin' that subversive, longhaired garbage?"

"Oh, come on, Fats, get with the times, man." Joey raised his hands.

"Figures you like it," Hugo shrugged.

"It's all my fourteen-year-old niece listens to." Johnny kept his eyes glued to a newspaper. "Though I don't understand the stuff myself."

"Yeah, Johnny," Hugo pulled on Ferdi's leash. "Instead of reading up on losing racehorses, read up on how the commies have infiltrated the record industry. Understand this," Hugo pointed his finger. "The Beatles came from overseas with a mission to corrupt our youth."

"I like the twist. Come on baby, let's do the twist ..." Spanky McMullen sang and danced the twist with a freshly lit cigar in his mouth.

Johnny ignored Spanky and Hugo. After five seconds, he looked up from his newspaper and gazed at Dennis. "I know you like Jr. and the Jays. My favorite is Billy and the Essentials. Though I guess the kids aren't listenin' to doo wop anymore."

Ed handed Joey a beer.

"That's the problem with you guys." Joey gulped his beer. "You're all lost in the fifties. Come on, Hugo, Joseph McCarthy's crusade ended ten years ago. Doo-wop? The twist? Get used to it. The British invasion has arrived and it's here to stay."

Hugo motioned to Ed. He put a shot of Philadelphia Blended Whisky in front of him. "Jr. and the Jays? Billy and the Essentials? The British invasion? I say we should have stopped the clock after the big war. Glen Miller, Benny Goodman, The Dorsey brothers, Artie Shaw, and Harry James, now we're talkin' music." Hugo threw up his hands. "Thank God for Frank Sinatra." Hugo raised his chin. "And don't forget that Jo Stafford and Vera Lynn helped win the war."

"That music review coming from the man with fat in the ears," Frankie smirked.

"Up your hole with a Mello Roll."

"Yeah, well, up yours too. You're talkin' out of your hat, fat man. Because I heard you say, right here, at this bar, that you like Elvis."

"Yeah, Elvis is okay."

"Just okay?" Joey shook his open hands. "When Elvis first started, didn't you old farts call him subversive?"

"Yeah, well, he's American and served in the Army." Hugo saluted. "Can you picture those long-haired, foreign freaks in the U.S. Army? They're commie insurgents, I'm tellin' you."

"Oh, come on, Hugo," Dennis sipped his beer. "They're not subversive. A lot of their songs are Chuck Berry, Buddy Holly, or Little Richard covers. I like their new song, 'I Wanna Hold Your Hand.'"

"That's coming on next," a young guy wearing a Beatles haircut chimed in.

"Another thing you missed, Hugo." Ed leaned on the bar. "Back in '61, a mysterious woman more beautiful than the finest work of art came here and faith healed my shoulder."

"Faith healed your shoulder?" Joey skewed his head and rolled his eyes. "What's McMullen been puttin' in his cigar smoke?"

"You were too young to drink, Joey. You and Hugo are arguing about music. Sinatra? Elvis? The Beatles? You had to have heard her. She could sing the birds out of the trees."

"I will never forget her voice for as long as I live. Her singing is even something McMullen and I can agree on. And Joey," Dennis stood and faced Joey, "I'm skeptical of faith healers myself. But I saw her touch Ed's shoulder. The next day, he was practicing with the Iggles."

"Whoof, whoof," Ferdi the bulldog barked.

"Hey, I don't know about some mystery broad, but even my dog sings better than those long-haired foreigners, the cockroaches, or whatever. P.U." Hugo fanned away Spanky's cigar smoke. "I thought after the Bay of Pigs and the Cuban missile crisis those damn things were banned."

"Just more expensive." Spanky buffed a billow of cigar smoke.

Johnny looked down at a magazine. "Yeah, well, they shot JFK for his troubles. Nothing's been the same since, and I don't reckon it ever will be again…"

Hugo interrupted, "They is right. I used to believe in our government. Now I don't believe nothin', outta Washington no more. It's Bimboville I'm tellin' ya. Those com-symps want us to believe some crazy acted alone? All those bimbos can stick it where the sun don't shine. I know damn well it was a commie plot."

"Just like the Beatles." Joey pulled his face and shook his head.

"Yeah," Hugo pointed at Joey. "That's right."

Johnny continued talking without raising his volume or tempo. "I don't know what to think about Johnson and this whole Vietnam thing." He looked up from his newspapers, eyeing no one in particular. "Hey, I fought in the big one myself. I'm a patriot. I'll always support our boys. Still, I've got a seventeen-year-old nephew and an eighteen-year-old cousin. I don't want Johnson sending them over there . . ."

"LBJ is a Bimbo." Hugo gulped the rest of his beer.

"Don't tell me you're voting for Goldwater?" Joey finished his bottle of Schmidt's Beer and put it on the bar.

"I ain't votin' for nobody. I'll vote for Ferdi before I vote for any of those Bimbos."

Johnny continued, "…I can't see anything worth dying for over there. Who can figure out where this world's going? Everything's coming apart at the seams. Hey, I ain't prejudiced or nothing but take the Negroes. All this marching and protesting. They never acted like this before."

"Yeah, well, I ain't prejudiced either," Hugo said. "But I still wanna see some big white guy jam a fist right down that loudmouth Cassius Clay's throat."

"Thank you, Spanky." McMullen jutted his jaw. "If it wasn't for my bowling a 228 on my last game, that black team from North Philly would've beat us last Thursday night."

"Hey, speaking of North Philly, it looks like the Phils are going to win." Dennis pointed at the TV.

"Hell, yeah, it's four nothing, and Art Mahaffey's pitching." Joey folded his arms. "It's about time Mauch takes a break from his Bunning, Short thing."

Eighth inning. The Braves have cut the Phillies' lead to four-three. The Phillies would be up by two runs, save an ugly passed ball by catcher Gus Triandos. Still having a chance to catch a Braves baserunner trying to score, the Phillies catcher tripped over himself chasing the ball. Art Mahaffey did make a brilliant defensive play to escape a bases-loaded jam. Felipe Alou dribbled a ground ball between the pitcher's mound and the third-base foul line. Mahaffey dove on the ball and threw it to the plate from his belly for the force out.

The Braves opened their final at-bat by putting their first two batters on base. Pinch hitter Frank Bolling then smashed a sure hit up the middle. Phillies shortstop Ruben Amaro dove for it like a gallant soldier flopping on an enemy grenade. He speared it and flipped it to Tony Taylor. The sure-handed second baseman, unfortunately, treated the ball like an explosive. He dropped it for an error. The Braves loaded the bases.

"Here we go again." Dennis threw up his hands.

Gene Mauch went to a former Philadelphia A's great, lefthander Bobby Shantz, to face the Braves' hot-hitting right-handed batter, Rico Carty. He hit a tremendous drive off the center field wall, four hundred and forty-seven feet away for a triple. Rico Carty stood on third.

Dennis Waldron dropped his head, then slammed down his scotch.

Johnny McCusker walked around in a small circle before sitting down and silently staring into his beer.

Ed stared at the TV, mouth agape.

"Bimbos…Bimbos!" Hugo pounded the bar. "Damn bimbos."

Spanky puffed his cigar and laughed, "Looks like the Yankees ain't coming to town after all."

"You shut the hell up!" Ed pointed at Spanky. One of the patrons threw a handful of peanuts at him.

Mike De La Hoz followed Carty with a line drive to the left-center field gap. Center fielder Cookie Rojas valiantly chased, diving for it with the desperation of a soccer goaltender for a penalty kick. Caught! Umpire Ed Vargo ruled that he trapped it. Rojas charged Vargo as if riding in on a Kentucky thoroughbred. He bumped, jostled, and spewed verbal venom at the umpire. Vargo ejected him.

"Stupid, blind bimbo! Look! He caught it!" Hugo pointed at the TV instant replay.

"Damn!" Dennis bit his lip. "What next?"

Gene Mauch, coach George Myatt, and Ruben Amaro circled the umpire like marauding Indians in a John Wayne movie. Their howls of protest were like war cries.

Unlike Western movies, Gene Mauch and his war tribe won. The umpires reversed their call and declared De La Hoz out. He, like Rojas, bumped, jostled, and cursed the umpire. The umpire ejected him too.

Pandemonium ruled Shibe Park.

"It's falling apart." Johnny slapped his racing form on the bar. "It's like I keep saying, everything's going to hell."

Gene Mauch kept fighting. He argued that if Rojas had caught De La Hoz's liner, Carty was also out for leaving third early. The home plate umpire agreed.

Braves manager Bobby Bragan and his third base coach's dispute of the umpire's call raised the scene to another level of pell-mell. Umpire Vargo also ejected both.

"Now I know what you're saying about everything going to hell," Ed jutted his head toward Johnny.

More Braves joined the fracas. The umpires ejected more Braves, including catcher Joe Torre and pitcher Tony Cloninger.

Like an overload blowing all circuits and fuses, the drama ended there. Future Hall of Famer Warren Spahn retired the Phillies in the bottom of the ninth without incident. Final score: Braves six, Phillies four. Their sixth loss in a row. Defying all reason and logic, the Cincinnati Reds won their seventh straight. The St. Louis Cardinals also won. Now the Phillies' National League lead had evaporated to a threadbare half-game.

Over fourteen thousand emotionally drained mourners filed out of Connie Mack Stadium.

Most McCusker's Tavern patrons left with their heads down, muttering to themselves or one another. They tipped Ed less than usual. The last person to go home? Phillies skipper Gene Mauch.

# Chapter 6

Sunday, September 27, 1964

This morning, the Waldrons ate a late breakfast. Patricia prepared mounds of scrambled eggs, fried potatoes, and scrapple. Another Philadelphia specialty, scrapple, resembles a flat sausage. A piece of scrapple is about the size of a quarter-inch-thick playing card. It's delicious until you know its composition. Bill and Marie still managed to argue over the Froot Loops cereal. Dennis cloistered himself behind the Sunday Bulletin sports page. He muttered, "Why does this only happen to Philadelphia? Can't the Phillies win just one game and end this nonsense?"

Between slurps of Froot Loops, Bill pleaded with his father. "Please, Daddy, please, we have to go to the Phillies game today."

"Forget it." Dennis remained behind his newspaper.

"Please, if they don't win, they fall outta first place."

"What makes you think you're going to make any difference?"

"But it might be their last chance."

"Don't bother me."

"Please?"

"Shut up Bill. I'm reading the paper. Why don't you stay home and listen to the Iggles on the radio? They haven't blown anything yet."

"But, the Phillies haven't either."

"Yes, they have." Dennis finally appeared from behind his paper. "The sooner we face it and forget Mauch's phlops, the better for all of us. So, listen to the Iggles on the radio. They're playing Cleveland, so that means Jim Brown's coming to town."

"No, Daddy. Please. I wanna go to the Phillies."

"Bill." Dennis prodded. "I'm warning you. Shut up."

"It's great that you're not going to the game with Bill," Patricia put her arm around Bill. "Now you two can join Marie and I and visit my mother. My sister Claire will be there too. You know, Dennis, the one you nicknamed AT&T, for Always Talking and Talking. Of course, she'll also be with her husband, Massimo. The one you nicknamed Gluteus. Then, of course, Little Albert. The one you call Al Capone Jr."

"Get your cap and glove, Bill."

"AWL-right! Yeah! Thank you, Dad."

***

Dennis's North Philly reconnaissance for a parking place ended when two black youths waved him into an opening. "Watch your car for a buck, mister?"

Dennis sprang from his car and slammed the door. "Why don't you two get lost?" He put his hands on his hips and hunched his head. "If you want money, get a job. Now beat it!"

The two youths scowled at him before leaving.

"Extortion. I'm fed up." Dennis marched southbound with Bill on Twentieth Street. "Hey, I'm already supporting those welfare-gouging leeches as it is. I'm the one getting taxed to death. This time the cops can watch my car. I pay their damn salaries. It's about time I get something in return."

The Marvelettes' 'Beechwood 45789' radiated through a window. Six houses down the block, they heard Kim Weston's, 'Looking for the Right Guy.' Unfortunately, the music couldn't repair the many vandalized or abandoned structures. Dennis, nevertheless, spotted an oasis amid the North Philly blight. Across the street from Connie Mack's 34' spite fence stood Charlie Quinn's Deep Right Field Cafe.

Dennis and Bill sat at the bar. The jukebox played a harmony from a female group called the Toys, 'A Lover's Concerto.' The twenty other patrons at Charlie Quinn's worked on their drinks glumly.

Dennis ordered, "Scotch ... er ... make that a double Granddad. Straight up. The hundred proof, please."

The huge, gruff bartender's beefy, unshaven face sported a horse jaw and a spiked flat top. 'He's a military recruit's worst nightmare,' Dennis thought as he looked over his dark blue tank top exposing a thick, hairy arm tattooed with a snaggle-toothed bulldog, bayonets, and the acronym U.S.M.C. He acknowledged Dennis by standing over Bill. The bartender crossed his arms.

'That dog's opening his mouth to bite me,' Bill blanched.

"I know, I know, can my son at least have a root beer?"

The bartender grimaced at them while sizing them up. The jukebox played Darlene Love's 'Wait Until My Bobby Gets Home.' He silently poured Bill a root beer and Dennis a double bourbon.

"This sure beats listening to your Aunt A T&T's motor-mouthed gossip and your Uncle Gluteus's stupid wisecracks." Dennis downed his bourbon. "He's almost as obnoxious as Spanky McMullen." Dennis drank half his bourbon. "Keep my remarks between us as two men. No need to upset your mother."

"Do you think the Phillies can win, Dad?"

"They can." Dennis finished his bourbon. "But they won't." Dennis signaled to the bartender for a refill. "If you're going to be a Philadelphia sports fan, you must accept this as your fate. What we did to deserve this, I don't know. The sooner you accept that it's only a game and enjoy it anyway, the better. Look at Mets fans. All those great Yankees teams, but they have more fun with the loser Mets. Go figure?"

After the Darlene Love number, two Diana Ross and the Supremes songs, 'Where Did Our Love Go' and 'Stop In The Name of Love,' played on the jukebox.

"I guess you figure this will bring the Phillies good luck," the bartender scowled and poured. "Don't worry, you're not the only one. It's increased my business. For now. If there's no World

Series, I lose big time. I smelled this thing coming, and that steal of home with Robinson batting stank like a dead skunk on the road." He put the bottle on the bar and folded his arms. "Who's your favorite player, kid?"

"Richie Allen."

"He's only a rookie, but I say he's the best Phillies power hitter since Del Ennis. No, make that Chuck Klein. My father used to tell me about his hitting balls through, not just over, but through the tin wall at the old Baker Bowl. As for Richie Allen, the old timers who come here tell me he hits 'em like only Jimmie Foxx did. So, kid, can you bring 'em good luck today?"

"I know I can. The Phillies got to win today, and they will. I just know it. They got to."

"That's great, kid, but Mauch's bringing Jim Bunning back on two days' rest, the third time in a row. It hasn't worked yet, and I say he should stop it."

"I guess it's the same as in 1950. I surely remember Eddie Sawyer pitching Robin Roberts three times in five days?" Dennis sipped his bourbon.

"I've heard several customers talk about that, though it ain't the same. Robin Roberts was a durable, control pitcher with fluid motion. Jim Bunning's a power pitcher. Look at how he throws his body to hell and back with his crazy follow-through. That's got to take a drain the gas outta ya. Besides, Robin Roberts was ten years younger in 1950 than Bunning is now."

"Yeah, but what's left for Mauch to do?" Dennis asked. "Heck, before last week, it was only talk that Dennis Bennett, Art Mahaffey, and Ray Culp had sore arms." Dennis shook his head. "Now we know they're shot."

"And Jack Baldschun and Ed Roebuck don't do nothin' outta the bullpen no more," Bill pointed upward.

"Good point, Kid. Oh, what's your name by the way? So, I don't keep callin' ya kid."

"Bill."

"I'm Dennis." He extended his right hand, "the boy's father."

"I figured that." The bartender shook Dennis's hand. "I'm Duke. Yeah, Dennis, Gene Mauch doesn't have much left to work with, does he? Even so, this Bunning, Short thing is a proven loser. Seems to me Mauch's like a gambler who's lost his touch. Instead of trusting his instincts, he's chasing money by throwing it on favorites, only 'cause they're the favorites. I'll tell ya what he ought to do. Take a chance with Rick Wise. Okay, so he's only eighteen. But he's big and healthy. Strong as an ox. He can throw gas out there. I say put him in. Better yet, I say bring this Ferguson Jenkins kid up from the minors. I hear he's got great control. How many young pitchers have that? Put the kid in, I say. You know he's gonna throw strikes. Hell, the hitters don't know him yet. That's even more reason for him doin' good. The kid probably won't even know what's going on, so I bet he won't feel the pressure. That's the kind of daring Mauch used to get 'em here. I say he's gotta run with it. Not run away from it."

"I see your point, Duke," Dennis sipped his bourbon. "Hey, what's the worst that could happen? If Wise or Jenkins loses, they lose. At least they can give you nine innings. That not only gives the bullpen rest, but you can bring back Bunning and Short at 100 percent strength."

"Exactly!" Duke filled Dennis's glass. He waved off his attempt to pay for it. "Take a chance with Wise and Jenkins." He folded his arms. "That's what I say."

"Unfortunately, if the hitting and fielding don't start moving north, it's not going to matter what Mauch does," Dennis raised his palms.

"And all this bad luck's got to stop. They need a break," Bill chipped in.

"I must say kid, I mean Bill, after a week of hearing nothin' but bitching and moaning and all this 'Fizz Kids' and 'Mauch's

Phlops' talk, it sure is refreshing to hear something positive. So, you think the Phillies are gonna get some good luck today?"

"Yes."

"Tell you what. Maybe good luck is contagious." Duke took Bill's root beer away to a back room. When he returned, Bill's root beer had a scoop of vanilla ice cream, covered with whipped cream, and topped with a cherry. "I hope this gets you off to a good start. Bring good luck to the Phillies, why don't you?"

Is Baseball luck superstition or is it something deeper? The wise King Solomon wrote in Ecclesiastes 9:11: "I again saw under the sun that the race is not to the swift, and the battle is not to the warriors, and neither is bread to the wise, nor wealth to the discerning nor favor to men of ability; for time and chance overtake them all."

The Washington Senators won their only World Series in 1924, when with two outs, bottom of the twelfth inning, seventh game, Earl McNeely hit a sure out to Giants third-baseman Fred Lindstrom. A tiny pebble, however, deflected the grounder away, thus ending the Giants' season. A minute divot made Bill Mazeroski's seventh game, ninth inning walk-off 1960 World Series-winning home run possible. The Pirates had trailed by three in the bottom of the eighth when Bill Virdon hit a routine double-play grounder. Only it took a freak hop, striking Yankee shortstop Tony Kubec in the throat. Everybody safe, brand new ballgame. Bad hops. Bloop hits. Booming outs. Whimsical weather. Umpires making split-second decisions on plays indeterminable from multiple angles of video replay. Those factors and superstition are part of baseball.

A large banner reading, "Help!" hung from Shibe Park's upper deck.

Cold, steel-gray weather beset the final 20,569 of the 1,425,891 fans to attend Phillies games at Shibe Park in 1964. Fate again slapped their hero's faces. Felipe Alou initiated the Braves' fortunes by tapping to Tony Taylor. The second baseman's throw barely pulled Frank Thomas off the first base bag. Safe. Arthur Lee Maye next bounced a high chopper just over the reach of third baseman Richie Allen for a double. Jim Bunning then fooled Hank Aaron with a nifty curveball. He could only cue it off the end of his bat. It landed millimeters fair for a two-run double.

The Phillies fought back like a badger cornered by a grizzly bear. They took the lead on a Clay Dalrymple double, a Tony Taylor triple, and a Jim Bunning sacrifice fly.

Then came the inning that wasn't. Joe Torre started the Braves fourth with a routine infield ground ball to the left side. Crowd noise distracted third baseman Richie Allen and Shortstop Ruben Amaro. Safe at first. Rico Carty appeared to kill the rally by hitting a double-play ball to the second baseman. It took a bad hop over Tony Taylor's head. What should have been the inning's final out became the first run when Dennis Menke hit a grounder that jumped over the Shortstop's head. After a clean, run-scoring double, pitcher Tony Cloninger hit a high pop-up. An unexpected gust of wind played havoc. The ball dropped between outfielders Wes Covington, Tony Gonzalez, and shortstop Ruben Amaro. Two more runs. Felipe Alou next nicked the third base bag with a groundball, fair by a millimeter. A double and a run. More to come. The umpire called Tony Cloninger safe on a disputed play at the plate following Arthur Lee Maye's infield grounder for the final run of a six-run inning.

The Phillies didn't quit. The Phillies' pitching staff was shot, and Frank Thomas battled a broken thumb. Now, Johnny Callison had the flu, evaporating their top run producer's body weight from 189 lbs. to 161 lbs. In the sixth inning, the penicillin-injected ball player dragged his pallid and weakened body to home plate. Out of courage and instinct, he slugged a homer over the high and distant rightfield wall.

By the eighth inning, he played on primal anger alone. What else could explain him hitting another home run?

The last of the Ninth inning found the Phillies losing fourteen to six. Among both his fans and opponents, for both him and his teammates, Johnny Callison had inspired a paradox of admiration and pathos. With his body reduced to inflamed bone and sinew, and a mind hazy as the clouds shrouding Shibe Park, Johnny Callison achieved the impossible. He hit a third home run. Oh, so beautiful! The Phillies lost fourteen to eight. Oh, so ugly! No team tried harder. No team played harder. No team worked harder. No team was braver. Maybe they tried too hard? The final 20,569 witnesses filed out of Shibe Park looking like evacuees from a natural disaster.

***

"Fourteen years, Bill." Dennis shook his fists. "Fourteen damn years just for the Phillies to compete, much less win anything. We had it, Bill, we had it." Dennis spotted an empty Ballentine Beer can on the sidewalk. He kicked it clear across the street. "A-six-and-a-half-game lead," Dennis squeezed his temples, "Gone in under a week. Did you look at the scoreboard, Bill?"

"Yes, Dad." Bill looked down and shuffled his feet through a discarded milk carton, hot dog wrapper, and paper cup.

The Reds didn't just win. They took a doubleheader. Damn Mets! They couldn't beat a Little League team." Dennis stomped on an empty cardboard orange juice pint, making it pop. "You know what that means, Bill."

"We've fallen out of first place?"

"That's right." Dennis shook his head. "And a full game back at that."

"They can still win." Bill grabbed his father's arm and smiled. "They still have a chance."

"I hope you're right. Just three short years ago, you were only eleven; I watched the Phillies break their 23-game losing streak on TV at McCusker's. We all decided to greet the Phillies at the airport to celebrate winning a game. 5,000 others had the same idea. We carried Gene Mauch through the airport like he defeated death and taxes. Now losing is not so fun."

"I hope the Eagles won."

"I don't know the score. Look," Dennis pointed ahead, "that Black guy has a radio. I'll ask him." Dennis walked ahead of Bill. "Did the Iggles win?"

"Jim Brown whipped your cracker asses. Jim Brown's the baddest dude alive." The black tough prodded. "Now he's gonna whoop every honkey in the city."

Denis avoided eye contact with him and turned back to his son. "You heard his answer. The Iggles lost too. If the Phillies don't win the pennant," Dennis glanced back at the black tough. He scowled back. "At least we don't have to return to this neighborhood until next Spring."

A few blocks later, a sight stunned Dennis. "Oh my God." His jaw slackened; his arms dangled at his side. His car sat on four blocks with no tires, hood agape, and engine stripped.

# Chapter 7

Monday, 28 September 1964

Bill sat alone at the breakfast table. He cut his pancakes into small pieces and stirred. Patricia helped Marie with the top button of her catholic school uniform. Dennis stood in the foyer, briefcase in hand and a newspaper tucked under his arm. "Are you going to walk Marie to school? Or shall I drop her off?"

"I'm going to walk with her. The fresh air will do us both good."

"Tell ya what, Bill, hurry up and eat those pancakes instead of staring at them, and I'll give you a lift to school."

"Yo, thanks, Dad." Bill wiped a smudge of maple syrup from his mouth with a paper napkin.

The family exchanged pleasantries before Patricia walked away with Marie, and Dennis drove Bill to school in a rented Ford Fairlane. Dennis tuned into Jerry Blavat's radio show in time for him to introduce Marvin Gaye's, 'Too Busy Thinkin' About My Baby.'

Dennis spotted Bill with his head down and eyes glazed. "Hey, Bill, let me cheer you up. What do you say I swing around and pick up Jeff?"

Bill kept his head down, "He don't need a ride."

"Why don't we go and ask him?"

"Nah. Really. He doesn't."

"Is there anything wrong? After all, you, Jeff, and Frank have been like peas in a pod since you were little."

"No, Dad. Nothin's wrong."

"Okay, Bill, if you say so. Tell me, how is the algebra coming?"

"Nah, not too good. Heck, how can anyone learn anything from Old Man Arsenic? Besides, algebra is useless."

"Well, firstly, judging by how you and Frank throw around baseball statistics, I know you can do well at math..."

"Why bother? Algebra is useless."

"You don't know that yet. Don't find out otherwise after it's too late. Regardless, learning algebra is your responsibility. There are no free rides in this world. You better get used to working hard now, even at things you don't like, because work in one form or another doesn't end until you die. Even sitting on a street corner and begging is a form of work. The hoodlums call theft 'pulling a job.' Some job. Get caught and you go to jail. Now you get to spend your life smashing big rocks into little rocks for no pay. Bill, money's not everything. Nevertheless, you need it to live, and you'll work just as hard, if not harder, for low pay, or in prison- no pay, as you will for high pay. The next time you see some guy sweating his life away, digging a ditch on the hottest day of the year, remember, his boss is sitting in an air-conditioned office sipping coffee and making ten times more."

"What's that have to do with Old Man Arsenic's algebra class?"

"The educated man is the one who gets to be boss. Even if you never care about being a boss, the educated man has more choices. Education gives you a better chance of finding something you like. I think you know that already, Bill."

"What I know is that no one can stand Old Man Arsenic."

"Another thing you'll find out as you get older is you can't always choose who you work for or with. You had better learn how to work with difficult people." Dennis glanced at Bill. "I didn't like all of my teachers either, and I know Mr. Arsegio's methods are a bit old-fashioned..."

"You can say that again. Frank says they're from the Spanish Inquisition."

"Bill, like I've been saying, listen to him and try to learn. If nothing else, you'll gain people skills. Trust me, son." Dennis smiled. "You won't be sorry. Learn how to use that mind of yours."

"Yeah, sure, Dad," Bill grumbled. "I'll try."

"Bill, I can tell you're upset about the Phillies. That goes for the entire city. You've got to separate your personal and professional life. Right now, school is your profession. Okay. I admit that I've allowed it to get to me as well. Your Grandad and I went to games at Shibe Park long before you were born. Let me tell you something," Dennis raised his right hand, "I've waited for the Phillies to get another crack at the Series since the Whiz Kids in 1950. We cannot let it interfere with what's important in life."

"It's no fair."

"When did I ever say that life was fair? Baseball always has next year. I'll tell you what's unfair. When I was your age, my favorite team was the A's. Your Grandad and I used to go to their games and cheer for them, no matter how often they lost, and it was often. But we loved them anyway."

"But they moved out of town."

"That's right, Bill. The A's leaving town was complicated. What is simple is that no one asked me or my father about it. No next year. No nothing. What they did to Brooklyn a few years later was worse. Appreciate what you got. Your youth. Your health. Your family. Everything. 'Cause it can be taken away from you without notice, and no one will ask first." Dennis smirked. "Like with the car yesterday."

"Yeah, okay. I get it, Dad."

"Here we are." Dennis smiled at Bill. "See you tonight."

"I will, Dad." Bill alighted from the car. "And the Phillies are only a game back. We've still got five to play. Just watch. We're gonna win this pennant yet."

"That's the spirit!" Dennis waved while driving away.

***

South Philadelphia Jr. High's schoolyard seemed less convivial than usual, though hardly resembling a wake. The same groups of kids congregated, and the same conversations and youthful rituals persisted. Bill spotted Frank and Hank and ran toward them. "Yo guys! How ya doin'?"

Frank and Hank, not having seen Bill since the fight, scrutinized him before returning the salutation. Bill mustered his diplomatic best. "How is your history paper coming?"

"Okay," Frank cradled his books. "I'm almost three-fourths into the rough draft. The teacher only asked for five pages, though it looks like I'm going to end up with at least ten. She better give me an A. I'm working hard enough on it."

"What's it about?"

"It's about the Lincoln assassination. Mostly the aftermath."

"Oh boy!" Hank tore open a pack of baseball cards. "Richie Allen! I gotta Richie Allen!"

Bill examined Hank's lucky find like a curator would a rare, lost masterpiece. "I'll give you two Willie Mays's and a Hank Aaron."

Hank held the card close to his chest. "No way, Jose, I'm keeping this one."

Bill thought for a minute before saying, "Two Willie Mays's, a Hank Aaron, plus a Don Drysdale and a Pete Retslaff football card."

"Throw in a Micky Mantle and ya gotta deal."

"All right."

Just as Hank started handing over the coveted card, Frank made a counteroffer. "I'll give you these chocolate Tastykakes." He pulled a fresh, unopened pack of three chocolate cupcakes from his lunch bag. "My ice cream at lunch, and a piece of my mom's homemade pumpkin pie after school."

"Yeah!" Hank snatched the Tastycakes from Frank and gave him the card.

"Hey, no fair," Bill protested.

The school bell rang.

"See you at lunch." Frank and Hank walked away.

***

Myron Arsegio was a tall, stout, taciturn man in his late fifties with a large oval face, bald scalp, and hard, piercing eyes. He wore gray flannel slacks, a white shirt, and a bow tie two decades out of style. He spoke in a dry monotone, always making liberal use of a pointer while lecturing.

After a five-minute attempt at paying attention to the algebra lesson, Bill started doodling baseball diamonds in his notebook…Tony Taylor punched a single to left off Cardinal ace Bob Gibson. Johnny Callison followed by pulling a harder single to right. Dick Allen then slammed a screaming line drive, nearly decapitating Gibson en route to center field. Bases loaded. Bill came up to bat, his Phillies uniform fitting like stripes on a tiger. Gibson's glare burned through him before firing his nastiest fastball. Bill swung his bat with deft and courage. Deep to left, he drove the baseball. The left-fielder turned and watched it go ...

"You. Mr. Waldron. Mr. Waldron, I'm speaking to you," Myron Arsegio rapped Bill's desk with his pointer stick.

"Um…Yes, Mr. Arsegio."

"Welcome to my class, Mr. Waldron." Some braver students giggled. "Now…You." Mr. Arsegio aimed his left index finger toward the center of Bill's eyes. The teacher then tapped his pointer stick on an algebra problem chalked on the blackboard. "What is this?"

"I don't know," Bill squeaked.

123

"You don't? I've been explaining it to the rest of the class for the past twenty minutes. Where were you, young man? Somewhere out in left field, perhaps?"

"No, um, that's Wes Covington," Bill answered sincerely. The class laughed at him.

"Since you find my class so amusing, young man, perhaps you'd like to work on some problems on your own. After school. In detention?"

"Um, no, sir."

"Three o'clock. Mr. Waldron."

***

That evening, Bill gulped down his dinner of veal Parmesan and scalloped potatoes too quickly for his taste buds to register the fine home-cooked meal. Dennis excused himself to the lounge; Marie cleared the table.

"You make sure that you finish your homework before listening to the Phillies game," Dennis turned away from his TV program, the Hy Litt show, an "American Bandstand" spinoff where Hy Litt played records for a dancing studio audience. At this moment, they enthusiastically bee-bopped to Martha Reeves and the Vandellas, 'Heatwave.'

"Okay, Dad, I'm almost finished."

"Do a good job. Don't forget what we talked about this morning."

"Okay... Hey, I like that song," Bill said as Hy Litt spun Marvin Gaye's, 'Can I Get a Witness.'

"Say, why don't you go to the next school dance?"

"Nah, I don't go for that stuff."

"Well, you surely like the music. Hey, I saw Jeff today at Oregon Steaks with a cute girlfriend. Why don't you ask him if she's got a friend you can meet?"

"Yeah, so what? I bet any friend of hers is ugly, fat, and with braces."

"Only a suggestion.""Yeah, well, a bad one. I'm going upstairs to my room to finish my homework."

Bill ran slipshod through his homework, eventually resorting to fabrication. Much like a child anticipating Christmas morning gift-opening, time dragged as Bill awaited the start of the Phillies game. The moment arrived at last. "A must-win for the Phillies," broadcasted Byron Saam.

"Oh brother, is it ever!" responded Richie Ashburn.

"But it won't be easy for the Phillies tonight. They're up against one of the best. Bob Gibson."

"Yes, By. Bob Gibson's probably the strongest pitcher in the National League right now. For the Phillies, it's Chris Short returning on two days' rest. This is his fourth start in ten days."

"It looks like a mismatch on paper, but as we're all well aware, funny things can happen down on the field, Richie."

"Mismatch!" Bill said to himself. "Why not just give 'em the damn game without even playing it? You two are jinxing 'em."

Karma or not, the game did prove a mismatch. Chris Short battled overwork and a painful left forearm like a trooper. Courage and effort were not enough as the Cardinals hit him for three earned runs in five and a third innings. Yet the Phillies' only chance at winning would've been to borrow Sandy Koufax from the Dodgers. Bob Gibson dominated the Phillies' tired, sick, and injured batters, yielding just five hits and one run in eight full innings. Veteran knuckleballing relief ace Barney Schultz slammed the door on the Phillies by hurling a perfect ninth. Final score: St. Louis 5, Philadelphia 1.

The soporific eighth Phillies loss in a row coaxed Bill into dreamland before the game's forlorn conclusion. He was at his paternal grandparents' house in South Jersey's rural Cumberland County, the southern edge of the Pine Barrens. Over a century old, the large white, double-story, colonial farmhouse spooked him as a child. Its dark, musty basement terrified him as it had rats, black widow spiders, and possibly rattlesnakes. As a child, Bill firmly believed it housed the Jersey Devil. He still wondered.

Bill sat on an antique, creaky pastel couch in the family room. He cursed the TV while watching the Phillies lose. The floor started to wobble like sea swells. It next folded, converging with the walls at a forty-five-degree angle. It funneled Bill through the basement door. His butt dribbled down the craggy old spiral stairs, soon dumping him on the hard, filthy cellar floor.

Black widow spiders with bodies the size of softballs danced atop his body. A block broke off the wall. Columns of cat-sized, brown-bodied, screeching, red-eyed rats charged him. Bill knocked the spiders away, sprang to his feet, and ran to a corner. The first rat jumped on him and tore his arm open. "Ahh!" His scream got stuck in his throat as he shook the rat from his arm. He gasped. The other rats attacked him. Pain. Terror. A trap door dropped him...Down...Down…Falling…Falling…Thud. Bill crashed into a deeper, unknown chamber of the stygian, even darker and filthier. Cobwebs infested its ashen black boulder walls. Like resting in the eye of a hurricane, he gained a moment's asylum. 'Where am I? The rats are gone.' He sighed and wiped his brow. His peace was short lived, like a jack in the box from hell, it popped up from a trap door: a ten-foot-tall, red, dragon-like creature with an oversized lupine head. The beast's red eyes scorched him with hatred. Its lower jaw jutted forward, sporting eight-inch-long viper fangs. Flames blazed from conical horns. The creature flapped its reptilian wings. It roared as if from the depths of Hell. The Jersey Devil attacked.

Bill tried to run. He felt like he was wearing concrete shoes. He labored his way through a dark, narrow, head-high tunnel. He started to move faster. A little faster until the floor turned to goo. He sank up to his knees. The Jersey Devil's breath stank of excrement and corpses. It brandished a green-scaled, talon-drawn claw. Bill tried to scream but could only grunt as the Jersey Devil slashed his chest. Its forked tongue slurped up his blood.

Bill managed to run. 'Run faster! Faster! Please run faster!' He reached the end of the tunnel. Gene Mauch, Johnny Callison, Jim Bunning, and Chris Short had collapsed among the sharp rocks. "Run! Come on! Run!" Bill shook his fist.

"We can't," Gene Mauch raised his head. "We can't run anymore."

"But you must! Come on, please! The Jersey Devil! It will kill us all!"

"It's all over, we can't go any farther," Gene Mauch shook his head.

"Yes! You can! Come on!"

Gene Mauch, Johnny Callison, Chris Short, and Jim Bunning stood and trudged forward.

"Please! Faster!" Bill led them through a dark forest. Barren trees, gnarled limbs, and stripped vines hung like live electric wires. "Come on. Faster! It's gaining on us!" Sounding like a diesel locomotive, the Jersey Devil burned and destroyed everything in its path.

At last, they stumbled onto a beautiful beach with white sand like mineralized snow. The five laughed and cheered as they rolled and frolicked. "We made it!" Gene Mauch. Shouted. We made it! You're our hero, Bill."

"I told you we'd make. Didn't I? Next week the World Series." Bill lay back, allowing the sun to heal the spider, rat, and Devil-inflicted wounds. They relaxed and admired the tranquil, cobalt sea. The sun shimmered in technicolor rays off the water.

"You're going to be there," Gene Mauch beamed, "aren't you, Bill?"

"Of course!" Bill sat on the sand. "My father got us tickets. All my life I dreamed of seeing the Phillies play in the World

Series. I can't wait to see Connie Mack Stadium packed with cheering fans. I can already see it decked out in red, white, and blue bunting?"

"Where will you be sitting?"

"I don't know."

"Well, give those tickets to a friend. You and your dad will sit right next to me in the Phillies dugout—that goes for the away games too. Do ya know what else, my good man? I'm going to drive you two to Yankee Stadium myself."

"I've only dared dream of pitching at Yankee Stadium in a World Series," Chris Short held up his left arm.

"My arm hurts like hell, but I won't let it stop me. Sixty-three thousand people. The same grounds as Babe Ruth, Lou Gehrig, and Joe DiMaggio. Now it will be me on that mound, staring down Mantle and Maris with the entire world watching."

"Here, here," Johnny Callison and Jim Bunning concurred. The five of them next touched raised fists in a salute. "The World Series!"

"We never would have made it without you, Bill," Gene Mauch smiled.

The four Phillies tossed Bill skyward. "Hip hip hooray! Hip hip hooray! Hip hip hooray! For Bill's a jolly good fellow, for Bill's a jolly good fellow, for Bill's a jolly good fellow, which nobody can deny, which nobody can deny." They rode Bill on their shoulders and marched around the beach. They all fell and laughed.

A deep, guttural roar unexpectedly boomed like tropical lightning on an Arctic tundra. The forest erupted into a raging inferno. Heat seared their skins. "No! The four Phillies yelled before retreating into the sea. Bill stood at the ocean's edge, watching helplessly as giant, prehistoric crocodiles and sharks devoured them. The sapphire water turned crimson. A crocodile had Gene Mauch's entire body in its jaws. The sound of teeth crunching bone cloaked his screams. A shark tore Jim Bunning apart. His severed pitching arm momentarily floated on the surface before a crocodile swallowed it. Paddling like a cat thrown in a swimming pool, Johnny Callison swam from the shadow of a shark. It caught up to him and ate him in one bite. Sharks and crocodiles reduced Chris Short to a seething mass of human offal.

Bill retched all over himself. He turned. The Jersey Devil faced him. Cytotoxic venom dripped from its fangs. Bill's attempt to scream was a rasping gasp. At last, he could scream, loud and hard, with all his strength. His eyes opened. His bedroom was a hazy blur. Dennis, Patricia, and even little Marie ran into his room.

"Wake up! What's wrong?" Patricia hugged Bill. "What's wrong?"

"A nightmare. I had a horrible nightmare."

"You sure had a doozy." Dennis grinned and shook his head. "What nightmare got you this upset?"

"I'm sure he doesn't want to relive it." Patricia continued to hold Bill.

The now third-place Philadelphia Phillies' nightmare continued.

# Chapter 8

Tuesday, 29 September 1964

McCusker's Tavern.

Anthony Rocca Sr. leaned against the bar. The thirty-eight-year-old boasted a lean, rangy physique featuring well-developed biceps. Dark, navy blue cotton slacks topped steel-toed working boots. A light blue cotton shirt emblazoned "Anthony" across the chest. He put his drink on the bar and spoke to the bartender, "I'm tellin' ya, Ed, I know more about cargo in the head of my dick, than that son-of-a-bitch Hennessey's got in the head on his shoulders." Anthony grabbed his double shot of bourbon and downed it. "I don't know how in the hell those idiot losers up in management could make that useless loser supervisor. But I'm tellin' ya right now, if that loser tries riding my ass one more time, his shit's gonna be on the toes of my boots."

"Did you complain to the shop steward?" Ed refilled Anthony's shot glass.

"Yeah, and the useless loser told me Hennessey's now management, and that I've got to prove he's breakin' rules before the union can act. Rules my dago wop ass! I pay my dues. So, what do they ever do? Nothing. Do ya wanna know why? It's because the unions in this town are a bunch of candy-ass losers. Not like Pittsburgh. Their unions kick ass. Well up the whole damn system," Anthony snapped his right arm and fist upward, bracing his inner elbow with his right hand. "That goes for everything in this loser city. The government, the unions, and especially management, they're the worst kind of knuckleheads, 'cause when their stupidity and incompetence lose money, they keep their jobs while working men like us lose ours."

"Hey, and can you believe that Schuylkill Expressway?" George Mueller wore his Puddin' Head Jones Whiz Kid jacket. "Only in Philadelphia is a civil engineering project outta date before it's even finished. Today I got stuck in another traffic jam-an hour and a half this time."

Dennis Waldron signaled for a drink, "I went to pick up another Buick today, and guess what? They've built a freeway exit directly to the dealership. Hell, we're talking out in the middle of nowhere. I mean, nothing else is out there. You tell me some palms at City Hall weren't greased before they built it."

"This city's more corrupt than Al Capone's Chicago," Ed polished a glass. "Mayor Tate's so crooked he screws himself to the floor when he walks."

"Yeah, and the P.T.A., the Philadelphia Transportation Assholes. I'd still rather rot on the Schuylkill expressway than in one of their late-running, rat trap, sorry-assed excuses for buses." George's eyes lowered.

Spanky McMullen jumped in with a WC Fields mimic, "I came to Philadelphia, but it was closed." He puffed on his stogie, "I won a contest. It won a week in Philadelphia. The loser got two. Ha! Ha! Ha"

"Oh, will you look at this?" Anthony pointed to the TV. "Mauch's flops are losing again." He crossed his arms. "Who did the fool start tonight? Bunning or Short?"

"Dennis Bennett," Johnny McCusker put his beer on top of his racing form. "I think Gene Mauch's managing is the League's best in over twenty years. Without Mauch, they don't even come close. I sent him a telegram telling him, and I thanked him for a great season."

"You run a great bar, but you haven't won a bet since 1961. That was only because that California guy with his crazy-assed computer system gave you a winner. So, it figures. I'd expect that out of a chronic loser like you." Anthony pointed at him. "Face it. The team blew it. They choked. The buck's gotta stop somewhere, and I say it stops at Gene Mauch."

"It wasn't his fault his pitchers all hurt their arms. It wasn't his fault Frank Thomas broke his thumb. Do you know Johnny Callison is so sick, he's laid out in the clubhouse like a stiff in the morgue?"

"Too bad that California guy couldn't bring back his mysterious girlfriend." Ed filled Johnny's glass. "I swear she faith-healed my shoulder. Maybe she could do something for Johnny Callison and the Phillies' pitching arms."

"Yo, Ed, and where the hell is she now? Can she faith heal the Phillies of loser-itis?" Anthony threw up his arms, "This city is Loserville. It's beyond help. And, Johnny, you know what we call people who have everything happen to 'em at once, and at the worst time? Losers. A loser always has some candy-assed excuse. I'll tell ya something. This team never had me fooled. I knew all along they'd blow it. Hell, when that little spick stole home with Frank Robinson batting, I knew it was over right there and then. And another thing, the next time those damn the spades riot up there in North Philly riot, they can burn down that damn shit hole of a stadium." Anthony downed his bourbon.

"Hey, what do ya get if ya cross a spick and a spade?" Spanky, puffing a stogie, asked Anthony.

"I don't know."

"Someone too lazy to steal. Ha! Ha! Ha!"

"Hey, good one!" Anthony laughed and slapped Spanky on the back. "And the Iggles, what another bunch of lame losers. They go from World Champions to dog meat in less than four years. From Norm Van Brocklin to Sonny Jergenson to this numb-skull Norman Snead. Take Joe Kruharic, what a bum in every sense of the word. Hell, if ya mix water with a champion from this city, ya get instant shit."

"I Played for Nick Skorich." Ed Braceland served Anthony another double bourbon. "He was a great coach. I don't know why the Eagles let him go."

"Of course, you don't know," Anthony slammed down his double shot, "You didn't play for him. You warmed his bench."

Frankie Maresco, this time wearing a dark blue Izod shirt, walked back from the jukebox. "Yo! Everybody. I've put on a song in you guy's honor." The Rolling Stones, 'I Can't Get No Satisfaction', played.

"Look Smart Ass." Anthony brandished his index finger at Frankie. "You turn off that damn nigger music, or else I put you, and your damn record, outta here with my boot up your ass.

"Yo, cool it, Antny," Frankie held up his palms. "That's the Rolling Stones. They're white."

"I know who the Rolling Stones are, smart ass." Anthony leaned on the bar, "They sure don't sound white. They don't look white either. Did you get a load of the lips on that Mick Jagger guy?"

Spanky asked, "Yo, what's tattooed inside Mick Jagger's lips?"

"Don't know," Anthony gulped his drink.

"Inflate to fifty P.S.I.! Ha! Ha! Ha!"

"Yo good one!" Anthony slapped Spanky's back. "Good one. Hey, you're on a roll tonight." Anthony laughed. "Yo Ed, give Spanky here a refill on me."

"Yo Johnny. How'd your big bet at Belmont go today?" Frankie asked.

"I thought you knew everything." Anthony shook his head. "Why do you need to ask him," Anthony pointed at Johnny, "how his bet went? Shouldn't it be obvious to you?"

Johnny winced and crumpled his ticket. "I guess it serves me right, betting on a horse bred in this area."

"Yo, how come every time one of you suckers blows your money at the track, you blame the horse?" Anthony asked. "Why don't ya start puttin' the blame where it belongs? On the crooked little wetback jockey."

"Yeah, Johnny," Spanky puffed his cigar. "Instead of betting off track with da bookies, why don't ya go to the track in person and yell: Immigration! Every time your horse runs by?"

"Here we go again." Dennis Waldron muttered at the TV. Barney Schultz again nailed down the Phillies, saving the game for left-handed starting pitcher Ray Sadecki and the Cardinals. Final score: Cardinals four, Phillies two. The Phillies' ninth loss in a row and the Cardinals' seventh consecutive win. Like a condemned man  learning that the blade is extra sharp for a quick kill, the Phillies received a shred of good news: the Pittsburgh Pirates ended the Cincinnati Reds' nine-game winning streak. Final score: two to zero. The Cards and Reds are tied for first. The Phillies are third, a game and a half back, with three games to play.

Johnny walked to the bathroom in disgust. Dennis, Frankie, and George promptly left the tavern. Anthony uttered more colorful language, slammed down his bourbon, and bought himself and Spanky another round of double whiskey shots and a beer back.

# Chapter 9

Wednesday, September 30, 1964

Another school day down the drain. Bill, Frank, Hank, and Tony brimmed with energy. Tony stood on his Porter Street door stoop, leaning against a black wrought-iron balustrade. He shuffled a football from his left hand to his right hand. By tacit agreement, the boys wouldn't mention the Phillies and their nine-game losing streak. Tony said, "Two-hand touch, rush on three Mississippi."

Hank stepped forward, "Me and Tony stand." No one objected. Tony was the fastest and most athletic with Hank the slowest and least athletic. Bill and Frank fell somewhere between.

They marked out their gridiron on Porter Street. A yellow Ford Fairlane obstructed their playing field. "It's unlocked," Tony said, "I'll release the handbrake and steer. You guys push da suck'a outta da way." Tony climbed into the car. "Yo, all right! They left the keys in the car! You guys don't have ta push. I'll crank this baby up and drive it outta da way."

"I don't think you should," Hank wagged his finger."

"Oh, shut up your fat face. Stop being a candy-assed loser. Get in."

"I don't want to," Hank said while climbing into the car; Frank and Bill got into the back seat.

"What do you say I drive this baby around the block a couple of times, just for the hell of it?"

"No way, Jose." Frank grabbed the door handle. "I'm getting out."

"Hank and Frank are right." Bill leaned on the back of the front seat. "We can get in big trouble."

"Will you guys quit bein' a bunch of chickens?" Tony cranked up the car and drove it in reverse. "Let's have a little fun."

"Hey, really, Tony, stop this thing. Let me out," Bill grabbed Tony's right arm.

Tony pulled his arm away and flapped his elbow. "Bock, bock, bock, bock." Tony steered with his left hand."

A split second separated the shrill of the trolley horn and the screech of crunching metal and shattering glass. The crash jolted the boys. Uninjured, they staggered onto the street. The trolley driver confronted them. Wearing a blue Philadelphia Transportation Authority uniform, the short, overweight driver's round face sported a walrus-like mustache. He prodded, "Freeze! Don't any of you even think about moving!"

Frank, Hank, and Bill stood mannequin still.

"Screw him!" Run!" Tony darted like a startled trout.

Frank responded next; Hank followed, lumbering off in a different direction. The trolley driver lurched forward, grabbing Bill by the arm. "Gotcha, Punk!"

"No!" Bill jerked away his arm. His shirt sleeve tore. Three staggering steps later, Bill sprinted. The trolley driver chased him. Bill looked back and screamed. The faster he ran, the closer the trolley driver pursued. Bill veered through a narrow alley separating two blocks of row houses. He slept poorly the night before, lest slumber return the Jersey Devil. In the dream, his feet are mired in molasses or concrete. Now it was no dream. He ran like Mercury. Each vision of reform school quickened his pace. Visions of whippings from burly guards, tough black kids beating him up and stealing his possessions, and worst of all, older, hardened criminals forcing him to play girl and commit unspeakable acts. It meant separation from his mother, father, and little sister. 'No time to think—run!' The trolley driver closed the gap to two steps. Bill toppled over a trash can. The trolley driver tumbled over it, scoring a perfect ten for a high-flying bellyflop into the alley's dirt, broken glass, and refuse. Bill cut a sharp left down another passage. Dead end. A six-foot-high brick wall. He looked back. 'No one.' He turned a trash can upside down and boosted his body over the wall. He ran across several postage-stamp-sized townhouse backyards, hurdling fences from two to four feet high. He ended up in a larger yard. Garbage, rusted auto parts, and old tires splayed the grounds. A large brown rat scurried over his feet. Bill jumped three feet back. He started to scale a six-foot-high chain link fence. A growl. A Doberman pinscher curled its lip and brandished its teeth. Leaping off the ground, the dog sank its teeth into Bill's buttocks. He screamed in terror and pain as the dog hung from his ass in midair, trying to shake him off the fence, much like a great white shark dislodging a side of beef from a rope. Bill's feet fell from under him. Knuckles locked into the mesh saved him from a fatal mauling. The dog let go, only to bounce back as if from a trampoline. Bill raised his body six inches higher. The dog snapped its jaws. Its teeth fanned the air millimeters away. At last, he scaled the fence, falling over to the other side. The barking and growling Doberman repeatedly crashed into the fence. Adrenalin deadened the pain as Bill limped through a labyrinth of back alleys until finally emerging onto Snider Avenue. A police car with flashing dome lights caused Bill to duck back into the alley. He squeezed into an empty trash can and prayed. 'Please God, forgive me. Spare me from reform school.'

After hiding and praying for over an hour, Bill climbed out of the trash can and ventured through mazes of back alleys until reaching home. He crept through the rear kitchen door to avoid his mother's detection.

"Is that you?"

Bill didn't answer his mother.

"Why are you late?"

Bill froze.

"My God! What happened?"

"Um…Nothing." Bill covered his mouth.

"Nothing? My goodness, look at you!" Patricia examined the cuts and abrasions on his head. "Are you hurt? Are you all right?"

"I'm fine, Ma." Bill jerked his head away. "Stop babying me."

"Bill." Pat grabbed Bill's shoulders and looked him in the eye. "What happened to you? Tell me."

Bill shook his head. "I was…um…just playing tackle football…with my friends."

"You must be more careful."

"Oh, come on, Ma." Bill looked away. "Stop treating me like a baby. After all, football is a man's game."

"All right. Now that you're a man, you can replace your torn clothes with your allowance."

Trudging up to his room, Bill thought, 'Small price to pay to stay out of reform school.'

Shortly after tuning in to the Phillies game, he heard a distant police siren. Bill hid in the closet and listened to the Phillies lose their tenth straight.

The Cardinals blasted tired, unrested Jim Bunning for an eight-to-five victory. In a cruel twist of irony, Curt Simmons, a former Phillies whiz kid's hero, shut down the Phillies batters, who scratched all their hits and runs after the seventh inning. Cardinal's president Branch Rickey afterward assessed the Phillies' plight, "I don't think I'd ever seen a group of able-bodied men, thirty of them I'll say, walk off the field a sadder spectacle."

Combined with another Cincinnati loss in Pittsburgh, the victorious Redbirds seized first place. The third-place Phillies dropped to two and a half out. They had two games to play. The Reds and Cards each had three. Sportswriter Ray Kelly wrote, "A fool wouldn't give a nickel for the Phillies' chances."

# Chapter 10

Friday, October 2, 1964

Bill managed to survive the remainder of the school week. If not embarrassingly squirming on his injured buttocks, he lingered in fear of the police kicking the door in Gestapo or KGB style and hauling him to reform school. He walked to and from school via alleys and back streets, avoiding all authority figures. Playing outside was out of the question lest someone identify and report him. Bill ate his meals in hurried gulps. Conversations were clipped. His parents detected something amiss but couldn't decide what. They chose not to press the matter.

The Phillies had a two-game series against the Cincinnati Reds remaining. The Redbirds had a three-game set with the hapless, last-place New York Mets. Any Phillies loss or Cardinals win eliminated the Phillies. Gene Mauch stayed the course and scheduled Jim Bunning and Chris Short to pitch the final games. Thursday's and Saturday's scheduled off-days gave Bunning and Short their normal three days' rest. Bill turned the game on his radio and prepared for the inevitable.

Chris Short opened the Reds' first inning by walking Pete Rose. After two outs, Frank Robinson batted. By Saam described it. "Pop-up to the right side; Uh oh, it's trouble. It falls in for a base hit. Pete Rose is going to score."

"Oh brother," Richie Ashburn chimed in.

"Oh crap." Bill threw up his arms, "Here we go again."

Bottom of the sixth. Aided by yet another Phillies error, the Reds put Vada Pinson on first and Chico Ruiz on second. Two out, Frank Robinson batting. Bill's radio broadcast, "Ruiz breaks for third."

"What?" Bill said to himself. "Nobody tries to steal third with two outs."

"They're gonna get him this time ..."

"Serves him right." Bill punched his desk.

"Oh no," Bill heard on the radio. "The throw skips under Richie Allen's glove and into shallow left field. Ruiz is coming home; Wine recovers the ball; he throws...Over Dalrymple's head. Everybody safe. Oh no, it goes into the Reds dugout. Pinson will score as well. Phillies trail three to nothing."

"Oh Brother," Richie Ashburn said.

"Oh Shit," Bill added.

The Phillies offense was just as bad. By the seventh inning, they only had two singles and no runs against Reds' southpaw Jimmy O'Toole.

The Reds threatened again in the bottom of the seventh. Deron Johnson reached second base with only one out. By Saam described the next at-bat, "Hit him. Leo Cardenas is hit by the pitch. Ugh oh, Cardenas isn't too happy about it. He's coming after Chris Short with his bat!"

"Oh Yeah! I'll take care of those losers for you!" Bill grabbed his bat. "Here's to loss number eleven and blowing the pennant." He smashed his radio into oblivion. Plastic, metal, glass, and wire sprayed into the corners of his room like atomic particles in a reactor. That night, he dreamed of the junkyard from Wednesday afternoon, except instead of a dog, an alligator crunched on his limbs.

# Chapter 11

Saturday, October 3, 1964

Bill plodded downstairs to the breakfast table while rubbing his eyes. Marie, slurping down spoonfuls of Froot Loops, ignored him. Patricia emerged from the kitchen with a platter of piping hot, freshly cooked pancakes. "Good morning, Bill."

"Good morning, Mom."

"What was all that racket coming from your room last night?"

"Um ... I tripped into my desk and the radio smashed on the floor." Bill covered his mouth.

"Tripped? It sounded more like an earthquake. Are you sure everything's all right?" Patricia placed the pancakes on the table.

"Yes, mother, I tripped, okay? And no, mother, nothing is bothering me." Bill sat and looked away. He forked a small helping of pancakes, doused them with maple syrup, and sawed them into tiny pieces without eating them.

Dennis's arrival through the front door broke the stony silence. He carried a large jug of black coffee in one hand and a white paper sack in the other. "Daddy's home!" Marie sprang from her seat. "Goody! Oh Goody! Donuts!" She jumped up and down.

"Hi, honey." Patricia pecked Dennis on the cheek. "What did you bring us?"

"Well, let's see ..." Dennis opened the bag and placed the donuts on a plate at the table's center. "I've got glazed, chocolate frosted, grape jelly, and ...Bill's favorite ...Vanilla cream!"

"Thanks, Dad," Bill looked down and mumbled. "But I'm not hungry." He picked at his syrup and pancakes.

"Not hungry? Well, how about I call you a doctor? These are cream donuts from Vinny's Bakery we're talking about."

"I said I wasn't hungry, okay?" Bill stirred his pancakes and syrup.

"Seriously, Bill, are you feeling well?" Dennis put the donuts on a plate. "You've eaten like a bird lately."

"I said I'm fine."

"Are you sure?"

"Yes, I'm fine! What is it with you two? Geez ... I feel like I'm on trial around here or somethin'. Okay, if it makes you happy, here," Bill held up a donut as if it were a placard, "I'm eating." He exaggerated his chomp. "Maybe it'll choke me to death like the Phillies officially have."

"Choked to death? They're right back in it."

"Geez, will ya look who's telling me to bear down and learn math from Old Man Arsenic? The Phillies are two and a half out with only one to play. The Cardinals only have two to play. Do your math, man. They're eliminated, as in choked to death."

"Try one and a half out. They won last night."

"What?"

"They won four to three. The ten-game losing streak is over. I think that fight..."

"Yeah, I heard it."

"The fight fired them up, 'cause they came back with four runs the very next inning."

"No way, man. I don't believe nothin' no more."

"No way, huh? How about betting next year's allowance? Here ya go." Dennis placed a Philadelphia Inquirer sports page in front of Bill. "Your favorite player, Richie Allen, got the big hit. A two-run triple. Then Alex Johnson drove him in for the winning run. Read for yourself. Hey, can you believe it? The Mets beat the Cardinals one zip. Try and figure. The Cards had won eight straight; the Mets had lost eight straight. Gibson was pitching too.

I guess one-to-nothing is the only way he loses. Hey, you're the superstitious one. What do you think? Maybe someone up there's just tryin' to put a scare in us, huh? The Mets and Cards are on the game of the week this afternoon, and, hey, if the Mets can do it again, we've got a real shot after all."

Bill's jaw dropped as he read the newspaper account of the game.

"Yo Bill, what do ya say we go outside and toss the old pig skin around? Better yet, why not bring the guys around for a little two-hand touch? Not tackle." Dennis chuckled, "I can't afford to keep replacing your clothes."

"Um. No, Dad. I don't feel like it. I think I'll stay in and watch cartoons until the baseball game."

"Stay in and watch cartoons? Oh, come on. Since when did you become a homebody, boob tube fiend?"

"I said I feel like stayin' in, okay?" Bill stood and marched from the table.

Dennis joined Patricia and Marie, who were busy washing the breakfast dishes. "Honey, what can I do with that boy? He's never acted like this before. Sometimes I wonder if maybe I shouldn't just put him over my knee…"

"Don't do that, Dennis."

"It's not just any one big thing. It's his attitude in general."

"He has reached a difficult age. It's just a phase. Give him the benefit of the doubt." Patricia placed a dish on the rack and turned to her husband. "Although, I'll admit I'm also a bit perplexed. He isn't communicating with me lately either. For now, let's just be patient. If it doesn't sort itself out, well, we'll cross that bridge when we come to it."

Bill, stuporous, stared at the TV. An hour later, Patricia announced a visitor.

Jeff stood at the entrance to the TV lounge. "Hi, Bill."

"Um, hi." Bill glanced at Jeff, then turned back to the TV.

"I thought you might like to have my Godzilla statue. Remember, the one I made in Goodman's shop class? Remember how I formed it out of wax, then used it to make a mold in that special sand, then poured in molten lead?"

"I don't want it," Bill mumbled at the TV.

"No really, Bill." Jeff walked over and placed Godzilla in Bill's hands. "I want you to have it."

Bill rubbed the statue. His pupils dilated. "Gee ... Thanks, Jeff."

"Say, do you wanna watch the Cards, Mets game at my house? My mom's gonna cook up some lasagna for lunch."

"Thanks anyway, Jeff. But I think I'd better stay in." Bill again admired the peace offering. "Tell ya what." He smiled. "Why don't ya watch it here with me?"

Jeff inched forward and whispered, "Tony told me about the trolley crash. He says you got the driver something good. Hey, don't worry. You know I won't squeal. He says there's nothin' to worry about. No cops have been comin' by, and none of the neighbors are talking about it. Say, let's go over to Girard Park and toss the football around."

"Okay," Bill chirped.

Restored friendship and lifting the yoke of reform school buoyed Bill's steps like a thermal under a condor's wings. He raced his buddy to the park. They played football for over an hour, first playing catch, then gently tackling each other, rolling with laughter. The boys frolicked to the point of forgetting that the big game had begun.

Finally realizing the time, they sprinted to Jeff's house, eventually stumbling through the front door. Nick Giordano greeted them while smoking a pipe. "You missed it, boys. The Mets scored four runs in the top of the first."

"All right!" The boys beamed at each other.

Bill White dampened their joy by belting a long two-run homer onto the right field pavilion roof of ancient Sportsman's Park.

"Uh oh," Nick groaned and placed his pipe in an ashtray as Ken Boyer followed with a homer to left. "Shoot! I guess here it ends." Jeff slumped into his chair

"No way, Jose! The Mets are gonna do it!" Bill smiled and pointed to the ceiling. "Not just today, but tomorrow too! I got a feelin'. I never stopped believing." He punched his palm. "The Phillies will win the pennant."

"I hope you're right." Nick lit his pipe. "It surely has been a long time in coming."

***

October 3rd, 1964. Autumn in Philadelphia. Yet, it should've been spring as the day became one of eternal hope. The Mets' George Altman answered right back in the top of the second by clobbering a home run. The Mets hit four more home runs before the game finished and hung a shocking fifteen-to-five loss on the Cardinals, beating their twenty-game winning pitcher, Ray Sadecki.

"That's it." Nick puffed his pipe. "We're just one back with one to play. Huge game tomorrow, boys." Nick left the room.

"Yo Bill, if you're not doing anything tonight, and if your parents will let you…Dawn and me are going to Chuck Rossicelli's party, you know, the football team's quarterback. Why don't you come along? All the cool kids are gonna be there."

"Nah. I wouldn't feel right, you know, just hanging around you and Dawn."

"No. She's got a friend, and she really wants to meet you."

"Why would she want to meet me? She's never even seen me."

"Dawn told her a lot of cool things about you."

"But I've never been nice to Dawn."

"That's okay. She can tell you're cool."

"Cool? Me?"

"Yeah, Bill. You're cool. Why don't ya come along? Her friend's name is Andrea and she's real good lookin'."

"I don't know about blind dates."

"How would you know? You've never been on a ... I mean, trust me, she's real cute."

"Well ...I gotta admit, Dawn's real cute." Bill scratched his head. "Okay. I'm in."

"Great! Meet me here at seven. We'll walk over together. The girls will be there. Do you think it will be all right with your parents?"

"Yeah, I'm sure they'll let me."

"All right! Put it here, pal! Jeff shook Bill's hand.

***

That evening, Bill and Jeff walked down Sixteenth Street to the first block north of Shunk Street. The Beatles, "Eight Days a Week," blared from the window. On entering, the company astounded Bill. His school's most popular kids attended--athletes, cheerleaders, and student council leaders--even the ravishing Mary Beth McGovern. Bill winced. Her boyfriend looked five years older. "How did you ever get us invited to this party?"

"I helped Chuck out with his science project. You know, those scale-model dinosaurs and a working volcano. He's just an everyday guy."

"Yeah, an everyday guy who's a football star and can pick and choose any girl he wants. Is Frank coming?"

“Nah. You know how he does nothing but study these days. I figured you'd have a better time anyway."

“Gee, thanks, Jeff. By the way, where's Dawn?”

“She's coming ... There she is.”

Bill shyly looked her way. This time, all tomboy pretenses were history. She wore an emerald green gown and a gold necklace. Newly styled raven hair, adult makeup, and a rosy complexion, Dawn looked like a young movie star. Next to her was Andrea. Bill's first date. Her hair wasn’t as dark as Dawn's, but twice as long. Taller and slenderer, she wore a dark black velvet jumpsuit. Bill stared with wide eyes. ‘She’s gorgeous.’

“Come on over, Bill.” Jeff grabbed Bill's wrist and pulled him to the girls. Bill’s knees wobbled. Jeff greeted Dawn with a peck on the cheek, then introduced Bill to Andrea.

“I've heard so much about you,” Andrea looked Bill over.

“Um ... What did ya hear? I mean, um, thank you, um, I heard a lot about you too.”

“Jeff tells me you’re a big baseball fan.” Andrea arched her eyebrows.

“Um…Yeah.”

“I like baseball too. My uncle played minor league ball with Mickey Mantle in Joplin, Missouri.”

“Mickey Mantle! Wow!”

“Yes. Mickey Mantle. They're still friends. Sometimes he even gives us free tickets to Yankee Stadium. Though, unfortunately, not World Series tickets.”

“My father's got us World Series tickets for not only Philadelphia but New York too!” Bill grinned.

“You must be some kind of pulling for the Phillies. Are you watching the big game tomorrow with Jeff?”

"Yeah, probably."

"Hey, I like that song." Andrea grabbed Bill's arm and tugged toward the dance floor as Smokey Robinson's 'Goin' to a Go Go' played. "Let's dance."

Bill stood still like a zombie. He often watched Dick Clark's "American Bandstand," and Jerry Blavat and Hy Litt's local versions on TV, but he never danced with a girl.

Andrea pulled harder on Bill's arm. "Oh, come on, Bill."

Bill stumbled to the dance floor.

Andrea's feet were light enough to dance on thin ice. Her movements were free and uninhibited, yet never out of sync with the music. Bill nervously shifted his arms in an unrhythmic gyration; his feet stayed glued to the floor.

After the song, Dawn whispered in Andrea's ear. Both giggled. "Excuse us." Andrea and Dawn walked away, still giggling.

Bill walked over to the punch bowl and poured himself a cup. Tony Rocca soon joined him. "Yo Bill, how's it goin'? Yo, wasn't it great how we beat that dumb sucka' trolley driver?"

"Great?"

"Yeah, great. I peeked around the block and saw how you tripped that sucker. I don't know how ya did it, but way to go." Tony shook Bill's hand. "Yo, how's the punch?"

"Not bad. It tastes like ginger ale, root beer, and I think cinnamon. I taste orange sherbet ..."

"Boring! This'll liven it up some." Tony revealed a half-full bottle of Jim Beam bourbon hidden in his jacket. "I swiped it from my old man." He poured the contents into the punch bowl. "He has so much of the crap that he'll never miss it."

"You can't do that!" Bill prodded.

"I just did," Tony smirked and folded his arms.

"You'll get in trouble."

"Only if ya squeal. You ain't a squealer, are ya?"

"No. Never."

"I didn't think so. I'd never have a squealer for a best buddy." Tony gulped more spiked punch. "Ahh ... good shit. Here," Tony handed the cup to Bill. "Try some."

Bill took the cup, looked at it for three seconds, and sipped. The multi-flavored punch softened the taste of bourbon.

"Finish it," Tony leaned on the table.

Bill downed the concoction.

Tony filled two more cups, handing one to Bill. "Here's to good pals." Tony toasted Bill. Both downed their drinks.

Bill sighed and wiped his brow as Andrea returned. The Beach Boys' Surfin' U.S.A.' now played. "Would you, um, like to dance, Andrea?" This time, Bill's feet shuffled in something resembling rhythm, his arms moving far less spasmodically. Marvin Gaye's 'Hitchhike' played next. The young teen partygoers formed a line dance. Bill took the lead with Andrea, confidently waltzing her through the procession. Their song and dance concluded with self-congratulatory applause. Smokey Robinson's ballad, 'Could You Love a Poor Boy,' silenced them. The other couples clung to each other like pairs of koalas. Bill stood agape before Andrea. She tilted her head and grinned. Stepping forward, she pulled him close to her, leading him through the slow dance. Bill's body went limp. Five seconds later, he squeezed her and rested his head on her shoulder. Halfway through the song, he snuggled his head closer to hers. The song ended way too soon for Bill. Andrea slipped through his grasp and thanked Bill for the dance.

"Um ... would you like some punch?" Bill smiled.

"Sure."

Bill gritted his teeth, clasped Andrea's hand, and led her to the punch bowl. After handing her a cup of Tony's mix, he raised his glass, saying, "Salute."

Andrea tipped his cup and took a sip. "Woo! What's in this?" She pulled a face.

"Ginger ale, root beer, cinnamon, and I think some of that bitter adult soda."

"Adult soda? My eye! Someone spiked it with booze."

"No way. It just tastes a bit funny. That's all. Drink up, Andrea. It's not so bad once you get used to it."

"Who wants to get used to this stuff?"

Bill chuckled and took another sip. "So, how long have you and Dawn been friends?"

"Are you kidding? I can't remember back that far. We're practically sisters. How about you and Jeff?"

"Believe it or not, the same."

"I don't believe you. How can you two be sisters?"

"I mean, we're like brothers." Bill flushed as Andrea laughed at him. "Very funny, very funny."

"You're not going to believe this, but my father knows your father."

"Really?"

"Yes, really. My father's a buyer for Sears and sometimes deals with your father."

"What does he say about him?"

"Good things. He said that your dad's smart and knows more about baseball than anyone. That's sayin' a lot, 'cause my dad thinks he knows more about everything than everyone."

"Wow. That's something. My dad's swell, but sometimes gets nosey. Take the other night…"

"Hey, it's Bill Waldron," a male voice interrupted.

Bill gasped. Chuck Rossicelli, the football star and coolest kid in school, greeted him. Even better, he had head cheerleader Debbie Mackenzie on his arm. She looked ravishing to Bill with her long, honey-blond hair, twinkling sapphire eyes, and a very adult figure. Chuck snapped Bill out of his haze. "Yo, Bill, that was so cool the way ya stood up to old man arsenic. I mean, you were boss, man. Like, you know, he's always putting us down with that, 'You are out in left field' crap. Putting the old fart in his place took guts. Your Wes Covington line did it. It was so cool, man. How'd ya think it up so fast? You're okay. Put 'er here." Chuck shook Bill's hand. Smokey Robinson's Mickey's Monkey' t played over the hi-fi.

"Hey, great dance song," Chuck nodded. "Yo, Bill, you don't mind if Andrea and I dance, do ya? You can dance with Debbie."

Bill figured he was on a roll that could ram through Vegas, Reno, and Tahoe combined. He seldom attended school football games. When he did, Debbie Mackenzie's cheerleading interested him more than the game. Now she gyrated directly before him. Sometimes her enticing sapphire eyes even ensnared his bashful brown ones. The D.J. faded the fast "Mickey's Monkey" to the slow Beach Boys ballad, 'Surfer Girl.' Bill's heart pulsated as her arms circled him.

Andrea stepped in with as much finesse as an offensive lineman between a blitzing tackle and his quarterback. She seized him and led him through the slow dance. "I don't blame you for thinking she's pretty; everybody thinks so. But you don't want her; she's such a bitch. She's so conceited and stuck up. The only reason she hangs out with Chuck is because he's the football star, and everyone thinks he's the coolest guy in school. She doesn't even like him. She's only in love with herself. All she ever talks about is how she's gonna win Miss Teenaged this and Miss

Teenaged that. All the girls in school hate her 'cause she's only into herself." Andrea squeezed Bill tighter and continued leading him through the dance. Andrea peeked out of the corner of her eye. She smiled upon spotting Debbie dancing with Chuck. After the dance, Bill poured them both a couple of cups of punch. Jeff and Dawn soon joined them.

Dawn smiled pertly at Bill and asked, "Do you think the Phillies will win the pennant tomorrow?"

"They can't win the pennant. Just a tie for the pennant. To win the pennant, they must win a round-robin playoff with the Cards and Reds. But they will beat the Reds tomorrow, and the Cards are gonna lose to the Mets. Plus, the Iggles are gonna beat the Steelers."

"Gosh, you sure sound confident."

"That's because I can feel it. Like that E.S.P. or something." Bill raised a cup of punch to his lips.

Andrea leaned on Bill. "Will you please excuse me for a moment? I want to talk to Dawn."

"Sure, Andrea."

"What do ya think of the party buddy?" Jeff punched Bill's arm.

"Best one I've ever been to." Bill finished his punch.

"It's the only one you've ever been to."

"Oh, so you're the seasoned veteran at this? When was your First one? Last week?"

"No, the week before." Bill and Jeff laughed with each other. "I think ya got the lucky touch there, Bill. So, how about coming over to my house and watching the Phillies game with me? My dad's got a powerful radio. It can pick up New York stations. We can listen to the Mets beat the Cardinals."

"Great! Thanks Jeff"

"By the way, how are you getting along with Andrea?"

"Fantastic! She's a swell chick. She's pretty, and lots of fun too."

"Stick with me and you can't go wrong." Jeff turned his head. "Tony! How's it going?"

"Not too bad. But it would get a lot better if I could get that chick in the green dress," Tony pointed, "drunker on Jim Beam punch and get her alone."

"Good luck, Tony." Jeff smiled.

"Yo," Tony jutted his jaw. "Luck's got nothin' to do with it, pal."

"Say, why don't ya come on over to my house tomorrow and watch the Phillies game with Bill and me?"

"Geez, what's with you guys? Haven't dem bums tortured ya enough already? I can't anyway. My old man's taking me to Franklin Field to watch da Iggles. I kinda hope they lose. 'Cause whenever they start losing, he starts drinking and yells fun curse words at 'em."

"Well, look who's back," Jeff said as Andrea and Dawn returned.

"Hi Tony. Hope you didn't get these two in too much trouble while I was gone," Andrea chuckled. "Pretty song, don't you think, Bill?" The Safari's 'Image of a Girl' played. Andrea motioned with her head toward the dancing area. They slow-danced. After the song, she grasped Bill's hand and led him to a couch. She held Bill's hand as they talked for half an hour. She checked her watch. "Gosh, look at the time, and I see a few others leaving. Will you walk me home, Bill?"

"Thanks for inviting us, Chuck. It was a swell party, and we had a terrific time." Bill and Andrea walked out hand in hand. The temperature had dropped ten degrees. Misty rain made it feel colder. They walked the final two blocks without saying a word.

After turning north on Camac from Oregon, Andrea broke the ice. "Here we are, Bill."

They stood in front of her house, a double-story red brick row home with a green fiberglass awning over the front veranda. She gazed into his eyes. He looked back. His nerves vibrated like a tuning fork. His stomach felt like it was filled with helium. His mind went blank. 'She's so pretty.' He lurched his head forward and pecked her lips.

"Do I remind you of your aunt or your sister?"

Bill fidgeted with his watch. "Um…I don't understand." He scratched his neck.

"You're silly," she chuckled. "Don't worry if you've never kissed a girl before." She smiled. "I like you."

Bill shuffled his feet. His lips twitched.

Andrea braced Bill's shoulders, kissed his lips, and darted her tongue into his mouth.

Novel waves of pleasure swept over him. Bill stood back. He looked at her with glazed eyes for three seconds before wrapping his arms around her and pulling her close. He embraced her and kissed her. Their tongues mingled like violins.

"Goodbye, Bill. Thank you for the lovely evening. I'm glad you and Jeff are friends again. I hope the Phillies win the pennant tomorrow. Would you like to hang out with me at school on Monday?"

"Yes, Andrea. I'd love to."

"Bye." Andrea blew him a kiss before going inside.

He gamboled home through the cold, falling rain, singing the Temptations My Girl.'

# Chapter 12

Sunday, 4 October, 1964

Visions of Andrea buoyed Bill's confidence for an outcome beyond his control. He banged on the Giordano's door. "Come on in," Jeff's voice muffled through the door. Bill rushed into the house, finding Jeff, his father Nick, and Frank gathered around the TV.

"Yo. It's the Saturday night swinger," Frank turned to Bill. "Hope ya wiped off the lipstick," Jeff chuckled.

"Ha. Ha. Ha." Bill smirked, "Very funny. Hey, who's pitching for the Reds?"

"John Tsitouris," Nick answered, pronouncing it zittourist. The correct pronunciation is known only to the pitcher's immediate family.

"Oh no." Bill raised his hands. "Not Tit-saurus again."

"That's not a nice thing to say." Nick's eyes narrowed.

"You ought to hear what Tony's dad calls him. Starts with a 'c'." Jeff giggled.

"I'm your dad, not Tony's dad. You know better than saying bad words. Anyway, Jim Bunning's pitching for us with his full three days' rest. I like our chances."

The Phillies' chances to share first place required a dual outcome. They had to beat the Reds, while the Mets had to win against the Cardinals. The revered baseball adage merits repeating: "Hope springs eternal." Getting both outcomes was close to owning a winning lottery ticket. The Mets trailed the Cardinals by a full thirty-nine games. Nevertheless, Bill, Frank, and Jeff lived in life's spring.

Chico Ruiz's preposterous theft of home triggered the Phillies' descent. Thirteen days and eleven games prior. Their inability to fathom the awkward delivery of John Tsitouris, a pitcher of underwhelming achievement and ability, also haunted the team. The Phillies took ten games and thirteen days of Hell out on John Tsitouris and six other Cincinnati pitchers. They battered the Reds for ten runs, all earned. Richie Allen spearheaded the onslaught by banging two long home runs off the Superior Towel and Linen service, across the street from Crosley Field's left field wall. He also hit a double, drove in four runs, and scored three.

Pitching on his normal three-day rest, Jim Bunning was a revelation. He threw a shutout, allowing only one walk and six harmless singles in winning his nineteenth game.

With victory secure, the Phillies put their derailed Pennant-bound express back on track. The Mets led the Cardinals three to two in the fifth inning. Nick Giordano said, "Well, we now know that Bunning and Short can only pitch like Bunning and Short on their full rest. Yeah, I guess Dennis Bennett, Ray Culp, and Art Mahaffey couldn't pitch anymore. Yet if they would've won one, just one of those ten, they wouldn't be in this mess." Nick tightened his lips and shook his head. "You know what's crazy about all of this?" Nick looked at the boys.

The boys shrugged.

"The Phillies' last pennant, the Whiz Kids." Nick smiled at the boys. "They won it right before you three were born. The two mainstays on that staff were Robin Roberts and Curt Simmons." Nick tapped his pipe bowl upside down into an ashtray. "They win this thing in a breeze if they keep Simmons and Roberts." Nick scraped out the excess tobacco with a silver pipe cleaner. "You guys know Simmons won seventeen games for the Cardinals. And Robin Roberts," Nick lit his pipe, "who's gonna ever think of him as anything other than a Phillie? Has anyone mentioned that he won ten games for the Baltimore Orioles?" Nick puffed a tobacco cloud. "Think about it, Roberts and Simmons joining Bunning and Short in the World Series. Oh no ..." Nick groaned as the radio described the Cardinals' Ken Boyer doubling home Bill White with the tying run. They remained silent as the Cardinals scratched across two more runs, seizing the lead at five-three after five full innings.

The Mets didn't quit. Next inning, they scored a run and loaded the bases. The Cardinals summoned Bob Gibson for a rare relief appearance. He ended the threat.

Next Cardinals' at-bat, Bill White hit a two-run homer into the right-field pavilion. Nick placed his pipe on the table and said, "That's it, boys, it's over. I wish we could say it ain't so, but there ain't gonna be a World Series in Philly." He then switched the radio to the Eagles game.

"Turn it back. Please. It's not over 'till it's over," Bill pleaded.

"Dad's right, Bill, it's over. The Mets can't come back against the Cards, especially not against Bob Gibson. It's just ain't gonna happen." Jeff dropped his head.

"No! Please! Turn it back."

"Okay, Bill. If you want to prolong the agony." Nick pinched the dial and tuned in to the baseball game. "I've had enough. I'm gonna listen to the Iggles on my portable radio." Nick left the room.

The boys huddled around the radio like evacuees in a bomb shelter listening to details of their town's destruction. The Cardinals built their lead to eleven to four in the ninth. Nevertheless, the Mets went down fighting. They put two runners on base. Bill shook his crossed fingers. "Here we go, here we go, miracles happen, miracles happen." Barny Schultz fanned the Mets' Charlie Smith for the second out, yet Bill kept his fingers crossed. "Yeah!" He yelled as Rod Kanehl followed by driving home a Mets run with a single.

"What are you getting so excited about?" Frank glowered at Bill. "The Mets have as much chance of scoring six two-out runs as Sammy Davis Jr. has of knocking out Muhammad Ali."

"Face it. Frank's right. It's all over. It's all stinkin' over." Jeff stood and squeezed his head. "They blew it. I'll never forgive Mauch for as long as I ..."

The radio announced Ed Kranepool hitting a high pop-up on the left side of the infield. Bill was breathless. The pop-up had a longer hang time than an NFL punt. Bill wished it could be fixed in the firmament. It fell harmlessly into the glove of Cardinal catcher Tim McCarver. The three boys silently stared at the radio, oblivious to descriptions of the Cardinals' celebration.

"Son of a bitch." Jeff snapped off the radio. "I never truly thought they'd blow it, but they did."

"At least they knocked off the Reds. No team that steals home with Frank Robinson batting and gets a shut-out from a pitcher named," Frank raised his voice with rancor, "Clitoris, deserves to win nothin'."

Bill lifted his head and looked at his friends with damp eyes. "I gotta go. See ya at school tomorrow." He bolted from Jeff's home, slamming the door behind him. The unseasonably cold weather, replete with dark clouds, captured the mood. They soon rained cold tears.

Bill walked half a block before breaking into a gallop. He paid no attention to pedestrians and vehicles. After reaching Stephen Girard Park, he collapsed on a bench. His lips quivered on hearing a distant radio playing Chad and Jeremy's melancholy ballad, "A Summer Song." Each lyric, lamented Love, like summer and all good things, coming to an end. Bill openly cried. All hope, any reason for optimism, every pennant dream, was dead. The '64 Phillies season had ended.

***

Dennis and Patricia uncomfortably conversed as Bill barged through the door. "Tough luck today," Dennis turned to Bill. "I'm tempted to say, these things happen, but this one's an all-time first. Look, I'm upset too, though I've experienced worse things, and

158

unfortunately, you will too. So, we'll keep our chins up and do what we must." Dennis grinned and playfully punched Bill's shoulder.

"Yeah, the Phillies stink out the joint?"

Patricia then gave Dennis a long look. "Bill. Something else. I'm leaving for New York on business. I'm sorry, but I must use the extra World Series tickets for company clients. I'm sorry… I am. However, I did warn you."

"You did not." Bill prodded. "You're a liar."

"Hey, look," Dennis prodded. "I'm not gonna take lip out of you." Dennis furrowed his brow. "I am not lying. Last week, I expressly told you the tickets were conditional on my not having to use them for work." Dennis wagged his finger. "After all that's happened, I'd think that seeing the World Series would be the last thing you'd want to do. Heck, I don't even want to think about watching the Cardinals."

"Yeah! Well, I do! And you're a liar." Bill jutted his jaw.

"That did it!" Dennis lurched forward and throttled Bill's shirt and shoved him into a lounge chair. Dennis wagged his finger.

"Young man, you've been walking a narrow line the last few days. This time you've tripped over it!"

Patricia pulled Dennis away. "Bill," she prodded. "Go to your room. Now!"

Bill trampled to his room,

"Honey, I just don't know what to do with that boy … If he thinks he's too big for a smack on the behind, he's got another thing coming." Dennis then shouted up the stairs. "You're staying up there till I get back! Then we're going to talk. A long talk."

"I never want to talk to you again." Bill stuck his head from his bedroom door. "You liar!" He slammed the door.

"Come on, honey. We'll all settle this when you get back," Patricia kissed Dennis goodbye.

***

McCusker's Tavern sounded like a monastery. George Mueller sat slumped over a draft beer and shot of bourbon. Ferdi the bulldog soundly slept by Hugo Tubbs's feet. Hugo drank beer from his second full pitcher. Frankie Maresco sat at a table with his girlfriend and another couple. They shared a pitcher of beer and softly conversed. Spanky McMullen played a coin-operated bowling machine, stoically sliding a metal puck over sensors that activated plastic pins.

Dennes entered the corner door of McCusker's tavern. "How are ya doing, Ed?"

"Okay, I guess," Ed grunted.

"Six pack of Miller to go."

"Going away?" Ed reached into a cooler and took out a six-pack.

"Yeah. New York."

"New York? To Hell with New York," Ed put the six-pack in a brown paper bag. "Those morons take the World Series for granted."

"I agree with Ed." Johnny McCusker put his racing form on the bar. "Do you know how many World Series games the Phillies have won in their eighty-one-year history? Not Series. Games? One. Just one. In 1915. Forty-nine years ago, at the Baker Bowl. Both my father and grandfather were there. Grover Cleveland Alexander, Alex, topped Ernie Shore, three to one. Nineteen-fifty. Johnny closed his eyes and lowered his head. My grandad was gone by then, but my father took me to both of those games at Shibe Park. They lost both!" He tightened his lips. "I had tickets to take him this year, but they blew it. They blew the whole damn thing ..."

160

Ed mumbled to Dennis without moving his lips. "Did ya have to trigger this guy? This is his third time already."

"... Unbelievable. Un-dam- believable. Six and a half up, and they lose ten straight. My dad's almost seventy-five now. I hoped. I hoped just maybe, he would see 'em get another shot at the Series. But no. Mauch goes out and blows it. Bunning and Short, Bunning and Short, Bunning and Short. Hell, look at how well they pitched on their normal rest."

"Oh, cut the blubbering," George snarled. "This is the third damn time I've heard it."

"What do you mean?

"I mean, shut up and run your bar. Next thing you know, you'll use the Phillies as an excuse for serving warm beer."

"Yeah, I'm with Ed and George." Dennis placed his package on the bar. "Two weeks ago, you sat there talking like they were only better than the Mets and the Colt 45s. Hey, weren't you the one saying how Mauch was a genius? That no one managed better in over twenty years? Didn't you say that you sent him a telegram telling him how great he managed? Hey, wasn't it you who said Bunning and Short were the way to go? And weren't you the big profit of doom the moment Ruiz stole home?"

"Yeah, but I never thought that they'd actually lose the pennant. This hurts more than the twenty-three-game losing streak in sixty-one. That team was like the sixty-two Mets—nothing but a joke. But I ain't laughing this time. They took our hopes and dreams right up to the sky only to pull the plunger and flush 'em down the toilet. We were proud of this team. They were bringing the city a World Series. Now we're again a laughingstock."

"How can you say that? Back in sixty-one, who would've thought Gene Mauch could've taken 'em from only forty-seven wins to ninety-two in just three short seasons? How can you compare this with that? Ninety-two wins. Only one team in the National League won just one more game. I'll deck anyone who tries laughing at that." Dennis raised his fists like a boxer. "If they had the ten-game losing streak, say, back in June, and came back to finish within one game of the pennant, how would you feel?" He spread his arms "It's like you said, they only had four good players yet damn near took it. So, I'm damn proud of this team." He pounded the bar with his fist. "Hell, those damn New Yorkers can afford to laugh at the Mets. Afterward, they can hop on the subway and watch Mantle, Maris, Ford, and company win a hundred games and the pennant. Well, the Phillies are all we've got, and I'll take a winner like this over the losers we've been stuck with any day!"

"Yeah!" Hugo held up his beer mug, "I second that! Hey, I'm not like one of those damn New York bimbos who takes everything for granted. I can damn well appreciate a great effort. The sixty-four Phillies were the most exciting baseball team I have ever seen. Beats the hell outta da cellar."

"You know something?" George stood. "He's right. I've followed the A's and Phillies all my life. This is the most interesting season of all. Maybe even better than the Whiz kids. We watched Jim Bunning throw a perfect game, the first one in the National League in nearly a century. We saw Johnny Callison win the All-Star Game with a bottom-of-the-ninth three-run homer. And Richie Allen, no one's seen anything in this town like him since Jimmie Double X. It hurts. But I agree with Fats. This does beat the hell out of finishing last."

"Absolutely!" Dennis smiled. "For better or for worse, we saw a history-making team. Hell, who's ever going to remember the '64 Cardinals or the '64 Yankees? What do ya say, guys?" Dennis raised his glass in a toast. "To a great effort and a great team ... Gene Mauch and the sixty-four Phillies."

"To Gene Mauch and the sixty-four Phillies," toasted the entire tavern in unison.

# Chapter 13

Wednesday, 8 October 1964

Bill sat at his desk perusing Captain Marvel comic books. The clear autumn weather and golden foliage made this third day of room incarceration even more frustrating. He regretted his remarks and accepted his punishment. A glance out of the window abruptly ended his boredom. Two police cars pulled up in front of his house. Shock and fear dizzied him. His throat felt as if he had swallowed a walnut whole. 'I didn't get away with the trolley crash after all. The police are here to take me to reform school.' Grasping his head with two hands, he circled the room, jaw chattering. He sat in the closet and hid his head between his knees. 'Is this how John Wayne and James Bond would act? How about Clark Kent, Bruce Wayne, and Peter Parker? How would they handle this? Would they cower in a closet like a yellow sissy? Hell no! They'd take it like a man! If I go to reform school as a crying, scared baby the guards and inmates will beat me and maybe rape me. As a tough guy, that ain't happening.'

Bill left the closet. He raised his head and descended the stairs. He felt like a condemned convict taking his last steps toward Old Sparky. 'I'm going to take it with honor.'

What greeted him in the living room was even worse than expected. Four policemen waited. One comforted his wailing mother. Another restrained Marie, who screamed repeatedly, "Daddy! Daddy! Daddy! Daddy!"

Two of the others approached him. One looked out of a Marine Corps recruiting poster. His military haircut enhanced his square jaw. The other was shorter, older, and plumper. He had an olive complexion, short dark hair, and a bald spot. The young one asked, "Are you Bill Waldron?"

"Yes, sir," Bill looked back and forth.

"You better come to the other room with us."

The policemen escorted Bill to the kitchen. He felt like Old Sparky was waiting, charged and ready.

"Better sit down," the older policeman put his hand on Bill's shoulder.

"I'm going to tell you everything," The younger cop towered over him. "You're old enough, and I think you have a right to know. Your father was drinking in a New York bar. Two of the customers started mocking the Phillies' collapse. Your father told them to shut up. An argument ensued. He punched one of them. The report says he hit him squarely. Bill, the other one had a knife. I'm sorry, Bill. Your father is dead."

Bill turned white as a cave newt. "Dead?" He gasped for air.

"I'm sorry, Bill." He put his hand on Bill's shoulder. "Your father is no longer with us."

"No! No! It can't be! No!" Bill's vision blurred, although the policemen's faces told the truth in crystal clarity. 'My father is dead.' He bolted from the kitchen and out the front door. The young cop lurched three steps toward him. The older cop grabbed his arm and nodded his head, tacitly saying to let him go.

Bill ran aimlessly. 'Why does the sun still shine? Why do the cars still move in all directions?' His world was spinning. Spinning.

"No! No! It can't be. It can't be.'

Bill slowed to a walk, although his throat still felt as if a noose was choking him.

He arrived at Stephen Girard Park and scanned the scenery. "Everything's the same. Dad's coming back in just a couple of days." He sat on a park bench and overheard a loafing teenager's radio. It played two straight Righteous Brothers tunes, 'You've Lost That Lovin' Feeling' and 'Just Once In My Life.' Next, he heard Brenda and the Tabulations, 'Dry Your Eyes.' The final song he heard was an Intruders recording called 'Come Home Soon.'

His delusion ended. His father is dead and will never come home. He fell off the bench and onto his knees. Resting his forearms on the bench, he buried his face into his arms and bawled. An unexpected aroma of a lush flower garden seeped through his sniffles. His eyes, blurry from emotion and tears, first saw wings with luxuriant feathers white enough to reflect sunbeams. A gentle arm of feminine grace wrapped around his shoulder, comforting him immeasurably. Her eyes sparked like sapphires, and her florid cheeks and lips glowed with vitality. Her indigo hair flowed like a waterfall. "Fear not, Bill. I am Isolde Maria. Heaven sent me to you. Your father may have told you about me. Three years ago, I appeared at McCusker's Tavern. Heaven permitted me to heal Ed's shoulder."

"I don't remember nothin'." Bill continued to bawl.

"It's good to cry, Bill. Don't worry. Your father is with us now. You will see him again. I know a long parting is sad. I will stay here for now and be sad with you."

Bill grasped the angel's thick tress and held it to his eyes. He wailed into the angel's hair as she rubbed his back. "Daddy! Daddy! Tell my Dad I'm sorry. I don't care about no World Series. I just wanna be with my Dad." The Angel kissed Bill's cheek.

# Part III

# Chapter 1

"Daddy! Daddy!" Bill bawled. "I don't care about no World Series! I want my dad!"

Nurse Ruth Jackson pressed a button and spoke into an intercom microphone. "Dr. Greenberg! Come quick. He's regaining consciousness!"

"I don't wanna see the Cardinals. The Phillies will win next year. We'll go to the World Series then." Bill's vision started to clear. He saw a plump black female nurse looking at him with furrowed eyebrows and pursed lips. "Hey! You're not the angel. I want the angel to bring back my dad!"

Dr. Solomon Greenberg ran into the room.

"Hey! You're not my dad! I don't want you!" Bill pointed. "I want the angel to bring me my dad!"

"Bill, she's your nurse and I'm your doctor."

"No! I'm in reform school! I don't wanna be in reform school. Tony made me get in the car. He drove it. Let me go home!" Bill's shaking rattled the IV bottle.

"Take his pulse."

Nurse Jackson held Bill's arm.

The doctor looked in Bill's eyes through an ophthalmoscope. "His pupils are dilating wildly. What's his pulse?"

"A hundred and ten BPM."

"Let me go home! I didn't do nothin'. I want my mom and dad!"

"He's not ready yet. Give him a single dose of Midazolam."

Nurse Jackson injected the sedative into Bill's IV drip.

Bill passed out.

***

The next morning, glare seared Bill's eyes. At first, the light drilled his eyes like a basketball-sized solar flare against a white-hot background. The glow ebbed to baseball size. A minute later, multiple needles of light buffeted his cornea like pinpricks. Interminable seconds later, it eased to a haze. A blurred image came into focus. Bill saw a lanky man about his age. He had an olive complexion and wore a white overcoat. He stood with his arms at his side. A black female nurse who looked about ten years older flanked him. "What's happening? Where am I?"

"Do you have any idea who I am?" The man put his hand on the rail of Bill's bed.

"You look like a doctor. Where am I? What happened to me?"

"We'll talk about me later." Dr. Greenberg leaned closer. "What's the last thing you remember?"

"My father…World Series…I don't want my daddy to die…The angel…She said never to worry, my father is with them."

"How old are you, Bill?"

"Thirteen."

Doctor Greenberg and Nurse Jackson exchanged glances. The doctor's brow furrowed slightly. Nurse Jackson met his gaze and pressed her lips in a thin line. Doctor Greenberg craned his head forward. "What do you do for a living, Bill?"

"Um…Yeah…I'm starting to remember. A teacher…Yes, a teacher. I teach English at Filbert High School." Bill shook and cried, "I wanted to make a difference, but nobody cares. Nobody!"

"I'm sorry nobody appreciates you as a teacher. You can't be a high school teacher if you're only thirteen."

167

"No, no, I'm starting to remember. I'm forty-two. My wife is divorcing me. Burt Jenkins!" Bill narrowed his eyes and shook his fists. "She's with Burt Jenkins. I'm alone. It's not fair."

"So, you did what you did to yourself because you thought life wasn't fair." Dr. Greenberg pursed his lips and nodded."

"Just who are you anyway?"

"I am Dr. Greenberg. A neurosurgeon. You are at Jefferson Memorial Hospital."

"A neurosurgeon! You didn't lobotomize me, did you?" Bill rubbed his forehead to ensure no surgical stitches. His thoughts started to crystallize. He saw an I.V. needle in his arm connected to a glucose bottle dangling on an aluminum pole. The walls were whitewashed. The odor of antiseptic clogged his nostrils. He moved his legs and sighed in relief. "What happened? Was I in a car crash?"

"You can say that. Only if you were driving, the courts would tear your license into confetti and save it for when the Eagles win a Super Bowl."

"What do you mean?"

"Your level of intoxication shocked me, and I've seen it all. Neighbors report that you were talking to yourself. The bad news is that a van struck you. The rest is good news."

"Confused. I'm so confused."

"People who have just awoke from seventeen days in a coma tend to be confused."

"A coma? What do you mean, a coma?"

"It means you were unconscious for seventeen days with no response to your environment, and you couldn't be awakened. The van striking your head on the pavement caused a severe concussion. It didn't fracture your skull. It should have. After all, you're a teacher, not a caveman. A brain scan found no indication of an embolism, or swelling of brain tissue, or any sign of cranial pressure, or fluid in the skull. You'll recover from your physical injuries. Whether you recover from yourself is out of my hands." The doctor leaned on the steel bracing of Bill's bed and looked into his eyes. "What drove you to drink the amount you drank, only you know. Step one to recovery is acknowledging how fortunate you are. You didn't even break any bones or suffer internal injuries. Do you have any idea of what could have happened to you?"

"Um, uh, I guess, uh, I could be dead."

"You demonstrated a death wish. Now, what is the last thing that you remember? As an adult?"

"Um…What do you mean by adult?"

"Do you remember regaining consciousness yesterday?"

"No, Doctor."

"Well, yesterday, you thought you were still thirteen years old. Suppose that regression was permanent? Then what? I want you to try and recall your last memory as an adult."

"I don't know. My brain feels exhausted…Uh…Yes, now I remember. I left Filbert High after teaching my last class."

"Bill, what do you know about global amnesia?"

"Global amnesia?"

"Global amnesia happens to many victims of similar trauma. It is total memory loss. Total. You forget your family and friends. You have to be re-taught to read and write, even how to eat with a fork."

"I'm so tired and confused…So confused."

"I'm sure you are tired. No need for confusion, however. When you're well enough, we'll wheel you around to see other patients who suffered similar accidents. Accidents. Not the results of their stupidity. The permanently brain-damaged. The forever confused and disoriented. Speech reduced to gibberish. Loss of all motor functions. Bill, I don't think you need much imagination to picture a human vegetable."

"I don't want to."

"Maybe you should. It could've been you. For the rest of your life attendants aid your every biological function, feeding you, helping you shit and wiping your ass. I think you get the picture."

"Ouch." Bill moved his hip.

"Oh, so you're also complaining about your bruised hip. You should visit a paralysis and amputee rehabilitation clinic. I will leave you now, Mr. Waldron. Other patients need me. Mrs. Jackson is the chief nurse for your ward. She can do more for you than I can." Dr. Greenberg left Bill's room.

The nurse took Bill's pulse and temperature with an electronic thermometer. "Where did he get his bedside manner? The Devil's Island infirmary?"

"I heard you're a big baseball fan, Bill."

"Yes, I am, Nurse Jackson."

"You can call me Ruth. Anyway, Bill, think of Dr. Greenberg as an umpire. He calls them exactly as he sees 'em. You know that everybody always yells, 'kill the ump.' Yet the ump's usually right. Every day, I deal with patients exactly like the ones the doctor described. Believe me, it would break your heart. Dr. Greenberg never worked the Devil's Island infirmary," she chuckled." Yet you are one lucky devil." Ruth then clasped Bill's hand. "Keep that in mind. You'll need a positive mental attitude to get through this. The doctor did say your life has finally turned for the better."

"Why am I so tired? After all, you said I've been asleep for seventeen days."

"A coma is not sleep. Real rest is exactly what you need. So, rest up. Get your strength back. Many people want to see you."

"You're a wonderful nurse, Mrs. Jackson."

"I'm sorry I'm not the angel."

"What angel?"

The nurse beamed, "I think you just reached step two." She laughed.

"I'm so tired, too tired to think."

Nurse Jackson turned out the lights and left the room.

# Chapter 2

Bill's second day of consciousness began with less of a jolt. He could focus and had fewer headaches. Three floral arrangements broke the room's sterility. He tried to sit, but dizziness caused him to collapse. Rolling his head left, he saw an ancient old man with networks of tubes connected to his frail body. *'He looks* dead *three times over.'*

"Good morning, Bill." Nurse Jackson, wearing a light-blue sweater over her white uniform, turned on the lights and opened the curtains. The sun shone through the window. "Feeling any better?"

"I feel like I'm alive anyway."

"Have you tried sitting?"

"Yes, and it was horrible." Bill laid his arms on the railings. "I almost vomited. My head felt like it was vanishing into thin air."

"Expect that, Bill. You've been lying on your back for a long time, and your blood pressure is low. I'm going to increase the incline of your bed. Tell me how it feels." Ruth pushed a button on a small control box beside Bill's bed.

"Better, yes, much better."

"That should give you a better view of your room; after all, you have some lovely flowers to see. Oh, look, Bill. Nurse Haskins has brought you some breakfast."

A petite female nurse with strawberry blonde hair smiled. Bill smiled back and made eye contact with her. *'Cute.'* She blushed and lowered her head before placing a small dish of lime gelatine, a cup of strawberry yogurt, and a glass of water before him. "Thanks…"

"Nurse Haskins." She smiled and nodded.

"It's not exactly gourmet fare from Bookbinder's," Nurse Jackson smiled. "But it will put meat back on your bones and help you regain some strength."

Bill nibbled on the gelatin. "You're right about it not being Bookbinder's. But not bad. Not bad at all."

"It's hard to believe. Here I am, asking you to eat that to gain weight. I should be eating it to lose weight."

"You look fine, Ruth."

"Thanks anyway, Bill, but I can't remember the last time someone mistook me for Vanessa Williams."

"Well, don't feel too bad. No one ever accused me of being Tom Cruise in the best of times."

Ruth clasped Bill's hand. "Well, Bill, wit and charm like that will have you walking out of here in no time."

"When can I get visitors?"

"Visitors? When you were unconscious, this room was like the waiting room at Grand Central Station."

"Really? Who came?"

"Well, let's see, your mother came from Florida and your sister from Buffalo, she brought your oldest nephew with her, some people from school, and some of your buddies from McCusker's Tavern."

"Did Laura visit?"

"Oh yes! She is so well-dressed and classy! She was very concerned for you, too. She brought you these flowers." Ruth presented a bouquet featuring orchids and chrysanthemums.

"Was she alone?"

Nurse Jackson winced.

Bill jutted his head forward. "Was she with a man named Burt Jenkins?"

"As a medical professional, I am legally bound to confidentiality." She smiled, "Here." The nurse handed Bill a card. "She wrote you this."

Bill grabbed the card. *'Get well soon. Talk to you then. Love ya, Laura.'* He gobbled his gelatine and yogurt. "Oh, yeah, Ruth, did my son, Rory, visit?"

"I didn't know you had a son."

"Never mind," Bill snapped.

"Is there something you'd like to talk to me about?"

"No!" After ten tense seconds, Bill continued, "I'm sorry, I really am. I had no right to take it out on you."

"That's okay. Bill, but when you're ready, you can talk about it."

"You don't want to hear about it. It would take too long."

"Well, honey, you did nothing but listen for seventeen days. It's your turn to talk."

Bill chuckled. "Thanks. No, really. I don't feel up to it yet."

"Well, whenever you're ready, I'm all ears."

"Thanks." Bill took a long gulp of water. It tasted like wine to his drought-stricken throat.

"I'm not surprised that you're enjoying the water. If it weren't for this I.V. drip," Ruth pinched the tube connected to his arm, "you would have died of dehydration. So, drink up. You need it."

"When can I call everyone?"

"Dr. Greenberg has spoken to your family. They all know you're conscious and recovering. Dr. Greenberg would rather you wait until you're stronger and more alert before they visit again. Besides, don't you want to look your best?"

"What do you mean by look my best? Where's a mirror? What do I look like?"

Nurse Jackson handed Bill a small mirror.

"Huh! Egad! My face looks like a dirty rag." He had jaundiced skin, eyes that drooped like a bloodhound, and black circles hanging underneath that looked like an oak stump's annual rings. Poorly shaven cheeks wilted like November leaves. "My frazzled hair! I look like Larry of the Three Stooges." He put the mirror on the bedside table. "Sure, nobody ever asked if I was Tom Cruise, but Hollywood never asked me to play Quasimodo either."

"Don't you worry. You'll look good as new in no time! Even better." She pointed upward. "Hey, I wouldn't mind a little knock on the head, if it meant losing twenty pounds. Maybe this will cheer you up." Ruth handed Bill several telegrams. "They're from all over the country. Here's one from Pittsburgh."

"Gee, thanks." He looked down at the telegrams. "Yo, it's from my old buddy Tony. He owns four semi-trucks. And, hey, from Jeff out in California. Did you know he's Hollywood's most sought-after special effects man? Here's one from my buddy Frank. His father was a history professor at U of P. Now he's an economics professor at Northwestern."

"Yes, of course, I saw him on TV. Larry King had him on while you were unconscious."

"Yo, guess what? He's coming to town. He wants to meet me at McCusker's." He paused. "You won't believe this, Ruth, but I don't know today's date."

"How does May 15 sound?"

"Sounds strange. I last remember sometime in late April. Anyway, Frank wants to meet me at McCusker's Tavern in June. Do you think I can be outta here by then?"

"All depends on you, Bill. It will give you something to shoot for anyway. Promise me one thing, though."

"What's that, Ruth?"

"When you meet Frank at McCusker's, please don't drink alcohol. Remember what the doctor said."

"You have my word on that." Bill's face drooped. He remained silent for twenty seconds. "Geez, it's not fair."

"What's that, Bill?"

Bill dropped his head. "All of my friends. They're more successful than me. Okay, Frank was an Einstein and always studying. No surprise there. But Jeff's a damn millionaire. I never considered him smarter than me. But Tony? He dropped out of tenth grade. My dad said he'd land in jail. Now here I am, six credits short of a master's degree, and, damn, do you know how much more money he makes than me?"

"Do you see me as a failure?"

"No way, Ruth! I think you're the greatest. I surely need you to help me get well."

"Well, Bill, I had to study three years of basic nursing, and two more years for this specialty. It took me ten years to pay back all my student loans, and guess where I live? West Philly. Sixty-third and Walnut. Right where I started. That's far from a four-bedroom house in Wayne on a wooded acre. Bill, I feel successful in helping people in need." She smiled, "Like you right now. It's my calling. I have three kids in public schools, and I think you guys do a great job." Ruth clasped his hand. "I sure appreciate it when smart people like you choose to teach my kids rather than pursue money. You teach people who need you. What kind of future would we have if all the good teachers aspired to university posts? I know it sounds corny but put that chin up." She tapped an affectionate punch on his chin. "Be proud. Here, I brought you something to pass the time." Ruth put a radio next to Bill's bed.

"Gee, thanks, Ruth! Oh, I was wondering, how did the Phillies do while I was out?"

"Don't you worry about them. They kept the cellar warm for you. Well, I've got other patients to visit. Should you need me, just push that button."

"Thanks. I'll do that. Goodbye."

# Chapter 3

Bill had shifted his hospital bed to full upright. He ate scrambled eggs, mashed potatoes, and toast while listening to the all-sports-talk radio station.

Dr. Greenberg entered the room with Nurse Jackson. "Look at our Patient, Doctor. He's sitting up and eating solid food."

The doctor glanced at a chart on a metal clipboard. "Your physical progress is excellent. You seem alert. Are you still experiencing any disorientation?"

"No Doc. My memories end with finishing a class at Filbert. Memories of my unconscious experience are fading. Yet it seemed so real. I was thirteen again. Is there any chance of my signals crossing again?"

"As stated, Bill, you suffered no permanent brain or neurologic damage. That is the extent of my department. Therefore, I've arranged for Dr. Tryvyé, a psychiatrist, to examine you."

"Hey, I'm not crazy."

"I didn't say you were. Nevertheless, you did suffer a severe concussion, and you've experienced regressive episodes. It may involve more than physical trauma. Furthermore, a chapter of Alcoholics Anonymous meets at the hospital on Thursday evenings. I've arranged for an orderly to wheel you in."

"Alcoholics Anonymous? I'm no alcoholic."

"You think not? Drink landed you here. It should have put you in the morgue. Bill, people without a drinking problem don't go out and get drunk three times over on a work night. You'd better get a grip on it. Next time, you may not get so lucky."

"Yeah, sure, Doc. Hey, I promise that I haven't spiked my orange juice with vodka." Bill held the cup.

"That's okay," Dr. Greenberg grinned, "because that's not orange juice. It's a urine specimen."

Bill spewed a mouthful of orange juice.

"Don't get too cocky," Dr. Greenberg laughed. "Now finish your orange juice, Bill."

"By the way, Doc, are you related to the Hall of Fame first baseman, Hank Greenberg?"

"Yes, I am. Distant. Although, unfortunately, I never had an opportunity to meet him."

"Are you a baseball fan?"

"Bill, I wish I could enjoy the national pastime. Although in my profession, a pastime is finishing a meal in the hospital cafeteria or getting four consecutive hours of sleep."

"What do you think, Doctor?" Ruth asked. "Can he see visitors yet?"

"Tell you what, Bill. I'll examine you first thing tomorrow. If you're doing as well as today, I'll send you some visitors by the afternoon."

"Gee, thanks, Doc."

"Don't thank me yet. See you tomorrow morning."

***

Nurse Jackson and Nurse Haskins helped Bill prepare for his first visit. The nurses dry-washed his hair by sprinkling powder to absorb the oil, afterward brushing it out. They also acted as his surgical assistants, handing him grooming instruments as he sat in bed and shaved and splashed his face with cologne. Grasping a hand mirror, Bill scrutinized his reflection. His complexion had improved from jaundice to pale. The annual rings under his eyes had improved to a sappling. After the shave, his face looked like a clean rag. Ruth held a mirror in front of him. "What do you think?

"Well, I better not think about auditioning for a modeling agency. I guess this truly is a face only a mother could love. We'll put that to the acid test momentarily. Won't we?"

"You'll do fine, Bill." Ruth patted the top of his head. "Just relax and enjoy their visit."

"What do you think, Miss Haskins?"

"You look like what I imagined you'd look like when healthy." She winked. "Keep up the good work."

*'She was thinking about me.'* Bill smiled.

Dr. Greenberg escorted Patricia Waldron and Bill's sister, Marie, into his room.

Bill blinked three times before rubbing his eyes. He gawked at the two for several pregnant seconds. "Hi Mom."

"Hello, Bill. I worried about you so much."

Bill rubbed his eyes again. "Grandma Marconi! What a surprise! I hope you baked me some chocolate chip cookies. Did Mom tell you? Daddy got us World Series tickets."

Patricia inaudibly murmured to Dr. Greenberg before looking at Marie with pinched eyes and slightly parted, jittering lips.

"Aren't ya listening? Grandma? World Series tickets! Daddy got me World Series tickets!"

Dr. Greenberg gently shook Bill.

"Yo! Why are you shaking me? Who are you? What am I doing here?"

"Come back to me, Bill. You're still at Jefferson Hospital…"

"Ahh!" Bill screamed. "There's a needle in my arm!" Bill tried to dislodge the I.V. needle by whipping his arm like a fly-fishing rod. "Get this thing outta me! I don't want it!"

Dr. Greenberg clenched Bill's arm before motioning to Nurses Jackson and Haskins. Nurse Jackson put her right arm around a crying Patricia. Nurse Haskins put her left palm on Marie's back and directed her out of the room.

"Hey! Yo! Where's that fat lady taking my grandmother? Where is the skinny woman taking my mother?"

Dr. Greenberg restrained Bill with both arms.

"Yo! Get off me! I want my mother! Get off me! I wanna go home! That needle hurts!"

Dr. Greenberg nodded to Ruth, who injected a sedative into a junction in the I.V. tube.

Bill passed out.

# Chapter 4

Dr. Eduardo Tryvyé, psychiatrist, sat diagonally from Bill's bed. Ruffled black hair contrasted with his trimmed Van Dyke beard angling over his pointed chin. Thin wire-framed, half-eye glasses rested low on his Byzantine nose. He wore a loose-fitting, sandy-brown tweed jacket sporting Earth-brown corduroy elbow patches over a snug white turtleneck shirt. The psychiatrist took notes on a pad resting atop legs crossed at the knees.

Bill sat upright in his bed. "No offense, but I don't much believe in shrinks."

"I'm a professional. Colloquial contumelies don't upset me. Bill, a second brain scan reconfirmed that your problems are not physical. Therefore, we must conclude that your regressive episodes are symptomatic of a psychiatric disorder. We aim to identify it and ascertain why. Dr. Greenberg informs me that your episodic regressions are as a thirteen-year-old."

"It's like this, Dr. Tryvyé, when I was unconscious, I relived a chapter of my life, as a thirteen-year-old in 1964. The final two weeks of the Baseball season, to be exact. It was all so real ... Everything. Sights. Sounds. Even tastes, smells, and feelings."

"Nineteen-sixty-four? Wasn't that the year of the collapse?"

"Yes."

"What role did baseball and the collapse play during your hallucinogenic state?"

"Well...I'd say a major role. I re-lived every detail. My father was with me throughout. I regained consciousness right after he died."

"So, baseball did play an important role."

"Yes. Yes, it did."

Dr. Tryvyé pinched his chin. "Hmm ...Ahh ... Now I can construe and codify your delusions. You see, Bill. All sports represent manifestations of man's primal urges. Primitive man hunted and gathered for his survival. He had no control over his environment, yet its challenges stimulated him. As the human populace advanced to agricultural and later industrial societies, the stress of mundane drudgery supplanted the threat of wild beasts. Mankind's environmental alienation became irrevocable. Thus, as a primitive manifestation of that alienation, he devised sports." The psychiatrist grinned and flapped his hands like an infant playing with a rattle. "Can you see Bill? No longer needing to hunt for survival, man created games of pursuit and aim. Ancient man was also tribal; therefore, as the industrial revolution split and scattered family units, mankind substituted team sports as a manifestation of that phenomenon."

"Yo! Speak English! What does that have to do with me?"

"Bill, a manifestation of your testimony is that your hallucinogenic episodes involve a primordial fixation with baseball."

"Huh?"

"Do you agree, Bill? Baseball involves aim and pursuit."

"Yes. So?"

"Is not the goal of baseball a return to home? Now, Bill, that ties into Baseball's psychosexual manifestations. Isn't a baseball bat the ultimate phallic symbol, and a baseball testicular? What does a leather glove enveloping a baseball represent?"

"Oh no," Bill raised his hands, "come on."

"And why do baseball people pine for thick, natural grass?"

Bill smirked, shook his head, and waved his right hand.

"Now, Bill, would you agree that your father's murder manifested an abrupt end to your childhood?"

"Yeah, okay, I agree."

"Hmm...Ahh...Can't you see?" He shook his hands and beamed. "Can't you see? Your infantile fixation with baseball represents your fear of leaving home. Now your conscious mind has rejected the reality that you have left home; thus, it conflicts with your subconscious mind, which still recognizes reality. Therefore, an oppressed state of regression exists, and you resolve this conflict by deluding your ego through an inhibited awareness of reality; thus, your compulsive need to return home as a thirteen-year-old. Home. Home-plate. Same thing you see." Dr. Tryvyé beamed and pointed to the ceiling. "That you are obsessed with a stretch of collapse and defeat is a classic manifestation of a neurological incapacity to manage the dynamic phenomenon of present circumstances. The psychosexual aspects of this fixation with losing baseball are a manifestation of your subliminal fear of sexual dysfunction. After all, your pending divorce contributes to your inner conflict. Correct?" The psychiatrist nodded in parrot-like twitches. "Correct? Hmm ...Ahh...Yes. A classic case for shock treatment and Thorazine therapy. I'll relay my findings to Dr. Greenberg." Dr. Tryvyé left the room.

Bill shook his head, *'That session was a manifestation of my need for Jack Daniel's treatment and beer therapy.'*

# Chapter 5

The Flamingos sang their rendition of the Warren and Dubin standard, "I Only Have Eyes for You," from the monophonic speaker of Bill's radio. A ringing telephone clashed with the harmony. Bill put aside his *Philadelphia Daily News* sports page and arced the receiver to his ear. "Yo."

"Hello, Bill? Peter Capolino from Mitchell and Ness. It's great to hear you speak. We were all worried about you."

"Thanks."

"Are you feeling better?"

"Fine. Just fine. Although I'm still not on my feet yet."

"Do you think you can get outta there by June sixth?"

"Yeah, I'll sure try. Unless my shrink zaps me with shock treatment first."

"Shrink? Shock treatment? I always knew you were a bit crazy...but not that crazy."

"No, it's nothing like that. It's a manifestation of the physiological trauma, as he would put it."

"Here's some positive motivation to get you back on your feet. You know that we're sponsoring the memorabilia show in Valley Forge and that Dick Allen is the celebrity host. And since you're one of his biggest fans, I'd like to invite you to meet him at my shop."

"Dick Allen? At your shop?" Bill shook the phone as if shaking a cup of dice. "Hey! Yo! I'll be there, even if I must use a sheet to rappel out my window."

"Great. Get there in the morning."

Ruth Jackson entered the room. "Sorry to interrupt you, Bill, but you have a visitor."

"Yo, Peter, I'll have to give you a rain check. Got a visitor." Bill hung up the phone. "Good morning, Ruth!"

"And a good morning to you, too! I think this visitor will make your morning even better!"

Bill looked back at his newspaper. He almost whiplashed himself. *Laura*! Spring sunshine waltzed upon her auburn hair. Her cheeks radiated zest and color, yet they were so soft, like a bed of rose petals. Enticing lips seemed to drip apple nectar. She adorned no perfume, yet her fragrance was palpitating. She was casually attired, yet even loose-fitting denim pants failed to hide her thin waist and straight legs. A V-neck white cotton blouse exposed tanned gossamer skin. Bill reflexively moistened his lips.

"Hi Bill."

"Um, uh, hi, Hi Laura." Bill's jaw chattered.

"I worried about you." Laura tapped Bill's left hand. "You know that, don't you?"

"Um, no, um, I thought, um, you'd want to get rid of me." Laura clenched Bill's hand.

"No, Bill. Never. I married you. Would I have done that if I didn't love you? I've given you eighteen years of my life. I'd have to love a man an awful lot to do that." Laura strengthened her grip on Bill's left hand. "Do you know that else? When I saw you lying there helpless in a coma, I realized that those years were darn good ones. When summer turns to winter, the sun only seems cooler, yet its heat still burns. The trees lose their leaves, yet they sprout new ones in spring. My love for you will never fade; it only changes and grows anew. We've created a wonderful, intelligent son with so much potential. That will never change. I do love you, Bill." Laura kissed Bill's forehead. "Goodbye, Bill. I'd love to stay, but I really can't. Get well soon."

Bill's jaw stopped chattering. It now hung agape like an unmanned ventriloquist dummy. Laura had departed. He spoke to the air, "I love you, Laura. I love you. I love you, Laura, with all my heart." *'She has to hear me say it.'*

Bill pulled his body upright. He swung his legs over the bed's edge. Attempting to stand for the first time, Bill's love for Laura conquered the pain and vertigo. The I.V. pole served as a walker. His legs felt wobbly as a boxer's would after taking a Mike Tyson straight right. *'I love you, Laura.'* With strong resolve, he plodded into the hallway. *'Laura. Where's Laura? Is there enough time to say, I love you? There she is.'* He spotted her getting into the elevator ... Hand in hand with Burt Jenkins!

Feeling as if Mike Tyson followed his straight right with a haymaker, Bill collapsed. The chrome I.V. pole toppled like a toy soldier. The glucose bottle shattered. Glucose solution and glass shards flooded the floor. He tried to regain his feet, but dizziness and nausea defeated him. He slipped in a puke puddle. Bill wallowed in the vomit, glucose, and shattered glass. Grasping the IV pole, he waddled into his room on his knees. He swung the IV pole overhead and repeatedly hammered his mattress, yelling in sync, "No! No! No! No!"

# Chapter 6

With feline grace, Burt Jenkins's black Porsche stalked along 6th Street. Burt soon pounced on a parking space facing Laura's 6th and Locust Street townhouse. Built during the Federal period of the late 18th century, her society Hill townhouse sat on the southwest edge of Washington Square. Designed by William Penn, the town square was across from Independence Hall and the Liberty Bell. Washington Square is famous for the Tomb of the Unknown Revolutionary Soldier. People have reported seeing Leah, a ghost of a colonial Quaker girl, carrying a lantern and guarding the Square's unmarked graves.

Burt's Porsche door opened smoothly and silently. With a chivalrous right hand, he helped Laura alight from the passenger side. High-spike Italian shoes added length to her legs, tapering to proportional knees and ankles. Her designer brown silk wrap skirt maintained an aura of dignity while being tantalizing. A white silk shirt and a linen jacket perfected her attire.

A rumbling like the locusts of the fifth trumpet.

Four chopper motorcycles whipped around the corner of 6th and Locust, soon circling Burt's Porsche like hungry sharks. The lead bike stopped between the Porsche and Burt and Laura. A gruff bearded, professional wrestler-sized biker wearing a Nazi helmet dismounted. Brown western boots, torn denim pants, and a black leather vest exposed tattooed, python-thick arms. He rubbed the Porsche. "Hey ... nice car. How about ya guard my bike, while I take your baby here for a little ride."

"I don't think so," Burt said. "And I'd appreciate it if you would please not touch my car."

"Oh, please, pretty please," the biker taunted Burt. "If I wanna drive your damn car—I will. Give me the Gawdam keys!"

Burt stepped back three steps.

"Back off, Scorpion!" Laura prodded.

"Uww ... Tough lady. Hey Laura, I like that. Now I know who wears the pants around here. Too bad. Don't want ya to cover those sexy legs." Scorpion slipped his hand under Laura's skirt, grabbing a mound of buttocks.

Laura slapped Scorpion's face crisp as ringing a bell.

"Look ya fookin' bitch!" He rubbed his stinging cheek.

"No! You look! You son-of-a-bitch! Next time I scratch your damn eyes out!" Laura unsheathed her fingernails.

"Hey…I think she's Mama material." Sleazette, Scorpion's girlfriend and riding mate, blew and popped a bubble from a wad of chewing gum. Clad in vacuum-tight black leather, she set her hair in coal-black spikes and wore matching black lipstick. A sleeveless top showed off her tattoo of a black widow spider in a web.

"Shut up bitch." Scorpion glowered and pointed at her. "There's only one reason, and one reason alone, that you open ya filthy mouth."

"Who are these people?" Burt put his hands on his hips.

"Just some friends of Rory's."

"Oh ... Just some friends of Rory's? How uncouth." Scorpion crossed his arms. "Why don't ya be the proper Society Hill hostess?" He smirked at Burt and Laura. "This little tramp is Sleazette ..."

"Shut the hell up!"

"No. You shut the hell up ... Or next time ... Bitch ... I rather stick the tip of my boot in that big mouth of yours." Scorpion turned back to Laura. "The freak over there is Space Case." Scorpion pointed to a wire-thin biker leaning against his motorcycle in a crocodilian stupor. His long hair hung like greasy strands of linguine. "He may be skinny ... but don't mess with him. Even he doesn't know what he's high on. There's Rat Fink." Scorpion nodded to a squat, neanderthal looking man sitting on a chopper. The unshaven, round-faced biker wore a German World War I pickelhaube helmet. "We call this one Cockroach." Scorpion pointed at a tall biker whose belly jutted bare navel between his belt and shirt. His straggly hair and trollish beard oozed oil. "And I think you know this young punk..."

Next to Cockroach stood Rory Waldron. Thin and gaunt, the teenager's black T-shirt hung loose over his shoulder-length, dark brown hair. His shirt had the logo of a black metal band called Lucifer Jack. The logo featured a Dante's Inferno-like creature with an angular face, fiery eyes, a pointed chin, and a goatee beard. Two conical horns extended from its forehead. A red, upright reptilian body ended in a pointed tail. Two three-fingered claws played a hexagon-shaped electric guitar.

Rory's face boasted Laura's angles, although his father's coloration and Mediterranean nose. The teenager's eyes looked like a road map of red highways and byways.

"My God. What have you been ... Just get inside. Get inside now."

"Oh, Mom, not here."

"Mommy, oh mommy," Rat Fink and Cockroach taunted Rory.

"I mean, like, man, I'll go when I feel like it."

"No. You'll go when I feel like it."

"Ah, shut up."

The bikers cheered Rory.

"No. Not man ..." Laura lunged forward and grabbed Rory's ear. "Ma'am. And you're the one who's going to shut up. Now you're going inside the hard way." She pulled him toward their front door by the ear, to the derision of the motorcycle gang. After closing the door behind Rory, she turned to Scorpion. "Why on Earth do you want a sixteen-year-old boy in your gang?"

"Hey, the younger the member, the better the chance of a young, sexy mother." Scorpion put his arm around Laura's shoulder.

Laura knocked it away as she would an insect. She put her clawed hand an inch from his eyes. "You don't value your eyesight? Do you?"

"Woo..." Scorpion backed away, shaking and waving his fingers like a sorcerer casting a hex. "Tough lady. I like that. I like it so much…" He grabbed Sleazette. "That I'll ditch this bitch." He impertinently shoved her at Burt Jenkins. "And make the switch."

"Aw, right." Sleazette nodded. "Aw, right. Ya asshole. Say ..." She leaned on Burt. "I'll take a strong, silent type over a loudmouth, and he's got money." She then touched her tongue to Burt's cheek.

Burt pushed her away.

"What's a matter?" Scorpion, hands on his hips, glared at Burt. "Ain't my woman good enough for ya?"

Burt's voice dropped a decrescendo, "I'm, um, sure she's a lovely lady, um, she's just not my type."

"Lovely lady." Scorpion threw up his hands. "She's a piece of garbage."

"Not your type, huh?" Sleazette massaged Burt's crotch. "Don't say that till you've had me in action, rich boy. 'Cause I think I'm gonna like this setup." She rubbed her hands over Burt's Porsche and embarked. She stuck her head out of the window. "What are you waiting for?"

Burt twitched his head back and forth.

Scorpion, meanwhile, saddled his Harley, revved it twice, and patted the seat behind him. "Come on, Laura, babe. Take a chance. Hop on the hog. Get a life. Find out what a real man is all about."

Laura sneered at him. Turning to Burt, she said: "I'll talk to you in the office Monday."

Burt nodded.

Sleazette jumped out of Burt's Porche. "Yo Scorpion. Ya lazy bum. I'm dumpin' ya broke ass for da green." She clamped Burt's crotch like a cliff purchase, shocking him. She then kissed his quivering lips and shot her tongue into his mouth.

Scorpion mock-charged like an African bull elephant. "So, you're gettin' off on my woman ..."

Burt dove into his car. He left a vestige of burning rubber as he drove away.

"Yo, Laura, babe. Did ya see rich boy foolin' with my broad?"

Laura turned and marched to her front door.

Scorpion flagellated his crotch. "So, what do you ya say ya switch from a weenie to a kielbasa?"

The rest of the gang mocked her.

***

Rory sat in a lounge chair and pondered the ceiling as if it were a planetarium.

Laura trudged through the front door. "Rory. We need to talk. Right now."

"I ain't sayin' nothin' to you." He pointed. "You made an ass outta me in front of the gang, so piss off!"

"Look," she prodded. "As long as you're living under my roof, you will do as I say."

"I don't care about nothin' you say." Rory started climbing the stairs.

"Young man, until you graduate from high school…

"What makes you think I'm gonna finish high school? You graduated from a loser to a wimp." Rory reached the top of the stairs and locked himself in his bedroom. He cranked his stereo volume louder than a 747 takeoff. The screeching electric guitars and vocal screeches of a "Lucifer Jack" number shook the walls.

"Five and sixty-nine times nine; six in and fate is mine."

"Five and sixty-nine times nine; my power will shine."

"Five and sixty-nine times nine; being your master is my design."

Laura had not smoked a cigarette in ten years. Nevertheless, she knew where to find R.J. Reynolds' most toxic. She lit up and sucked nicotine into her lungs.

# Chapter 7

During the next few days, Bill's health improved. The headaches had all but disappeared; the dizzy spells were fewer and less severe. He no longer experienced episodic regressions. The I.V. needle was gone, and Dr. Greenberg put him on a normal diet.

Bill sat upright in his bed with the receiver to his ear, holding to recommend to sportscaster Howard Eskin's radio audience that the Phillies fire their manager. The patient chuckled while listening to a caller going by the handle "Baseball George" humiliate the host. Bill's receiver immediately got the hook as his son, Rory, entered the room.

"Rory! What a surprise! It's about time!"

The only sound from Rory was screeching guitars from tiny speakers jammed into his ears. Bill yanked out Rory's earphones.

"Hey! Yo. man. Whad did ya do that for?"

"It's bad enough you haven't visited me in over a month. Don't ask me to compete with that noise."

"Noise? This Lucifer Jack's heavy stuff, man. You know, like dig this guitar ..." Rory aimed the speakers at Bill and raised the volume to maximum. "No one plays guitar like Bud Z. Beal, you know."

"What about Chuck Berry?"

"Who?"

"Geez ... Never mind. Hey, where were you anyway? Don't you think you could've visited sooner?"

"Why? You weren't awake."

"Well, you could've at least shown your father some concern."

"Why? You're not even living at home...Hey, cool contraption." Rory grabbed the hospital bed's remote control and scrunched Bill in and out.

"Cut that out." Bill snatched the remote from Rory. "Now I haven't heard a thing about you in almost two months ... How did you do in school?"

"School sucks."

"I didn't ask you for your opinion on school." Bill raised his hands. "I asked how you did in school."

"It still sucks."

Bill took a deep breath. "How did you do?"

"Hey man, get off my case. Like, look at it this way, they didn't kick me out. And, ya know, they're not holding me back."

"That's not going to get you very far." Bill pointed.

"School never got you anywhere."

"Hey! I'm earning a living. If you want to do the same, you better bear down."

"Yo, that's for *losers*. As for me, I'm gonna get me a hog and ride where the wind blows."

"Yeah, sure. That's where trash collects."

Rory pulled a face and brushed his father off with his right hand.

"Yo...Bigshot. Where do you think you'll get the money to buy a motorcycle with no job?"

"Ha! Grandma Chilton gave me enough on my birthday to buy two."

"That's no way to get ahead."

"It's a way...Shoot, man, you're just jealous because she thinks you're a loser. She hates your guts, and she likes Burt."

"Don't talk to me like that."

"Yeah, well, it's true. And even if you could get outta that bed and kick my ass, I can avenge it by getting Scorpion to take you apart."

"Dammit Rory. When are you going to learn the meaning of the word, respect? You can start by realizing that the mark of a man is not the ability to kick ass. While you're at it, try learning some discipline. Character. Responsibility."

"Ya Voe." Rory gave his father a stiff-armed Bellamy salute.

"I'm serious."

"So am I. Hey, ain't this a bad assed number?" Rory directed the Walkman speakers at Bill, assailing him with a Lucifer Jack "*song*" about patricide.

"Yo! Get that out of my face."

"Okay, Man. You asked me." Rory jammed the speakers back into his ears and backed out of Bill's reach. Rory spent the next two minutes shaking his head to the clamor. He left without saying goodbye.

Bill gritted his teeth, called the sports talk station, and blasted the Phillies manager with "Baseball George" fury.

# Chapter 8

The following Sunday was Bill's final night in the hospital. The lights were off as he sat in a chair and looked southwestward out the open window of his eighth-story room. He viewed Doc Watson's Pub, a place of his many hours, and many people he counted as friends. He turned his radio dial to Jerry Blavat's Sunday night doo-wop program. The first song that Jerry played was a Harptones' doo-wop interpretation of the standard, *'When the Real Thing Comes Along.*

The song heightened Bill's reflective mood as he watched the coming and going outside Doc Watson's Pub.

"Hi there, Bill. I hear you're leaving us tomorrow."

Bill turned to nurse Elizabeth Haskins. He beamed. *'She looks cuter than an Easter bonnet.'*

"Yes. I am, Nurse Haskins.

"You must be glad."

"Yeah. A little bit."

"You don't sound overly enthusiastic." She moved closer.

"It's like many things in life. Bittersweet. I'm gonna miss you people, and I admit I'm uneasy about what awaits. So much has happened. Before the accident, my life was headed straight down the toilet." Bill spread his arms. "Now what?"

Nurse Haskins sat on a chair next to Bill's bed. "At least now your life's not in the toilet."

"You're sure about that, nurse…?"

"Elizabeth. Those close to me call me Liz."

"Thanks, Elizabeth. You and Ruth were a great help. Lucky for you, you don't know what I was going through before I got here and what I must deal with tomorrow."

"You can be negative about the past." Elizabeth smiled. "But be optimistic about the future. You've proven you can overcome. After all, I first saw you wheeled in while strapped to a gurney. Now you're on the eve of walking out of here." She tapped his hand. "You're an inspiration."

"An inspiration? I've been called many things. Many of them bad." Bill chuckled. "But never an inspiration."

"You are an inspiration, Bill. You've overcome just about the worst that life can dish out. Your progress even impressed Dr. Greenberg."

"Thanks, but there's still a lot more to overcome. My wife, who's soon to be my ex-wife, is already with another man. My son? I've lost him to God knows what."

"You'll reach him. I know you will."

"I surely hope so."

"You've proven your determination, and I admire you for it. I know you will never quit. Soon, your son will follow your example."

"Maybe I should quit. Maybe Rory should sink or swim on his own. Learn the hard way. Like I had to. The easy way has taught him nothing... You are right about one thing, though, Miss Haskins."

"Liz." She tapped his hand.

"Liz." Bill smiled and squeezed her hand. "I've learned a great deal about myself these past weeks. I guess it's from reliving a major chapter of my life."

"I heard about that."

"Yeah, Liz. While I was comatose, I may have looked dead, but inside, I was very much alive. It was so real. I still can't fully sort it. Sights. Sounds. Even touch and taste. Most of all, the people. Liz, my boyhood friends and foes, especially my father, all came back to life or got about thirty years younger. I spoke to them; I lived with them. That must affect you.”

“It sounds fascinating.”

“Fascinating ... You can say that, Liz. Although, like my present life, it all came unraveled and ended badly. I never want to experience it again.”

“What about the angel?” Liz let down her long, strawberry blonde hair. “Nurse Jackson said something about an angel visiting you?”

“She said something about it to me, too. It was a female angel. I can’t recall it, though.”

Don't you remember what Dr. Greenberg said? Maybe your life was unraveling, but it didn't end. Badly or otherwise. You're walking out of here tomorrow. Not only with a sound mind but with a richer one.”

“That's a sweet thing to say. Nevertheless, I still must live at the Kesmon, and Laura,” Bill dropped his head, “is still seeing someone else.”

“Well, Bill, you're not the only one to suffer a broken heart.”

“It goes beyond that.”

“That’s how anyone who’s suffered lost love feels.”

“No, Liz. It’s more than that ...Okay, look at it this way...How old are you?"

“That's a personal question for a lady.” Liz laughed.

“Please, Liz.”

“Okay, Thirty-four.”

“Liz. Laura's been my whole life since you were in high school. Now she's gone. Gone into the arms of another man." Bill clenched his teeth and pursed his lips.

"I'm sorry, Bill. I am. It stinks. It's rotten. But what more can be said? Okay, you got it worse than most. Fair enough. But where do you go from here?"

"Can't you tell me?"

"You can either overcome and make a life for yourself, or you can crawl into a hole and wait for death."

Bill snickered. "I'm afraid I'm already living in a hole. Better you visit Dracula's dungeon than the Kesmon."

"Why do you stay there?"

"Because it's all I can afford."

"Oh, come on." Liz raised her hands. "I know an experienced teacher makes about the same as a nurse. My apartment won't please a sultan, but at least it's respectable. Don't tell me the Kesmon is all you can afford?"

"You make a point. Maybe I stay there as a reflection of how I'm feeling."

"Why punish yourself, Bill?"

"Punish myself? Isn't my life punishment enough?"

"Losing Laura hurts. I can feel it from here. I also sense your frustration over your son. But playing the martyr won't help your son or bring your wife back."

"Wow, Liz. What can I say? You again make so much sense. Yet what awaits me out there?" Bill pointed out the window. "I'm middle-aged with nowhere to go but down."

"I disagree. You're an intelligent man, well-established in a noble vocation. You can still make a difference."

"Yeah. Sure. I often said that to myself. Besides, who'd be interested in me? As an attractive nurse, you must get to date doctors."

"Doctors? Well, I'll admit. I used to have a crush on Dr. Greenberg." Liz blushed and lowered her head. "Unfortunately, he lacks the time to look at his watch, much less look at me."

Bill again looked at Liz. His pupils widened. "No time to look at you? Now that's what I call total devotion to work."

"Thank you, Bill." Liz blushed. "That was sweet. Still. No one ever notices me."

"Maybe that's because you never give them a chance. During my entire stay here, you came in and out of my room too fast for me to get so much as a word in. Yet here I am speaking to a beautiful young lady, and I don't just mean the outside."

Liz blushed and took Bill by the hand. "Thank you, Bill. Thank you very much. You're a kind man. I wish more were like you. It's just that each time my heart goes out, someone stomps on it."

"Impossible. Many guys are just dreaming of meeting someone like you."

"That's nice of you to say. No, Bill. I've given up on romance. I find my sense of purpose and fulfillment in caring for people. Just as you aim to do as a teacher, I want to make a difference in the lives of others." Liz closed her eyes and lowered her head. "Moreover, I won't get hurt."

"Hmm…" Bill put his hand on his chin. "Ahh." Bill pictured Dr. Tryvye and laughed. "Do you like oldies?" Bill pointed to the radio. The Spaniels, *A Hundred Years From Today*", played.

"They're okay. Although they're not my thing."

"Just as long as Lucifer Jack ain't your thing." Bill laughed.

"No, Bill, nothing that radical," Liz chuckled, "although I like rock like Guns and Roses, Pearl Jam, and Nirvana."

"I like some modern rock, although too many new songs either assail the senses or are sterile and pedestrian. The oldies convey a natural feeling and spirit."

"I like some oldies. I still listen to my David Bowie, Led Zeppelin, and Aerosmith albums from the Seventies."

"Yes. I like some of their songs too. I like songs that tell a story along with the music. I even learn from their basic wisdom. Jerry Blavat plays the soundtrack of my life ...You've made me think, Liz ... Dr. Greenberg is right. I am self-defeating. Maybe we all are. Liz, I heard what you said about yourself. I want to dedicate a song to you. Smoky Robinson wrote it for the Temptations. I'm sure Jerry will play us the Persuasions' du-wop a cappella version." Bill turned away and called the radio station. He then gave Liz a thumbs-up. "It's coming on next."

Jerry Blavat broadcasted, "Come on in, we're in the du-wop room. Philadelphia Pennsylvania. Street Corner Sunday. Give me a call. You say it, I'll play it. This is from Bill, dedicated to you, Liz. The Persuasions and their rendition of ... "Don't Look Back."

The Persuasions' deft lead singer, Jerry Lawson, commanded an earthy, masculine voice. He sang as a suitor, encouraging a broken-hearted girl to leave the past behind and give love another chance.

After the Persuasions hummed the final bar, Liz said, "You're too sweet. No one's ever been so thoughtful of me." She leaned across and planted a firm kiss on Bill's forehead. He clasped her hands. Their eyes met. Slowly, like two docking spacecraft, their heads moved closer. They kissed. This time, their tongues entwined. Their kiss was brief while seeming eternal.

Liz pulled her head away and looked downward, avoiding eye contact. "What must you think of me? I've been a nurse for 14 years. I've never come close to kissing a patient." She turned away. "Moreover, I could get in serious trouble."

"Don't worry. I won't snitch." Bill chuckled. "I still blame it on you." Bill laughed out loud. "Never has anyone given me enough self-confidence to do that. I think the world of you for it. After all, you're the first lady, other than Laura, that I've kissed in over twenty years. I want to see you again. I really do."

"I would like that." Liz took a pad and pen from the table beside Bill's bed and scratched her home phone number. "This is also something I've never done." She handed it to Bill and squeezed his hand. "Let's not get carried away here. I'd better go. Call me."

Bill felt a special warmth as he tucked Liz's note into his wallet. He listened to Jerry Blavat on his radio. "Here's a never-released record. I had earlier played a dedication to my long-time friend Bill. I suspect this one is also for him and his new lady. The Skyliner's Jimmy Beaumont sang it with the Ray Charles singers. It's called "Blossoms in the Snow."

Bill clutched the paper scrap with Liz's phone number and closed his eyes while the song played.

"It's time for this week's doo-wop quiz," Jerry Blavat said after the song ended. "I'm going to play two songs. Tell me each artist's name and what makes them both alike and unique. This week's prize is the original 45 records of both songs. I'll take the eighth caller. Don't call until the second record. I'm not answering the phone until then. This week's prize is compliments of Val Shively's R and B warehouse. He's got possibly the largest 45 record collection on Earth, over three million in stock."

The first record was a ballad devoted to a lost love that will forever echo in the heart. Bill closed his eyes. He pictured his twice-lived experience with the '64 Phillies. Gene Mauch the peerless leader, Bunning and Short, Tony Taylor, Alex Johnson, and Tony Gonzalez, Johnny Callison slugging a homer over the spite fence, Shibe Park, Dick Allen slamming a ball over the Coke sign… "I know that song." Bill opened his eyes as the song reached its coda.

"Some people are already calling the station," Blavat broadcasted. "Now we're not taking any calls until the next song. Okay, here it is. I'll take the eighth caller."

The second song was also a love ballad. It sang about a desperate lover's search for the girl whose heart he had broken.

Bill grabbed the phone and hastily dialed the station. He heard ringing. "All right!" Bill shook his left fist.

"Hello, you're the eighth caller. What's your name, please?"

"Bill."

"Bill? You again. I was just talking about you. I hope you and your new lady enjoyed the dedications."

"Yes. Thank you, Jerry. I want to answer the quiz."

"Go for it, Bill."

"Echoes of November" was sung by Dick Allen. "Moonlight" was sung by Arthur Lee Maye. Both played big league baseball."

"Correct. Tell you what. Give me the name of Dick Allen's back-up group and I'll throw in the original label 45 of the Intruder's *Come Home Soon* also compliments of Val Shively."

"The Ebonistics."

"Correct again. You know your oldies and your baseball, Bill. Where do I send your prizes?"

Bill hesitated, "... Um ... Uh ... One Washington Square."

"One Washington Square? You live there?"

"Um…Uh…Yes."

"If you live there, you can afford to buy the prize package! No problem. You're our winner. Thanks for playing. We'll send it right out ... Arthur Lee Maye. Great centerfielder with the Milwaukee Braves. Batted over .300 and led the National League in doubles in '64. He hurt us late that September. And Dick Allen. Crash. Number 15 in your program, number one in your heart. "Echoes of November," that song sums up the end of an era. The '64 Phillies. That's what this show's all about, folks. Some listen to remember, some listen to forget. We'd all like to forget about how the Phillies lost today! If you don't know about it, you really don't want to know. Enough baseball! Back to the heavenly harmony. This one is dedicated to the Phillies' last winning season. The Pastels and "Been so Long.""

# Chapter 9

Late the next morning, a firm Dr. Greenberg handshake and a firmer Ruth Jackson bear hug launched Bill into the city. Bill had to shield his eyes from the sun. Ninety-five degrees Fahrenheit heat and high humidity glued Bill's shirt to his body. Honking horns, bus engines, sirens, and air hammers clanged and banged in his skull.

Mack Pittman beamed and circled the front counter to greet Bill as he entered the Kesmon. "Hey, great to see you." Mack shook Bill's hand. "How are ya feeling?"

As well as can be expected.

"Your room is waiting for you. All your stuff is intact. Laura came in and paid your rent. You also got a call from that summer camp . . ."

"Camp Greenbriar? I work summers there as a counselor."

They rode up in the jail cell looking elevator.

"Yeah, they want you to phone 'em and tell 'em if you're coming."

"Thanks."

"Yeah, that Laura is one lovely lady."

"Ya. Sure. I know." Bill grunted. "Was she alone? Was she with a tall, fancy pants guy?"

"Yeah, they were both well dressed."

Bill scowled, turned, and faced Mack. "Was his name Burt Jenkins?"

"Hey, don't take this out on me." Mack shrugged. "He didn't introduce himself."

"I'm sorry, Mack." Bill placed his hand on the old man's shoulder. "I had no right to take it out on you."

"How long were ya married?"

"Eighteen years." They exited the elevator and strode down the dusky hallway.

"If it's any consolation to ya, all the men stayin' here, can never even hope for one day, with a woman like her, much less eighteen years."

"Thanks, Mack. I know you mean well."

Mack unlocked Bill's room. "Well, here you go."

Bill's steam sauna of a room was an entomologist's dream of flying and creeping things. He first inspected his baseball memorabilia collection. Bill nodded. '*All there, nothing damaged*'. He caught three cockroaches congregating on a bureau top. Drawing a shoe like a samurai, he stalked forward.

Slowly. Silently. "BAM!" He smashed all three with a single blow. "My all-time record!" Bill victoriously raised his shoe overhead.

# Chapter 10

Doc Watson's late afternoon patrons clapped and cheered as Bill entered. Like autograph hounds, the regulars competed for a handshake and a chance to slap Bill's back. Bill stood up straight, smiled, and nodded. "Thanks, everyone. I'm feeling fine and doing great." Cynthia loped over and pecked his lips.

"Yeah! All right!" A customer wearing a shirt with a name tag embroidered, James, slapped his back.

Jill, Doc's alluring manager, who, to Bill's chagrin, seldom noticed him, kissed his cheek. Jill flicked aside a cascade of honey-blond hair, wrapped her arm around his waist, and led him to a table. "Chris. Two free drinks for our hero."

Chris beamed. The tanned bartender wore a white shirt with Doc Warson's logo. A sporting person, yet his body looked as if someone h a d  locked him in a bakery for the past year. "What'll it be?"

"An O'Douls."

The bartender fetched the non-alcoholic beer. Bill soon realized that his fame had vanished as fast as a U.S. president's popularity.

Chris leaned on the bar and craned his head toward the door. "Uh oh. Trouble is here."

A man no more than five feet, five inches tall with an oversized oblong head and a never-exercised body walked into the pub. Although the outside thermometer registered ninety-two degrees, he wore a long, khaki trench coat. "Vincenzo," Chris pointed at him, "I told you not to come in until you pay your bar tab."

"I'm not Vincenzo. I'm Julius Camillus."

"Last week, you were Flavian Fury." Chris folded his arms over his chest. "Good God, how about you answer to the name on your unpaid bar tab? Vincenzo."

"God? Did you say God? I told you before. I'm too smart for that Sky Daddy, superstitious stuff." He raised his chin. "I'm an Atheist."

"If you were so much smarter than me, because I believe in God, why do you owe me money?" Chris pointed at the door. "Now pay your bar tab or get out."

"It's okay." Bill stood and raised his palms. "He can have one of my free drinks."

Chris pursed his lips and shook his head. "Okay, Waldron, if you want to be a sucker, fine."

"Give me a Heineken." Vincenzo pointed at Chris.

"You get a Budweiser," Chris smirked.

"You gotta drink one too." Vincenzo picked up Bill's bottle of O'Doul's. "This stuff is for sissies. It's overpriced, lousy-tasting soda pop."

Bill grimaced, slid his bottle of non-alcoholic beer to the bar's drop ledge, and held up two fingers to the bartender.

Bill returned to his table with two bottles of Budweiser. "You're having trouble here. Why don't you go to McCusker's Tavern in South Philly? I heard you had a connection."

"Don't ever mention that place again." Vincenzo took a long chug. "Let's finish these quickly. Your reminding me of that place, has me needing to fill the empty with something a hell of a lot more potent." Vincenzo looked in every direction. He narrowed his eyes and looked downward. Bill followed his gaze. Vincenzo reached into his trench coat.

"That's Austin Nichols' Wild Turkey Kentucky Legend." Bill pointed. "It's the best damn Bourbon on the market. How did you ever afford it?"

"I went to the bottle store." Vince ticced his head back and forth. "The clerk wasn't looking. I got it on five-finger discount."

"You stole it." Bill narrowed his eyes. "Besides, you can't sneak in outside liquor."

"That's what's great about being an Atheist. Idiotic rules puritanical morality doesn't apply to me."

"Going to jail or getting banned from the pub stops me."

Vincenzo filled his and Bill's empty Budweiser bottles with bourbon. He slid Bill a bottle. Bill held the bottle to his nose. "These smells are so piquant and lush. I'm tempted to drink it."

"The best way to resist temptation is to yield to it. Bottoms up." Vincenzo chugged from the beer bottle of bourbon. He grabbed his bottle of Budweiser and drank half of it as a chaser.

"Are you insane? You drank the equivalent of half a dozen shots. That booze is 114-proof!"

"What's stopping you?"

"For one, doctor's orders." Bill looked around. Jill and Cynthia were gone. Chris was busy serving other customers. Bill again sniffed the premium hooch. He stared at the bottle for four pregnant seconds. Feeling detached, he took a long swig and chased it with the rest of his Budweiser.

"Was that good or was that great?" Vince wiped his mouth. "Finish it."

"You're right. It's mellow and hearty at once. The taste of charred oak lingers oh so sweetly. But let's slow down. I want to enjoy it. Besides, we need more beer. I'll buy us a pitcher. I don't want Chris paying attention to us." Bill walked over to the bar.

"Yo Chris." Vincenzo stood. "Your music sucks. It's not even singing. It's just talking."

"That's Dr. Dre and Snoop Dog." Chris rolled his eyes at Vincenzo. "It's popular. The pub is a business. We cater to the public. I play what the people want."

"It's a bunch of musical masturbation."

"Oh, really, Vincenzo. I was here last week for your little karaoke performance. What do you call singing that song, '*Look at Your Game Girl*'? A cappella? I call it musical mass murder." Chris filled a pitcher with Budweiser and handed it along with two glasses to Bill.

"Yeah, well, that song's singer and writer makes more sense than you ever will," Vincenzo shouted back, "or any politician for that matter."

Chris mumbled to Bill. "Will you at least keep him quiet?"

Bill returned with the pitcher of beer. Vincenzo had already refilled his empty bottle with the premium Bourbon. "Finish it."

"Slow down." Bill held up his hand in a halt gesture. This Austin Nichols Wild Turkey Kentucky Legend is the finest hooch I've ever drunk. Let me enjoy it."

"You'll enjoy it more if you drink it rather than just talk about it." Vincenzo held his bottle aloft. "Bottoms up." He downed the rest of his booze-filled beer bottle and chased it by drinking a pint of beer.

Bill quaffed the rest of his bourbon and chased it with beer. "Woo!" Bill shook his head. "That hit the spot."

"It helps me drown out the government."

"Government?" Bill shook his head. "You used to claim you were a Communist. A month later, you were a National Socialist. What are you now?"

"I'm an anarchist. It's time to overthrow the entire system by any means possible. Tax and spend. Tax and spend." Vincenzo banged on the table. "Tax and spend. That's all they're good for."

"I'll drink to that." Bill held aloft his bourbon-filled beer bottle. "Tax and Spend is to politicians what Bunning and Short were to Gene Mauch and the '64 Phillies."

Vincenzo refilled their beer bottles with bourbon. He chugged the entire thing and chased it with half a glass of beer. Bill chugged half his bourbon bottle but chased it with an entire glass of beer.

Vincenzo stood and yelled, "Hail Errico Malatesta!" He collapsed and lay passed out on the floor. The bottle of Austin Nichols Wild Turkey Kentucky Legend rolled away. Bill gasped. Vincenzo's coat was open; his pants were unfastened.

Bill braced himself against the table to prevent himself from joining him on the floor. More customers had entered the pub. They clamored for service without noticing Vincenzo. Chris was too busy to see him. Bill trudged out the door and onto the sidewalk. He felt himself bobbing and weaving. *'Great job, Bill. You'll get banned unless Vincenzo gets all the blame. Stay away until the heat is off.'*

Plodding like Boris Karloff's Frankenstein, Bill joined the creatures of the night.

A tattered panhandler accosted him. "Give me some change."

Bill shrugged his shoulders and raised open palms.

"Come on, man, I can tell you're drunk. Give me something so I can at least have one."

Bill reached into his pocket and handed him a dollar bill.

"That's more like it."

Bill staggered on, hoping he was headed toward the Kesmon. A long-legged streetwalker whose red, spiked shoes lifted her three inches taller than him approached, "Looking for a date, sugar?"

"I can't afford you."

"How much you got?"

"Not enough for you."

"Maybe this will help you find the funds." The hooker lifted her ultra-short, white leather skirt. Bill managed to turn the corner without stumbling onto the street.

"Hey, buddy, I got what you need." A weasel-faced Spanish guy reached under his silk shirt and showed him a clear bag of white powder. "Colombian."

"I'm not into it."

"Bullshit. Look at ya now. This'll at least spare your liver."

Bill crossed the street to avoid him.

He never looked. He never saw the oncoming delivery truck. The skidding vehicle's horn blared; its brakes screeched.

Facing the truck, his face looked as if it were made of putty and someone pulled it downward. His eyes opened like light sockets.

*Thud.*

The truck knocked Bill backward. He somehow kept his footing.

The driver yelled, "Watch where you're goin'! Ya drunk, dumb jerk!" The driver circled him and drove away.

"Ah, screw you!" Bill flicked his middle finger.

Bill trudged on. He staggered into a man wearing a white tank top shirt and painted-on tight denim jeans. He shoved Bill to the sidewalk. "Watch where you're goin' ya damn drunk."

Bill looked up and saw the Kesmon. The man's partner took Bill's hand, rubbed it, and helped him stand. He patted his back. As Bill staggered into the Kesmon, he heard the two men yelling at each other.

***

An aviary of flying insects buzzed about Bill's room. He heaved on the floor. Strangely, the vomit didn't seem to make his room any dirtier. Bill passed out face-first on his bed.

At three o'clock in the morning, a teenage gang awoke him with high-decibel rap music from a Honda Civic-sized *ghetto blaster*. A fresh puddle of puke shared his bed. Cockroaches feasted on the earlier regurgitation. He stumbled to the window and futilely yelled, "Yo! Cut the noise! I'm trying to sleep!"

The teens danced on.

"The city. I must get out of this city." Bill groped for the phone and dialed a West Virginia number.

The phone rang five times before a groggy voice answered. "Hello."

"Smooty? Is that you?"

"Yes. Who is this?" Lee Smoot, Camp Greenbriar's director, answered.

"It's Bill. Bill Waldron."

"Bill!" Lee's voice came to life. "It's great to hear from you, but whatever inspired you to call at this ghastly hour? It's three o'clock in the morning."

"Oh ... Um ... Ah ... I'm sorry. Um ... It's eight o'clock here. Um. I didn't realize the time…"

"Where are you calling from?"

"Um…Switzerland. I went to see a specialist. I forgot the time difference. My apology."

"No problem, Bill. Are you joining us this summer?

"Yes. That's why I called. My specialist gave me the all-clear."

"That's great news, Bill. We heard about your accident and kept you in our prayers. The camp wouldn't be the same without you. Can you be here on June eleven?"

"Absolutely! Another thing, Lee. Can you fit my son, Rory, in as a junior counselor?"

"If he's got even half your spirit, sure."

"Fantastic, Lee. These overseas calls cost a fortune so I'd better go. See you then?" Bill lay back and fell asleep over the city noise.

***

Awakening late the next morning, Bill's head felt like a gang of gandy dancers were sledgehammering spikes into his brain. He switched on his bedside radio to the sports talk station. A half-hour later, he pulled himself out of bed, took three aspirins, and soaked a towel in steaming water. *'At least the hot water works in this place.'* He wrapped the towel around his head, collapsed into a chair, and craned his neck on the backrest.

"I think the Sixers should trade up for a higher draft pick." A caller said on the radio.

"Who would you trade?" asked the talk jockey. "That will have to wait. First, some business, then back to your call."

Three grating commercials later, the talk jockey spoke, "It's one o'clock. The sixth of June. Now, back to our caller. So, who do you think the Sixers can trade for a draft pick?"

"Oh no! Dammit!" Bill pulled the towel over his eyes. *'Today's Dick Allen day at Mitchell and Ness.'* Ignoring his headache, he threw on his clothes. "Dammit!" He donned last night's puke-encrusted shirt. After putting on clean clothes, he sprinted three blocks through the early heat wave's 90-degree heat and 95 percent humidity.

***

Bill bolted through Mitchell and Ness's front door looking like a near-drowning victim. He panted and gasped for breath. The three blocks felt like a marathon. He handed his number 15 peppermint pinstriped Phillies jersey and 45 rpm. record disc of *'Echoes of November'* to Mitchell and Ness manager, Ray Jannelli, like a relay baton.

"Bill! Great to see you!" Ray took Bill's items. "I'm sorry, but you just missed him."

"No." Bill closed his eyes and jerked his head back. "Tell me you're kidding."

"Don't worry about it. He'll be at the memorabilia convention next week. We'll introduce you as if you're important."

Bill winced.

"I'm sorry. I didn't mean it that way…It's just that…"

Bill held up the halt sign. "It's okay. I'm used to it." He gritted his teeth and shook his head. "I'll be in West Virginia next week."

"I'm sorry, Bill. I told him how you were a devoted fan, and I told him about your accident. He waited an extra hour for you."

"Bill! How are you?" Peter Capolino, Chief Executive Officer of Mitchell and Ness, loped down the mezzanine steps. "I heard you were back on your feet," He laughed. "I didn't know that you were swimming already."

"I could use a cool swim." He chuckled. "Now that I missed meeting Dick Allen, I feel like using the Ben Franklin Bridge as a diving platform." Bill smiled. "It's good to see you, Peter."

"Don't worry. Dick Allen will be at the memorabilia convention."

"Yeah. I know. Ray told me. Unfortunately, I'm going to miss the convention as well. Terrible disappointment."

"He waited an extra hour just for …"

"Yeah, I know. I only have myself to blame."

Ray walked over and handed Bill his jersey and record.

"I'll tell you what," Peter took the jersey and record from Bill. "Leave the stuff with me. I'll see to it that he signs it. I'll keep it here for you until you get back."

"Yo, thanks."

"I've got some fantastic new items. Come on back. I'll give you an exclusive."

Peter and Bill walked through the array of sports treasures. "You don't know how great it feels to be here again. Instead of selling this stuff, you ought to charge admission just to come in and look."

Peter smiled. "Thanks."

It stood in the corner of the back room.

Its backrest had three horizontal slats placed about six inches apart. Five-seat slats tightly fit like sections of an Acropolis column. The wood was chipped. The red paint was faded. Patches of rust on the steel frame couldn't rob the double ribbon-shaped armrest of its beauty.

"My goodness! Is that?" Bill pointed to the item.

"Yes, it is," Peter said. "Skip 'Memory Lane' Clayton confirmed it for me. It's authentic. It's the real thing."

"Where did you ever find it?"

"At a barn sale in Amish country. The funny thing about it is that sports artifacts were the farthest thing from my mind. Yet there it stood."

"Is it for sale?"

"No ...It's a get-well gift for you."

"A gift? I can't just take it."

"Yes, you can. Now, stay healthy and look both ways the next time you cross the street."

Bill missed meeting his boyhood hero that day. Yet he took home a piece of history. Baseball and his own. A genuine Shibe Park seat.

# Chapter 11

The June heat pushed the mercury to near-record highs. The circles of Dante's Inferno best gauged the humiture. *'Thank God I'm leaving this combustion chamber for West Virginia's mountains.'* Bill took a deep breath. *"Rory joining me depends on you, buddy, let's do this.'* Put a quarter in a payphone. *'Better not call her office. He might answer.'* He chose to punch her home phone number. An answering machine told him to reach her at a number with a suburban prefix. *'Just great. I paid a quarter for that. Now I must deal with only one worse than him.'*

Bill tapped the seven-digit number. A recording told him to insert another quarter. As it rang, he tightened his lips, saying under his breath, "Please, Laura, answer the phone. Not your mother. Please ..."

"Laura Chilton. Can I help you?"

He looked skyward, whispering, "Thank you, God. Laura. It's me. Bill. Could I please come out and talk with you? I wouldn't ask you if it wasn't important."

"Is it so important that we can't talk right now? On the phone. You know how my mother ..."

"In person, please. It's critical. It's about Rory."

"Very well, Bill. I'm also very concerned about him."

"Can I see you this afternoon? Say, two O'clock?"

"Yes. I'll be waiting for you."

"Another thing, could you please prepare your..."

"You still like pinning the tough ones on me. Don't you?" Laura paused before chuckling, "Don't you worry. I'll handle my mother. See you at two. Goodbye."

*'Mission accomplished. That's boot camp. Now for the war.'*

Bill chose the Paoli Local train over jamming his poorly air-conditioned Nova on the Schuylkill expressway. After a restive half-hour journey, he arrived at the Wayne, Pennsylvania, station. Built during the golden age of steam, the Wayne train station looks like something a master model railroader would design for his layout. Built between 1882 and 1884, it consisted of two Victorian buildings flanking the rail lines connected by a tunnel. The main building sat on the south, or windward side of the tracks, and was integrated into the business district. Facing the tracks, the main station featured a two-story Victorian square tower with a pyramidal turret. Facing town, a second-story section had two windows and a gabled roof. *'I'm here for a purpose. A purpose too important to tackle on an empty stomach.'* Rather than take the tunnel under the station, Bill went to a tiny wooden structure across the street, north of the station. Bill considered John's Village Market the Italian Hoagie champion of the Philadelphia area.

Slabs of Italian meats and cheeses topped with lettuce, tomato, and onions, enhanced with tart spices and sweet peppers, all inside an Italian roll, make a sandwich more delectable than even a Cole Porter song could describe.

Bill sat on the westbound platform of Wayne Station, ate his hoagie, and psyched himself for a life-altering meeting. He wiped his mouth, tossed the hoagie wrapper in the trash, and walked to Laura's family home.

Bill prided himself as a neighborhood guy, yet he enjoyed walking along Wayne's meandering, narrow streets and its leafy, asymmetrical lots. The spacious turn-of-the-century homes of Queen Anne, Tudor, and colonial revivalist styles contrasted with the city's compact row houses. *'Here we are. The Chilton home. Veronica Chilton... Upper class my eye! The old bag. Incapable of the slightest civility to her son-in-law. Eighteen years. For eighteen years, I was married to her daughter. Never once, no, not once, did I ever cheat on or strike her precious little princess. Yet she thinks I'm worse than Hannibal Lecter. And what the Hell is wrong with my family anyway? We expressed more love and put in more hard work in a day than that bitch in an entire decade. Here we are, Bill,*

Bill walked down a driveway toward the Chilton's bucolic double-story home. Ivy climbed its stone walls, much like those of Wrigley Field. Wooden blue-gray window shutters added to the house's charm. Bill took a deep breath and rapped on the front door.

A slender, elegant, white-gloved woman in her early sixties answered. She gawked at Bill as if a stray cat deposited him. "Laura ... He's here." Veronica pulled a face and looked away. Laura appeared and mumbled into Veronica's ear. She got in one last sneer before departing.

A light green sun dress delicately draped Laura's lithe figure. "Why don't you wait on the patio? I'll meet you there in a moment."

Lounging on the slate patio, Bill smelled the flower garden and listened to songbirds and a distant dog barking. Two minutes later, Laura joined him. She handed him a cold glass of lemonade.

"Thanks, Laura." Bill inhaled deeply through his nose. "I'll give your mother credit. She is one heck of a gardener."

"Remember the arrangement I left in your hospital room?"

"Yes. Thank you. They were lovely."

"Guess where I picked them?" Laura laughed gaily and steered her gaze toward the house. "But don't tell you know who." Laura's quip broke the tension. They laughed together. "Well, Bill, I know you're not here for my mother's hospitality, or to talk about gardening."

"Yes ... Um ... About Rory ... Uh ... You know that I'm going to West Virginia to work as a camp counselor ... Um ... I've arranged for Rory to come with me ...As a junior counselor ...I of course need your ..."

"Yes. I can't think of anything better."

"What?"

"I said yes…"

"That's what I thought you said…"

"Yes, Bill. I can't think of anything better." Laura leaned forward and placed her right hand on his.

Bill's heart sputtered.

"A summer in West Virginia is what our son needs. At first, I denied that a problem even existed." Laura retracted her hand, looked upward, before inhaling deeply. "Next I blamed you." Laura's pupils dilated as she gazed at Bill. "Yet I realized that you were always there for him and that you gave him your best." Laura grasped Bill's hands. "I'm sorry, Bill. I really am."

"You have nothing to be…"

Laura held up her hand. "I fell into a trap, Bill." Laura closed her eyes and sighed. "I thought I could find fulfillment through my career. As a wife, as a mother, I thought that would fall into place. After all, I believed I could do it all. Now, I look at you ... No, no, I'm sorry." Laura looked downward and shook her head. "That didn't come out right."

"It's okay. It's okay." Bill squeezed her hand.

She reciprocated. "You were right, Bill. Rory is running with a bad crowd. Very bad. We're losing him, Bill. Please take him to West Virginia. He's only sixteen, yet he is at a crossroads. Bill, I'm entrusting his future to you."

Bill and Laura embraced.

"I'm sorry to interrupt, Laura," Veronica placed her white-gloved hand on Laura's shoulder, "it's time for your hair appointment. After all, it's not every night that one sees Hildegard Behrens perform the lead in *Tristan and Isolde*. Not everyone has the connections to get such an exclusive invitation. So, look your best for Burt."

# Chapter 12

Bill strolled into McCusker's tavern's north entrance. "Hey! Look who's here." Ted Bodanski walked around the bar and slapped Bill's shoulder almost hard enough to knock him over. The other patrons lined up to shake Bill's hand. "Maybe I should get hit by a car." Ted folded his arms. "The only time I got such a reception was after making that scoop and score against Nebraska."

"If a car hit you, it would be totaled, and you would walk away." Bill laughed. "Look at you. What did you do to yourself while I was out, and I mean out?"

"I went on a new training regimen. I lost twenty pounds while increasing my bench press by thirty pounds. Even better," Ted smiled as wide as his shoulders, "I passed the Eagles' physical. In just two weeks, I'll be in training camp."

"He did it himself. He didn't even have a mysterious female faith healer help him pass his physical like me in '61."

"Ed Braceland! What brings you back?"

"I heard you came back from Never Never Land." Ed shook Bill's hand. "So, I had to see for myself. Someone else made a special trip to see you." Ed pointed to the south entrance. "There he is."

A small bespectacled man walked into the tavern.

"Oh my God!" Bill beamed and darted over to the door. "Frank! Frank Cipparone! Great to see you." Bill shook Frank's hand.

"Yo Ted!" A patron shouted. "Ed's here, but he hasn't bartended in years. That leaves only you. How about it?" He held up an empty glass.

Ted turned to Bill and Frank, "I'd better take care of business."

"So, how are you, Frank? I've often seen you interviewed on TV."

"You first. After all, you're the one who just left the hospital."

"Where do I begin? I can't believe I'm sitting here talking to you. This may sound crazy, but when I was in a coma, I relived the final weeks of the 1964 baseball season."

"Nineteen-sixty-four? You poor guy. How about I knock you over the head again? Maybe this time you'll get lucky and relive October of 1980."

"Hey, I relive Tug McGraw telling New York to take this World Series and stick it, every day. Seriously. When I say re-lived, I mean re-lived. Sights, sounds, touch, but not just baseball. You as well, Frank. Try to understand what I'm saying. Here I am talking to Frank Cipparone, the distinguished economist. Yet just a few weeks ago, I spoke to Frank, the thirteen-year-old. It was so real—too real. I gotta admit, I'm still having trouble sorting it out."

"Have you spoken to anyone about this?"

"Yes." Bill laughed. "The first one wanted to give me shock treatment and Thorazine. The second kissed me. I don't want either from you."

"I absolutely won't kiss you. I'm not packing a cattle prod either, but would you settle for a beer instead of a Thorazine?"

"Sure. Thanks."

"Kissed you, huh?"

"Yeah, she's a nurse. As sweet as they come. Cute too. I'm still legally married to Laura and doing everything possible to reconcile with her. Yet it all seemed so right."

"Have you called her?"

"I've called her a once. I know Laura is seeing someone else, but I'm still confused about whether to ask her out. She's a great gal. Understanding. Caring. Easy to talk to. Common sense...Good sense says, 'ask her out.' But I still love Laura, and if there is a sliver of hope ..."

"Even so, you shouldn't let this new girl ..."

"Liz."

"You shouldn't let Liz slip away. Ask Liz out. You say she understands your situation ..."

"She does."

"Then what is stopping you? Hedge your bets, so to speak."

"Hedge my bets? Is that economic advice?" Bill Chuckled.

"I get it." Frank laughed. "Seriously, you've told me Laura is seeing that lawyer, Burt Jenkins, so why not Liz for you?"

Bill tensed his lips before downing his beer. "My concern is that seeing someone else would fully release Laura to that Jenkins creep. Would I receive a favorable custody arrangement with my son if I were to go up against two lawyers? I see fighting for Laura as fighting for my son. This is my last night here. Tomorrow, Rory and I are going to West Virginia for the summer. I hope a summer at Camp Greenbriar will sort both of us out. Although the stakes are higher for him."

"No, they are just as high for you."

"Like Rich Ashburn would say, 'Oh brother, you can say that again.'"

"Pardon the interruption, but Bill, it's great to have you back." Joseph Loviglio extended his right hand. Bill shook hands without looking at him. Joseph then turned to Frank. "How will the administration's latest tax hike affect..."

As Joseph and Frank engaged in an esoteric exchange on law and economics, Bill ordered his first bourbon.

Five minutes later, Joseph slapped Bill's arm. "Glad you landed on your feet. Hang in there." He walked away.

Bill skewed his face, "Geez, Frank, can you believe that guy? Only a Burt Jenkins associate...Not only does he come wearing a custom-tailored three-piece suit, but he doesn't even loosen his tie or undo his top button. 'Glad you landed on your feet?' 'Hang in there?' I never knew law school taught clichés 101." Bill wryly shook his head and sipped his bourbon. "Well, I've talked enough about myself. How about you? You surely lead an interesting life."

"That depends on your perspective. More than a few accuse me of being a boring stuff shirt. Traveling, family separation, airports, hotels, restaurant food, it gets old in a hurry. Despite the recognition and respect ..."

"Better your two R's than my two K's. Krap and the Kesmon."

"Touché." Frank smiled. "Although, unlike you, I'm not making a difference."

"What? How can you say that? I've seen you on national TV."

"Yes, but each time I devise a new idea, someone else has an equally qualified counter. You're the one making a difference. You teach. I don't teach. I give a monologue in front of several hundred blank faces. Have you seen the movie, *Stand and Deliver?*"

"Yes, of course. The movie about a teacher who teaches disadvantaged Los Angeles youths calculus."

"Well, not only have I bought the video, I've almost worn it out. That's what teaching is all about, Bill. Heck, that's what living is all about."

"Then why don't you do it?"

"I always ask myself that. Maybe I'm a coward? Maybe I'm selfish? I've got a tenured university post, I'm locked into a

mortgage, and I've got my kids in expensive private schools."
Frank gulped his beer. He  signaled for another. Bill slid a five-
dollar bill forward. Frank waved him off. "I just can't bring myself
to give it all up." Frank quaffed  more  beer.  "Quite  a  world  we
live  in.  It's  like  the Middle Ages again. Only  now  the famous
are  the  lords  and  the  obscure  the  serfs.  The  masses honor the
famous, even if they're dishonorable people. Many esteem me for
reaching the top of my profession. Yet the  truth is, I don't  have
what it takes to make a difference."

"Nonsense, Frank. Surely you can serve the community in
other ways."

"Oh, sure. I give to charity and do volunteer work." Frank
sipped his beer. "But is that enough?"

"It sounds to me like you're doing all you can. How did
today's lecture at Penn go?

"Fine. The usual. I say my thing; they listen and take notes.
After the exam, I'm forgotten."

"Don't be so cynical."

"I'm  not  being  cynical,  I'm  being  truthful.

Bill, I came back to do more than lecture. Wharton offered
me a post a year back. A f t e r  a l l ,  m y  f a t h e r  w a s  a
h i s t o r y  p r o f e s s o r  a t  P e n n .  Now I'm  seriously
considering joining the economics department. I have no qualms
about life in Illinois. We're living in a quiet suburb with good
neighbors. Nonetheless, things have changed,  and  not  for  the
better. The residents are so paranoid about burglaries that they've
turned their houses into compounds. Wooded areas and playing
fields are now condo developments or strip  malls.  You  need  a
permit  to  play  on  what's  left  of  the  green  areas.  The  only
games  or  sports  my  kids  play  are  school  or  community-
organized. All  that  regimentation and, win, win, win." Frank
downed his drink. "I taught my son half-ball in our backyard. Yet
never will he experience the joy that we had." Frank winced.

"Kathlene and I have hankered to move back to this area for some time now. I even did some advanced house hunting. I checked out the suburbs. The Main Line. Elkins Park. Jenkintown."

"I wish you wouldn't mention the last one."

Frank chuckled. "Unfortunately, they're the same as suburban Chicago. Yet our old neighborhood. Right here in South Philly. It hasn't changed since I left over fifteen years ago. I received more salutations on my first day back than I would in a year in the suburbs. If not with a kind word," Frank chuckled, "a good-hearted one anyway. South Philly will always be South Philly." Frank signaled for another round of drinks. "This is my point, I still don't see much evidence of crime or drugs. Heck, the residents take pride in this community. They'll never allow it. I see kids playing fun games of pick-up half-ball, basketball, or street hockey ..."

"They even sometimes sing du-wop on the street corner."

"Yeah. That too. Bill, I think I want my family to live here. Maybe I'll accept that offer from Wharton and buy a big house in Girard Estates. My kids can attend St. Joseph's Prep or Central. I've seen all that I need to see. Now I realize that our old buddy, Jeff, is right. South Philly is the Garden of Eden ..."

"Jeff's a bimbo. If he thinks dispatching taxis to pay rent on an unairconditioned row house is the Garden of Eden, then why don't he swap me his place in Belair and let me sit around making T-Rexes?"

"Hank! How are ya, buddy?" Frank stood and shook his hand. Bill did likewise. Frank's 145 pounds and Bill's 180 pounds combined fell short of Hank Tubbs's weight. "I'm doing O.K.—for now. How I am in five minutes depends on that overgrown bimbo." Hank pointed at Ted.

"Overgrown? Talk about the pot calling the kettle black. Yo! I can bench press your weight." Ted pounded his Sasquatch chest. It thudded like a bass drum. "And lift mine overhead. A big difference, Fats."

"Am I supposed to reward you with a banana for that? Now make me three cheese steaks and three orders of cheese fries. If ya manage to keep the stinkin' mayo off my steak, I'll rehang your tire from the ceiling." Hank looked at Frank and Bill. "Mayo on a cheesesteak? Can you believe that simian bimbo? Last time he put mayo on my cheese steak."

"Three cheese steaks?" Frank asked. "Three orders of cheese fries? Are you sure you need all of that?"

"Need? What does need have to do with it? Stick to the numbers, Prof. Life's too hard to deny myself the good things."

"It's also too short, to shorten it with too many good things."

"Hey? Who do you think you are? Dick Gregory? Richard Simmons? Just how long do you plan on stickin' around? Bones. My old man just turned 70. He ain't been under 350 pounds since he was fifteen years old. He says a day without a cheese steak is as bad as a day without beer. Besides, the older I get, the younger and cuter the girls get. That's all I need to do...Lose weight so that one of them likes me. Then my wife will kill me for sure."

"Good point, Hank." Frank chuckled. "I'll let you in on a little secret. After first arriving at the airport, I had the cab driver detour to Geno's Steaks before taking me to my hotel."

Hank said, "If ya love cheese steaks so much, and you keep sayin' that South Philly's the Garden of Eden, why don't ya move back here?"

"Believe it or not, Hank, I was just saying to Bill..."

"Hey, everybody!" Spanky McMullen, puffing a huge stogie, crashed through the door like a runaway steam locomotive.

"That's the reason why not," Frank muttered.

"Bill! Bill Waldron! How much did they fine you?"

"What?"

"The city. How much did they fine you? For splitting their road with your head! HA! HA! HA! Oh, look who's here. The professor. Yo Frank, how much did ya make this year at Northwestern? For tellin' the students how to run a business. How much for your *Wall Street Journal* column? Tellin' businessmen how to run their business. And for your spots on cable news? Tellin' the entire country how to run their business?"

Frank shook his head

"Come on prof. How much? A hundred grand? A quarter of a million?"

"All right. I'll give you a hint. Less than the Phillies' futility infielder."

"Still too much. You've never run a business in your life. Tell you what. I got a hundred. Run this place for a week. Even money says ya bankrupt the joint." Spanky clouded Bill in cigar smoke. "I'll give ya two to one—if ya don't serve this one! HA! HA! HA!" Spanky slapped Bill's back. "And ten to one, i f ya let the man who indulges gastronomically, astronomically— eat free! HA! HA! HA!" Spanky billowed cigar smoke on Hank.

Hank said, "You know sumptin? You who could mate with a horse and sire a mule. There are three things worse than mayo on a cheese steak. Hot beer. Wet toilet paper. And a smart ass!"

"Better my ass be smart, than big enough for a howdah."

"How—what?"

"Howdah. An elephant saddle! HA! HA! HA! Yet another reason why my ass is smart, and yours is ..Ju m b o ! HA! HA! HA!"

"Yeah, well I got 405 reasons why your ass is gonna be grass. Here's the first five." Hank put a beefy fist before Spanky's face. "The other 400 battery rams it through your bowling ball head! Next, I sit on ya bowling ball body!"

"Sit on me?" Spanky then feigned like a professional wrestler begging for mercy. "No! No! Please! Okay. truce! truce!"

Ted returned and placed Hank's food tray on the bar.

"Yo, professor?" Spanky puffed on his cigar. "How much you say Jeff's getting for making movie dinosaurs?"

"I'm not sure," Frank answered. "Look at it this way: Jeff lives in a swank house in Belair."

"Well, what do you say, we crate Bodanski and send him to Hollywood. We can all split the take and buy ourselves vacation homes in Wildwood! HA! HA! HA!"

"Do you know the address of a movie studio?" Bill put his hands on his hips.

"No. Just put down a Polish return address. At least that will get rid of the lug-head."

"I bet you don't know a Polish address." Bill pulled his face.

"Just slash an 'X'! HA! HA! Ha! Even the loafers at the Post Office can figure out it's for Poland. HA! HA! HA!"

"Look, Chucklehead. I'm about this close," Ted held his thumb and forefinger a half inch apart, "to giving you a lunar address."

"Yeah. Well, why don't ya make like an Eskimo—and get yourself a polar address!" Spanky guffawed. The others didn't. "Get it? Polar—Poland?" Spanky winched his head forward, face frozen in anticipation of Bill, Frank, and Hank's laughter.

"We got it," Frank nodded. "It just wasn't funny. Yo Ted. You've heard every Polish joke in the book. On a scale of one to ten, where do you rate that one?"

"About a negative three. Yo, McMullen, if you want to piss me off, you got to get better material."

Frank placed his arm around Spanky's shoulder and led him away. "I'm afraid your gags are getting a bit stale. You better sit over here and recharge."

Upon Frank's return, Ted said, "Way to go, professor. You truly are a genius." Ted drew a frosty draft beer and gave it to Frank. "This one's on me. Heck, for shutting him up, you ought to get the Nobel prize."

"How are ya guys?" George Mueller, clad in his red Phillies Whiz Kids jacket, asked. "Glad you're all right, Bill. You must like Chicago, Frank. Now, instead of one losing baseball team, you get two."

"Yeah, George, but even if there's an all-loop series, I'll remain a Phillies fan."

"You're still lucky. At least you get to watch meaningless games in a meaningful place. The first time I saw Wrigley, the green grass, ivy climbing the walls, all that history, even I said, 'Let's play two.' Hell, by the time I reach the hinterlands of that concrete glob called the Vet and squint at the ant-sized players, toilin' on that funny-colored, phony turf, I say, 'Why didn't I stay home and watch the game on TV?' I heard you guys talkin' about the '64 Phillies. Got a question for ya. What seasonal defensive record did the '64 Phillies set?"

"Most triple plays. Three," Bill beamed.

"Very good, Bill." George sipped his whiskey. "I'm sure you know the first player to win Rookie of the Year and Most Valuable Player in the same year."

"Yeah," Hank put his cheesesteak on his plate. "Fred Lynn. The '75 Red Sox. Even I know that one."

"Well, if the '64 Phillies didn't blow the pennant, Fred Lynn would've been the second. For my money, Dick Allen was the 1964 National League M.V.P."

"We've been fortunate," Frank smiled. "Just three years after Dick Allen left, Mike Schmidt arrived."

"Don't forget. Dick Allen returned to Philly and joined Mike Schmidt and Greg Luzinski." George folded his arms "It didn't work out as we wanted. Nevertheless, it was still cool."

"That's exactly what we need now," Bill said, "another Mike Schmidt or Dick Allen. Someone to make an uninteresting game interesting. No matter how dull the game, I never left until Allen or Schmidt got their final licks."

Frank added, "Can you imagine if Dick Allen had Mike Schmidt's temperament."

"I'll say," George downed his whiskey. "I don't want to get into the problems Richie had here. Still, other than possibly Mantle, Richie Allen had more talent than any ballplayer I'd ever seen. And I've seen them all. My father always compared him to Jimmie Foxx. I agree. Remember, Jimmie Double X once hit 58 homers in a season. Allen never hit 58 homers in a season, but he had that kinda power."

"Everyone always talks about what Dick Allen would've done," Bill signaled for another beer. "Let's talk about what he did do. Frank Robinson won the American League Triple Crown in 1966. Yet one can make a case that Dick Allen hit better per at bat. He hit over 350 career homeruns and slugged a career .530 something. Not too shabby."

Frank pinched his chin, "No, it isn't. Yo. I've got another trivia question for you all. Who, that once was a Cardinal, has a monument in Yankee Stadium?"

"It can only be Johnny Mize," George answered.

"Not even close."

"How about Roger Maris?" Bill shrugged his shoulders. "He finished his career with the Cardinals."

"No. Not Roger Maris either."

"Let me take a wild stab at this," Hank dipped a French fry in cheese. "Enos Slaughter. He played some for the Yankees."

"He spent fifteen years with the Cardinals, and he did finish his career with the Yankees," Frank grinned. "But they never erected him a monument. Okay. Give up? Pope John Paul II. They honored him with a monument after he celebrated mass at Yankee Stadium."

"Boo." Ted leaned on the bar. "That's something McMullen would come up with."

"Yo. Guys. Speaking of the bimbo...it didn't take long for him to 'recharge." Hank pointed to Spanky, lividly cracking jokes at other patrons.

"Why don't we talk to him?" Frank raised his hands. "See what goes on inside his head."

"What?" Bill shook his fists. "Talk to that chucklehead? He used to annoy my father as much as he annoys me."

"You, Spanky." Frank stood. "We want to talk to you."

"All right. What are we going to talk about? Baseball or economics. How about both? After all, the Phillies' deficit in games under .500 is deeper than the country's deficit in dollars! I overheard you guys say you never left a baseball game until Dick Allen or Mike Schmidt got in their licks. Well, I never leave a tennis match until Martina Navratilova gets in her licks! HA! HA! HA! Martina Navratilova? Licks? Get it? HA! HA! HA!"

Bill clenched his teeth and shook his head. "Geez, Frank, you just had to call him over."

"Come on, Spanky." Frank threw his arms up. "Enough. You run your own plumbing company, and you're the commissioner of a bowling league. Surely you didn't get that just by cracking jokes."

"It helped." Spanky's demeanor changed. "If everyone tried some laughter, surely there'd be fewer ulcers, hypertension, and heart attacks. Quite a world we've got. Look at the news on TV. It's like a 24-hour snuff movie. And what about this politically correct nonsense? Oh no, black people don't have higher butts than white people. Oh no, the Asians are great drivers. Oh no, the Irish never drink too much. Oh no, the Scottish aren't cheap. Oh no, Puerto Ricans never shop at K-Mart. Oh no, Bodanski there is smart. Oh no, Hank here is thin. Oh no, Frank has a he-man body. Oh no, Bill always gets life's lucky breaks. Give me a break." Spanky opened his arms. "Maybe someday we can learn to not only laugh at ourselves but at each other as well. Waldron, do you think your family," Spanky jabbed his finger at Bill, "was the only one to suffer a loss?" Spanky craned his head at Bill. "Let me tell you something. By the time I was your age when you lost your father."

"Thirteen."

"Before I was thirteen, I had lost a sister to polio and my father to the war. If you think my father died just doing his patriotic duty, think again. Times were so tough for some back in the day that going to war was the only way to earn a paycheck and keep their family fed. Believe me, without laughter, my family never would've survived."

"Fair enough," Bill nodded. "But why do you have it in for Bodansky and the Polish?"

"I don't have it in for the Polish. I nail everybody. Especially those with no sense of humor. Bodanski's father and I were co-captains of McCusker's bowling team. He was some kind of bowler, and he cracked a mean joke too. But unlike his lug head son, he could also take a joke."

"Come on, Ted's not a lug head," Bill sipped his beer. "After all, he went to college for four years."

"Phys Ed."

"So." Bill pointed at Spanky. "You didn't even finish eighth grade."

"Let me tell you something, Waldron. I was the oldest surviving male in my household. When my uncle offered me a job as a plumber's apprentice, I took it. I'm glad I did too. I may not hold fancy degrees like you and especially Frank. But I've got an honest, money-earning trade, and I'm damn proud of it."

"No one suggested otherwise," Frank opened his hands. "Nonetheless, why can't you get along with Ted? You both lost your fathers at a young age, and you both worked hard to support your mothers. I know you have differing personalities and temperaments…Still . . ."

"I don't hate Ted. I'm glad he's here. After all, He's the easiest target in the joint."

"Yo Ted." Frank waved to Ted. "Why do you always get so angry with Spanky?"

"I don't know. Maybe 'cause he's an asshole."

"Come on, Ted. Get real. Try again."

Ted put his hands on his hips and looked Spanky over. "Well …compared to a serial killer, rapist, or thief."

Ed Braceland looked over from the end of the bar. "As you know, Ted, he used to say the same things to me." Ed laughed. "The exact same things. Frank, you're a second-generation professor. You've got smarts. How do such cheesy jokes still upset people after so many years?"

"I'll answer for him." Bill sipped his beer. "I'm an English teacher, but I know it was a Frenchman, Jean-Baptiste Alphonse Karr, who said, 'The more things change, the more they stay the same'."

"So, what do you say, guys?" Frank also lifted his glass. "A toast to our neighborhood. South Philly. The Garden of Eden."

Frank, Bill, Hank, George, Ed, Ted, and Spanky touched glasses.

# Part IV

# Chapter 1

Jerry Blavat played the Intruders' *'Love That Is Real'* for Bill's final mile in Philadelphia. Flags of every nation flank the Ben Franklin Parkway, where the Franklin Institute, the Museum of Natural History, and the Rodin Museum are found. Bill drove along the Parkway toward the Philadelphia Museum of Art. Each turn of his Chevy Nova's balding tires enlarged the colonnaded Acropolis-like structure. Magnificently perched atop a hill, its cascade of steps arose between dancing fountains as an ascent to paradise.

Rory looked back at the multiform Philadelphia City Hall. A statue of William Penn stood over 500 feet on top. He cocked his right arm at a 90-degree angle with a scroll in hand. "Hey, look! William Penn's got a hard-on!"

Bill chuckled. "When I was your age, my buddies and I used to joke about that too."

"Really? No Kidding?"

"Yeah. No kidding. It looks as if we share something in common after all." Bill smiled.

"No. What I meant was, I didn't think city hall was built back then."

Bill laughed. "Okay. Very funny. Good one, Rory. I owe you one."

"Yeah, well, you and your buddies are getting pretty fuckin' old, ya know."

"Hey. Hey. Enough of that. Let's not start cursing in my car."

"Woo! Like this thing's a holy chariot or somethin'. Come-on man. Mexican illegals ride around in better than this. Burt's got a brand-n e w Porsche. Now *that* is a car. This is a shitmobile."

"Rory! I'm warning you."

"Hey, chill out man. Don't start acting like I asked to be here. Ya know, like, it's you and mom that condemned me to your hick camp for the summer. Don't act like you're doin' me a favor."

"Just wait until we get there. Then you'll thank me. Have you ever imagined real mountains and real roaring rivers?"

"Yo, Mom and Burt took me to the Poconos. I didn't think it was so great."

Bill grimaced and wrung the steering wheel. "Poconos are just hills and streams. I'm taking you to mountains and  rivers. Believe me, anyone in the city would gladly trade places with us."

"Yeah, right, like, you know, ain't Fairmont Park country enough?"

Bill stopped at a red light. "Ain't? Who taught you to talk like that?"

"When in Rome, do as the Romans. You are banishing me to hillbilly country, ain't ya? And ya know somethin' else, man? I don't know what ya think draggin' me off to Hicksville's gonna accomplish. But if you think Scorpion's gang can't haul out there in half the time your shitmobile takes—you is wrong man."

Bill pulled his face at Rory, "Yeah, man. Well, I know he ain't gonna. 'Cause you mean as much to Scorpion's gang as the batboy does to the Phillies."

Rory fast-forwarded his Walkman c a s s e t t e  t a p e p l a y e r  to Lucifer Jack's patricide song. He upped the volume to full blast and pushed the speakers an inch from  his father's nose. Rory next pantomimed the speakers into his ears and turned away.

*Honk! Honk!* "Yo! Greenlight pal!

"Yeah! Yeah! Yeah!" Bill yelled back as he stepped on the accelerator. The Parkway soon veered east around the Art Museum, becoming East River Drive. The tree-skirted route twisted beside Fairmont Park's Schuylkill River. Bill admired the river's waterfalls and colorful boathouse row. Although still within the Philadelphia city limits, he felt he was in the country. The 8,000-plus-acre Fairmont Park is the planet's largest intra-urban park. Herds of white tail deer roam its woods like impala on the African savannah. Fishermen often catch huge bass, catfish, and pike in the Schuylkill and Wissahickon Rivers.

Bill drove his Nova beside the Schuylkill River barely faster than the crew teams rowing on the river. He felt a tinge of sadness in leaving Philadelphia, yet excitement for West Virginia. He felt like a boxer entering the most important fight of his career. Glancing at Rory staring at the floormats while black-metal rock rattled his skull, Bill knew round one was lost.

By mid-afternoon, Bill and Rory had crossed Pennsylvania Dutch country, driven down through Western Maryland, and into Virginia's Shenandoah Valley. They could still receive the Phillies radio network's 50,000-watt clear signal. Bill listened to Harry Kalas deliver the Phillies' ninth inning.

The Phillies trailed the New York Mets by two. The Phillies were down to their last out. They had runners on first and second base. "Long drive!" Kalas yelled. "It has a chance! Outta here! Homerun! Unbelievable! The Phillies win the game, 5 to 4, on a two-out, three-run homer! What a great ending to a great game!"

"Yeah! Yeah! All right!" Bill yelled while honking the horn.

Rory jerked the Walkman speakers from his ears. "Hey man, what are you having a spaz-a-taz over?"

"You should've listened! The Phillies just won on a two-out, bottom-of-the-ninth, three-run homer!"

"Big deal man. So, they're what? Now, twenty-eight games out of first place instead of twenty-nine, and what's that guy's problem?" Rory pointed at the radio. "He acts like the chumps just won the World Series."

"Actually, they're only twenty-one games out."

"Wow, man. I'm impressed. Now don't bother me unless it's important." Rory stuck the Walkman speakers back into his ears.

Bill pulled out the speakers. "You've been listening to that stuff for five straight hours. Isn't it branded in your brain yet? Don't you think it's time you talk to me?"

"Branded on the brain? Look who's talking. Hey, this music just came out. You've been branding your brain with the same songs for thirty years. Now I've got some catching up to do." Rory returned the speakers to his ears.

"I mean it." Bill pulled out his speakers. Give it a break. Why don't we listen to the post-game show?"

"Yeah, right. Baseball sucks."

"Well, they play a lot of it where you're going. So, get used to it."

"Yeah, sure, and I bet they also listen to," Rory mocked country singing, "Your cheatin' heart," Rory smirked. "Give me a break. And, ya know, the way the Phillies play, the batboy is their MVP. The next sound you hear may be Scorpion's gang overtaking this shitmobile." Rory drilled his Walkman speakers back in his ears.

Bill sighed and listened to the post-game show. By dusk, he wound along a West Virginia road that meandered through the mountains like a stream. Driving high on a ridge gave a sensation of flying. Low in a valley was like driving through a sea of greenery. He stopped, s t r e t c h e d, a n d t o o k i n a cliffside view. Admiring the tourmaline sky and riverside village far below, Bill said to Rory, "I agree with the John Denver song, *'Almost Heaven.'* What do you think?"

Rory's eyes opened wide before mimicking W.C. Fields. "All in all, I'd rather be in Philadelphia."

Bill sighed and threw up his hands, "Come on, let's go. I want to reach camp before dark."

Rory gazed at the view again,

Bill and Rory approached from the highway. His first view of the camp to Bill made him think of how Columbus felt on first sight of the New World. Camp Greenbriar rests on a level valley, ensconced in the Blue Ridge Mountains and beside Greenbriar River. The camp had Canvas tents over wooden floors, seven tennis courts, an outdoor and indoor basketball court, three baseball diamonds, and winsome, Fenway Park green, wooden buildings.

Bill pulled his Chevy Nova next to the camp office. Camp director Lee Smoot waited on the office's porch. Lee walked up to Bill's car and shook his hand an instant after alighting. "Great to have you back." Lee was mid-thirties, squat, and robust. A perpetual smile crowned his triangular face. Lee was Camp Greenbrier's spirit.

"Thanks," Bill beamed. "It's great to be here."

Rory climbed out of the car.

Lee walked around Bill's car. "This must be Rory."

"Yes, it is." Bill walked over to his son.

"This is Lee, the camp director.

"Hello, Rory. What do you think of West Virginia thus far?"

"It's okay, I guess."

"Just okay? I imagine it must be a letdown for you as well, Bill."

"Um..No…What do you mean?"

"Compared to Switzerland."

"Oh, yeah, yeah, not at all. The Greenbriar Valley is every bit, if not more, beautiful than Switzerland."

Dave Boettger, Lee's second-in-command, joined them.

"Dave!" Bill shook his hand. "How are you?"

"I'm fine, Bill. I'm glad you could make it. I understand you had some drama over the winter." Dave was almost identical to Lee in height and build. Dave, however, had shaggy red hair as opposed to Lee's short, dark brown hair. Dave's red mustache and poorly shaven face also clashed with Lee's clean-shaven face. Dave, furthermore, had a more serious demeanor. If Lee was Camp Greenbrier's spirit, Dave acted as its conscience.

"You're a master of understatement, Dave."

"Look, Bill, we don't want you to take any risks on our behalf. Should you experience complications from the accident, tell us. We may be in a rural area, but there is a good hospital nearby."

"Thanks for your concern, Dave. But I feel great, and my doctors gave me the a-okay." Bill pointed his right thumb skyward.

"Glad to hear it."

Lee wore a white T-shirt boasting a Fenway Park green canoe fronted by two crossed paddles. Above it were the letters *Camp Greenbriar*. Lee looked over Bill's "Sixers" tank top. "Glad you came prepared. I'm putting you in charge of basketball again."

"I was hoping you'd say that. Thanks, Lee." Bill glanced at Rory, who was staring at a mountain. "Oh, I'm sorry, Dave. This is my son, Rory."

Dave extended his right hand. "I'm Dave Boettger. The director of the senior camp. I'll be working with you more closely than Lee."

Rory looked away as he limply shook Dave's hand.

"Your father is one of our best counselors. I expect no less from you. You'll be working with Sayres Dudley in the craft hall."

"I don't know nothin' about crafts."

"That's not important." Lee added, "Cooperate with Sayres, set a good example to the campers, and you'll do fine." Lee beamed. Most importantly, have fun. It's contagious."

"Yeah, sure. 'Fun, fun, fun 'till daddy took the T-Bird away.'"

Lee pointed. "Hey! Here comes Sayres."

"How was your winter, Sayres?" Bill shook Sayres's hand.

"Fine, thank you." The handsome, crew-cut, clean-shaven Sayres Dudley looked like a white-hatted co-star from a Roy Rogers western.

"I'd like you to meet my son, Rory. He'll be working with you in the craft hall."

Sayres looked at Rory's Lucifer Jack T-shirt. His smile dropped as if two fishing sinkers were hooked to his mouth's edge.

Rory glowered back at him.

"I run a tight ship at the craft hall." Sayres's eyes hardened. "The campers arrive tomorrow. Their safety and happiness depend upon us."

A bugler played taps.

"We've got a big day tomorrow," Sayres continued. "I don't know about you guys. But I'm turning in early."

Dave smiled, "Let's make this a memorable summer."

"The best," Lee nodded.

# Chapter 2

"Everyone put the basketballs away." Bill tossed a basketball to a camper and watched them put the basketballs in a large wooden box. "Same time tomorrow, kids. Race to the river. Last one eats boogers. The big waterslide is waiting."

Bill walked to his tent, grabbed his disassembled Shibe Park seat, and took it into the craft hall. Busy campers hammering and sawing vibrated the craft hall's wooden plank walls like a tuning fork. Sayres pitched in to help two twelve-year-olds build a model sailboat. A Junior counselor conducted four younger boys banging metal sheets into the coda of a dish. Rory sat on a chair, one foot on the floor, the other on the tabletop. His Walkman drowned out the clamor. He shook his head to the music. Bill leaned his Shibe Park seat against an adjacent table.

"Yo! Rory!" Bill shouted. "Why aren't you working with the kids?"

"Huh?" Rory's head jerked upward.

"Pull out your headphones." Bill pantomimed removing headphones. "The kids. You ought to be helping the campers, not sitting on your ass listening to what you call music."

"Ah, lay off, man." Rory brushed him off. "What do the little nose pickers need me for?"

"Rory, you've got a job. A responsibility. You're a camp counselor. The kids are what you're all about."

"Excuse me. The kids are what you are all about. Like, who signed me up for this? Not I, Jack."

"Don't tell me you're complaining again. You tell me, Rory, what better place to spend a summer?"

"Wherever a hog can take me. Which is anywhere, man. That beats the hell outta getting stuck in this noisy barn with a bunch'a brats."

"Yeah, yeah, yeah. Look. When you actually own a motorcycle, I'll listen to your whining. 'Till then, give a little something back to the camp. Start by helping me with this."

"What's that?"

"A genuine 1909 Shibe Park seat."

"Looks more like a shithouse seat." Rory pointed to the seat. "Cut a hole in the middle, put a tin pot beneath it, and you'll make it useful."

Bill took a deep breath and counted to ten. "You won't say that after we restore it." Bill  took two pieces of sandpaper from the adjacent table.

"Who is we, white man?"

"One for you," Bill smirked and handed Rory a seat slab and a piece of sandpaper. "And one for me. Go to it, Rory." Bill clasped the slat in his left hand and sanded it vigorously with his right hand. He paused. *'An essence? An energy?'* Bill closed his eyes. *'Do not baseball exploits—Frank Baker, Jimmie Foxx, Del Ennis, or Dick Allen slugging a long ball... Eddie Plank, Lefty Grove, or Robin Roberts blazing a fastball...Eddie Joost or Tony Taylor spearing a grounder...Richie Ashburn running down a 440-foot fly ball—result from a capacity to do work? Energy?'* Bill tapped the seat slat on his right palm. *'How many people? How many thousands of people energized this piece of wood? The tension of the 1950 and 1964 Phillies pennant races? Their joy over the Whiz Kids' triumph and their despair over the '64 collapse. Did I ever sit in this seat? My father? His father? Maybe notorious fans like the Huckster, or Bull and Eddie Kessler, or Pete "Foghorn" Adelis. What of their outrage over serial losing? What about the energy of Martin Luther nailing his 95 Theses to the door of the Castle Church in Wittenberg, or Thomas Jefferson writing the Declaration of Independence, and John Hancock and 55 others signing it? Their passion changed human history. Is this just a piece of wood, or did it absorb the energy of the thousands who sat on it?'* Bill closed his eyes and looked upward.

*'Yes. I can feel its essence, its energy. It's not just imperceptible; it's tangible.'* Bill again closed his eyes. This time, he squeezed the seat slat at full strength. The clamor of the craft hall and the Greenbriar River buffeting against rocks became crowds cheering, and the beat of clapping hands and stomping feet.

"Mr. Bill. Will you help me paint my canoe paddle?"

"Huh?" Bill's head snapped sideways.

Rory was gone.

"Help me paint my canoe paddle. Please?" A nine-year-old, red-freckled boy with a canoe paddle longer than himself stood before Bill. "What color do you think I should paint it?"

"How about blue, like the river?"

Bill painted his Shibe Park seat red, like the Phillies, instead of green, like the A's. After reassembling, the seat seemed to dare Bill to sit in it. He dared not. Instead, he locked it in his trunk.

# Chapter 3

Three evenings later, Bill teamed with two teenage Junior counselors and a slew of eleven and twelve-year-olds for a softball game against Lee and his junior counselor teammates. Lee had assigned Rory to help with the activity. He failed to appear.

In adult games, Bill mostly hit singles. Against kids, he belted 'em like Jimmie Foxx and Dick Allen. The youngsters expected no less. They relished the chance to better a counselor.

Bill stepped up to the plate. He stood tall and straightened his shoulders upon seeing the young outfielders move back.

Lee lobbed Bill a fat pitch. He stung a crisp line drive. At best, a double in an adult game. Here, the eleven-year-old left fielder ran in a circle before waving his glove no closer than 20 feet of the ball.

"Hi-yo!" Bill yelled before running the bases.

"Come on, Jimmy! Let's get him!" Lee shouted.

After chasing down the ball, Jimmy relayed it to a junior counselor, who threw it to Lee. Bill headed home. Lee tossed to a twelve-year-old catcher. He tagged Bill.

"You'rrre out!" Lee raised his thumb.

"All right! All right!" The twelve-year-old jumped up and down, holding glove and ball upward.

"I doubt you'll brag about getting tagged out by a twelve-year-old." Jim "Turtle" Palmer, a senior counselor, slapped Bill's arm. "But you can brag about this afternoon's baseball game and getting struck out by Jim Palmer."

The fun-spirited game continued after the sun descended behind the mountains. They played into the gloaming until Lee called the game on account of darkness. Everybody won. After all, they stopped keeping score at 20 each. Lee slowly collected the equipment, giving the campers ample time to disperse. "Bill. May I have a word with you?"

"Sure, Lee. Shoot."

"You are aware that I assigned Rory to tonight's activity."

"Yes. I am"

"Bill, this isn't the first time he's gone AWOL."

"I'm sorry, Lee."

"I know you are, but is he? Apologizing on his behalf won't solve the problem. Bill, our policy is that we never hire a sight unseen counselor. Anything else would be negligence on our part. Rory's chronic absences are bad enough. But that's only part of the picture. We make a huge impact on these youngsters. Our obligation to the kids and their parents is to set a good example. Bill, you know Rory's behavior and language fall short of our standards."

Bill pursed his lips and nodded.

"I don't have to tell you that I only gave Rory this opportunity because of you."

"I realize that Lee, and I appreciate it."

"Okay, please, Bill. For everyone's sake. Talk to him. Don't let things get out of hand."

Bill marched across the athletic fields as if fitted with blinders. *'What now? Scorpion is gone. Burt Jenkins is gone. No Veronica Chilton to indulge him, none of Laura's progressive child-rearing methods, now it's me and I'm the one failing.'* Bill bee-lined to the junior counselor shack. Like the other Camp Greenbriar wooden structures, the JC shack was painted Fenway Park green. Bill marched in. Four junior counselors were playing cards. "Do any of you know where I can find Rory?"

A tall, slender boy put his cards on the table. "He usually hangs out at Richmond Dock with John and Ricky."

Camp Greenbriar has two swimming areas. The main waterfront abides on a wide, deep, and still stretch of the Greenbriar River. Here, an L-shaped wooden dock floats on barrels extending almost 50 yards into the water, providing a protected, current-free bathing area. A square dock, a spring diving board, and a lifeguard stand float within it. A fleet of canoes are moored beside it. The campers' favorite feature is an eighty-foot water slide. About 200 yards upstream, Richmond dock plays into a narrower, faster river frontage divided by Woofus Island. The campers opting to swim here stack stones into a makeshift damn that channels the river into a small rapid that the kids ride in inner tubes or air-bagged pillowcases. Descending the riverbank path, Bill heard Rory's voice above two other boys.

"Shit! Someone's coming! Throw it in the bushes."

Bill arrived. Six bloodshot eyes met him. A stench like burning hemp steeped the air.

"Throw it in the bushes, huh?" Bill pointed at Rory. "Get it, now!"

"Yo, Dad? What are you talking about?

"Don't mess with me. Get it!" After a four-second pause, Bill lunged to the weeds and picked up a plastic bag filled with parsley-like leaves. "What's this, John?" Bill shoved the bag inches from a pimpled boy's face. "How about you Ricky?" He did likewise to a black teenager. "Okay, Rory. You know everything. Why don't you tell me?" Bill sprinkled the substance into the river.

"Hey, man! That's Columbian! It cost me a hundred bucks a lid!"

"Take it out of your motorcycle fund."

"Up yours man. I'll get more money from Grandma Chilton. She'll do anything to fuck you over." Rory hunched his shoulders. "Man, even Burt's cooler than you."

"Don't talk to me that way! You get your ass to your tent and in bed! Now!"

Rory looked at John and Ricky. "Woo! He's sending me to bed without my milk and cookies."

John and Ricky sniggered.

"What's so funny? I'm sure Lee and Dave will laugh themselves silly over this." Bill held up the remains of the marijuana. "Your choice. Either go to your tents or get on the next bus home." John and Ricky opted for tents.

Rory stayed. He hunched his shoulders and narrowed his red eyes. "Yada, Yada warden, yada, yada. Just because you sentenced me to this peanut gallery, don't mean I gotta take gettin' treated like a child."

"First, stop acting like a child. Do you think you're tough? Don't make me laugh. Talk this way to a real warden and watch how fast your ass gets kicked. And believe me, you are on the express lane to prison."

"Ha, ha, ha. I'll laugh even harder when it's your ass getting kicked by Scorpion."

"Scorpion will be your cellmate."

"Huh! Scorpion can kick any Philly cop's ass. And he's teaching me everything he knows."

"Oh, so you two are invincible. Well, I have bad news for you. When you and Scorpion wind up cellmates, you won't be his apprentice." Bill paused for effect. "You'll be his wife! Now beat it! You're not worth anything to me stoned. Tomorrow, when the dope has worn off, we'll talk."

Rory sneered, spat a gob of phlegm into the dirt, turned, and walked away.

# Chapter 4

The sunny Camp Greenbriar days swiftly flew. '*If only I could get through to Rory. At least he's here. No more bad influences.*' Bill stood by the outdoor basketball court and gazed at the mountain's morning mist. '*I know I'm healing. The camper's love and respect sure beat Laura's rejection and worrying about her non-rejection of Burt Jenkins.*' Bill stood up straight and thrust his chest. '*Yes. Almost Heaven. I'm finally getting a grip on my life.*" Bill bounced a basketball to a ten-year-old boy. "Come on, Michael Jordan! Take it to the hoop!" The boy clanked a lay-up off the rim.

"Charles Barkley in for the rebound." Bill cruised in and snatched the ball. "Back to Larry Bird." Bill chest-passed the ball to a tall, blond eleven-year-old. He made a bucket. "All right!" Bill shouted. "Swish!"

Lee's voice came over the loudspeaker. "Bill Waldron, please report to the office."

"Okay, guys, I gotta go. Everybody over to Rusty's side of the court." Bill pointed to Rusty Milligan. His junior counselor assistant was playing H.O.R.S.E. with three campers.

Bill wandered toward the camp office, figuring it was routine.

Lee, Dave, Sayres, and John Rand, the head counselor and a welterweight college wrestler, sat around a table. Their faces met Bill as the Policemen's faces waited in his living room on the fateful October of '64 afternoon.

"You Better sit down, Bill." Lee pointed to a chair behind the table.

Bill's buttocks sat; his stomach remained standing.

"Bill," Lee closed his eyes and took a deep breath. "This is my toughest duty as camp director. It is always my last possible resort. This is the first time in four summers ..."

"Cut to the chase, Lee."

"Bill, we are left with no choice. Effective immediately, Rory is dismissed from his duties as a Junior Counsellor."

"What? Dismissed?" Bill's throat clenched.

"I'm sorry, Bill." Lee pursed his lips. "Rory left us no choice."

"Bill," Sayres folded his hands. "Rory's attitude toward the craft hall is appalling. I've never encountered anything like it. If he shows up at all, he sits in a corner smoking cigarettes, reading comic books, and shutting himself out to his music. If I ask him to do anything, he swears at me. Even worse, he swears in front of the campers."

"He misses his duty assignments so often," John added, "that we assume he's going to skip. When making my duty rosters, I'm forced to appoint an extra counselor."

Lee made eye contact with Bill, "If laziness and irresponsibility were the only issues, we'd be willing to carry him for your sake ..."

"For my sake." Bill threw up his hands. "What other favors are you going to do me?"

Dave turned to Bill, "Lee is trying to say that his influence on the campers and other junior counselors is unacceptable. I know that he's drinking and smoking pot with some of the older campers. That alone is cause for summary dismissal. I've done my best to work with him, but his response is always the same. Flagrant insubordination."

"Insubordination? Come on, Dave! What kind of hard ass do you think you are? You walk through the tent area like a damn drill sergeant. You flip over kids' beds if they're not made right, and you turn over their trunks if they fail your damn inspection. Give me a break! This isn't the army. You're doing more than dishonorably discharging my son." Bill raised his palms. "You're putting him before the firing squad!"

"We're not punishing him," John said. "It's more like removing a cancer."

Lee stiff-armed the halt signal. "Nobody is pulling rank, Bill. Your son is openly hostile to authority. What if his attitude rubs off on the campers? Can we allow them to take it home to their parents and teachers? Bill, I've explained this to you before."

"I'm not being picky, but that music he blasts from his tape player." Sayres tightened his lips and shook his head. "The parents send their children here to remove them from such influences, not have them reinforced."

Bill felt as if he was watching the proceedings from the ceiling.

"We're holding this meeting for your sake," Lee folded his hands. "Do you want to tell him yourself, or would you rather we tell him?"

Bill breathed heavily, remaining silent.

Lee continued, "You can put him on a bus or you can drive him home yourself. We want you to remain; although, if you feel Rory's dismissal will make staying awkward, we'll release you from your contract. I'll leave that decision to you. This entire matter grieves me. However, our foremost obligation is to the campers and their parents."

"Come on, Lee. What about me? Please. You're a parent. You must understand. You're signing my son's death warrant. This summer is both of our last chances. Please Lee. One more chance."

Lee looked downward. He raised his head and looked at Dave, Sayres, and John's glum faces.

Bill's face froze.

"I can't give him another chance." Lee looked deeply into Bill's reddened, misty eyes. "What I will do is delay enactment until Wednesday morning. If your son changes markedly, we'll delay one more day. If he stays on track, we'll delay another day. Otherwise, he's gone. No further debate."

"You better go, Bill. Lee just overrode my judgment." Dave looked at his watch. "You've wasted five precious seconds."

Bill plowed toward the craft hall. "This is just great. Okay, Scorpion, take my son. I failed to mold him into a good citizen. He's all yours now. Help him be all the delinquent he can be. Hello Laura. You know that chance you gave me with our son. Guess what? I blew it. Go live your new life with Burt. Don't worry about me. I'll be at the Kesmon waiting to die. That won't take long."

Bill blitzed into the craft hall. He asked Kit Holland, a skinny, squirrel-faced junior counselor, "Have you seen Rory?"

"Rory? Are you looking for Rory in the craft hall? You gotta be kidding. This is the last place you'll find him."

"Do you know where he is?"

"Does anyone?"

Bill marched to Rory's tent. No luck. He marched to his tent, reached into his wall locker, and grabbed his Shibe Park seat. Next, he rifled through his duffle bag. It was hidden under stacks of clothes, untouched since his Camp Greenbriar arrival. After dumping the contents on the floor, he found his bottle of Wild Turkey bourbon. He hid it under his shirt, took his Shibe Park seat, and loaded it all in his car. He drove out of camp, his rear tires propelling pebbles.

# Chapter 5

Bill placed his Shibe Park seat on a cliff edge. Several thousand feet above the Greenbriar Valley, the viewing site is called Indian Lookout. As it did for Native Americans centuries before, the post rendered Bill a virtual magic carpet ride over the Greenbriar River, Camp Greenbriar, and the picturesque town of Alderson. He sat in his Shibe Park seat and slugged bourbon straight out of the bottle. *'Drown it out, Bill. Drown it out.'* Bill jammed earphones into his ears and cranked up the volume to Rich Allen and the Ebonistics, *'Echoes of November.'* Bill closed his eyes and let his head drift backward. He floated away. Far away ...

He awoke in the back seat of a luxury Limousine.

"Welcome, Mr. Waldron," said a voice with a mild British accent.

"My name is Carruthers. I am your guide." Curruthers's black suit was custom-tailored, uncreased, and unsoiled. Bill tilted his head, *'It looks like something you'd wear to your own funeral. He looks sixty-something.'* His Gray hair was full and groomed, yet dry and brittle. His piercing, deeply grooved eyes sheened like gray alabaster. A blank expression revealed no emotion. Bill reached for the door. *'He looks like a cross undertaker and Dickenesque hanging judge.'* Bill moved his hands to the sides of his head and closed his eyes. He opened them again. Carruthers remained. "You're still in my car."

"No! This is impossible."

"Believe it."

Bill smelled the leather upholstery. Even in his distressed state, he admired the craftsmanship of the car's interior. He rapped his knuckles on the door and felt a gentle yet palpable vibration. Urban blight passed by the window. "Hey, we're in a city. No way Jose. I'm still in the mountains of West Virginia."

"You're in North Philadelphia."

"How? Why?"

"We were expecting you."

"Who?" Bill again surveyed the car's handcrafted, gold-trimmed leather interior. "Are you the mafia? Why would you want me? I never gamble; I've never borrowed money. I'm just a teacher."

"I am not the mafia."

"KBG? CIA? Am I a guinea pig in a mind control experiment? If so, why me?"

"I assure you, I represent no temporal government."

"Have I gone insane?" Bill again squeezed his head and slumped downward. After ten seconds, he jerked his head upward and looked to his side. *'He's still here.'*

"Perhaps. Perhaps not." Caruthers looked straight ahead.

"What am I doing here? Assuming I am actually here."

"You are actually here. We have special plans for you."

"Plans? What plans? Why won't you tell me who you are?

The car stopped. "Look out the window." Carruthers leered at him.

Bill gazed out the window. Shibe Park. "Jesus Christ!"

"Ahh! Don't you ever—ever—say that name! Never again!" Carruthers prodded. Before Bill's eyes, Curruthers aged ten years. His facial lines increased in number and deepened in magnitude. His hair erupted as if electrically charged. Curruthers's eyes pierced him, yet Bill felt a wave of relief.

"Now I know what happened to me," Bill patted his chest. "That van never hit me. I never went into a coma. Nor was I ever in the hospital. Rory and I didn't go to West Virginia. I never left Philly. Some Jim Jones, David Koresh-type cult brainwashed me!

Shibe Park is just an illusion from deep in my memory bank. Well, the jig is up. Now I know who you are and where I am. You can't hold me hostage. I'm getting out of this car right now and taking a taxi home. Don't try to stop me!"

"Get out! Get out now! I never want to see you again!"

"Fine." Bill alighted, slamming the door behind him. He looked back and saw Carruthers signal to a stoic, onyx-colored, Frankenstein-looking chauffeur. Their shiny black Bentley vanished into *traffic. 'Did they dump me into a movie lot, or what? This Shibe Park is no illusion.'* Shibe Park still stood in all its arched and gabled glory. Scores of horn-blaring mid-twentieth-century automobiles jostled on the streets. The sidewalks teemed with a mass of people wearing out of fashion attire. He banged on the wall of Shibe Park. A solid thud. Bill's Urban Oz was no movie set. He wasn't in West Virginia anymore.

"Get your pennants! Get your souvenirs!" Another hawker yelled, "Peanuts! Popcorn!"

Bill gasped; his body stiffened. A vendor tried to sell him a pennant emblazoning a Phillies cap and orbiting baseball with the inscription, "Phillies 1964 National League Champions." "How much for a program?"

"Fifteen cents, pal."

Bill gave him a nickel and a dime and grabbed a program. The game: The Philadelphia Phillies vs. the Cincinnati Reds. The date: 21 September 1964. He asked two passersby, "What year is it?" No one answered. They gawked at him with skewed faces and scampered away. Bill soon noticed many people ogling him; some laughed openly. A chill ran down his spine. Fear and cold. Satin basketball shorts and a cotton "Camp Greenbriar" tank top T-shirt generate little warmth on unseasonably frigid Philadelphia fall night.

The mythical Oz at least had warm weather; the fictional Dorothy at least had her dog, Toto, as a companion. Bill felt more helpless and alone than a lost child. Sitting against Shibe Park's facade, he draped his shirt over his knees and pulled his legs to his chest. He shivered. His mind numbed to a stupor. Several pedestrians tossed him their spare change. One charitable couple sent over their ten-year-old daughter with a dollar bill. "Awww ... You poor man." She dropped the note beside Bill.

The midnight black Bentley reemerged, floating down Lehigh Avenue like a dark cloud across the twilight. The car stopped at Bill's curbside. Its door creaked open. Inside, it was dark as a crypt. Nevertheless, sitting like a cold, abandoned ragamuffin made Bill scurry into the vehicle.

"You're back." Curruthers's hair was brushed. Yet the ten extra years of wrinkles endured.

"What have you done? Where have you taken me?"

"I'm taking you to a ballgame. I think you'll find this more suitable attire." Curruthers handed Bill a pair of long trousers, a flannel shirt, a pullover sweater, and a khaki jacket. "Unless, of course, you prefer cold and ridicule."

Bill started pulling the garments over his shorts and tank top.

"I didn't think you'd enjoy the cold. The ridicule, I'm not so sure."

"This is insane."

"Insane? Enough! We've proven that without me you're a helpless child. From here on, I expect unswerving obedience."

Entering Shibe Park elevated Bill's state of mind to euphoria. The Cadillac and Coke signs perched upon the leftfield bleacher roof seemed like Renoir's and Van Gogh's at the D'Orsay. Billboards advertising Goldberg's Peanut Chews, Wise Potato Chips, and Alpo Dog Food hung on the left field walls as Giotto's, Rembrandt's, and DaVinci's at the Louvre. The Ballantine beer scoreboard surpassed a Renaissance tapestry; what a miraculous sight! A young Tony Taylor and Cookie Rojas tossed a ball to one another. *pop, pop* echoed each catch. Bill gazed upward at the light tower's multiple suns. He admired Pete Rose, Johnny Callison, Frank Robinson, Dick Allen, Vada Pinson, and Alex Johnson stretching on the green grass. Bill clutched his program. He opened it and stared at the date: 21 September 1964. Bill spotted the Reds John Tsitouris warming up in the left-field bullpen. Art Mahaffey warmed up for the Phillies in the right-field bullpen. Bill still doubted his sanity, but not his whereabouts. He followed Curruthers down the aisle, lower deck, third base side. Arriving at their sixth-row seats, directly online with third base, Bill noticed his seat was freshly painted. It was also a slightly dissimilar shade of red. Bill stared at the seat.

"Yes, it is." Carruthers sat in the seat next to him.

"You mean, it's the same seat that Mitchell and Ness gave me?

"Yes. Now stop asking questions and sit."

Bill reluctantly sat.

"You do know what game you're watching?"

"Yes."

"Nauseating, all these happy people. I wonder how cheerful they'd be if they knew what we know. Don't expect anything different this time either." Carruthers pointed to the field. Tony Gonzalez again opened the first by slapping a single. Dick Allen again sacrificed him to second. Just as almost three decades prior, Johnny Callison and Wes Covington failed to drive Gonzalez home.

"Why am I here?

"Don't question me. Show gratitude. I am granting you the impossible. How many baseball fans wish they could experience a Shibe Park game again? To see deceased or elderly ball players again in their prime? Millions? Besides, I'm going to allow you to right an injustice."

"Right an injustice? What do you mean?"

"Patience."

Several times, Bill tried looking upward. Each time, a mysterious force paralyzed his neck.

"I know what you're thinking. Watch the game. I decide when or if you see your father."

Next inning, Bill watched the Phillies again strand Clay Dalrymple on second and Tony Taylor on first.

Top of the third. The loudspeaker announced, "Now batting for the Phillies. Number fifteen. Richie Allen."

"I remember exactly what happens next. He's going to scorch one off the scoreboard."

Carruthers glanced at Bill in stoic silence.

Dick Allen swung his 42-ounce ash bludgeon easily as cracking a willow switch. He redirected Tsitouris's slow screwball into a rising missile. It crashed against the scoreboard.

The fans leapt and yelled. Bill merely stood and smiled. Like a true connoisseur, he cherished every microsecond of his fantastic vision—Dick Allen—again the consummate 22-year-old athlete. Instead of watching the Frank Robinson to Pete Rose to Chico Ruiz relay, Bill admired Dick Allen sprinting around the basepaths. *'What a superb fuse of power and speed.'* Bill already knew the outcome. Last time he witnessed from the upper deck. This time, his viewing angle exceeded umpire Augie Donatelli's. He called Allen out. *'Son-of-a-bitch.'* Bill threw up his hands. *'He was safe.'* While Gene Mauch argued the call, Carruthers asked, "Bill, have you ever wanted to kill somebody?

"Kill somebody? What? You're crazier than me."

"I bet you'd like to kill that umpire. He just cost your hero the M.V.P. and your team the pennant. Isn't 'kill the ump' a baseball maxim?""You're insane."

"Am I? How about Burt Jenkins? I bet if you watched him intimately knowing Laura, and you know he does, you'd like to grab Richie Allen's forty-two-ounce bat and bash his brains out."

"How did you know about Burt Jenkins?"

"I know everything about you. You only imagine it. I've seen it. Burt doesn't just do Laura in her bed. Sometimes they do it on top of his desk during office hours. He stole your wife. What have you done about him? Nothing. Scorpion took your son. Again, what did you do about him? Nothing. Now, Augie Donatelli just gave St. Louis your hometown's pennant. Why should St. Louis win again? Not counting this one, they've already won nine pennants to the Phillies' two. So, who do you hate most, Bill? That umpire or the city of St. Louis?"

"Hate?"

"Yes. Hate. Don't try to kid me or yourself. I bet you wish you could murder the umpire, then watch the Mississippi burst its banks, like brimstone from the depths of Hell, and sweep St. Louis and all their goddamned pennants into the Mississippi River. Hundreds of thousands of those pricks losing their lives and homes."

"No. No, I don't feel that way. I don't hate them at all. I think St. Louis is a great baseball town. And they brew Budweiser. There's no bad blood between St. Louis and Philadelphia. New York? That's a different matter."

"We'll deal with New York later. That umpire just gave St. Louis the pennant. Tell me, how much do you hate him? Enough to do to him, what you want to do to Burt Jenkins?"

"What?" Bill shook his head. "You're sick."

Caruthers grinned like a hyena.

"All right, look." Bill's head jittered. "I'm angry with the ump. Okay? Big difference. He missed a call. Heck, I make mistakes in my work too."

"You got that right. Ha! Ha! Ha! Why do you think your wife left you for Burt? Because of your technique or an anatomical failing? What else is new? You also failed as a parent, a teacher, a camp counselor, and even as a baseball fan. Face it. You're a do-nothing loser. You'll always be a loser. How fitting that you dwell in the city of losers."

"Shut up! Shut up, you old bastard! I don't have to take this." Bill stood and tried walking away.

"Ha! Ha! Ha!" Carruthers laughed. An Arctic cold blast of wind quavered Bill's bones. "Just where do you plan on going? Man from the future? You're not in the Twilight or the Outer Limits. You're here with me. Ha! Ha! Ha!"

Bill stared at him.

Curruthers's smile bared no emotion. It looked like a leering gloat molded onto a waxwork. "Lack of common sense is not among your many weaknesses, Mr. Waldron. Sit down."

Bill sat.

"I think you know the score. Smoke?" Carruthers opened a gold cigarette box.

Bill shook his head and held up his hand.

"Surely you won't refuse a drink. What's your preferred brand these days? Does this look familiar?" Carruthers, like a skilled illusionist, pulled a bottle from his coat.

"Wild Turkey. Wait a minute ... The upper right-hand corner of the label is peeled back. That's the same bottle that I took to Indian Lookout."

"I thought you might miss it." Carruthers turned his right hand upward. Two glasses. After handing one to Bill, Curruthers poured.

"Words can't describe how impressed I am by your generosity." Bill shook his head, "sharing my own booze with me."

"I only reward obedience, Mr. Waldron. Besides, if not for me, your bottle would be lost in another dimension. Drink up. You need it to warm your bones on such a cold night. Tonight is the equinox. Winter draws nigh."

Carruthers stayed silent as the '64 Reds and '64 Phillies continued their scoreless 21 September duel. Bill enjoyed the experience, thinking, '*Instant replay was revolutionary in its time. Next came 'virtual reality'. I wonder what to call this. Einstein said it might be possible; so maybe I'm here—1964.*'

With one out in the Reds' sixth, Phillies M.V.P. candidate Johnny Callison gunned down Vada Pinson attempting to stretch a single into a double. Bill shook his fist triumphantly. "Yeah!"

"You act as if you saw it for the first time. You Philadelphians are surely optimistic tonight." Carruthers pointed at Chico Ruiz dancing off third base. "Need I remind you, of how he will steal your city's hopes and dreams and damn them to Hell. Unless you stop him."

Ruiz danced off third. He then bounced two steps closer to home. Phillies pitcher Art Mahaffey peered in for catcher Clay Dalrymple's sign.

"Stop him? Me? How?"

"Use your imagination."

Bill cupped his hands in front of his mouth and yelled, "Watch him, Art!"

"Shut up! Shut up, you fool! What is that going to accomplish?"

"I'm warning the Phillies pitcher."

"You fool! What if third base coach Otero hears you? He'll stop Ruiz from stealing home. So what? The best clutch hitter this side of Mantle is batting. Frank Robinson will drive Ruiz home anyway. No. I've got a better idea." Curruthers handed Bill the bourbon bottle. "Finish this." One shot remained.

Bill downed the final tot.

"Throw it on the field."

"What?" Bill tilted his head, raised his eyebrows, and slightly opened his mouth.

"You heard me. Throw the God-damned bottle on the field." Caruthers glowered at Bill. "Time is short."

Ruiz danced off third base. Mahaffey nodded to Dalrymple.

Everything stopped.

The players and fans froze like mannequins.

"What the…"

"I don't know who suspended time. It wasn't I. Now throw the Goddamned bottle before whoever did changes his mind."

"Suspended time?" Bill's jaw fell agape. "I have gone insane. Who commands such power?"

"Shut up and throw the Goddamned bottle."

"I can't throw a bottle on the field. I'm a baseball fan, not a soccer hooligan."

"So what? Hurry. Who will ever know?"

"I can't."

"I should have figured as much. We already know that you're a loser. Now you're a betrayer as well. Don't throw the bottle. Betray your city. Let injustice prevail. You coward! You traitor! Judas Iscariot lives again."

Bill cocked his arm, bottle by ear. A rich baritone voice spoke to him. "We trust the game in you."

Bill lowered the bottle.

"You sniveling bastard." Carruthers growled.

"We trust the game in you."

"We trust the game in you." George Kelly appeared to him wearing his 19th-century baseball uniform.

"Forget it." Bill handed the bottle to Carruthers. "The game does belong to me in spirit. But on the field, the game belongs to the players. I can never cross that gulf. Chico Ruiz stealing home was as much a baseball feat as Johnny Callison slugging a homer or Jim Bunning pitching a shutout. The Reds won this game fairly. The '64 collapse was horrible, to me, and to the city of Philadelphia. It's a game, not an injustice."

"What you are is a murderer. Is cold-blooded murder ever justified? Look up there." Carruthers pointed to the upper deck.

Bill looked. He gasped. His Father. Dennis Waldron. Seated with him as a thirteen-year-old. Frank and Jeff were also with him. Bill's heart skipped a beat. He clutched his chest and collapsed into his seat.

"Look at him! Stand up and look at him! He died because of you! You killed your father, surely as if it you stuck the knife in him. You're a pervert. A fiend."

"Don't listen to him." George Kelly floated above him. "You are here for a purpose. We trust the game in you."

"You knew it then and you know it now. You stabbed your father! Now you're killing him again! How vile! how loathsome is patricide? Hanging is too good for you."

The image of George Kelly had vanished. Bill again looked at his father and himself as a thirteen-year-old boy. He threw the bottle. During its descent, Ruiz broke for home. Bouncing on the cushion-like Shibe Park turf, the bottle remained intact. Umpire Donatelli ran onto the infield, arms upward. "Time!"

Mahaffey stopped his wind-up. Ruiz scuttled back to third. Only one player or coach noticed Ruiz's stunt. As Dick Allen retrieved the bottle, he concealed his mouth with his glove and advised his pitcher.

Art Mahaffey shook off Clay Dalrymple's sign. The catcher responded with a different sign. Art next made a pumping motion in his glove. Clay stood, hands on hips. Mahaffey steeled his face and repeated the motion. He now pitched from a stretch.

Ruiz broke for home.

Pitch-out!

The catcher stood between Ruiz and home plate like a barrel blockade. He tagged Ruiz out by the same margin that Andy Seminick tagged out Cal Abrams on 1 October 1950. Knocked aside, Ruiz kept his back to his teammates in the dugout.

Shibe Park was still as the bottom of the Mariana Trench.

Ruiz mustered the courage to face his teammates.

They shunned him. He crept back to the dugout. His teammates and manager treated him like a biohazard. His manager, Dick Sisler, grabbed his arm as he left the dugout to take the field. "Take the rest of the night off. Get dressed and take a cab back to the hotel."

When Ruiz reached his hotel room, his bags were already packed. A bus ticket to the Cardinals' AAA minor league affiliate in Jacksonville, Florida, was stuffed in his suitcase handle.

Carruthers laughed loud and sinisterly enough to scare Dracula and Frankenstein. Bill buried his face in his hands.

The sixth-inning dramatics leeched the life from the game. The remaining strikeouts, pop-outs, and weak groundouts did little to allay Bill's fear for his sanity and repulse over his dependence on Carruthers.

"Hotdogs, get your hotdogs," a vendor chanted.

Carruthers signaled to the vendor. Bill remained seated, gaze fixed ahead. Carruthers handed Bill two hot dogs. They warmed

Bill's hands. Their aroma perfected Shibe Park's mix of cigar smoke and stale beer. Chomping the appetizing tidbit reinvigorated Bill's awe. *'I am experiencing the impossible.'* Each week Bill played several lotteries. He dreamed of using his winnings to rebuild Shibe Park. After all, a Reds fan built a life-sized replica of Crosley field in Blue Ash, Ohio so actual that the Reds second baseman of the fifties, Johnny Temple, said upon seeing it, "First I got goose pimples, and then I started to cry."

Bottom of the nineth.  Like applying the paddles to a cardiac patient, Wes Covington jolted life into the scoreless game by nailing a Tsitouris delivery against the scoreboard. The speedy Adolpho Phillips pinch-ran. John Herrnstein batted. With the winning run on second and nobody out, Gene Mauch ordered Herrnstein to bunt. He laid it down the first base line. Tsitouris fielded, looked to third, then threw to first for the out.

"We want a hit! We want a hit!" the crowd yelled with hands clapping and feet stomping.

Clay Dalrymple hit the same routine grounder as he did decades ago. This time, the Reds drew in the infield to prevent the winning run from scoring on a groundout. Pete Rose charged for the short hop. It spun off his glove and into right field. Frank Robinson was playing shallow. He rushed in and barehanded the ball. He cocked his arm for the throw…He chose to hold the ball and trot to the dugout. Adolpho Phillips sprinted home with the winning run. The Phillies players left the dugout to greet him. The fans stood and cheered. "Congratulations," Carruthers extended his right hand, "You just won the Phillies the 1964 pennant."

Bill reluctantly shook his clammy hand. He felt himself fade like a film scene. Falling …Falling…Falling off the precipice of Indian Lookout. Bill's scream wisped through his throat like steam out of a smokestack. He snagged a shrub; its trunk bent like a fishing rod fighting a marlin as he dangled by one hand. The swaying landscape far below resembled a view through a stereoscope. Another yell, and Bill swung his other hand onto the shrub and shimmied himself onto the plateau. He lay in the fetal position, gasping and sweating. Five seconds later, he low crawled with his Shibe Park seat to safety. He drove back to camp on subconscious autopilot.

His search for Rory again proved futile. The camp appeared to exist on a different plane. Late afternoon light and shadows seemed as if screened by tinted lenses. The campers and counselors were playing baseball on each of the camp's three diamonds. Yet the attending banter and holler of the players, bat striking ball, and rawhide ensnaring horsehide, sounded to Bill as if seashells covered his ears.

He sat on a bench by the main basketball court and pondered asking someone to drive him to a hospital. 'Did a physical manifestation of the accident cause my bizarre episode? An aneurysm? A blood clot? Something potentially fatal? Fatal. Even worse—who would care? Sure, my mother, sister, and cousins would mourn for a few days. Laura will move in with Burt, and Rory will ride the back of Scorpion's chopper to jail or the morgue. If I check into a hospital, I'm outta Camp Greenbriar and my son's life. For how long would the tests take? How much later the results? The ensuing treatment could last deep into fall. Anyway, Dr. Greenberg confirmed no physical damage. Imagine telling the doctors about venturing into the past and talking with specters and voices. They'd send me back to Dr. Tryvye and commit me to a funny farm. No. I have one last chance with my son. I better seize it.'

Rusty Milligan, with basketball in hand, approached Bill. Rusty last year won a silver bowl for exemplary camp spirit. "Bill? Is something wrong?"

Bill looked up at the tall, slender, curly blond-haired junior counselor. "Um, no; just thinking."

"What about, Bill?"

"Nothing. Have you seen Rory?"

"Not since breakfast. Why?"

"It's important that I talk to him. When you see him, send him to me right away."

"Sure. Hey. How about a game of H.O.R.S.E.?"

"Okay."

Rusty sank a basket from the key. Bill followed with a brick. "An 'H' on you good buddy." Rusty grabbed the basketball and walked to the corner. "Are you ready for this one? Swish." Rusty tossed. "Ho!" he yelled as it caught nothing but net. "And if you can't match it, that's what you get—ho." Bill followed with an airball.

"What's the matter? Your mind surely isn't on playing."

"No, Rusty, it isn't. I must talk to Rory."

"I can see it's important to you. How about I help you look for him?"

Even with Rusty's help, the search again proved futile. *'My head feels like a helium balloon. It's not from drinking. This feels different.'* "Thanks for the help, Rusty. I think I'd rather be alone now."

"Sure thing, Bill. Would you like me to spell you as referee for tonight's senior basketball games?"

"Thanks. I'd appreciate that."

Bill took another look for Rory in the craft hall. He got an idea. He snatched a piece of rope. He went to his car, grabbed his Shibe Park seat, and went to the main waterfront. With the rope, he tied the seat, stern facing, to a canoe's bow thwart. He sat in the Shibe Park seat and paddled on calm waters behind Woofus Island until he reached a wide, calm hollow just past the island. Here lay Bill's favorite spot ... Pristine and natural, the cove's tree-sated escarpments secreted the outside world. He felt as if floating within a crystal bowl while meditating on the drifting white clouds on the azure sky. Bill turned up the volume as his Walkman and played Dick Allen's *'Echoes of November...'*

# Chapter 6

"You made me wait. Why? You changed history. You won the Phillies the 1964 pennant. Aren't you eager to see the World Series?"

Bill again awoke in a luxury limousine back seat. The same macabre-looking chauffeur drove. The leather and gold gilded interior of this car surpassed Curruthers' car. Moreover, Carruthers was not his host. Rather than a cadaverous old man, Bill's host looked in his prime. Trained jet-black hair topped his angular face. He had a hawk nose, a well-defined jawline, and a pointed chin with a trimmed Van Dyke beard. *'His narrow-set black eyes…They see right through me.'* Bill closed his eyes and shook his head. *'No. This can't be happening again.'*

"Surprised?" His host smiled, flashing polished, ivory white teeth. "My subordinate just finished with you."

"Carruthers works for you?" Bill's voice stammered at a higher pitch.

"Must I again apologize for him? I seldom approve of his style. Nevertheless, he has served me well for many a year."

*'How long? How long?'* Bill thought, *'Could a man in his mid-sixties serve under someone in his mid-thirties?'*

"Why the confusion? How long ago did Carruthers deal with you?"

"A couple of hours ago."

"Time moves differently in my dimension. The date is 11 October 1964. The Phillies, thanks to you, won the pennant. You arrived just in time. The Phillies lead the Yankees three games to none in the World Series. I am rewarding your service and obedience by returning you to 1964 so you can watch the Phillies win the World Championship at Yankee Stadium."

"Who are you?"

"Call me Drago."

***

The limousine braked parallel to Yankee Stadium's main entrance. A policeman opened the door for Drago and Bill. Bill shielded his eyes with his right hand from the sun glare off the Rolls-Royce Phantom. The car was gold. Not just the paintwork. Gold. Even more splendid than the car of Ian Fleming's Goldfinger. A police blockade parted the crowd for Bill and Drago. Bill gawked up at Yankee Stadium. Its exterior differed from Shibe Park's manor look. Yankee Stadium captured New York's skyscraper essence.

*'They're treating me like a star.'* Bill smiled and straightened his posture. Drago strolled nonchalantly to their lower box seats, three rows above the Phillies' dugout. Bill opened his eyes wide and raised his eyebrows as he looked up at the three tiers of seats filled to the brim with people. He admired the copper art deco frieze roof façade above and the Merrion blue grass and brown clay infield below. Bill stood proudly for the national anthem.

"Play ball!" The umpire shouted.

Tony Taylor led off the game with a single. Dick Allen flowed by scorching Whitey Ford's first pitch on a line over Mickey Mantle's head and into the Lou Gehrig, Babe Ruth, and Miller Huggins monuments. Mantle recovered it and threw it to cut-off man Bobby Richardson who relayed it to catcher Elston Howard. Too late. Dick Allen dove into home plate with an inside-the-park home run.

Bill beamed and quaked like a delighted child.

"Evocative?"

"I don't understand."

"Just a few weeks ago, you saw him hit a game-tying inside-the-park home run against the Milwaukee Braves."

"You mean in 1964?"

"You saw it again only a few weeks ago. Did this home run thrill you more?"

"This one seemed too unreal."

Chris Short struggled to hold the two-run lead. His fastball lacked velocity, and his breaking pitches had no snap. He sweated and panted after each pitch. Nevertheless, by changing speeds, the Yankee hitters battled to time his deliveries. His defense caught every solid opposition hit. Two timely double plays also bailed him out of jams.

Whitey Ford walked Bobby Wine to open the fifth. After a Chris Short sacrifice bunt, Tony Taylor drove Wine home with a single into center field. Dick Allen followed with a long single to right center, Taylor advancing to third. Ford then fooled Alex Johnson with a called third strike. Johnny Callison next stroked a drive into the rightfield stands. The Phillies led by six runs. The home run knocked Ford out of the game. Bill joined the scattered Phillies fans in a rousing ovation.

Chris Short continued winning his valiant battle against a tired arm, yielding only one run going into the eighth. With two out, Joe Pepitone lined a single to right. Tom Tresh walked. Elston Howard roped Short's first pitch foul passed third. Short froze him with a change-up for strike two. The next pitch came in at seventy-eight miles per hour, straight as an arrow. Howard smacked it down the left field line. Fair ball. Home run. The Yankees closed the gap to two runs. Chris Short leaned over, rested his hands on his knees, and gasped for breath. Gene Mauch didn't budge from the dugout. Short followed by hanging Cletus Boyer a curve. He drove it 420 feet ... into Alex Johnson's glove.

Al Downing retired the Phillies in order in their ninth. Pinch hitter Johnny Blanchard opened the Yankee ninth with a long flyout to left fielder Wes Covington. Phil Linz followed by popping out to Tony Taylor.

"How does this compare with the 1980 series?" Drago asked.

"Watching this is like living a dream. Of course, the 1980 World Series felt the same. Yet this is too surreal." Bill pointed to the Phillies players with one foot on the dugout steps, poised to run onto the field in celebration. Bill beamed. "But beating the New York Yankees is infinitely more satisfying than topping the Kansas City Royals."

"Considering what happened to your father, I can empathize with your bitterness. Nevertheless, don't allow prejudice to deprive you of life's greatest pleasures. New York is the world's greatest city. Period. Anything not found in New York does not exist."

Bobby Richardson walked on four pitches.

"You only hate New York because you're uninformed and unprivileged," Drago continued. "I want to change that. I must return you to your dimension when the series concludes. The Phillies don't need to win in a four-game sweep, do they? I can't control or determine the outcome of a game, but I can influence it. This morning, I incited a disagreement between shortstop Wine and Second baseman Taylor. Let's just say, they're not communicating."

Roger Maris rapped a game-ending groundball to Tony Taylor. He fielded and looked at second base to toss to shortstop Bobby Wine for the force-out. Bobby Wine hesitated to cover. Taylor's had to double-cutch before throwing it. Richardson slid in safely. Chris Short, looking exhausted as a polar explorer, glared with his hands on his hips. Wine and Taylor jawed at one another before resuming their positions.

"Chris Short looks distracted," Drago pointed at him. "I think you know what Mantle does to pitchers not exercising one hundred percent concentration."

The next occurrence did not belong on a baseball diamond but at a military testing ground. Chris Short hung Mantle a curveball. Mantle sprang his hips, torso, and arms like a medieval catapult. The baseball boomed off his bat like a light anti-armor missile. It crashed off the top of a steel support post in Yonkers (A leftfield upper-deck area so named because it's considered closer to the suburb of Yonkers than home plate) and rebounded clear to the infield. A tremor shook the stadium. Mostly owing to the ball's impact rather than over 67,000 screaming voices. Chris Short and the Phillies lowered their heads and trudged off the field.

"Admit it. Even though the Phillies lost, you enjoyed that Herculean feat."

Bill grinned. "Yup. Gotta admit it."

# Chapter 7

The Plaza Hotel's porters and doormen dashed toward Drago's Rolls-Royce, opened the rear doors, and made a promenade for Drago and Bill. Once inside the hotel, Bill marveled at the marble lobby and its enchanted forest of columns and thick pile rugs. Subdued lighting from crystal chandeliers suspended from gold-crested ceilings shone on knots of dapper people seated in plush chairs and sofas.

"I will not be seen with the likes of you. The Plaza Hotel is a far cry from Kesmon. It's time to dress you in a way that reflects my standard of dignity and class." Drago motioned to a porter. The porter hustled over like a dog for a treat. Drago relayed a covered suit of clothes from the porter to Bill. "Put these on. Here are the keys to your room. I checked you into the Vanderbilt suite. I expect you to meet that standard. Meet me here in half an hour."

Bill's room featured a grand arrangement of Renaissance furniture. He gazed with a pilot's perspective over Central Park's trees, trails, and reservoirs. New York's skyline arose from the green plain as concrete, glass, and steel Sierras.

Bill long ago ceded to his fate of average looks and paid little attention to dress. Nevertheless, he reacted to the mirror image of himself in a form-fitting, black sharkskin suit. He sported a Cheshire grin while adjusting his black tie by another millimeter.

***

The Matre'd of the Plaza Hotel's ultra-exclusive Edwardian room snapped to attention like a Marine Corps presidential sentry. The staff escorted Bill and Drago to their best table. Bill's eyes opened wide. "Is that…?" He pointed.

"I asked you to elevate yourself." Drago slapped his finger away. "You're staring like a trailer park wench." Drago pulled a cigarette from a platinum, jewel-encrusted box. "Yes. It's Doris Day, Rock Hudson, Liz Taylor, and Richard Burton. Over there are

Ronald Reagan, Angie Dickinson, and Samuel Goldwyn. And we have Barry Goldwater and some Secret Service gorillas seated at the corner table. Mortals. Mere mortals. Yet you'd still be arrested for even thinking of entering these premises without me. However, because you're with me, consider yourself above them all."

A high-nosed waiter poured them Dom Pérignon Champagne into long, slim crystal goblets. Drago snapped his fingers. Another waiter placed a vessel of Beluga caviar plus a plate of raw oysters on the table before Bill.

"What are these for?"

"You're going to need them."

"Why?"

"As I said before, I often object to Curruthers's methods. I reprimanded him for the way he handled you. All that talk of hate and murder. You're not a murderer, are you?"

"No . . ."

"So, the suggestion is ridiculous."

"I don't understand."

"To control a man, you prey on his weaknesses. Correct?"

"Huh?"

"Have you ever been prone to savagery? I don't mean a few punches. Genuine brutality. The urge to torture, or knife someone 64 times. Do those urges ever possess you?"

"No. No! Of course not."

"I didn't think so. Nevertheless, many unresolved conflicts gnaw upon your life like cancer. Not the least of which is gaining revenge on Burt Jenkins. You don't see violence or lawlessness as a solution, so what can you do? Ulcerous. Isn't it?"

"You can say that again."

"Is the fault Burt Jenkins?" Drago folded his hands in front of him. "Don't get me wrong. He turned over your marital bed as sure as Dave Boettger flipping over a cot at Camp Greenbriar. You're here with me in 1964. Right now, in your time, he's making love to Laura. Did she moan for you? I can hear her moan for Burt right now. It's a high-pitched sigh of delight. Burt's is deeper. He grunts like an animal." Drago grinned. "This is getting interesting. She's about to climax."

Bill turned pale. His expression froze.

"Give Burt some credit. He sure can please her." Drago tilted his head at Bill. "You look surprised. Why? Think about it. Burt and Laura are both lawyers. You're a mere public-school teacher in a rough district. Burt and Laura are Ivy League graduates and from upper-class families. Your family is lower middle class." Drago blew a smoke ring. "And I emphasis the lower. Laura's family adores Burt. They despise you." Drago prodded. "Need I remind you that Burt has a house in Ardmore and drives a new Porsche? You live in a hotel one step above a homeless shelter and drive a Chevy Nova with enough miles to reach lunar orbit. May I add that Burt is taller and better looking than you?" Drago leaned back and folded his hands behind his head. "Face it. You lost. Is that surprising? When's the last time you won anything?"

Bill gasped. He covered his face with his hands.

"Nothing to say?"

Bill remained silent.

"I'll give you a little credit. You got to kiss a cute nurse. Did you follow up on it?" Drago paused for effect. "I didn't think so. You'd rather masturbate and fantasize about getting Laura back."

Bill's jaw dropped.

"Don't think you're a moral lion by pretending you're honoring your marriage vows. I know it." Drago pointed at Bill.

"And you know it. Your marriage is over. Laura has moved on with Burt. You have no one."

A tear formed in Bill's eye.

Drago smiled. "I have the ultimate solution. One that will make you eternally grateful to me." Drago pointed toward the restaurant's entrance. "Here she comes. Introducing the companion that I've selected for you."

Bill's pupils dilated wildly. He broke into a cold sweat.

She sauntered toward the table. Her toga-style dress appeared to be woven from a gold thread. Her narrow ankles, diamond-shaped calves, small knees, lithe thighs, and heart-shaped butt flowed like an electrocardiac wave. A red swath girded her tight waist. A narrow X sheathed her body from hips to shoulders, baring her naval and presenting her melon-shaped breasts in their most spectacular light.

She sat beside Bill and arched her arms upward, lifting her breasts h i g h e r . With her right hand, she flicked half of her luxuriant tress of flaming red hair over her blouse. Her florid cheeks glowed above her rosy complexion. She had sharp, dark eyes and a Renaissance aquiline nose.

Bill's heart pounded faster and louder than a nightclub beat. He sweated like a circus fat lady walking the sidewalks of Philadelphia in August.

"She's a lot better looking than Laura, you will agree?"

Bill breathed in heaves. He nodded.

"I thought you'd like her." Drago arched his cigarette between forefingers. "Congratulations. Your life's first victory. You were close when Laura married you. Unfortunately, like the Phillies, you ultimately choked. Your companion's name is Lilith. She is yours if you pledge fealty to me." He puffed another smoke ring toward the ceiling. "Do you agree? That includes never so much as questioning me."

Lilith squeezed Bill's hand. He looked into her dark eyes, stared at her cleavage, and imbibed her black orchid perfume. He panted.

Lillith breathed minty breath into his nose and licked her lips.

"Do we have a deal?"

"Yes. Yes!" Bill kissed her. Long and wet. Embarrassed, he put his napkin over his lap as concealment.

"Enough! Where do you think you are? A drive-in burger joint? You will enjoy Lilith when I say you can. Common slobs are unfit to read the Edwardians' menu, much less order from it."

Two black-tied waiters brought silver-domed platters to their table.

"Therefore, I took care of it for you. Behold," Drago opened his hands. "Chateaubriand and Lobster Thermidor. Eat them both. Pretend they're tacos. Wash it down with the Dom Perignon. You can pretend it's Boone's Farm. Gluttony and libation are blessings."

***

"You devoured your chateaubriand and lobster Thermidor faster than a dog consuming Alpo. I like that."

Lilith snuggled up to Bill. She discreetly licked his ear.

"Ugh." Bill winced in pain while clutching his groin.

"I knew that would happen. So far, you've done all I asked. You're no use to me in that condition. You may take Lilith to your room. After you've sated your carnal appetite, rest up. Tomorrow, we celebrate the Phillies winning the World Series."

# Chapter 8

Bill, Lilith, and Drago claimed their seats three rows above the Phillies' dugout. Drago handed the usher a twenty-dollar bill. The usher bowed to him. Bill's second trip to Yankee Stadium again electrified him. Today, Jim Bunning faced the Yankees. His fastball c a m e  i n  a t  five miles per hour slower than u s u a l. He stumbled and fell after each pitch. His courage, determination, and guile kept the Yankees scoreless on ten hits and no walks entering the ninth. Johnny Callison had driven home the game's only two runs with a first-inning, two-run homer off Mel Stottlemyre.

Bunning started the ninth by striking out Phil Linz looking on a change-up. Mantle walked. Maris hit a flyball to Johnny Callison for the second out. While Elston Howard batted, several  hundred Phillies fans stood and applauded, many waved Phillies Pennants with a crusader's zeal. Several thousand Yankee fans sat in grim silence. Others headed for the exits.

"The Phillies contingent sure are excited. Are you?"

"Strangely enough, yes," He squeezed Lilith's hand.

"Hey ... Wouldn't you love to see Shibe Park again? Can you imagine the grand old lady decked out for the World Series? You missed it in 1964. Why miss out again? Don't end your trip now. Live this to the fullest. Experience a World Series at Shibe Park."

"No, sir!" Bill Beamed. "I've already experienced Shibe Park. Let's win it now."

Lilith started crying. "Bill, I've never met a man like you. I thought no one could ever please me or truly love me. I never dreamed of meeting a lover as skilled as you." She breathed minty breath on Bill. He imbibed her Shumukh by Nabeel perfume. "Bill." She kissed his cheek. "I think I love you. Please never leave me." She broke down and wiped her tears with her flaming red tress.

"I can never leave you, Lilith."

"I don't think you understand, Bill." Drago steepled his fingertips. "Once the Phillies win the 1964 World Series, I must return you to your time and place. Lilith must leave with me. You will never see each other again."

"Bill! Bill!" She pulled on his arm. "Don't make me go. Stay with me." She pulled harder on his arm and cried more tears. "Please, Bill, please."

"The separation is immediate. The instant the Phillies make the third out, you return to the Greenbriar River. Have you ever done Broadway?"

"Yes."

"As a tourist." Drago sniggered. "You've never experienced it with more than the proverbial thin dime in your pocket. I can show you Broadway as only the rich and famous know her." Drago grinned. "Moreover, you will have Lilith on your arm. What do you say, Bill?"

Bill looked into Lilith's teary eyes.

"I thought so. What happened to Mickey Mantle in the 1951 World Series?"

"A negligent groundskeeper left a storm drain uncovered. Mickey got his cleats stuck in the drain and tore up his knee. It permanently impacted his career."

"As well-manicured as the field looks, not every worker is at the top of the labor totem pole. I got a few of them drunk last night. They neglected to fully smooth out the infield dirt."

Elston Howard rapped a h a r d grounder to Dick Allen. It hit a divot, took a bad hop, and struck his face. Shortstop Rojas recovered and held the ball. Mantle and Howard were safe. Allen's face bled as if he had gone 15 rounds with Muhammad Ali. Gene Mauch and the Phillies trainer ran to the field and gave him a towel to cover his bleeding face. They helped him from the field. Ruben Amaro replaced Allen.

Joe Pepitone followed with a routine grounder to second baseman Tony Taylor. The ball deflected off a pebble and into right field. Callison charged and threw a tracer to catcher Dalrymple. Mantle held at third. With the bases loaded, Tom Tresh hit a routine groundball to first baseman Frank Thomas. It hit a pebble and bounced down the right field line. Mantle scored; Howard headed for third. Johnny Callison charged the hit. The ball struck a loose panel fronting the lower box seats and ricocheted away from him. Howard scored. Callison chased it down. Pepitone rounded third. Callison picked up the ball and threw a one-hop strike to home plate. Pepitone's slide raised a dust cloud. Dalrymple applied the tag. The umpire ruled it late. The Yankees beat the Phillies three to two.

Most of the 67,000-plus spectators roared like a departing 747. Bill spotted two Phillies fans with their faces buried in their hands, and another woman, sporting a Phillies cap, bawled. Bill stood in a shocked silence. He looked at Drago with his jaw agape. He spread his hands and shook his head.

Lilith beamed. "Thank you, Bill. I want to stay with you." She embraced him and kissed him. "I can't wait until we're alone."

"Don't worry, Bill," Drago grinned. "You and I both know the Phillies will ultimately prevail. Let's do Broadway."

* * *

Neon lights. Vapor lights. Spotlights. Strobe lights. Footlights. Headlights. Broadway at night was a dazzling wonderland of illumination. Golden prisms of rays glittered from the Rolls-Royce Phantom.

"Would you care to see Carol Channing star in *Hello Dolly* at the St. James Theater? Someone such as yourself would be lucky to get on a month-long waiting list for the last row, balcony. I obtained front row center."

281

The public, police, and theater staff received Drago's Rolls-Royce as a movie star for the Academy Awards. Six ushers led Drago, Bill, and Lilith down the center aisle. The audience on both sides stood and applauded. Bill straightened his posture and raised his chin. Each step felt lighter. Each applause lifted him higher. Watching the renowned musical from his front-row center seat, hand in hand with Lilith, proved a thrill equal to the World Series. The play even ended in marriage instead of defeat.

***

Afterward, the three rode the Rolls-Royce to Philadelphia. Riding through North Jersey, Drago lowered the window, raised his nose, and drew in the sulfurous industrial fumes mingled with swamp gas. "Ah...The aroma."

Bill held his nose. "You must be joking. This smells like Hell."

"Well said, my loyal servant."

***

American flag bunting and pennants decked the rafters of Shibe Park. Anxious Philadelphians filled every seat and jammed every aisle. Drago, Bill, and Lilith sat atop the Phillies' dugout.

"Play Ball!" The ump bellowed.

Chris Short retired the Yankees in order. He wiped sweat from his brow as he trudged to the dugout. Tony Taylor opened the Phillies' first by drilling a Jim Bouton curveball down the leftfield line for a double. Dick Allen, wearing a hardshell face mask, batted second. Bouton hung a slider. Allen lashed the pitch with Samurai Sword ferocity. The ball darted from his bat, rising at a 30-degree angle, still rising as it cleared the Coke sign perched atop the left-field bleacher roof.

"I don't believe it! I don't believe it! Of all the things I knew I could never see again, that's what I wanted to see most! Hey!" Bill leaped and yelled as Johnny Callison took Bouton's next pitch

282

deep over Shibe Park's rightfield wall. The crowd cheered and cheered some more. They were still cheering while Wes Covington banged a drive off the rightfield wall.

Alex Johnson followed by smacking a double into the left-centerfield gap. The crowd remained standing as Frank Thomas singled Alex Johnson home. The Phillies led five to nothing. The fans derided Yankee manager Yogi Berra as he walked to the mound with his head lowered and hooked Jim Bouton. Al Downing relieved and doused the Phillies' uprising.

Chris Short's velocity slowed even more since game four. The Yankees responded with extreme prejudice. A Roger Maris two-run homer spearheaded a three-run, sixth-inning rally.

Facing Elston Howard in the seventh, Chris Short threw one in the dirt. Even the lower box seat spectators heard his arm snap. He fell to the ground as if gunshot. Flopping about like a fish out of water, his face gnarled in agony, his wails were audible to the upper deck. Both the Phillies and Yankees' trainers rushed to the mound. Short's spasms of pain required restraint. Bill gasped. "What have we done? This is horrible! Do something!"

"I told you before: I can't control. I can only influence. Why do you care? Aren't you forever complaining about player salaries? Injury is such a small risk for such a great reward. He's got six months to recover. Besides, he'll be dead by the time I return you to your time. So, cheer up, the Phillies are still winning."

Chris Short's bravery overcame the intense pain. He left the field unassisted. The crowd applauded gingerly. Ed Roebuck relieved him.

The score remained 5-3 Phillies in the top of the ninth. Ed Roebuck started the inning by striking out Cletus Boyer. Next, pinch hitter Johnny Blanchard grounded out, Taylor to Thomas. Bobby Richardson then stepped to the plate. The audience stood and applauded their imminent world champions. Strangers shook hands, some even hugged.

Phillies boosters everywhere shed tears of joy. One more out. Just one more out. Bobby Richardson tipped a foul into the screen ... A Ball outside ... Strike two swinging! Just one more strike! The Phillies players were already congratulating each other. The clubhouse staff had the champagne waiting for them on ice. Roebuck froze Richardson with a belt-high curve, outside corner. Catcher Triandos pumped his fist victoriously. Roebuck leaped skyward. The stadium erupted into delirium.

The umpire called it a ball.

The crowd groaned, cursed, or booed. Triandos squawked. Roebuck lowered and spread his arms and yelled at the Umpire. "Where was that?" Gene Mauch shouted more severe things at the umpire. Nevertheless, Richardson still batted.

The next pitch again caught the corner. The umpire again pinched the pitcher. Gene Mauch grabbed a batting helmet and cocked his arm to throw it at the umpire. He instead gritted his teeth and placed it down. The manager remained poised, one foot on the field, one knee on the dugout steps. Instead of berating the umpire, he shouted encouragement to his pitcher. The umpire next got an easy call, Roebuck walked Richardson on a way high and outside pitch.

The Phillies' hopes still soared. The fans stood and applauded. A Phil Linz bloop single to shallow center failed to stop them.

Mickey Mantle ambled to the plate as the go-ahead run. Shibe Park hushed. Time slowed by three pulses as Gene Mauch replaced Roebuck with Jack Bauldchan. Mantle took his first pitch for a strike. The fans gingerly applauded. Their hearts abruptly stopped. Mantle hit a long one to right field. A reprieve. It curved foul. The Phillies again closed to just one strike of the world championship. Mantle hit the next delivery on a line no more than ten feet high. The crowd sighed in relief as the fence knocked it down. Mantle had a double, nonetheless. Richardson scored; Linz stopped at third.

Mauch relieved Jack Bauldchan with left-hander Dennis Bennet.

Drago turned to Bill. "What do you think of Frank Thomas?"

"Great power hitter. Losing him to a broken thumb cost us the pennant first time around."

"Forget about him as a player. Must I remind you that he hit your boyhood hero, Richie Allen, with a bat? That Thomas, the donkey, pinned the blame on Allen's tail. That incident kicked off Allen's problems in Philadelphia. Frank Thomas deprived Philadelphia of the joy of following a brilliant athlete. And what do you think of Bill Buckner?"

"Another great ballplayer. He made nearly 3,000 base hits. I heard he's a fine fellow too. What a pity he's only remembered for that error on the '86 World Series."

"If you don't know anything else, you do know your baseball, Bill. Lilith's looking lovely, isn't she?"

Bill looked over at Lilith, clad in tight jeans and a braless sweater. Her flaming red hair was spread over both her front and back. She penetrated Bill with her deep, moist eyes. He turned and nodded.

"I guess you never want to see her again."

"No." Bill shook his head. "But... The Phillies..."

"The Phillies," Drago smirked. "Well, I've got a triple-play for you. Run that son-of-a-bitch Thomas out of town before he fights Richie Allen, take some heat off Bill Buckner, and spend another night with Lilith. I know that would make her happy."

Lilith leaned on Bill's shoulder. Her minty breath mingled with her Chanel Number 5 perfume

"What do you say?"

"I don't know."

"After all I've done for you. After all I've shown you. You still don't trust me?

Lilith moved her left hand to Bill's thigh, rubbed her breasts against his shoulders, and licked his ear.

Bill grabbed Lilith tightly and kissed her. "Okay, okay, let's see your triple play."

Drago snapped his fingers. A grotesque winged reptilian creature with a rat-like head feasted upon first baseman Frank Thomas's cheek. He swatted his glove on his face. Maris slapped a low-ground ball. Thomas bent for the ball. It went between his legs and into right field. Linz scored the tying run, and Mantle scored the go-ahead run. The Medusa ugly misplay froze the fans into stone silence.

"Cheer up, Bill. Look to tomorrow and how exciting the Phillies' winning game seven will be. Let's go. The Yankees' Pete Mikkelsen will strike out the side in the Phillies' half of the inning. We have an exclusive banquet to attend. Your attire *will* match the occasion."

***

Bookbinder's Fifteenth Street Seafood House was the site of the Mayor of Philadelphia's banquet in honor of Gene Mauch. The diners looked more like mourners. Although they admired the sight of the famous seafood restaurant's spread of lobster, prawns, scallops, and crab meat, the events of the afternoon had sapped their appetite. Drago, Bill, and Lilith sat at their best table, ahead of the city's dignitaries and celebrities. After several addresses, the guest of honor, Gene Mauch, stepped up to the podium.

He looked a decade older than his 39 years. Bill never saw a photograph of the skipper with a face so lined, hair so gray, or eyes so bagged. He looked worn as an unpopular U.S. president at his term's end. "These losing streaks are like malaria—they keep coming back. Well, losing streaks are funny. If you lose at the beginning, you got off to a bad start. If you lose in the middle of the season, you're in

286

a slump. If you lose at the end, you're choking. I know watching these losses is like watching someone drown, and most one-run games are lost, not won. The worst thing is the day you realize you want to win more than the players do. Well, now is not the case. My players want to beat the Yankees more than anything on Earth. Tomorrow, they'll win it all. So, get your appetite back. Philadelphia is 24 hours away from its greatest triumph."

The city dignitaries and celebrities gave Gene Mauch a standing ovation.

"Trite," Drago shook his head, "those speeches and platitudes. Nevertheless, look around you. Under normal circumstances, these people might even put a coin in your cup. Never would they give you the time of day. Now you're the esteemed. Seize the moment. At this time tomorrow, you'll be nobody again. Lilith will be a memory while Burt Jenkins will still be sleeping with Laura." Drago smirked at him. "You can take credit for the Phillies' first world title."

# Chapter 9

The next afternoon was a golden Indian summer fall day. Jim Bunning's first pitch had batting practice velocity. Light hitting Phil Linz smacked it off the left field wall for a double. Bobby Richardson followed by jerking Bunning's fourth delivery of the inning into the leftfield corner for another double, driving in the first Yankee run. Maris casually stroked Bunning's next pitch over the rightfield wall. Bunning's first curveball to Mantle hung as if sitting on a tee. He whacked it to dead center field. The home run soared over the wall between the bleachers and flagpole, possibly rivaling the 565-feet of his 1953 wallop off Chuck Stobbs at Griffith's field. Easing up on Bunning, Joe Pepitone only hit one high off the Ballantine Beer scoreboard for a triple. Elston Howard soon scored him with a high-velocity line single to left. "What's going on here?"

Bill stood with wide eyes and open hands

"Why no faith? Don't you want to see a rousing comeback?"

"Yeah. Sure. But isn't this a bit much?" Bill pointed to the field as Cletus Boyer put a Jim Bunning delivery into the leftfield upper deck.

"You ingrate. How nauseating. Look at who's sitting next to you."

Lilith squeezed Bill's hand, smiled, and planted a wet kiss on his lips.

Gene Mauch removed Jim Bunning for Art Mahaffey. The Phillies fans groaned as Tom Tresh greeted Mahaffey with the Yankees' fourth home run of the inning. The first inning ended with nine Yankee runs.

In the Phillies' first, the fans booed after Mel Stottlemyre struck out the side in order. A tear formed in Bill's left eye.

By the fifth inning, Bill slouched over. He fidgeted and wrung his hands.

"Don't worry, Bill," Lilith put her arm around Bill and pressed her cheek to his. "I love you, Bill. I can't live without you."

The game deteriorated to atrocity. Another Roger Maris home run, this time off Ray Culp, upped the score to 16-0. Joe Pepitone followed with a pop-up to shallow right. Taylor gandered out; Callison loped in. They stared at each other as the ball fell between them. Pepitone motored for second. Callison and Taylor stood still, looking at the ball. Callison finally picked it up and lofted a soft toss over the shortstop's head. Pepitone churned for third. Allen recovered the errant throw and held it as no Phillie covered third base.

"Wait a minute," Bill clenched his fists. "You lied. The Phillies are going to lose. Look at them. They're down 16-0. No team comes back from that. Hell, they've already thrown in the towel."

"Liar? Who are you calling a liar? Thanks to me, you've ridden cars out of a fantasy novel, feasted better than a sultan, and stayed in hotels where you're unfit to scrub their toilets. You've worn outfits worth more than your year's pay. Even if you had the money, you don't have the taste to select them. "Ha! Ha! Ha! Think about it. Before you met me, you couldn't even wear a tie properly. Your wife dumped you. Your son would spit in your face before respecting you. Yet I had you honored among the elite. Most of all, I treated you to my queen herself. Ha! Ha! Ha! Lied? Lying is only wrong in your realm.  Ha! Ha! Ha!  I outsmarted you! I don't yet command the power to condemn you to my Hell." Drago's face transmogrified. His skin turned red with bullfrog texture. His forehead jutted and widened with ridges and grooves like grotesque valleys. Goat horns sprouted over reptilian eyes. His teeth became snarling strands of barbed wire. Ha! Ha! Ha! I can condemn you to the Hell of your making. Welcome to modern and new Philadelphia."

Bill suddenly lay on a sidewalk on Twelfth and Market Street in Philadelphia. Reading Terminal had burned to the ground. Trash filled the site. In place of the ARA building and the high-rise Marriott Hotel stood X-rated bookstores and movie houses.

Two muscular men stood over Bill. The black guy wore black slacks and a white tank top. The White dude had shaved the side of his head to show off neck tattoos of snakes and dragons. "You got something for us?" The black teen hunched his shoulders.

"What do you mean?"

"You a moron or somethin'." The white thug stepped forward. "Give us your money."

Bill looked up at them with blurred vision. He scrambled for his wallet, reached into it, and pulled out a five-dollar bill and two one-dollar bills.

The muggers grabbed his cash. "That's all you got?" They kicked Bill in the ribs and gut. He held his gut, gasped for air, and groaned. No one noticed him.

Ten minutes later, a burly policeman accosted him. "You can't sleep here. Get your ass moving."

"You don't understand, officer. I was mugged. Two thugs robbed me and kicked me. I'm in pain. I can't get up."

"That's not my problem." He brandished his nightstick. "Get your ass up and move outta here or I'll give you more problems"

Bill managed to stand. He staggered along the sidewalks of Center City, Philadelphia. Poorly dressed people jostled and jarred him. Many of the shops were barricaded with graffiti-strewn boards. Others sold down-market wares. Street vendors vociferously hawked used clothing and rancid vegetables. Bill raised his head. "Doc Watson's Pub. I've got lots of friends there. They can tell me what's going on."

***

"Come on in." Doc Watson's doorman stood at least six inches taller than Bill. The bouncer's crew-cut face was broad and flat. An orange leisure suit opened to flaunt a deep barrel chest with gold medallions suffocating in gorilla-thick fur. "We've got blonds with big tits. Black girls with high tight butts. And redheads with fires between their legs."

"Is Barry or Jill in?"

"Nobody named Barry works here. We don't have a Jill either. But we do have a Gizzelle. Give me a twenty and she'll crawl under your table and ..."

"I don't have any money."

"You don't have any money! Then what the hell are you doing here!" The bouncer lifted Bill by the shirt and tossed him into a parked delivery van. "Asshole."

The back of Bill's head hit the van first with a thud. A storm of electrical flashes seared his eyes. He sat against the van in a daze. Over the next fifteen minutes, he sat against the van in a stupor. His face started swelling like an over-inflated football, and the placekicker was setting for a long one.

"Get your ugly face off my van."

"Huh?"

"Move it, asshole." The driver drove away before Bill could stand. The rear tire rolled inches from severing his arm.

While wallowing in the gutter, he gained another insight. "My father. Yes. Of course. My father. That's why I threw the bottle on the field to begin with. The '64 Phillies still won the pennant. Therefore, my father was never murdered." Bill dragged his body upright. "If I can just make it to our old South Philly home, my mom and dad will be there. Everything will be fine."

Owing to bruised ribs and a concussion, Bill stumbled along like a hopeless drunk. He aimed southbound, although the derelict buildings and stolen or vandalized street markers foiled navigation. His broken nose was filled with phlegm and blood. He spotted four thugs on motorcycles parked on a street corner openly passing a cannabis pipe to each other. '*I know them.*' He squinted. '*Yes. I know them! Maybe they can make sense of all this.*'

"Scorpion! Sleazette! My God! I can't believe I'm so happy to see you guys."

"What the ... How the hell do you know my name?"

"Hey, you're famous," Sleazette drew on the pipe.

"Please. You know my son Rory. Can you tell me where he is?"

"Rory? Who the hell is he?" Scorpion dismounted his chopper and lurched toward Bill.

"My son. You know. The young guy who rides with you."

"Hey look, I don't know you, and I sure as hell don't know your damn son. Look asshole..." Scorpion spotted two approaching police vans. "If you know what's good for you, you'll fuck off right now."

The police vans screeched and skidded against the curb. Six policemen in riot gear rushed from each van. Scorpion took a chain from around his shoulders and used it to hit a cop's head and shoulders. The policeman dropped to his knees. Scorpion recoiled and struck him behind the neck. Two other policemen ran in and clubbed Scorpion's back. They pinned him against the van. A cop repeatedly speared his solar plexus with his riot club.

Two other cops restrained Sleazette with grips on her breasts and crotch. They disappeared with her into the back of the van.

Space case scrunched like a fetus as he received merciless clubs and kicks.

Cockroach shot a .38 caliber slug into a riot policeman's abdomen. Two backups disarmed Cockroach from behind and restrained him. A burly cop yanked off Cockroach's Nazi helmet and repeatedly bashed skull with it. It sounded like Dick Allen taking batting practice with a metal bat. Brain tissue sifted through shattered bone like gelatine between the fingers of a clenched fist.

The cops tossed a bloodied beyond-recognition Rat-Fink into a van.

Quickly as they arrived, the riot squads departed. A backup unit arrived and fetched the wounded cop. They threw a canvas sheet over Cockroach's corpse and left him on the sidewalk.

Bill slumped against a wall and retched. "Ugh." He groaned as his bruised and swollen jaw chattered. *'Walk on. Gotta walk-on. It will be all right when I get to Mom and Dad's home.* The mosaic of South Philly's small-town-like neighborhoods were now a diarrhea of gritty tenements. Many of the tenants lay on sidewalks or sat against the houses as the living dead. Others argued with unseen entities and unheard voices. Platoons of hate-eyed urban warriors girded with chains, brass knuckles, and switchblades patrolled each corner.

Bill emerged from the cloying black forest of slums to the garbage and debris-replete opening of Stephen Girard Park. He spotted a junky spiking himself in the overgrown, weed-choked grass. Three Vagrants sat on the benches snuggling brown-bagged bottles. Red paint depicting a gunshot wound marred the statue of Stephen Girard. Spray painted below: "Death to Blades." The sight of the park rejuvenated Bill's final steps to his family home.

The adjacent home's vandalized shell looked like a malignant tumor on Bill's semi-detached former house. Broken windows and graffiti punctuated the former Waldron household's condition. The front yard was a patch of weeds and rusted auto parts.

Drago and Lilith, in their humanoid forms, appeared on the porch. Drago laughed, "You're a fool beyond my most shallow estimation."

"What have you done with my father? Curruthers promised that if I threw the bottle…"

"Ha! Ha! Ha! Carruthers made no promises. Ha! Ha! Ha! He only stated a fact. You murdered your father."

"Yes. They won the pennant, only to choke the World Series in historic ignominy. Ha! Ha! Ha! You think New Yorkers said nothing about it?" Drago prodded. "You're the blame for your father's murder. You put the knife in his back! Only this time over a World Series choke."

"You bastard!"

"Ha! Ha! Ha! Bastard? Ha! Ha! Ha! I'm the king of bastards! Better to never know your father than to murder him. Ha! Ha! Ha!"

"No!" Bill fell to his knees and pounded the ground. "You're the Devil! You're Satan himself!"

"The Devil? Ha! Ha! Ha! The Devil. Beelzebub. The Prince of Darkness. Satan. The Deceiver. The Accuser. The Dragon. Lucifer. I go by many names. I thought of calling myself Lew, for Lucifer. Yet I figured even a moron as you might put two and two together. So, I called myself Drago. Short for Dragon. Ha! Ha! Ha!"

"This isn't real. I'm not in Philadelphia. You're deceiving me again."

"This time it is for real. This is Philadelphia. Like killing your father, you killed your city. You see, I hate baseball. Its geometric perfection makes me sick. A non-violent sport, yet a perfect avenue for man to quell his inner aggression. I enjoy pain, hatred, and violence. So, I will never allow a pastime that promotes health, friendship, and joy. I tried to destroy America's despicable game before. In 1919, I almost succeeded. I prayed on an owner's avarice and exploited others already under my thumb. But that fat, ugly, stupid baboon came along and saved the game. I tried ruining him with every possible temptation, and the fool succumbed every time! Yet he kept playing better. Before long, I discovered that I could use baseball to torment. Even wreck entire communities! So, I changed tactics. As I mentioned earlier, I cannot control the game, but I can influence it. Take the Brooklyn Dodger fans. They showed genuine love and affection for their team. Love? Affection? Disgusting! So, I used the owner's greed to rip the heart out of an entire borough. Ha! Ha! Ha!"

"No! No!" Bill stood. "You failed. They took their love and affection to the Mets! Who cared if they always lost? They got the game back and loved it! The A m a z i n g Mets won the World Series just seven years later. Seven. The number of days God took to create the world!" Bill pointed. "You lost!"

"Ha! Ha! Ha! I thought you hated New York? You're over New York because now you know it's you," Drago pointed at him. "Who killed your father. Ha! Ha! Ha! What a fool you are! Every game has a winner or a loser. The result is irrelevant. The loser will curse my enemy regardless. Ha! Ha! Ha! In your case, losing is no longer a torment. It's an accepted lifestyle. That's why I chose you. The perfect tool to destroy the City of Philadelphia."

"Philadelphia? Why Philadelphia?"

"The poet Thomas Gray penned, 'Where ignorance is bliss, 'tis folly to be wise.' Instead of playing half-ball on Sunday mornings, you should have gone to Sunday school and learned something. I possess all the World's kingdoms and their splendor. They're all mine. It's to everything a season. Kingdoms and cities rise. I can't control nature. So, I exploit human failings to bring their fall. And no one is a worse failure than you. I know the importance of sports to a city's culture and its effect on its economy. So, I devised a scheme to annihilate your city. Even though the enemy sent a good spirit to warn you, you proved an easy mark. I used you to reverse that September 21st, 1964 game. The Phillies still lost their next nine games. Gene Mauch again condensed his rotation to Bunning and Short. Not only did you miss Sunday school, but you also took up space in public school. You never learned simple arithmetic. Stopping Chico Ruiz from stealing home only gave the '64 Phillies a first-place tie. They still had to win a best-of-three playoff with the Cardinals. Guess the Phillies starting pitchers?"

"Bunning and Short?"

"Very good. The old dog knows some tricks after all. Getting the Phillies through that playoff was easier than you think.

All I had to do was stand beside the home plate umpire. That worked just as well in helping Bunning and Short win the first three World Series games."

"What's your point? Even though the Phillies lost the 1964 World Series, we still won the pennant."

"One of my greatest human servants said, 'One step backward, two steps forward'. Chris Short became a tired and hurting pitcher. His game six World Series injury was inevitable. Remember I said he would recover in six months? I lied. It took sixteen operations and five years of physical therapy before he even regained use of his left arm. Jim Bunning was luckier. He even pitched again. Then again, not everyone considers 1-9 with an 8.23 earned run average pitching. Dennis Bennett, Art Mahaffey, and Ray Culp already had career-spoiling sore arms. The Phillies needed pitching in the worst possible way. They got it in the worst possible way too. They traded Richie Allen, Johnny Callison, Alex Johnson, and Tony Taylor for pitching. Pitchers who bombed as badly as did Larry Jackson and Bob Buhl, whom they still traded Ferguson Jenkins for. Soon, the Phillies were losing 115 games or more a year. Ask yourself, who would brave North Philly to watch that? The Phillies were hemorrhaging money. They deferred all maintenance on Shibe Park, including security. Remember how two juvenile delinquents snuck into the place the year after the final game and burned the place down? This time, two juvenile delinquents snuck in during the season and burned it down. The Phillies finished the year playing in their spring training park. How fitting. At that point, they were a minor league team anyway. Philadelphia is infamous for its corruption and inefficiency. With no new stadium on the horizon, they moved. The National League expanded to Montreal. The league wanted a Canadian rival. In 1944 and '45, the Phillies called themselves the Blue Jays. The Phillies, thanks to you, became the Toronto Blue Jays. Franklin Field has many of Shibe Park's charms: wonderful architecture, sightlines, and acoustics. It also lacks parking, luxury boxes, and profitable concessions. "The NFL was now big time and big money. Franklin Field was no longer viable. The Eagles didn't get a new stadium either. How does the Phoenix Eagles sound? Ha! Ha! Ha!  The wind still blew off Spectrum's roof in 1968. The 76ers had already traded Wilt Chamberlain, and the Flyers were just a first-year expansion team. Once the do-nothing city council  figured out how to repair the roof, the elements ruined the place beyond repair. Ha! Ha! Ha! Bye-bye, Sixers and Flyers. You didn't answer my question about how The Phoenix Eagles sounded. After all, a Phoenix is a mythological bird while an Eagle is also a bird. But the Utah 76ers? It sounds nonsensical but, thanks to you, that's what they became.  Ha! Ha! Ha!  Your hockey team moved to North Jersey and renamed itself in my honor. The Jersey Devils. Ha! Ha! Ha! A man losing a limb is horrible enough. Imagine losing all four. Philadelphia lost its teams, its pride, and its soul. Soon its other industries and businesses left. People moved out with them. Unemployment, crime, and  drug abuse skyrocketed. The institutions became corrupt enough to shame a third-world city. Once the Liberty Bell and the Declaration of Independence were moved to Washington, DC, no one cared. Ha! Ha! Ha!"

"You bastard!"

"You think name-calling from the likes of you can bother me? You now know what you did to your city. You did worse to your family. Soon, you will face Laura with Rory and your Camp Greenbriar failure. You also get to tell her about your infidelity. What you did surpasses mere adultery. You enjoyed sexual congress with the Queen of Hell."

Lilith transmogrified. The bones surrounding her eye sockets grew grotesquely. Her eyes turned black with red pupils. Two conical horns with S-shaped curves sprouted from the jutted bones of her forehead. She sprang a slimy, reptilian black tongue. It telescoped into Bill's mouth.

Bill bent over a wretched.

"Ha! Ha! Ha!" Lilith mocked him.

After you turn your son over to Laura and Burt, you know where he is headed. They are lawyers. They can get him out of trouble until, of course, he takes it too far and catches a life sentence. Laura and Burt have careers and social reputations to protect. They'll act like he never existed. Rory will blame you for his predicament and not even write to you. After getting gang raped in the showers, he'll tie one end of a bed sheet around his neck, tie the other on a railing in the upper cell block, and take the plunge. Ha! Ha! Ha!"

"Ha! Ha! Ha!" Lilith also mocked him.

"Once again, I win." Drago pointed at Bill. "Rory will be mine forever. Ha! Ha! Ha!"

"No! No!" Bill closed his eyes and squeezed his head. "No!"

"It doesn't have to be that way. You still have time."

Bill opened his eyes and looked up. He encountered a woman more beautiful than anyone he had imagined or seen in photographs or artwork. She wore a pure white gown and wings of feathers so white and luxuriant that they reflected the sunlight into prismatic colors. Her breasts were a testament to creation. Her eyes shone like sapphires. Her thick, wavy indigo hair flowed to her waist. "Isolde Maria! Now I remember. I thought I had imagined you. You comforted me after my father died." He pointed at her with a jittering finger. "I've heard your name before at McCusker's, but I thought it was drunken ramblings."

Lilith's eyes flared at her. Her teeth became long and sharp like a tiger's. She bared them and hissed catlike at Isolde Maria.

"I am a Heavenly Angel. He is fallen," Isolde Maria pointed at Drago. "He was created as the Angel of Light but rebelled against God and was cast out of Heaven. He has more power than I. But you can call on the one more powerful than all."

Lilith returned to her human form. She stepped forward. "Yes, Bill, Isolde Maria is gorgeous. But am I not also beautiful?" Lilith thrust her chest forward and upward. She shook her head. Flaming red hair equal to Isolde Maria's indigo tress splayed about. "She can never so much as touch you sexually." Lilith licked her lips. "You were delirious when we made love. I thought I could never love a mortal." Lilith started crying. "I was wrong. I love you, Bill. I love you with all my heart." Lilith took two steps forward and extended her hand. "Take my hand, Bill. Come with me. We can make love whenever you want. Your ecstasy will never end."

Bill's jaw chattered; sweat drenched his face. He looked away from Lilith to gaze at Isolde Maria. "Oh Lord Jesus, save me." Bill felt his body crystallize into the wind. A warmth and sense of security accompanied his transformation. He awoke in the canoe, floating on tranquil water. His body bore no cuts or bruises. With a lucid and inspired mind, he paddled back to Camp Greenbriar.

***

Upon returning to camp, Bill first encountered baseball coach Bob Harris. "Yo, Bob."

"Yo? Is that a Philly greeting I hear? I only answer to a Carolina hello."

Bill chuckled. "Sure thing, Bob. Hey, have you seen Rory?"

"No. But I may have heard him. Try the big library. I heard his loud, heavy metal stuff coming from there. That makes it a good bet."

"Hey, thanks. Yo Bob. Who won the 1964 National League pennant?"

"The St. Louis Cardinals. How can a Philadelphian forget that one?"

"Thanks." Bill slapped Bob's shoulder. "Thanks a lot. Best news I've heard in years."

Bob scratched his head as Bill walked away.

***

The electric screech and violent howls of Lucifer Jack drummed the wooden walls and stone chimney of the old library. The green-planked building formerly housed books. Now serving as a clubhouse for the campers, it also functioned as the main baseball diamond's left-field wall. Bill barged in. He saw Rory smoking cigarettes with 13-year-old campers. Their conversation consisted mostly of "F" this and "F" that. Bill marched over and snatched Rory's ghetto blaster, opened its back, and dumped out the batteries.

"Hey! What did you do that for? Who the hell do you think you are?"

"Your father."

"No, you aren't. My father is a one-night stand mom had with a winner."

Bill grabbed Rory by the arm and pushed him toward the door. Rory turned and raised his fist.

"If that's the way you want it, let's go. Show me what Scorpion taught you."

"Oh, screw you." Rory waved both hands.

Bill pounced in and shoved Rory. "Screw you, huh? If you're going to curse at a man, you better be able to back it up. I'll give you a choice: The boxing ring or a canoe trip."

Rory sneered while keeping his hands to his sides.

"Wise choice. Let's go."

***

Rory and Bill paddled back to his favorite cove without speaking. Upon reaching their destination, Bill asked, "So you think I'm a loser? Why?"

"I don't know. You're just not cool." Rory spun around on his bow seat. "You're a schoolteacher. Mom dumped you. You live in that ratty hotel, listen to boring old music, and follow a last-place baseball team.”

“So, what you're saying is that a winner is someone cool? Who do you think is cool?”

“I don't know ... Scorpion.”

“Why?”

“I guess because he's tough. He rides a hog, bangs lots a chicks, and parties to ass kicking tunes.” He rested his crossed ankles on the mid-ship thwart and folded his hands behind his head.

“What does he do for a living?”

“He sells drugs.”

“Okay, you think dealing dope is cooler than teaching? I doubt you’d feel that way about scrubbing the floors of a cellblock. Where does Scorpion live?”

“In a trailer.”

“But he gets lots of girls?”

“Yeah, man. Sleazette will do anything for him, but he slaps ’er around and treats ’er like garbage.” Rory smirked. “Girls desperate for drugs do him certain favors right in front of her. But she takes it because he’s so cool.” Rory chuckled. “If you know what I mean?”

“I know exactly what you mean.” Bill nodded. “Would your mother go for that?”

“No way, man!” Rory snapped upright, causing the canoe to rock. “I mean ...I don't know ...No ... you're confusing me...Mom's way too good for him.”

“But you said Scorpion is cool. Why isn’t she good enough for your mother?”

"Hey, Mom's classy." Rory gripped the bow thwart and stretched. "She's pretty and makes piles of cash."

"Since she likes Burt, I guess he's the ultimate cool winner?"

"No way, man. He's a rich wuss. Scorpion can kick his ass."

"But isn't that good enough for your mother? After all, Scorpion can also slap women around with the worst of them."

"You're confusing me again." Rory flapped his hands.

"Am I? But I thought you already knew everything. Now that we know that you don't, I'll simplify. Do you think your mother is a winner?"

"Yeah. Okay. Mom's a winner."

"No. She's a loser."

"Say What?" Rory craned his head forward.

"She's a loser because she has you for a son. A winner doesn't raise a son who gets kicked out of two schools. Okay. The Phillies have had nearly a decade of losing. Well, you've had sixteen losing years in a row. That's it. I'll just do what Spanky McMullen at McCusker's Tavern did." Bill rested his canoe paddle on his thighs. "I'll abandon the Phillies and claim the New York Yankees as my team. Now that I've rejected the Phillies for a winning team, I'll disown you too. I'll adopt another kid. A winner. One who works hard at school; one not hell-bent on wasting his life."

"You can't do that."

"I can't? Just watch me. Your mother also once believed in you. Now she's fed up as well. She'll gladly cut you loose and start a new life with Burt. After all, do you think he wants a delinquent in his life? You had better think hard. Find out who loves you. Not Scorpion. Get locked in a jail cell with him and you'll hope not."

Rory slumped for half a minute, raised his head, and chuckled. "I guess you and Mom are the only ones who really care about me."

"My goodness! Are you agreeing with me?"

"Yeah. Guess so."

"Well, I do love you. I'm also your ally. If I can stay loyal to a team like the Phillies, I can remain loyal to a son like you."

"Thanks." Rory beamed. "Dad."

They paddled back to camp. Dusk added an amber gleam to the mountain river.

"Will you talk to Lee, Rory? Tell him you want to turn over a new leaf. If you will, we can make this a memorable summer."

"Must I?"

"I'm afraid so." Bill tightened his lips and lowered his eyes.

"Why not?" Rory beamed. "I think I can learn to like it here."

# Epilogue

October 13, 1993

Bill and Liz sat together in the living room of their South Philly townhouse. They squeezed each other's hands and crossed the fingers of their other hands. They inched to the edge of their couch. Bill pursed his lips and said under his breath, "One more…Just one more out and we win the pennant."

"Calm down, Dad," Rory chuckled. "The Phillies lead by three runs, two out, ninth inning. The Braves don't even have a baserunner. It's in the bag."

"It's not over until it's over. Afterall, Mitch Williams is pitching. When Wild Thing is on the mound, you never know what can happen."

Harry Kalas's voice resonated from the TV. "It all comes down to this. It's a full count on the batter. Two outs. Ninth Inning. Williams throws…He struck him out! Mitch Williams has struck out Greg Olson swinging on a three-two fastball! The Phillies have won the pennant. The Phillies have gone from worst to first to win the 1993 National League Pennant!"

"Yeah!" Bill, Liz, and Rory leaped to their feet and cheered. Bill and Liz exchanged a long kiss before they joined hands with Rory and danced in a circle.

"Let me get us beers to celebrate." Rory beamed,

"Thanks, Rory. That will be a Bud for me, Miller Lite for Liz, and a root beer for you."

"You got me again." Rory laughed. "Hey, look what I found." He held up an envelope. "It's from Burt Jenkins."

"Why don't you burn it or flush it down the toilet?"

Liz looked at Bill with droopy eyes and a creased brow.

"I'm sorry, babe." Bill hugged Liz. "Okay, Rory, open it. Let's hear what he has to say."

Rory perused the letter. "He wrote, 'Please accept this as a peace offering…' Dad!" Rory beamed. He sent you World Series tickets!"

"That's nice. But the Vet is a huge, cavernous stadium. I'd rather watch on TV in the comfort of our home than squint at the game from the Bob Uecker seats."

"No, Dad." Rory held up the tickets as if they were winning lotto tickets. "They're for Deluxe Box A-1!"

"Yes! Yes!" Liz leaped up and down before taking both of Bill's hands and kissing him.

"We all have much to be grateful for. Let's all go to church this Sunday," Bill arched his eyes, "as a family."

"Sure." Liz smiled. "Where did you have in mind?"

"The Deliverance Evangelistic Church."

"Where is that?" Liz shrugged.

"21st and Lehigh."